# DRIVEN

Lisa Nowak

*Lisa Nowak* (signature)

Published by Webfoot Publishing
Milwaukie, Oregon

Publishing

Driven

Copyright ©2012 by Lisa Nowak

All rights reserved. This book contains material protected under the International and Federal Copyright Laws and Treaties. Any unauthorized reprint or use of this material is prohibited. No part of this book may be reproduced or transmitted in any form or by any means without express written permission from the author or publisher, except in the case of brief quotations embodied in critical articles and reviews.

This is a work of fiction. All names, characters, places, and incidents, apart from those that are well-known, are products of the author's imagination or are used fictitiously. Any resemblance to current events, locales, or persons, living or dead, is entirely coincidental.

The text of this book is set in 11-point Georgia.

Book design by Lisa Nowak

Cover design by Robin Ludwig Design Inc.

ISBN-13: 978-1-937167-16-5

First Edition

## DEDICATION

For the teachers who have made an impact on my life, particularly Diane Harris, Jan Fagerberg, Bob Martin, and Thomas Rubick.

## ACKNOWLEDGMENTS

I'd like to express my gratitude to all those who contributed to my awesome cover: Mike and Maxci Jermann, Cari and Sam Myers, and their sons Jacob and Jared for providing a photo of Jacob's car. Hallie Lichen (who posed as Jess) and her mom Pat (who helped with the photo shoot). Sandy Fast and the rest of the crew at River City Speedway in St. Helens, Oregon, for allowing me to take photos of the track. And, of course, Robin Ludwig for putting it all together.

Special thanks to those who participated in the editing process of this book: Annetta Ribken, Bob Martin, Carol Sweet, and Amy Rose Davis. I'd be lost without you.

A tip of my hat to Dale Silver for her insights into alcoholism and children of alcoholics, and to Todd McCann for his expert long-haul trucker advice—not to mention spending all that time on the road away from his family so I can have my Newman's Own Thin and Crispy pizzas.

I'd also like to acknowledge the usual contingent of beta readers, critique partners, and other cheerleaders—the members of my critique groups, Chrysalis and Wow, Joel Schmitz, Barb Froman, Beth Miles, Paula Manley, Karen Champ, Roxie Matthews, Jenny Landis-Steward, Marian Meyer, Kayla Meyer Matsuura, Bob Douglas, Sylvia Potter, Bill and Ruth George, Bobby Shaw, Lois Lane, Gene Bradshaw, June Fezler, Josh Skinner, Mitch Hutchinson, Bill Graham, Roxanne Colyer Clingman, Eddie Kilgore, Laura Marshall, and especially Alice Lynn and my sister Angela Moist.

A multitude of appreciation to my fellow Indelibles, who have provided information, moral support, and friendship.

And finally, an extra special shout-out to my husband, Bob Earls. Thanks for cooking dinner all those nights so I could finish this book.

## CHAPTER 1

If it hadn't been for Teri Sue Cline's Southern drawl, I'd probably still be sitting in the stands at Eugene Speedway, wishing I had the nerve to talk to one of the drivers. It was pure luck that I was even in the pits to hear her. Every other race I'd been to, I'd waited until after the show to look at the cars. But for some reason on that last Saturday night in April, I felt oddly confident, so I slapped down twelve dollars for a pit pass instead of the usual seven for a seat in the stands.

It was a warm afternoon, sunny and blue-skied after a wet, gloomy week, and the loudspeaker blared a tinny rendition of *The Dance* by that popular new country singer, Garth Brooks. Just walking through the infield gave me goose bumps. My face stretch into a grin as the something's-going-to-happen electricity seeped through my skin and into my bloodstream. Some people might get that feeling at a state fair or rodeo, but it had always been the speedway that stirred it up in me. The excitement couldn't quite burn through my self-consciousness, though. Not one of the drivers knew me, and I doubted they'd want a stranger drooling all over their cars. Especially if that stranger happened to be a sixteen-year-old girl.

I headed for the Street Stocks first. Being the entry-level class, they were less intimidating than the Limited Sportsmen or Super Stocks. My Nike-wanna-bes scuffed the asphalt as I walked down the row, air pulsating around me in a symphony of growling engines, shrieking tires, and excited voices. With the bright, sharp odor of racing fuel teasing my nose, my nervousness began to melt away.

I stopped at a car I didn't recognize from last year, a baby blue Camaro with pink and yellow lettering. The number 70 blazed from the roof and doors in shocking pink. Even though I didn't think much of the current neon craze, I had to admit the colors looked good on this car.

"Son of a bitch!"

A wrench bounced across the pavement, landing inches from my toes. It was followed by a stream of swearing that made my cheeks go hot. The source of the tantrum, a guy with a beer-belly poking out from under his T-shirt, glared up at me from the ground beneath the rear end of the Camaro.

I took a step back.

The man's fingers curled around the bumper. He hauled himself up and wiped an arm across his forehead, leaving behind a streak of grease. Jerking down his shirt, he shifted his look of annoyance from me to a girl standing a few feet away. Her blue firesuit nearly matched the color of the Camaro.

Whoa. How had she wound up with a race car? She didn't look that much older than me.

The guy snatched a rag from his back pocket. "I can't get the damned thing loose," he said, rubbing at the grease on his hands so roughly you'd think it was the cause of his grief. "You're just gonna have to race it like it is."

The girl pushed herself off the wall. Hands on hips, she eyed him in a cool, disapproving manner.

"My daddy doesn't pay you to tell me to race it like it is, George. And he sure doesn't pay you to throw around tools he spent good money on."

My jaw dropped at the smooth, sweet lilt of the girl's voice. If it hadn't been for her drawl, I would've walked away. Who wants to stand around listening to other people's fights when there are so many you can't escape? But this girl was clearly from the South, and I had to know what she was doing at a rinky-dink speedway like Eugene when she could've been hanging out at Rockingham or Daytona.

Looking for an excuse to stick around, I bent down to pick up the shiny Craftsman wrench at my feet.

"I'll tell ya what your daddy don't pay me," the man said, dusting off his jeans, which sagged over a practically nonexistent behind. "He don't pay me enough to bust my knuckles and take your lip. If you're too proud to drive it the way it is, feel free to crawl under there yourself."

He stalked off, but I didn't see where to, because by that point, my attention was completely wrapped up in the girl. Like most, she had more going for her than I did, even though she wasn't what you might call beautiful. Along with green eyes, a pale, freckled complexion, and softly curling hair a little too red to be blonde, she had a figure that was sort of—well-padded. But she held herself with a confidence that brought those things together to make her look good. At any rate, she looked better than me, with my mousy-brown ponytail tucked through the back of my Eugene Speedway cap and a shape that would've let me pass for a twelve-year-old boy.

I realized I was gawking and held out the wrench, embarrassed I'd hung around eavesdropping.

The girl took it. "Thanks," she said, a friendly smile lighting up her face. Then, as if I'd blinked out of existence, she turned to rummage through the high-dollar toolbox sitting on one of her spare racing tires. After locating a can of WD-40, she lay down on the throw rug George had left under her car and scooted beneath the rear axle.

I'm pretty good with a wrench, and was tempted to offer my help, but I'd never worked on a race car. Besides, what driver was going to want an outsider messing with her equipment? Better to walk away.

I turned around, but before I could take a step, the girl swore in that sweet, twangy voice and reeled me back in. As if I could resist anything Southern. The South was where stock car racing was born. It was where I planned to move the second I got out of high school, so I could get a job on a Winston Cup pit crew.

Well, it couldn't hurt to stick around for a few more minutes.

I squatted to look under the Camaro. The girl was struggling with a nut on one of the U-bolts that held the springs to the axle. The wrench in her hand didn't offer much leverage. I glanced toward her toolbox, where a set of deep sockets gleamed in the slanting rays of late-afternoon sun. Not stopping to think, I picked one out, snapped it onto the end of a long-handled ratchet, and crouched beside her. When she turned to give me a curious look, my face prickled with heat.

"Uh ... here," I said, leaning forward to hand her the ratchet. "Try this."

Without speaking, she took it and attacked one of the four bolts, attempting to take it all the way off without loosening the others. I didn't want to tell her how to work on her own car, but I couldn't sit there and watch her make the job harder than it needed to be.

"You'll want to break them all loose, then take them off gradually," I said. "Back each one off just a few turns at a time."

She glanced at me, and my face did another supernova impression. *Good going, Jess. Just piss off the first person you meet.*

"Sorry." I stood up and backed away. "None of my business—"

The girl's hand darted out with a speed any cat would envy and latched onto the leg of my jeans. I took another step to keep from stumbling.

"Wait." She wiggled out from under the car and sat up, pushing pale red hair out of her eyes with the back of her wrist. "Where'd y'all learn so much about cars?"

I shrugged, uneasy about having her full attention. "Books, I guess. And I'm taking auto shop."

"You ever mess around with leaf springs?"

"Not much. What are you trying to do?"

"Add another leaf to this side. Only won't this spring jump when I let the tension off?" Her freckles crinkled up in frown lines.

I crouched down again and studied how the two jacks were arranged under the spring and axle. "Not the way you've got things set up."

The girl eyed the car as if it were a rottweiler that was simultaneously growling and wagging its tail.

"Maybe you'd do it for me?" Her eyebrows arched upward.

I blinked at her. Even with the howl of the Super Stocks hot lapping, I knew I'd heard right. I just couldn't believe the words. No one but my shop teacher ever took me seriously as a mechanic.

Hope drained from the girl's expression. "Never mind. I can figure it out my own self."

"No—I mean, I'd be glad to. You just surprised me."

"Well, I sure could use some help. That George ain't gonna be any use." She stood up and swatted her rear-end to get the dirt off her firesuit. "Name's Teri Sue Cline," she said, holding out her hand.

I had sense enough to shake it, even though I was so shocked it was all I could do to breathe. "Jess DeLand."

Teri Sue grinned. "Well, girl, let's get to work."

The spring didn't take long to fix. When I was finished, Teri Sue handed me a hot dog and Pepsi she'd gotten from the concession stand. I set them on the fender while I reached into my pocket for a couple of ones.

"Here you go."

"Aw, put that away." Teri Sue waved a hand at me. "I gotta show my gratitude somehow."

"That's okay. Like I said, I'm happy to help." I held out the money, but Teri Sue ignored it.

"Take a look at this." She lifted the hood and propped it up with a piece of aluminum tubing.

I had to give her credit. She'd known me less than an hour, and already she'd figured out how to get my attention. As uncomfortable as it made me to accept a free meal, I folded up the singles and put them away.

It was the first time I'd seen under the hood of a race car up close in full daylight. I drank in the details the way you gulp a glass of cold water on a hot summer day. All the unnecessary parts had been removed, leaving only what was needed to make the engine run. The brand-name, after-market equipment was clean and expertly installed. Nothing had been done halfway on this car. My hot dog disappeared without me even tasting it.

"Do people give you a hard time, being one of the only girls on the track?" I asked, stepping back so Teri Sue could shut the hood. While there were probably forty-five to fifty drivers between the three divisions, only four of them were women.

"Nah, not really. I've gotta put up with the occasional sexist comment, but I also get more than my fair share of attention."

"Teri Sue!" called an aggravated voice from the pit road. "You need to get lined up for time trials."

I glanced up to see the chief steward motioning toward the line of Street Stocks parked at the rear entrance to the track. He was scowling through a beard bushy enough to provide facial hair for three men.

"What's with him?" I asked, making a mental note never to get on his bad side.

"Ted? Aw, he's just naturally grumpy." Teri Sue fished a small notepad and pen out of the bottom drawer of the toolbox and slapped them into my hand. "Could you get my times for me? The easiest way is to write 'em down for all the cars so we can figure out the line-up ourselves. Sometimes it takes the officials forever to post it."

"No problem."

Teri Sue climbed into her car, tossed her strawberry blond

curls over her shoulders, and pulled on a baby blue helmet that matched her firesuit. Unable to hold back a prickle of jealousy, I watched as she hooked the shoulder straps of her safety harness through the quick release buckle on the belt.

The man in the next pit over was helping his driver secure the window net, so I pulled Teri Sue's from inside the door and clicked it into place.

"Thanks," she said, flipping the ignition switch mounted to the roll cage. She pushed the starter button, and the engine roared to life.

Once again looking to the guy beside me for a cue, I stepped onto the pit road to guide Teri Sue in backing up. I might not have any experience with race cars, but so long as there were people to watch, I'd have no problem figuring things out.

The Camaro pulled away, and I took a second to slip two dollars into a small drawer in Teri Sue's toolbox. By the time she found the money, I'd be long gone. It wasn't that I didn't appreciate her generosity. I just felt better knowing I didn't owe anything to anyone.

The loudspeaker crackled. "First up in our Street Stock division is Dallas Sauter. He got edged out of the 1989 championship, but it's a whole new decade, folks, and he's currently leading the points."

I sat down on a stack of tires and opened Teri Sue's notebook to a fresh page. One by one, the Street Stocks began pulling onto the track. I sipped my Pepsi as I wrote down each car number and its times.

Around me, drivers and crew from the higher divisions hustled to make last minute adjustments, working together like they'd known each other all their lives. That was something I'd always envied about people at the track. They were like one big family. Every week, as I sat alone in the stands, my ears would ring from all the whooping and hollering of wives, children, cousins, and friends, decked out in T-shirts and jackets that advertised their favorite driver. After the races, they'd hurry down to the pits, where kids would climb into cars or beg for autographs while everyone recounted the most exciting moments of the evening. I'd wanted to be part of all that since I'd started coming to the track when I was ten. I could hardly believe I was finally getting a taste, even if it was for only one night.

The purple #84 completed its second lap, and Teri Sue pulled onto the asphalt. She circled once to get up to speed before the flagman threw the green. Her first time put her mid-range in the pack. The next was less than three hundredths of a second off the first. That meant she was consistent—an important quality in a driver.

Using the best times, I made an ordered list of car numbers to get the lineup for the main event. The pack of fifteen would be split in two, with the top half in the fast heat and the bottom half in the slow one. The four quickest drivers from each heat would also race in the trophy dashes. Teri Sue had earned a spot in one of those. Even though she'd timed in slowest of the cars in her dash, she'd have the pole because at Eugene they inverted the pack. That stirred things up a little, giving the slow drivers half a chance and making the fast ones work for a win.

Teri Sue pulled into the pits. "How'd I do?" she asked as she climbed out of the car. I held up the notebook for her to see.

Her forehead scrunched up. "I'm in the slow heat and 'B' dash again." The irritation vanished as quickly as it appeared. "Oh well. Least I have a chance of winning there. In the fast heat, I'd really be outclassed."

She took the notebook and studied it. "Danny Lamar and Kit McKenzie are in my dash. They're pretty good. And then there's Cody Everett. He qualifies fast, but he can't hold his own in competition. Guess he doesn't have much experience." She shot me a grin. "He's only sixteen. Just a young'un, like you."

I fought off a twinge of annoyance. I was no "young'un." I'd been taking care of myself for years.

Teri Sue pawed through an old milk crate on the ground beside the toolbox, coming up with a ball cap that had a Charlotte Motor Speedway logo embroidered across the front. She shook it out and stuck it over her helmet-flattened hair, pulling her curls through the back so they formed a bushy ponytail. "Now, Cody's uncle—*he* can drive a race car."

"Who's his uncle?" I'd had to work the past few Saturdays, so I wasn't up to speed on this season's new drivers.

"Race Morgan. You know, in Limited Sportsman?"

"Are you kidding?" I looked across the pits to where Cody's Dart sat, and then over at the line of upper division cars waiting to time in. One glance confirmed it. The black #13 Street Stock was almost a mirror image of Race Morgan's #8 Sportsman. Both were '74 Darts with that distinctive squared-off body style. They also sported similar red, blue, and yellow graphics. The main difference, at least in outward appearance, was that Race's car was more than a little worse for wear, having been through a few encounters with the wall and one spectacular roll-over.

"I'd heard Race got saddled with his nephew last year," I said. "But I thought the kid was a juvenile delinquent."

Teri Sue shrugged. "Maybe Morgan reformed him."

"Maybe so. Everyone talks about what a great guy he is." I continued to stare across the pits, waiting for my favorite driver to take to the track. Race was young—in his mid-twenties—and drove with a smooth confidence that made him a lot of fun to watch. I'd never seen him back down from a challenge, but he wasn't one of those aggressive types who pushed everyone around. He just didn't seem to have any fear. Unlike myself. I'd never even had the courage to ask for his autograph.

"What—you like Race or something?" Teri Sue's voice was a teasing sing-song, and a smirk tugged at her lips.

"Who doesn't? He's an excellent driver." The defensiveness

in my tone was obvious, even to me. "He would've won the Sportsman championship last year if a wreck hadn't put him out for almost half the season. He's the only person who's passed Jerry Addamsen in the points in four years."

"I know," said Teri Sue. "He's leading his class now." Her smirk had mellowed into a humoring big-sister smile.

Not knowing how to respond, I froze. At school, the girls snubbed me because I had grease under my fingernails and didn't care how I dressed, so long as my shirt was right-side out. I had no experience with flirting or confessing crushes. Even if I'd been interested in that sort of thing, I'd have been laughed at for thinking I had enough class to attract a boy's attention.

Teri Sue's grin faded, and I realized my lips had stiffened into a scowl.

"Hey, I was just pickin' with ya." She punched my arm.

The last thing I wanted was for her to think I was an overly sensitive freak, so I forced myself to smile back. "I know. It's no big deal."

"Nothin' to be ashamed of, anyway. It's not like he's some dog that runs at the back of the pack. Matter of fact, he's got a real nice butt."

Laughter caught in my throat, almost choking me. Teri Sue was something else. I couldn't even *think* about Race Morgan's rear end without my face blazing, and here she was announcing her observations to the whole speedway.

"I hadn't noticed," I said. But any fool could see she didn't believe me.

## CHAPTER 2

While we waited for the first race, Teri Sue lounged on a stack of tires, and I looked over the Camaro, trying to memorize everything I saw. I wanted to tear a page out of her notebook and jot down details for when I built a car of my own, but I restrained myself. Some drivers got upset about that sort of thing.

"I'm glad the rain finally stopped," said Teri Sue. "I thought I was gonna grow moss on the north side of my body."

"You still might. It doesn't dry out around here until after the 4th of July." If there was one thing I knew besides cars, it was the weather.

"Really? It's always warm by this time of year in North Carolina. 'Cept in the mountains."

"Is that where you're from?" I straightened up, pulling myself away from the engine compartment.

"Yup. Hickory. It's about an hour north of Charlotte."

If I'd had to remember grade school geography to visualize that, I'd have been in trouble. But Charlotte was practically the stock car racing capitol of the world. It had a superspeedway, which meant I knew exactly where it was, just like I knew where Talladega, Darlington, and Atlanta were.

"You ever go to Hickory Motor Speedway?" I asked, lowering the hood. The short track in her hometown had the reputation of being the "Birthplace of the NASCAR Stars."

Teri Sue grinned. "Every Saturday night. We lived just a few miles away. From our front yard, you could hear the cars hot lapping."

"Wow," I said, instantly jealous. "That must've been so cool. I understand a lot of Busch and Winston Cup drivers live around there."

"Yup. We had Tommy Houston and Morgan Sheppard in Conover, and Dale Jarrett down in Newton. And then there was Harry Gant. He lived up the road a piece in Taylorsville. You get on the other side of Lake Norman, to Mooresville, and there's a whole pile of other drivers."

"Jeez." I shook my head. "That must've been heaven. Why'd you leave?"

"Daddy got a job teaching here at the University."

"Oh ..." I scrambled for a neutral comment, since there wasn't anything positive I could say. "I guess that's a good enough reason."

Teri Sue's face twisted into something that wasn't exactly a smile. "For him, I reckon. He always did want to come out west."

"Line 'em up, Street Stocks!" hollered the chief steward.

Teri Sue jumped up off her stack of tires like she'd sat on a bee.

Once she was in the Camaro and headed for the pit exit, I found a place at the front wall to watch the race. Unlike the heats and main events, trophy dashes weren't worth any points. But the four-lap sprints were fun to watch and good for bragging rights.

The cars pulled onto the track and circled twice, building speed. The second they got the green, Teri Sue's Camaro shot down the straightaway, making it to turn one ahead of the others. Danny Lamar stayed glued to her bumper, and Kit McKenzie dropped in behind. Stuck on the outside, Cody Everett didn't have a chance. The other drivers filed underneath, "freight-training" him.

Unfortunately, Teri Sue didn't have the muscle to hold Danny off for long. His red Mustang roared past her as they entered turn two for the second time. She managed to stay behind him until the final lap, when Kit overtook her coming out of turn four. Teri Sue wound up third, with Cody right behind her.

The Camaro rumbled into the pits and stopped in front of me.

"You drove a good race," I said as I unhooked the window net.

"I took *third*." With a scowl, Teri Sue unbuckled her neon pink racing harness and pulled off her helmet.

"But you didn't do anything wrong. Your car just wasn't as fast as the others."

"It should be, for the money Daddy's put in it." Grasping the roll bar that ran above the driver's side window, Teri Sue hoisted herself onto the edge of the door, swung her feet out, and dropped to the ground. "This was one of the top cars in this division last year. Brad Charleston drove it."

"This is his old car?" I handed her a quart of orange Gatorade I'd found in her cooler. I knew Brad had sold it and moved up to the Sportsman division, but I hadn't recognized it with the new paint job. Over half the cars in Teri Sue's class were Camaros or Firebirds. GM products were cheaper to race than Fords or Dodges because there were more performance parts available for them.

"Umm hmm." Teri Sue raised the bottle to her lips and drained it halfway. "Daddy bought it for me when we got here after Christmas, on account of how bad he felt for making us move in the middle of my senior year. Then he got George to help set it up. Not that *that* lasted long." Her mouth contorted at the mention of his name.

Even though I thought it was pretty heartless to make a kid move during her final year of school, I didn't say so. People were funny when it came to their parents. Lydia, my mother, was never going to win any parenting awards, but I wouldn't have let anyone get away with badmouthing her.

"So what's George's problem?" I asked.

"Just lazy, I reckon."

It was impossible to hold back my grin. I'd never heard

anyone say, "I reckon" in real life before.

Teri Sue boosted herself onto the front fender of her car. "Look, you seem to be pretty good at this. How 'bout taking George's place?"

"Are you serious?" For the past two years, I'd been trying to get work in a garage. After all that effort, it was hard to believe something so incredible could fall into my lap.

"Damn straight. Why wouldn't I be?" Teri Sue took another drink of Gatorade. "You could come by my place two or three nights a week to help get the car set up, and on Saturdays you could crew for me."

I gawked as if I'd been asked to sub for Dale Earnhardt at Daytona. Things like this didn't happen to me. They just didn't.

"So? Whaddaya think?" Teri Sue drained the rest of her sports drink.

For a second, I let myself pretend it could happen. That my life was normal, and I had a choice. But reality sent those thoughts into a skid.

"I can't. I work at Burger King, and they're always giving me a crazy schedule. This is the first time all season I've even made it to the races."

"So quit," said Teri Sue with a shrug.

Her indifference sent irritation rippling through me. Wouldn't it be nice to have things that easy? Why was it, when I finally got the opportunity of my life, I had to turn it down?

"That's not an option," I said. "I need the cash."

Teri Sue laughed. "Is that the only thing holding you back? Heck, my Daddy'll pay you. And believe you me, it'll be more than you're making now. Which would you rather do, flip burgers or turn a wrench?"

The offer toppled me like a tree in a windstorm.

"So? How 'bout it?" Teri Sue tossed the now-empty bottle at a trashcan, making a perfect two-point shot.

I took a deep breath and let it out in a rush. "I guess you'd better give me directions to your house."

Over the course of the evening, I discovered Teri Sue was friendly with everyone, and they seemed to like her right back. I couldn't believe someone that popular would take an interest in me. But then, George *had* left her in the lurch. There was no point questioning it. I just concentrated on enjoying every second I had in the pits. The best part of all was that I'd get to keep doing this all season.

In her heat, Teri Sue finished fifth out of eight cars, and in the main, she worked her way into seventh place. Cody came in nearly last in both events. The allegations about his lack of skill had left me curious, so I'd been watching him as closely as I'd watched Teri Sue.

The problem wasn't easy to pinpoint. Cody drove a good line and didn't let the faster drivers intimidate him. He just lost his edge when surrounded by other cars. His Dart handled well and had plenty of power, which was only to be expected. Kasey McCormick, Race's crew chief, sponsored both black Dodges. Since she'd started crewing for Race a few years before, he'd gone from being a fearless but underpowered mid-pack runner to consistently finishing out front.

If Race was my speedway hero, Kasey was a close second. At twenty-four, she already owned an auto restoration shop, Eugene Custom Classics. I would've given my right arm to work for her, but I'd never been able to drum up the nerve to ask.

"I've gotta say, you sure know how to pick 'em," Teri Sue commented as we watched Race charge across the finish line, stealing the win from Jerry Addamsen on the final lap. After being spun by a rookie halfway through the main, Race had fought his way back from last place. Teri Sue shook her head and whistled. "Talented and good looking. Definitely my top two qualities in a driver."

There was absolutely nothing I could say to that, so I didn't respond.

All through the Super Stock main, Teri Sue kept up the conspiratorial chatter, acting as if I were her new best friend. I stood rigid and uncomfortable, at a loss for words. It had been a long time since I'd hung out with people my age outside of school, and even there I kept to myself. But Teri Sue didn't seem to notice my silence, filling it with her opinions about living in Eugene, Oregon's incessant rain, and which drivers filled out the backside of a firesuit the best. The only topic I could hold my own on was the weather.

After the races, Teri Sue jogged across turn one to the field where the tow vehicles were parked. She came back pulling a car trailer behind a shiny new Chevy pickup. I had to wonder how her family could afford things like that with her dad teaching at the University. I knew college professors didn't make much, because Lydia had dated one until he'd gotten wise to her.

Wanting to earn my keep, I started loading equipment into the back of the truck. As I was lifting the toolbox, Teri Sue rushed over.

"Lemme help with that. It's heavy."

"I've got it." I lugged it over to the tailgate and slid it into the bed.

"Good lord, girl. Just 'cause I'm paying you doesn't mean you've gotta do it all on your own."

I shrugged. "I want to make myself useful."

"Uh huh. And *I* wanna keep my new crew chief from getting a hernia. Next time, say the word and I'll give you a hand."

I nodded, even though it wasn't likely to happen. I hated bothering people for help. Besides, doing things myself meant I didn't have to worry about anyone saying they were too busy.

When we'd finished loading the equipment, and had the car

on the trailer, Teri Sue turned to lean against the front fender of her truck. "Thanks for the help. I sure appreciate it. How 'bout we get a bite to eat? Most drivers go to this restaurant out on Highway 99 after the races. The Little R."

I would've loved another behind-the-scenes glimpse of the racing world, but it was almost eleven.

"I can't. I have to get home."

Teri Sue's mouth pulled into a knowing grin. "Early curfew, huh?"

If only it were that simple. "I've just got stuff to do."

"Okay. Well, I'll need your phone number so I don't lose track of you. Lemme grab a pen."

She opened the door of the pickup to get her purse, and while she dug through it, I scoured my brain for an excuse. I didn't need her calling and talking to my mother. I'd never hear the end of it if Lydia found out I'd taken a job working on cars. Could I say we didn't have a phone? Give her a number that was a digit off? Pretend I wasn't allowed to give it out?

Teri Sue turned around, a pen and address book in her hands. "Okay, let's have it."

"Uh . . ." My brain sputtered and stalled. There was no way out. Anything I said was bound to be suspicious. I'd just have to give her my number and hope for the best.

As I recited it, Teri Sue scribbled it in her book. "Great. So how 'bout comin' by my place tomorrow? I'll show ya what we've got to work with. Maybe around ten? I like to sleep in."

I forced a smile. "I'll be there."

# CHAPTER 5

On the way out to the parking lot, I almost regretted not taking Teri Sue up on her offer. *Almost.* Likely as not, she'd only invited me to the Little R to be friendly. Maybe she was even glad I'd turned her down.

I shivered in my lightweight jacket as I walked down the gravel driveway. The air, rich with the scent of freshly cut grass, was getting a bite to it. Even when we could squeeze a decent day out of our soggy Oregon springs, the nights stayed chilly. But at least I wouldn't have to walk back to the bus stop like I had for the past six seasons, ducking out of the Super Stock main early so I wouldn't miss the last bus home. Now, finally, I had my license and my car was street-worthy.

I grinned as I spotted the small, dark shape sitting in the field the speedway used as a parking lot. On the outside, the car was nothing but a '72 Pinto, fading red paint obscured by rust and primer. Under the hood, it was something else. I'd finished installing the new engine, a 351 Windsor, only a month before, working in the school's auto shop because I'd had no other options. That arrangement had its drawbacks, with my teacher practically ordering me to let the guys in class help, and threatening me with a lower grade when I refused. He hadn't understood that it was my car, and I wanted to do the work myself, in my own methodical way.

I opened the door and slid behind the wheel, the thrill of having everything completed after two long years still fresh.

The trip from the speedway in west Eugene to my apartment in Springfield was a straight shot through town with nothing exciting about it, but any opportunity to drive was pure bliss. As I sang along to my tape of hot-rodding songs, I kept a close lookout for cops—a skill I'd perfected after teaching myself to drive Lydia's Buick when I was ten. Even though I'd been legally licensed for nearly a month now, staying under the speed limit was beyond me.

My mood dimmed when I got home and saw that the college students in #106 were having another party. The parking lot was full. I grumbled as I backed out onto the street and found a spot between a Honda Civic and a jacked-up Dodge truck. Only residents were supposed to use the lot, but our manager was rarely home to enforce the rule. Even though I took offense to leaving the Pinto on a public road, I could hardly blame him. Mill Street in Springfield wasn't at the top of my list of favorite places, either.

I glanced at my watch as I hurried up the stairs to my second floor apartment. Quarter after eleven. If I hurried, I could get the place cleaned up and be safely in bed before Lydia got home. She'd asked me to do it that morning, but I'd gotten sucked into tinkering with the Pinto and hadn't had time before I'd left for the speedway.

Through the crack between the drawn curtains, I saw a flicker of blue television light. *Damn.* I tiptoed to the door, worked the key into the lock, and stealthily turned the knob. Maybe Lydia was already asleep and wouldn't notice me coming in. Usually, if she got home before one on a Saturday, it meant something had gone wrong between her and her boyfriend. She always drank too much when that happened, and if I got lucky she'd simply pass out. If not . . .

"Jess?" Lydia blinked at me from the couch, eyes bloodshot and make-up a tear-smudged mess. Her black mini skirt, worn over a sleeveless, neon-pink Spandex top, was as wrinkled as if she'd slept in it. Oh man. Definitely another argument with Jimmy. Why couldn't she tell that loser to get lost?

"Hey, Lydia." I said, giving her my helpful-daughter smile. Maybe it wasn't too late to salvage the situation. When she was sober, she was sweet as a kindergarten teacher, and even drunk she wasn't entirely unreasonable. Most of the time. "I'm sorry about the mess. I—"

"Just where the hell have you been?"

I glanced at the Budweiser can in her hand. Another sat on the coffee table in the clutter she'd swept aside to make room for her bare feet. Two beers here, and who knows how many at the tavern. There was no way I could risk telling her the truth.

"They called me in to work."

"And I suppose it was too much trouble to clean up around here before you left?"

"I had homework." That was an even bigger lie. I'd barely touched my assignments in a week. It wasn't that I was a completely hopeless student. Math and science were a breeze. But school seemed like a waste of time in comparison to getting enough hours at work to keep food in the cupboards.

"You always have an excuse, don't you?"

I vise-gripped my jaw to bite back a comment I'd only regret. My alcohol barometer told me she was just shy of passing out. If I could keep her calm, she'd drift off and everything would be fine in the morning.

"It's no big deal. I'll clean it up now."

"Damn straight you will, missy!" She drained her can and slammed it down on the end table. "And you can get me another beer while you're at it. I busted my ass at the restaurant all day. It'd be nice if your father bothered to send a child support check once in a while."

My fists clenched involuntarily at that last little snipe, and I forced myself to take a long, steady breath. Okay, so Dad didn't send any money. So he never bothered to write or remember my birthday. But as much as he'd let me down by abandoning us, I couldn't forget all the good moments I'd had with him, working on the Mustang he'd sold just before he left.

I wasn't about to get Lydia a drink, not even to keep the peace, so I escaped to the kitchen, where I could get started on the housework without upsetting her further.

Frustration welled up as I looked at the mess. It wasn't my fault. I put things away when I was done with them. Lydia was the one who left everything on the counter. Dirty dishes, used paper towels, empty food cans. Tonight there was even a gallon of milk sitting out. Milk I'd bought just the day before. Weren't things bad enough without her being wasteful?

I twisted off the cap and gave the jug a sniff. Still fresh. I stuck it in the fridge, resisting the urge to slam the door.

After throwing away the trash and wiping down the counters, I stacked the dishes and filled the sink, letting the rhythm of the work soothe away my annoyance. The window above the faucet fogged when I turned on the water. Lydia kept the thermostat at sixty and dragged her space heater from room to room to fight the chill. I'd tried to explain she wasn't saving money, but she didn't believe me. When I used my contribution to the electric bill as leverage, all it did was make her cry. She'd been a mess since Dad took off, and as difficult as that made things for me, I knew it wasn't her fault.

The hot water felt good on my hands. Running a sponge over the plates, I pulled Teri Sue's offer up from memory to savor the excitement of it. I still couldn't believe it was real. Just landing a job sweeping floors in a garage would've made my day, and instead I'd lucked into this. For the next five months, I'd have steady work doing something I loved. What could be better than that?

After scrubbing the last pan, caked with burnt chili, I drained the sink and wiped it clean. Exhaustion caught up with me as I ran a quick mop over the linoleum, but I called on my reserves and headed out to the living room.

Lydia was gently snoring, one arm draped over the edge of the couch and the other tucked close to her chest. Tomorrow she'd be sorry for yelling. She always regretted the things she said when she was drunk. It would've been easy to hate her for the roller coaster ride she'd made our lives, but how could I when I knew how miserably helpless she was at controlling her demons?

Figuring the rest of the cleanup could wait till morning, I pulled the afghan from the back of the easy chair and draped it over my mother. Things would be better now. I was finally on my way to achieving my dreams.

The next morning, I woke with an uneasy feeling, but I couldn't quite pinpoint the reason for it. Maybe it was because Teri Sue was so pretty and outgoing. As I blew my hair dry, I couldn't help thinking of her red-gold curls, which had looked perfect, even smashed down by her helmet. How long would it take her to figure out what a socially inept slob I was? At school, girls like her never gave me the time of day.

I tried to convince myself it didn't matter. I had something she needed: skills with a wrench. This was a job, not a friendship, and as long as I remembered that, I had nothing to worry about. Then I realized what was nagging at me. Sure, I could replace a leaf spring and do a tune up. I could even stick a small block V-8 in a compact car engine compartment. But I didn't know anything about setting up race cars, and eventually, that was what Teri Sue would need.

I wound a ponytail holder around my hair and stuck the brush back in the drawer. Maybe I could fake it, avoid telling her until I'd taught myself the basics.

I went out to the living room, where Lydia was still asleep, sprawled on the couch with the afghan hanging dangerously close to her space heater. Knowing she'd wake up feeling like she was in a sauna, if she didn't burn the place down first, I snapped the dial to the 'off' position.

How was I going to get out of this mess with Teri Sue? Maybe I could go to the library and check out books about race car suspensions. No, that wouldn't work. I'd already been through the entire automotive section, and I'd never seen anything like that. Oregon was woefully ignorant when it came to stock car racing.

After spending ten minutes straightening up the living room, I grabbed a sweatshirt and my Eugene Speedway hat and headed outside. The radio had forecast a high in the seventies, but the haze of thin clouds filtering the sun told me it wasn't likely.

I hurried down the steps, knowing there was only one solution to my dilemma. I'd have to tell Teri Sue the truth. But what if she changed her mind about the job? I needed the work, and now that I'd decided to quit Burger King, I realized just how badly I hated it there. Oh man, why hadn't I thought about this last night?

I pulled the scrap of paper with Teri Sue's address from my pocket. She lived on Fox Hollow road. From the number, I could tell her house would be on the back side of Spencer Butte. Eugene stretched east-west, so her place south of town was in the country, even though it was only about ten minutes from the city center.

My worries stayed with me the whole drive. It was only fair to be honest, but I hated the idea of losing such a great opportunity. With my stomach fluttering, I turned up a driveway that led to an old white farmhouse. The place was even nicer than the one we'd had near the University when I was little. A huge porch stretched along the front, its waist-high wall constructed from smooth river rock. Stone pillars marked the corners and each side of the steps, supporting a roof that slanted out almost flat from a multi-windowed second story room. The yard was a flurry of color, with flowerbeds outlining the porch and split-rail fence that encircled the yard. Off to one side, a weather-beaten barn sat surrounded by oaks and Douglas firs. Teri Sue's truck was backed up to its front doors, the race car behind it on the trailer.

I parked beside a Honda Civic and had one foot out of the Pinto when a boy with Teri Sue's strawberry blonde hair rushed through the front door and down the steps.

"Come back here, you brat!" hollered Teri Sue, hot on his heels.

The kid, who looked about ten, ran with a limp, and a closer look told me why. A leather and metal brace encased his left leg, starting at his thigh and wrapping down under his sneaker.

When Teri Sue caught sight of me, she gave up the chase. "Oh, hey," she said, tossing her hair back over her shoulder and trotting over to join me. "That's my kid brother. He ate the last pack of Pop Tarts, and it was mine."

"Ahh." I nodded as I took in Teri Sue's designer jeans and fitted T-shirt. She was going to work in that? Maybe I should've opted for a fresh pair of Levis instead of recycling the ones I'd worn yesterday. Of course, if she sent me packing, it wouldn't matter.

"He's a real pest," Teri Sue added, giving me a challenging look. "Don't make the mistake of feeling sorry for him. First off, he'd hate it, and second, he doesn't deserve the attention."

"Seems like it's you I should feel sorry for. He's the one who got all the Pop Tarts."

Surprise flashed across Teri Sue's face. She laughed, and the tension drained from her expression. "Oh, hey," she said, looking behind me. "Is that your car?"

I glanced over my shoulder, aware of how pathetic the Pinto must seem to the owner of a brand new Chevy pickup. "Yeah. Why?"

She shrugged. "I coulda sworn I heard a big car pull up out here. A Mustang or something."

"Take a look." I popped the hood, knowing I should be getting to the point about the job, but unable to resist grandstanding a little. Outside the kids in my shop class, no one had expressed the least bit of interest in the Pinto. Especially not

Lydia, who considered my fascination with cars to be a betrayal.

Teri Sue moved closer, her eyes widening. "Sweet Jesus. That's a V-8."

"351 Windsor." A grin tugged at my lips. The Pinto didn't just make me proud. Every time I looked at it, even thought about it, I was overcome by a swell of freedom, empowerment, and something a little harder to put a label on. My car wasn't just a vehicle to me. In some crazy way I'd never admit, it was almost a companion.

For several long moments, Teri Sue studied the engine compartment. There was nothing flashy about it, no chrome or anodized fittings. But every speck of grease had been scrubbed away, every part carefully painted, every wire tucked into place.

"You did this, didn't you?" she asked, turning to look at me with new respect.

My face went suddenly hot. "Yeah." I was glad she knew enough to realize what she was seeing. Most people would've wondered why I'd invested in something as lowly as a Pinto. They wouldn't have understood the appeal of a sleeper—a car that looked sedate and conservative, but was chock full of power.

Teri Sue grinned and shook her head, whistling in appreciation. "You just swap out the engine, or did you fix up the rest of it, too?"

"I've gone through everything mechanical: suspension, brakes, cooling system. All that's left is the paint." It hadn't been easy to come up with the money, even though I'd started saving when I was ten, lying about my age to hustle every babysitting job I could find. From day one, half my earnings had gone toward taking up Lydia's slack.

A curious face peeked around the hood of the Pinto, then Teri Sue's brother slunk forward to put his hands on the fender and peer at the engine.

"Hey," I said, smiling. Little kids were easy. They never set you up or laid traps like people my age did. The worst you had to worry about was having them rattle off whatever was on their minds.

"Hey," he answered, ducking his head and giving me a shy smile.

Teri Sue scowled. "You're not off the hook for stealing my Pop Tarts, y'know."

"I'll give 'em back if you want." The kid stuck a finger down his throat and gagged, pretending to throw up.

"Not on my engine!" I said.

The comment earned me a nervous giggle.

"Go find something to do," Teri Sue told her little brother. "Can't you see we're busy?"

He smirked. "Oh yeah, you look real busy." While Teri Sue's accent had intrigued me, her brother's piping voice sounded like music.

"Go on, you heard me," said Teri Sue, lifting her hands from the radiator core support and shooing him away. "Go work on one of your models or something."

He sighed and rolled his eyes, turning to trudge off dramatically toward the house.

"He's showing off for you," said his sister.

"I know. But he's funny. What's his name?"

"Rhett."

"Brett?"

"No, Rhett. Like Rhett Butler."

I looked at her blankly. Was that some sort of celebrity or something?

Teri Sue waved her hands in the air, as if that might somehow stir my memory. "You know, *Gone With The Wind*? Our Daddy's big on old movies. Reckon it comes from being a history teacher. I'm lucky he didn't name me Scarlet."

"Ohhh." I nodded, feeling like an idiot as I finally made the connection. "Sorry. I haven't seen it. I don't watch much TV."

"Prob'ly too busy stuffing big engines in little cars," Teri Sue said, giving me a grin. "So, are you ready to get busy on mine?"

My stomach lurched. "Sure."

As I followed her to the barn, I tried to work up the courage to say what I needed to. But somehow, I couldn't get the words to come out of my mouth.

"I don't have the most modern set-up for a shop," said Teri Sue, tugging the doors open one at a time. "But at least it's a roof to keep the rain off. And it has electricity."

Inside, the hard dirt floor was almost level and had been swept free of hay and loose soil. A big roll-away tool box sat along one wall. Next to it were a garage-style floor jack, a set of quality jack stands, and a metal shelf holding a variety of power and pneumatic tools. An air compressor had been tucked out of the way in one of the old horse stalls.

"What do you think?" Teri Sue asked, sticking her hands in her back pockets. A hint of anxiousness clouded her green eyes. *She* was worried about *my* opinion?

"It's great," I said.

Relief flickered across her face. "Daddy's gonna get cement poured in here eventually. George said we'd need a level surface if we wanted to get the car set up right."

I nodded, even though I had no idea what she was talking about. Why hadn't I just admitted I knew nothing about race cars last night and avoided getting our hopes up?

Teri Sue turned away. "Well, I guess we'd better get the car off the trailer."

As she backed the Camaro into the garage, I lectured myself. It was time to own up. Sure, working here would be great, but I'd have to risk losing that. It was better than misrepresenting myself. I hated phonies as much as Holden Caulfield did in that book they'd forced me to read for English.

Despite my good intentions, I couldn't figure out how to broach the subject. Instead, I let Teri Sue jabber away as I helped her put the car on jack stands.

"So where do we start?" she asked.

This was it. Time to come clean. I drew a deep breath and turned to face her. "Teri Sue, there's something I should've told you last night."

# CHAPTER 4

Teri Sue's smile faltered. "What—you're not gonna tell me you changed your mind, are ya? 'Cause I really need some help. Truth is, I never did like George much, and I don't know who else to ask."

I stood running my hand up and down the length of my arm. But I forced myself to look her in the eye. "No. I haven't changed my mind. I'm just not sure you'll want my help after you hear what I have to say."

"And what's that?"

"Well ... uh ..." I glanced toward the Camaro, and then back at her. "The truth is, I've never worked on a race car. I don't know anything about them. I'm sorry. If you want out of our deal, I understand completely."

Teri Sue frowned, but as though she were confused, rather than angry. "You fixed my spring, didn't you? And what about your Pinto? You gonna tell me the Engine Fairy dropped that 351 in there?"

My gaze slid to the dirt floor. "Just because I can turn a wrench doesn't mean I know how to set up a race car."

"You know more than I do."

I looked up at her. "So you don't care that I ... misled you?" How could she not be upset about that?

"Aw heck, girl," she said, waving a hand in my direction. "You didn't mislead me. I asked if you'd help with my car and you said yes. It's not like you tried to convince me you'd been crew chief for Richard Petty."

Surprise swept through me, followed by relief. I couldn't believe she was so willing to let it go. "Oh.... Well, okay. But that still leaves us with a problem. How are we going to figure out how to set up your car?"

Teri Sue hunched her shoulders up in a shrug. "I dunno. Maybe we can get some books. That's how you learned to do the other stuff, right?"

"Yeah, but I don't know where to find books about racing."

"Hmmm." Teri Sue studied the floor, rubbing a hand across the back of her neck. Then her head shot up. "Hey, I know. I've got three years of back issues of *Circle Track* and *Stock Car Racing* magazine. There's all kinds of technical articles in 'em. You wanna take a look?"

"Yeah. That sounds perfect."

I followed Teri Sue outside, where the clouds had thickened. A sprinkling of fat raindrops dotted the gravel.

"I thought it was supposed to be seventy-five today," she said, crinkling her nose at the sky.

"It's tough predicting the weather in Oregon. We've got the influence of the Pacific, and then there's the Cascade Range, which—"

"Whoa!" Teri Sue turned on her heel, arms raised in surrender. "Hold up with the science lesson. I get enough of that in school. Lemme guess—you're one of those geeky types, aren't you?"

I froze, chastising myself for not having the sense to keep my mouth shut.

A grin broke over Teri Sue's face, and she slapped my shoulder. "Hey, that was a compliment. One thing you're gonna learn about me—I'm dumb as a box of rocks. Hanging around someone like you will probably be a good influence. C'mon, let's go inside before we get drenched." Ducking her head, she made a dash for the house.

We stepped through the front door into a hallway with a staircase leading to the second floor. On the right was the living room, and on the left, the entrance to what looked like a den or office. Teri Sue poked her head through the doorway.

"Hey Daddy, I want you to meet my new friend, Jess DeLand."

*Friend?* She tossed that word around so casually. I'd known the guys in my shop class since September, and I wouldn't necessarily call them my friends.

I followed her into the room, where the walls were lined with floor-to-ceiling bookshelves and posters from old movies. A man with the same green eyes and red-gold hair as Rhett and Teri Sue sat behind a desk. Stacks of papers, cut flowers in a Mason jar, and a plate that held one chocolate chip cookie, along with the crumbs from several others, cluttered the surface.

"Hello, Jess," he said, giving me a smile that took twenty years off his age. He wore a green and yellow tie-dyed T-shirt with the words "How 'bout them Ducks" arching over the University of Oregon mascot.

"Hi, Mr. Cline." I stepped forward and held out my hand. "It's nice to meet you."

"It's nice to meet you, too, but there's no need to be so formal. You can call me Mark." He spoke with the same smooth drawl as his daughter. I could've stood there all day listening to it.

"You're gonna like her, Daddy," said Teri Sue. "She's real smart. But she doesn't know much about race cars yet, so we need to hit the books. Have fun grading those papers."

As she led me out the door and down the hall, she explained why I hadn't met her dad and brother the night before. "Daddy usually comes to watch me race, but he had to go to some history department shindig. They probably stood around talking about the Civil War and noshing on hard tack." She looked over her shoulder at me. "You want a snack? C'mon, I'll get us some tea and cookies."

In the kitchen, I expected her to go to the stove and put a kettle on to boil, but instead she opened the refrigerator and pulled out a pitcher. After putting ice in two glasses and filling them with tea, she handed me one.

"I've never had cold tea before," I said.

"No kidding? Give it a taste. See what you think."

I expected something plain and bitter. The sweet, rich flavor that coated my tongue completely startled my taste buds. "Hey, that's good."

"Sweet tea," said Teri Sue, opening a ceramic jar shaped like a bust of George Washington and pulling out a handful of cookies. "Grab some."

I reached in and got two. As I bit into the first, bittersweet chocolate melting in my mouth, my heart twinged. Before Dad left, when Lydia was still a real mom who read bedtime stories and kissed me goodnight, she'd taught me how to bake chocolate chip cookies. But I hadn't tasted a homemade one in years.

Shaking off the nostalgia, I trailed Teri Sue upstairs to her bedroom, which turned out to be the one at the front of the house above the porch. A row of old-fashioned double-hung windows made up the south wall, providing a view of the front yard, the barn, and the woods beyond. Envy knotted in my throat as I thought of all the sunlight that must stream through on a clear day. My bedroom had one small window that faced north and oozed gloom.

Teri Sue stopped short when she saw Rhett seated at her desk, pecking with one finger at the keyboard of a brand new Hewlett Packard 386 computer. "What on God's green earth do you think you're doing?"

He spun to face her, startled, and his face crumpled into a scowl. "Duh! I'm using the computer."

"Who said you could come in here?"

"It's my computer, too."

"But it's *my* room."

"So? You wouldn't let Daddy put it in the guest room."

The two of them stared at each other for several long moments, green eyes locked in contempt. Then Teri Sue slapped her tea and cookies down on the dresser, marched across the hardwood floor, and grabbed her brother by the back of his T-shirt.

"Out!"

"I'm in the middle of writing a letter!"

"To Mama I bet." Teri Sue glanced at the screen and nodded. "It figures. When are you gonna learn?"

"Just because you hate her doesn't mean I have to!"

"She won't write back."

"Yes she will!"

A pang shot through me at his hopeful insistence, but Teri Sue sighed and rolled her eyes. "I give up," she said, releasing his shirt and dropping onto the edge of her bed. "I swear, Rhett, sometimes you don't have the sense God gave a goat."

Hunching protectively over the keyboard, he rushed to finish his letter. After hitting the "print screen" key, he saved his file and popped his disk out of the drive while the dot matrix printer shrieked out a copy.

"There," he said, pulling back the bale and snatching his letter from the printer, "You can have your stupid room back." He gave his sister a glance that could've split stone before turning to stalk away.

I stepped aside to let him through the door.

"Sorry 'bout that," said Teri Sue. She stood up, gesturing behind her to the bed. "Come on in and sit down. I'll find those magazines."

The embarrassment of witnessing their fight had scrambled my stomach. I slipped across the room and sat, wishing she hadn't been so mean to Rhett. Was that how all brothers and sisters treated each other?

Oblivious to my discomfort, Teri Sue went over to the closet and began plowing through it. She emerged with a stack of magazines, which she dumped on the bed. "Here's some of 'em. You can get star—" Her eyes met mine and the words dried up faster than a mud puddle in July. "What's wrong? Oh Lord, you aren't gonna get all tore up because I gave the kid a hard time, are ya?"

Heat flushed across my skin. Who was I to judge her in her own house? But the stiffness of Rhett's posture, the grit in his expression, had set off flares of memory. I could hear the phone ringing, see my hands tugging at Lydia's shirt as I begged her to let me speak to my father. She'd finally get so frustrated she'd push me away. Later she'd say she was sorry, but Daddy didn't want to talk to me. The shock of it had been like discovering Santa Claus didn't exist.

"I'm sorry," I told Teri Sue. "It's none of my business."

She shrugged, her easy smile rushing back. "Don't worry about it. Anyway, we don't mean anything by it when we get on each other like that."

"It's just—I guess it hits kind of close to home. I haven't seen my dad in eight years." The words slipped right past the security center of my brain, leaving me slightly stunned. I'd never said anything like that out loud.

Teri Sue fired a stony look at me before shifting her attention to the magazines and shuffling them into a neat stack. "This is different."

"How?" I asked, ignoring the warning in her posture as she went back to the closet to yank a box from the upper shelf. "He's a little kid and he misses his mom. That's only natural."

Teri Sue turned abruptly and thumped the box down beside me on the bed.

"Natural? You think it's natural for a kid to love a Mama who crippled him then shut him out of her mind so she wouldn't have to face up to it?"

## CHAPTER 5

Teri Sue's eyes blazed. "Rhett didn't always wear that brace, y'know. Lots of people think he was born that way, and our family's not much on setting 'em straight." She glanced over her shoulder at the door, strode across the room, and shut it.

"It happened when he was six," she said, coming back over to the bed and looking down into the box of magazines. "Mama was getting ready for this big barbeque—some party for the people in daddy's department at the college. She'd been cooking all day and was about to have one of her breakdowns. She never was very strong. When she found out she didn't have any cinnamon for the peach cobbler, it sent her into a panic. She hopped in the car to go get some, and Rhett was riding his Big Wheel in the driveway. He didn't have time to get out of the way."

Ice pierced my gut—the way it does when you've smashed your fingers in a car door, but the pain hasn't yet registered. I stared open-mouthed at Teri Sue, who began snatching up magazines and slapping them down in stacks on the bed.

"Rhett's lucky he's even got a leg to put that brace on."

"Wasn't it an accident?"

"Of course it was an accident." She fired off a bitter look. "But shutting him out of her head afterward sure wasn't. Just because she's the sensitive type doesn't give her the right to abandon her son."

I wanted to ask what she meant by that, but how could I? It had been bad enough to put myself in the middle of a family squabble. Making Teri Sue re-live such a poisonous memory was unforgivable.

As she continued to sort magazines, her motions slowly losing their fury, I sat motionless on the bed and wished I'd minded my own business.

At last, the box was empty and Teri Sue looked up at me with a sad little shake of her head. "I reckon that's why I get so ill with him. I can't stand thinking about that boy worshipping a Mama who won't even acknowledge his existence."

We hung out for the rest of the morning, and as I read about camber, stagger, and cross weight, the shock of Teri Sue's outburst faded. While I did my research, she painted her fingernails, flipped through her history book, and finally went down to make us lunch.

"Pulled pork," she said, coming into the room with a tray that held two sandwiches and a pitcher of sweet tea. The food looked like it had come from a restaurant, the bread grilled and piled high with shredded meat, lettuce, and tomatoes.

"You made this?" I asked as she handed me a plate.

"Sure. It was no big deal. The pork was left over from last night."

I bit into the sandwich, my mouth watering at the best food I'd tasted all month. "Are you kidding?" I said after I swallowed. "You could open your own café."

"I just might have to. With the grades I'm making, I'll be lucky to get into the U of O. Even if Daddy does teach there."

I didn't want to get grease on Teri Sue's magazines, so I waited until I'd finished my lunch to go back to the article I'd been reading.

She stacked the plates and piled them onto the tray. "Y'know, you can take those home with you."

"That's okay. I don't want anything to happen to them." In a drunken rage, Lydia had once ripped some of my Hot Rod magazines in half because they reminded her of my dad.

"What's gonna happen to 'em?" asked Teri Sue.

Maybe she was right. I could always store them in the Pinto, where they'd be safe.

She tossed a stray pair of jeans into her laundry basket and picked it up. "Look, if you want to sit here reading, you're welcome to, but I've gotta get busy with my chores."

"That's okay," I said, taking the hint that I'd outstayed my welcome. "I should get going. I'll start with these and come back for the others another time." I set a stack of magazines aside and piled the rest into the box. Reading would be easier at home, anyway, where I'd have a pen and paper and could take notes.

Teri Sue led me downstairs. "You coming back tomorrow?" she asked, stopping in the hallway with the laundry basket hitched on her hip.

"If you want me to."

"Of course I do. I plan on winning some trophies before the year is out."

A few hours ago, that statement might've intimidated me, but now I felt more confident. "Okay. I'll be here right after school," I said before stepping through the front door.

Rhett was slouched in an Adirondack chair on the porch, reading a Teenage Mutant Ninja Turtles comic. "Hey," he said.

"Hey, Rhett." I gave him a nod and started down the steps.

"She told you about Mama, didn't she?"

His voice stopped me short. "Yeah," I said, turning to face him.

Rhett's eyes, big and sad, caught hold of mine, and he rubbed the leather band at the top of his brace. "It's not her fault, you know. It was an accident."

"That's what Teri Sue said."

He sighed. "Maybe. But she doesn't believe it."

On the drive home, I puzzled over what Teri Sue had said about her mother, trying to untangle the meaning of it. Had she really wiped the memory of Rhett from her mind? How could that be possible? I hadn't heard from my truck driver dad since he took off to haul a load of strawberries to North Dakota when I was eight, but even so, I was sure he hadn't forgotten me.

With my sympathy for Rhett so strong, it was easy to remember how I'd felt back then, stuck with a mother who no longer cooked—who cried all day and could barely hold a job. It hadn't been long before I'd learned to take care of her, teaching myself to fix tuna sandwiches, then Ramen noodles and macaroni and cheese. When she was out drinking, I stayed by myself, and when she came home in a daze, I tucked her into bed. In return, she'd call me "Mommy's Big Girl."

Scared as I'd been, not having a grownup to go to for comfort, when I'd learned how much she needed me, it was like discovering my bones were made of steel.

When I got back to the apartment, Lydia was waiting on the couch. She muted the TV and put on her best repentant smile. "Hi, sweetie. Thanks for cleaning the kitchen." She fidgeted with the remote. "I'm sorry about last night."

"I know."

"You want to order Chinese takeout? I feel like I should make it up to you. I was mad at Jimmy, but that's no excuse."

As always, something squirmed deep inside me, telling me the apology wasn't enough, but what could I do other than accept it? "That sounds good, Lydia."

Her expression brightened and she scrambled up to get the phone book.

At moments like this, she almost felt like a mother, but it had been years since the word "mom" had passed my lips. When I was nine, Lydia asked me to start calling her by her first name. "You've been such a big help since Daddy left. It's almost like we're sisters, don't you think?"

I'd been flattered by the privilege, and it wasn't until later that I realized what it meant. By taking her up on the offer, I'd given up my last chance to be a kid.

\* \* \*

I stayed up half the night reading Teri Sue's magazines and taking notes. The next day in English, my teacher threatened to take one of them away since we were supposed to be reading some boring poem by a man who had been dead for over three hundred years.

The second I got out of school, I drove straight to Teri Sue's.

"Okay, I'm ready to get started," I said, handing the stack of magazines back to her as she stood in the doorway. "I'll look over the suspension first to make sure nothing's bent or worn out, then I'll write down how you've got everything set up. It's really important to keep good notes so when you make changes, you know what worked and what didn't."

Teri Sue glanced at the dozen magazines in her hands. "You read all of these?"

"Yeah. And I'll get through the rest by the end of the week. There are a few things I'm not sure about, but I came across an ad for a book on suspension set-up. I'm going to order it tonight."

"No need," said Teri Sue, tossing the magazines on a table inside the door. "Just tell me which one you want, and I'll have Daddy get it."

"That's okay. I can buy it myself. I don't want to take advantage."

Teri Sue snorted. "Like he'd even notice. Daddy's got more money than he knows what to do with. He inherited half the family textile business when he was my age, but he didn't care a bit about it, so he let his brother buy him out. Anyway, he's not into fussing over money, and that's just fine by me. I'm happy to spend it for him."

We went out to the barn, where Teri Sue cranked up the country music. When we got to the point that we needed a gauge to set the castor and camber, she took off for the parts store to rent it.

Rhett crept in while she was gone. "Hey," he said, lining up cans of Coke, Squirt, and Mountain Dew on the workbench. "I thought maybe you'd be thirsty."

I wasn't, but my babysitting experience had taught me how badly it would disappoint a kid to say no to an offer like that. "Thanks." I said, picking up the Mountain Dew. "This is my favorite."

"Teri Sue hates it. She says it's a cheap knock-off of Sundrop. That's what we used to drink back home, only they don't sell it in Oregon."

I popped the top on my drink and leaned back against the workbench. "Do you miss North Carolina?"

"Sure, but I like it here, too. My teacher's nicer."

Rhett stayed in the barn talking to me until Teri Sue came back and shooed him away.

"You don't have to put up with him pestering you, y'know," she said as we got to work checking the alignment.

"He wasn't pestering me."

"Uh huh. Right. I've lived with that kid for ten years. Trust me, I know what a pain in the butt he can be."

I spent every night that week at Teri Sue's, trying out the things I'd read in her magazines. She had her foot on the accelerator when it came to getting to know people. By Wednesday, when we took the car to practice, she had no qualms about hooking an arm around my neck or giving me a hug, something I put up with, in spite of how uncomfortable it made me. But I didn't return the gestures. As much as I liked Teri Sue, Rhett, and even their dad, I had no intentions of letting them get too close. That would just be asking for trouble.

Each afternoon, Rhett brought me a can of Mountain Dew, and Teri Sue chased him off to play in the woods or work on his fort in the hayloft. She never believed me when I told her I liked having him around.

Every night, she'd invite me to dinner, but I'd beg off. It was bad enough accepting the free drinks Rhett was plying me with. I didn't need to con the Clines out of meals, too. After the first day, I started bringing a sandwich so I wouldn't have to stop working when Teri Sue went in to get dinner going.

I was curious about Rhett and Teri Sue's mother, but neither mentioned her again, and I was far too aware of the graveyard rattling around in my own closet to broach the subject. Instead, I minded my own business and hoped Teri Sue's friendliness wouldn't keep her from returning the courtesy.

# CHAPTER 6

Saturday afternoon, Lydia stopped me as I was heading out the door for Teri Sue's.

"Where are you going?" she called from the couch. She'd spent the whole day there, drinking Budweiser and flipping through the five TV channels we could get.

"To work." I'd stayed quiet about my new job all week, crossing my fingers Teri Sue wouldn't have reason to call. Two years ago, when I'd bought the Pinto and Lydia caught me working on it, I'd found out just how much she hated the idea of me being a mechanic. "How could you do this to me?" she'd hollered. "You're turning out just like your dad. Always working on cars and ignoring me. Well, I'm not going to put up with it, you hear?"

Ever since then, I'd kept my passion to myself.

Lydia looked imploringly at me across the living room. After the fight with Jimmy last Saturday, and getting written up for coming in late to work the next morning, she'd started slipping into one of her dark moods. "Do you have to go?"

"Yeah, Lydia. I'm sorry."

Her gaze drifted away to fix blankly on the TV. "Sometimes I wish I could go to sleep and never wake up."

I sighed, knowing I was powerless to pull her out of her funk. "I have to work. The electric bill is due next week."

When Lydia didn't answer, I stood there another moment before slipping out the door.

I tried not to let the problems at home follow me to Teri Sue's. There was nothing I could do about Lydia. Dwelling on it was a waste of time. And yet her gloom seemed to hover around me, dimming the bright May sunlight. Now that I finally had something good in my life, I couldn't escape the nagging worry she'd somehow mess it up for me.

After Teri Sue and I loaded up the Camaro, we squeezed into the front seat of the pickup with Rhett and headed for the track. He could've caught a ride with his dad later, but he liked to come early to watch practice and time trials. In spite of Teri Sue's constant complaints about what a burden he was, I'd noticed she always indulged him on matters like this.

At the end of the long, dusty driveway that led from West 11th to the speedway, Teri Sue pulled into line behind the other drivers waiting to buy pit passes. Rhett scrambled out of the truck, took three steps, and stopped to call over his shoulder. "See ya, Jess!"

"Oh sure," said Teri Sue as we headed for the pit gate. "I'm the one who goes to the trouble to bring him out here, and he can't give me so much as a 'good luck.'"

When we reached the front of the line, Teri Sue put twenty-five dollars on the counter. "Two please."

"I can buy my own."

"Oh hush." She dismissed me with a wave. "Entry fee's part of your paycheck."

"We didn't agree to that." I pulled a ten and two ones from my pocket and set them beside the clipboard that held the release forms.

"Didn't we? Well, we have now." Teri Sue slid her money closer to the lady in the booth.

I clamped my jaw shut, trying to head off a surge of annoyance as two opposing forces warred inside me. Pride said I needed to let her know how serious I was, but my desire to stay under the radar argued that making a scene at the pit gate was not the way to start the night. Sighing, I pulled my money off the counter, folded it neatly, and tucked it into my jeans.

In the infield, I glanced around, expecting everyone to know I was an outsider. Nobody gave me a second look. *Stop being so paranoid*, I told myself. The changes I'd made to the Camaro would show I knew what I was doing, and Teri Sue's friendly nature had proven she'd take care of the social niceties. There was nothing to worry about.

When she timed in two cars ahead of Cody Everett, a rush of satisfaction quelled the last of my uneasiness. Without a doubt, the car was handling better. That was probably why, when she took third in her dash, she came in off the track thoroughly disgusted with herself.

"I know the car's faster," she said, swiping at her sweat-dampened bangs with the sleeve of her firesuit. "You'd think I'd do better this week."

"You'll get it figured out. Just give yourself a chance. Anyway, it's not like you came in last."

"Right." Teri Sue rolled her eyes. "I finished ahead of Cody Everett. What an accomplishment."

I looked across the pits, to where Race's black Dart was lined up with the rest of the Sportsman 'A' dash cars. Cody leaned against the passenger door, his head poked through the window as he talked to Race.

"I guess he didn't inherit his uncle's driving talent," I said.

"No," Teri Sue agreed, grinning as she followed my gaze. "But he *did* inherit his cute butt."

After the heat, Teri Sue's spirits rebounded. She finished third again, but this time out of eight, and she had to work for it. As soon as the green flag fell, she shot under Cody's Dodge to methodically pick off three slower cars that had started in front of her.

"Good work!" I said when her #70 Camaro rumbled into the pits. "That was some smart driving."

Teri Sue climbed out of the car and took the bottle of lime Gatorade I had waiting for her. "Maybe so," she said, hooking an arm around my neck. "But I couldn't have done it without my new crew chief."

Her good spirits lasted until twenty minutes later, she went scrabbling through her toolbox for the black tape. When she opened one of the smaller drawers, she found the two dollars I'd hidden there the week before.

Her face crinkled up in a puzzled expression. "What's this?"

*Uh oh.* I held my breath. Maybe she wouldn't make the connection. But after the fuss I'd made over money at the pit gate, that was too much to hope for.

Teri Sue pulled the bills from the drawer, holding them up between two fingers. "This is yours, isn't it? From last week?"

I stared at her, afraid to answer.

She shook the money in my face. "What's the deal with you, girl? Don't you know it's rude to give back a gift?"

"I like to pay my own way."

"No kidding. How 'bout getting over it and letting someone do you a favor once in a while?"

I shifted my weight from foot to foot, sticking my hands in my back pockets. Favors meant you owed somebody, and that they'd always be watching, waiting until you'd settle up. Who needed that kind of attention?

"I don't want any favors."

Teri Sue shook her head. "I swear, you're more stubborn than Rhett. And that's saying something."

"I'm serious, Teri Sue." I gave her the steeliest look I could conjure. "You pay me good money for the work I do, and I appreciate it. But I'm not comfortable letting people buy me things."

Teri Sue held my gaze for a long moment before shaking her head. "Okay, fine. No more hot dogs." She stuffed the money in her pocket. "But pit passes are something else. It's only fair I cover those."

"No pit passes, either." I couldn't believe I'd found the grit to stare her down.

Teri Sue sighed like a radiator springing a leak. "Okay. No

pit passes, either. Damn, you've sure got your pride."

What I had was a life where I paid my own way and didn't give people cause to look at me too closely. I wasn't going to let anyone threaten that. Not even the girl who'd offered me the job of my dreams.

With Lydia dampening my mood as I'd left the apartment, and Teri Sue drowning it further with her arguments about money, it wasn't turning out to be the best night of my life. But I had high hopes for the main.

Apparently, Cody did too. When Teri Sue attempted to squeeze by him at the start, he slammed the door on her. She found a way around him before long, but he made her do it on the outside.

A wreck on lap ten eliminated three of the leaders. That, combined with smooth driving, put Teri Sue in sixth place. Amazingly, Cody stayed right on her bumper, displaying some of the most intelligent driving I'd seen from him so far. He made several bids to pass Teri Sue on the straights, but she wouldn't let him squeak underneath, and he didn't quite have the power to take her on the outside. In a case like that, a driver's only chance is to stay on the tail of the car ahead and hope for a mistake. Cody took that strategy a step further. As they charged into turn one, he stuffed the nose of his Dart under the rear quarter panel of the Camaro. Teri Sue held her groove. The two cars bumped. The Camaro spun off the front end of the #13 Dodge, and as Teri Sue came around, Todd Griffin's Firebird nailed her right front fender. Both cars slid to a stop in the dust and pebbles at the top of the track.

In the space of a heartbeat, my temper hit redline. Why hadn't Cody backed out? It was obvious Teri Sue had the groove. He'd cost us sixth place, and who knew how many hours in repairs, simply because he didn't have the sense to let off the throttle.

The flagman threw the red, and once the string of cars maneuvered around the wreck, they pulled to a stop along the front stretch. I ran across the infield to the battered Camaro, glaring at Cody as I passed in front of the Dart. He pulled away, his flat tire and crumpled front fender not enough to keep the car from moving under its own power.

Teri Sue wasn't so lucky.

"Are you okay?" I asked.

She wiggled through the window and dropped to the ground. "I reckon," she said, her voice wobbling. "At least I hope so, 'cause I forgot the number you dial to get 911."

While we waited for the tow truck, we circled the car, taking inventory of the damage. Aside from mangling the right front fender, the impact had torn a gash in the tire's sidewall, bent the wheel, and tweaked the suspension enough to give the Camaro a pigeon-toed look.

"I'm going to strangle that guy," I said.

"Who, Todd? It's not his fault. He didn't have anywhere to go."

I shook my head. "Not Todd. Cody."

"Aw, it wasn't his fault, either. Stuff happens on the track."

That was no excuse for stupidity.

Back in the pits, Teri Sue babbled cheerfully to everyone who came by to inspect the Camaro, acting like she'd won, rather than been wrecked. Why wasn't she mad? All I could think of was that sixth place finish, and how Cody's poor judgment had robbed us of it. Through the last laps of the Street Stock race, and the entirety of the Limited Sportsman main, I replayed the scene in my mind, willing him to back out of the throttle. I knew things like this happened, and it was just part of racing. Yet somehow, I couldn't let it go.

Maybe I needed to confront him about it. At home, my resentment smoldered because I never had the guts to tell Lydia how I felt. The few times I'd confronted her, it ended with her dissolving into a crying heap or threatening to do something desperate. But I was tired of swallowing my feelings. I'd been doing it for eight years, and the speedway was supposed to be my refuge.

After the Sportsman main, while Teri Sue was off foraging at the concession stand, I went over to Cody's pit. I'd tell him what I'd thought, and that would be the end of it. I could forget it happened and start concentrating on next week.

Race and Kasey were a few cars away, watching the Super Stock main with some of the other drivers. Good. I didn't feel brave enough to speak my mind in front of an audience.

I walked up behind Cody as he dug through an ice chest, the sleeves of his black double-layer Nomex firesuit pushed up over his elbows. Nomex? What Street Stock driver wore a Nomex? Most guys were lucky to afford flame-resistant cotton. The pretentiousness of it sent irritation rippling through me. I had to scrimp and save for every five-dollar part I needed for my Pinto, and this joker was wearing Nomex to race a car that topped out at seventy miles per hour?

"Nice driving," I sneered before I even realized I'd opened my mouth. Well, that wasn't how I'd intended to start things.

Cody's head snapped up and he turned to stare at me. His eyes were like Race's, a warm brown, rich as dark chocolate. In fact, he looked so much like Race, he could've been his brother. He was shorter, though—only about as tall as me.

"Who are you?" he asked, chin raised at a cocky angle. Unruly brown hair hung in his eyes, tousled and damp with perspiration. The fact that he was good-looking only fed my annoyance. He was probably one of those boys who got everything he wanted, simply because he was hot.

"I work for Teri Sue Cline," I said. "You know, the driver you spun out? She could've taken sixth if it wasn't for you."

Cody's stare hardened into a glower. The anger lasted only a second before fading. He shrugged and stuck his hand back in the ice chest, bringing out a can of Pepsi. "That's racing," he said, smooth as molybdenum gear lube.

"That's bullshit," I shot back.

"If you can't take a little rubbing, you don't belong on the track."

The smirk was what did it. I had to put up with girls scorning me in school, and Lydia mocking me when she was drunk, but I'd be damned if I'd take attitude from some arrogant punk at the track. My outrage rumbled from a simmer to a full boil, and in a flash I was slugging him. Or trying to. My fist made only the briefest contact with his jaw before his arm flew up to knock it away. Furious, I flung myself at him. He pulled off a quick ducking maneuver that left me lying behind him in the dust.

The realization that Cody might know a little more about fighting than I did didn't stop me from scrambling up to launch myself at him again. His foot snapped forward to catch me on the shoulder. It didn't hurt, but it put me back on the ground. I leapt to my feet in a red haze, ready to attack again. I would've, too, if someone hadn't grabbed me from behind.

"You really don't wanna do that. Cody's been studying karate, and his sensei says he's a natural."

There was something in that easy-going voice I thought I recognized, and it stopped me cold. I peeked over my shoulder. Oh no. How utterly mortifying. The person I'd have done anything to impress, the driver who'd been my hero for the past four years, and our first meeting had to involve me making a complete fool of myself. My anger drained away like hot 30 weight from a punctured oil pan. I shook my shoulders so Race would let go and turned to face him, struggling to maintain what little dignity I could muster.

"What's the trouble?" he asked. In spite of my attempt to whale on Cody, Race looked more amused than angry. He, too, was wearing a double-layer Nomex firesuit, but on him it didn't look pretentious.

"He spun out our car." I tried to look Race in the eye, but couldn't. Instead, I stared at his feet, noticing that he wore real racing shoes, not the work boots or sneakers most drivers got by with. He and Cody had some of the best safety gear I'd seen. In a flash, I realized the reason for that. The big wreck last year ... of course they weren't going to take chances.

"You work for Teri Sue?" asked Race.

I nodded and forced my eyes to meet his.

"Well," he said, flashing me a full-throttle grin. "I don't know what to tell you. Rookies make mistakes. I understand why you're upset, but if you go around starting fights, you're just gonna get kicked out."

I glanced over my shoulder at Cody, wondering how he'd react to his uncle's assessment of his driving. He didn't look the least bit bothered by it. Face calm and unreadable, he met my gaze evenly. He hadn't even dropped his drink during our scuffle.

"For your information," he said, "I was coming over to apologize."

I barked out a laugh. *Yeah, right.* "I hope you're better at apologizing than you are at driving. Teri Sue and I won't be holding our breaths."

Oh wow. Where had that come from? I'd never said anything so catty in my life. Of course, I'd never attacked anyone, either.

"Whatever." Cody shrugged, pulled the tab on his pop can, and took a slug of Pepsi.

I realized Race was still watching me. It was a little late to make a good impression, but I didn't want to look like a complete jerk. "Forget it," I said.

Without waiting for a response, I turned and walked away.

## CHAPTER 7

When I got back to the Camaro, Teri Sue was parked on a stack of tires, crunching ice from her Pepsi. A hot dog in a little paper boat sat in her lap. "Where've you been?" she asked.

Too humiliated to venture an explanation, I shrugged.

Teri Sue squeezed mustard onto her dog. "I wanna take Rhett over to the Little R when we're done here. You up for that?"

I wished she'd thought to ask before I caught a ride with her. With the mood Lydia was in, it was best to get home. Besides, I didn't want to run into Race and Cody again. "Do I have a choice?"

"Sure. Daddy can give you a ride." Teri Sue followed up the mustard with two packets of ketchup.

"I don't want to impose on him."

"How's that imposing? He lives there, remember?" She looked up, licking ketchup from her fingers. "What's up with you? You're a total Miss Grumpypants."

I darted a glance at the Camaro's crumpled fender, my emotions still tangled up in the fight. "Maybe I don't take well to people causing us extra work."

"Oh, heck. Are you still tore up about that?" Teri Sue shook her head. "Like I told you, stuff happens. Cody didn't do it on purpose."

"He's a pompous little jerk who cost you sixth place."

She raised an eyebrow as if trying to fathom how I'd come to that conclusion. "Just let it go. If he didn't mean to do it, it's no big deal, and if he tries it again, I'll stuff him in the wall."

After Teri Sue finished her hot dog, we began getting things together so we'd be ready to leave when the Super Stock race was over. Cody wandered into our pit as I was returning a ratchet to the toolbox. His dark hair hung disheveled in his eyes, and the leather jacket he'd slipped over his firesuit made him look like a delinquent out of a '50s movie.

"Uh ... Teri Sue?" he said, stuffing his hands into the front pockets of his jeans.

I froze, crouched in front of the toolbox.

"Yeah?" she asked.

"I just wanted to tell you that I'm, like, sorry for sticking my car under yours." He looked down at his feet, scuffing one of his racing shoes in the dust before raising his eyes. "I wasn't trying to spin you out or anything. I guess my judgment was a little off."

Well, he certainly had the contrite routine down to an art. And Teri Sue bought right into it.

"Aw, thanks, Cody. I 'preciate it. Not too many people woulda had the gumption to come over and apologize." She grinned, extending her arm, and he pulled his hand from his pocket to take hers.

Oh, *please*. Snorting, I snatched up a perfectly clean adjustable wrench and began rubbing it with a grease rag.

Teri Sue glanced in my direction and lowered her voice. The conversation continued as I got up to toss spare parts into a milk crate and pitch an empty Gatorade bottle at the trash. Naturally, it missed. I stalked over, picked it up, and slammed it into the can, meeting Cody's glance with a glare.

After far too long, he cast me a final mysterious look, said goodbye to Teri Sue, and took off.

A thunderous roar rose from the grandstands as the Super Stock main came to an end. Teri Sue turned to face me. "What's wrong with you?" she demanded, subjecting me to the irritation that should've gone to the guy who spun her out.

I couldn't think of a response that wouldn't sound pathetic. "Nothing."

"He apologized, Jess. Isn't that enough?"

*No.* The word popped into my head, and I barely kept it from finding its way to my lips. "Just forget it, okay?"

"Jess..."

I shot her a deadly look. "I don't want to talk about it."

"All right, no need to get so ill."

She left to retrieve her truck, and I sank onto a stack of tires, wallowing in my mood. The whole night had been a disaster. I didn't understand it. Sure, Cody was annoying. His quiet air of cool made me feel like something stuck to the bottom of his shoe. But I'd *never* hit anybody. Through all the tongue-lashings I'd received at home, and taunts I'd gotten at school, I hadn't felt the slightest impulse to react with violence. So what was it about Cody that had sent me into such a rage?

"Are you the girl who's helping Teri Sue?"

I jumped. When I looked up and saw Ted Green, the chief steward, I spooked all over again. Uh oh. After the way he'd barked at the drivers, it didn't bode well that I'd attracted his attention.

My teeth worked at my lip as I pulled together the courage to answer. "Uh...yeah."

"I'm already hearing rumors about you scrapping with Cody Everett." He paused, his eyes boring into mine. "You're lucky they were only rumors. I catch you throwing a punch at someone, and you're out of here. Understand?"

I nodded, the lump in my throat making words impossible.

"Good." He poked a finger in my face. "And don't think I won't do it. If you have doubts, ask any driver out here just how much I'll put up with."

The humiliation of Teri Sue's disappointment, Ted Green's reprimand, and worst of all, my fight with Cody, stuck with me into the next morning, making me happy to stay home and tackle my overdue schoolwork. Trig was the only subject I'd stayed on top of. The problems were so easy, I could work them out in class during the lecture. But in English, I was hopelessly behind. I started with that to get it out of the way. When I got bogged down in boredom, I switched to physics to give my brain a break.

My mood lifted a little when Lydia pulled herself up off the couch to get ready for her shift at IHOP. Her drinking and depression had cost her more than one job. At least I wouldn't have to worry about that today.

When I got to Teri Sue's after school on Monday, the gloomy overcast subduing my mood, she was already in the barn, knocking dents out of the Camaro's fender with a sledgehammer.

"Hey, girl" she said. "I got that tie rod end and ball joint you wanted. They're on the workbench. But how 'bout giving me a hand with this first?"

"Sure." I rooted through the toolbox, came up with a body hammer and dolley, and got to work.

It didn't surprise me when Teri Sue started in with a stream of friendly chatter, as if our argument at the track had never happened. Nothing unpleasant seemed to stick in her head for long.

While we were finishing the fender, the throaty rumble of a big-engined car sounded from the driveway. A Ford Galaxie 500 with oxidized yellow paint pulled up outside the open barn doors. 1965. I know my Fords.

I was too busy admiring the enormous grill and dual headlights to notice who was behind the wheel. Then the driver's door opened and Cody Everett stepped out, spoiling the picture.

What was *he* doing here?

Wearing faded jeans, black Converse high tops, and a T-shirt that read *Outcast*, he sauntered into the barn as if he were six feet tall instead of 5'6". His dark bangs, which on Saturday had been flattened by his helmet, now arched over his forehead like the tail of a proud rooster. "Hey, Teri Sue," he said, ducking his head in her direction.

"Cody!" She smiled so big you'd think he was a rock star, blessing us with his very presence.

He flashed a grin that rivaled one of his uncle's, yet had its own distinctive bad boy edge. It didn't impress me. I'd seen his type in action. They flirted with the homely girls to get their hopes up, and then laughed about it with their buddies behind their backs. Why did all the good looking ones have to be such arrogant jerks?

Maybe if we ignored him, he'd go away. I sank down beside the car to begin dismantling the steering linkage. That tie-rod end needed replacing, and it sure wasn't going to replace itself.

"Looks like you're getting her back together," Cody said, nodding toward the Camaro. He leaned against the barn doorway, hands jammed in his pockets.

"Yep." Teri Sue went on smiling. What was that all about? If she had any sense, she'd run him off with a tire iron.

I finished loosening the nut on the tie-rod end and dropped the wrench in the dust with a thud. "Teri Sue," I said, trying to reel in her attention. "I need the pickle fork."

"Sure thing." She got it from the toolbox and slapped it into my outstretched hand.

"Thanks." The word came out sharp, causing Teri Sue to raise an eyebrow. Well, what did she expect? There was work to be done. This was no time for chit-chatting with the competition.

"So . . . you were running pretty good Saturday night," Cody said, facing Teri Sue but cutting a sideways glance at me.

"Yeah, until you slammed into her."

"Jess!" Teri Sue's eyes flashed a warning. "Cody apologized for that."

"He wouldn't have had to if he hadn't done it to begin with." And what was he looking at, anyway?

"Well, as far as I'm concerned, that's water under the bridge." She beamed at him, and he granted her a lazy grin in return. Good Lord, if she got this friendly with a guy who spun her out, what was she going to do when someone stuffed her in the wall?

I wedged the pickle fork between the tie-rod end and center-link. The hammer felt dangerous in my hand as I slammed it against the end of the tool, popping the joint loose with a single blow.

"It's nice to know you can channel your anger," Cody said.

I nailed him with a poisonous look. He might've kept the smirk off his lips, but I could see it in his eyes. For a moment, I let myself savor the idea of chucking the hammer at him.

He raised an eyebrow at Teri Sue, and she shrugged. Great. One brief conversation in the pits, and now they were best buddies. I hoped this wasn't heading where I thought it was heading. The last thing I needed was Teri Sue hooking up with him.

"So . . ." Cody said, rocking forward on his toes, impervious to the waves of loathing I was sending in his direction. "You guys wouldn't happen to have a gear puller for a pitman arm, would you?"

He could *not* be serious. In what demented universe did he think we'd fall for such a feeble line? "Yeah, sure," I said, waving a hand toward the back of the barn. "It's right over there by the welding equipment, just this side of the paint booth."

"Jess!" Teri Sue gasped.

I ignored her and turned to face Cody head on. "I should think if anyone was going to have something like that, it would be your sponsor. This isn't exactly a Winston Cup garage we're running." Too late, I realized it must sound like I was belittling Teri Sue. Fortunately, she was so exasperated she failed to notice.

"Why are ya givin' him such a hard time?" she demanded,

hands parked on her hips and feet planted wide. "If I'm not mad, why should you be?"

It struck me that I was being entirely too vocal. Raising a fuss would only draw out Cody's visit. "Forget it." I said, getting up to grab the new tie-rod end off the workbench.

Teri Sue sighed and shook her head. Grasping Cody by the wrist, she dragged him outside, where their conversation resumed in low tones peppered by occasional laughter.

Good. Now maybe I could get some work done. I tried to lose myself in the rhythm of replacing the part, but something kept compelling me to glance toward the doorway of the barn. Whenever I did, I caught Cody grinning at me, his dark eyes taunting. What did he have to grin about? And why did he keep staring at me? I swiped at my cheek with the sleeve of my sweatshirt. Did I have grease on my face or something?

It was nearly dinnertime, and I'd single-handedly repaired the steering and removed the upper control arm, when Cody finally found it in himself to leave. Teri Sue stood in the doorway, waving as if he were a favorite relative departing after the holidays.

Once the Galaxie had growled away, she turned to face me. She didn't have to say a word. Her mile-wide smile made it clear what was going on.

"Next thing I know you'll be going out with the guy," I said, wiping my hands on a grease rag and throwing it at a box near the door.

"I dunno about that."

"Oh, come on." I cocked my chin, annoyed that she was so intent on playing the clueless role. "Couldn't you tell he was blatantly flirting with you?"

Teri Sue laughed. "Wake up, Jess. It's you he likes."

## CHAPTER 8

I wasn't sure what to make of Teri Sue's claim about Cody. She had to be teasing. Nobody like him would have the slightest interest in me. Not that I cared. I could name three boys in my shop class who I'd put ahead of him on any potential dating list. Ones whose egos didn't rival the size of several major planets.

Tuesday afternoon, I was pulling one of the Camaro's spark plugs when the yellow '65 Galaxie crunched through the gravel, exhaust rumbling like an approaching thunderstorm. A light mist slicked the car's generous grill, making it glisten.

"Not again," I grumbled.

"Ah-ah! None of that." Teri Sue's eyes continued the lecture as she shook a quart of bright blue automotive paint for the fender we'd straightened.

Ignoring her, I scrutinized the spark plug, noting the light tan color of the electrode. Perfect.

Cody slid out of his car and strolled into the barn, moisture slicking his leather jacket. Today his T-shirt read, *I'm the person your mother warned you about*, but he wore the same black Converse high tops and the same outlaw grin. I was beginning to wonder if he slept with that smirk on his face.

"That's an awful lot of car for such a little guy," I said. "However do you manage to reach the pedals?" Maybe if I was mean enough, he'd take the hint and leave. I stuck the spark plug back in its hole and spun it clockwise.

"I have this little monkey that works them for me," he said, leaning against the undamaged fender of the Camaro and grinning even more smugly.

I had to hand it to him—he was cool. I slipped the socket over the end of the spark plug and snugged it up.

Always the diplomat, Teri Sue stepped in to break up our

verbal sparring. "Sounds like she runs good. You do the work yourself?"

Cody didn't take his eyes off me as he answered. "Me and Race. He found her last summer in some old dude's yard in Veneta. We're hoping to get to the bodywork and paint next winter."

I looked down, fussing with the plug wire. After what Teri Sue had said the night before, Cody's attention made me feel like a cow being sized up for market. I snapped the wire into the plastic clip that held it away from the exhaust manifold.

"So what do you want to borrow today?" I asked. "A cup of sugar for your Mommy?"

Cody chuckled. "Nah, my Mommy lives in Phoenix. I just stopped by to see how y'all were doing with the car."

"Y'all?" I raised an eyebrow. Sure, I'd caught myself picking up some of Teri Sue's expressions, but Cody barely knew her.

His grin stretched wider. What a jerk. I glanced at Teri Sue and was disgusted to find her smirking at me. Snorting, I went out to her pickup to get the paint gun she'd borrowed from one of the Limited Sportsman drivers.

"Don't you have any friends to hang out with?" I asked Cody when I came back into the barn.

"Sure.... What—you think I should drag 'em around with me like some kind of posse?" He stroked his chin and let his expression go distant. "That's not a bad idea. I wonder if my buddy Quinn would go for it?" He held the pensive routine another moment before plopping down on a toolbox and twirling his keys on a finger. "I can't stay long," he told Teri Sue. "I've got karate practice at seven."

"That's almost two hours from now," I said. "Were you planning on inviting yourself for dinner or something?"

"Wouldn't bother me," said Teri Sue. "Maybe he'd actually join us, instead of sitting alone in the barn with a peanut butter sandwich."

Cody placed a hand over his heart and made his eyes go big. "I would never *dream* of insulting you by turning down a dinner invitation."

"And I'd be honored to give you one," said Teri Sue, throwing me a so-there look. "But we eat late. Daddy's got office hours till six-thirty on Tuesdays and Thursdays."

Not wanting to touch that conversation with a ten-foot pole, I made myself busy experimenting with the paint gun. I'd never used one before, but it wasn't difficult once I figured out that if I kept it a constant distance from the fender, and didn't apply too much in one coat, the paint wouldn't run.

I tried to pretend Cody wasn't there. It was nearly impossible with him goofing around and shooting unnerving little grins at me. A person would've thought he was Rhett's age, rather than mine, the way he played with the floor jack, raising and lowering it while standing on the pad. He distracted Teri Sue so much she was worthless at helping me with the fender.

After a while, Rhett came out to pester us under the pretense of bringing a snack. He carried a six-pack of Coke hooked through his fingers, a Tupperware bowl under his arm, and a single Mountain Dew in his free hand.

After giving me the bright green can, he popped open the container to reveal homemade peanut butter cookies. "They're really good," he said. "Teri Sue made 'em."

I savored my cookie while Cody bolted one down and grabbed another.

"Who's your waiter?" he asked.

Teri Sue laughed. "I wish he was my waiter. The only time he makes himself useful is when he's trying to nose into something I'm doing."

"Liar," said Rhett, sticking out his tongue.

"Huh! Cody, meet my obnoxious little brother." Teri Sue's statement was gruff, but her eyes held the same challenge she'd leveled at me the week before. I didn't think she had anything to worry about. So far Cody hadn't even glanced at Rhett's brace. He'd been too busy ogling me. Not that I could believe Teri Sue's explanation for that. The two of them had to be messing with my head.

Cody reached for yet another cookie. "What's your name, dude?"

Rhett gave him a wary look. "Rhett."

"As in Rhett Butler?"

"You got it." His green eyes dared Cody to make a joke about it.

Cody didn't. "That's cool," he said with a nod. "Your name's almost as original as my uncle's."

The tenseness melted from Rhett's expression. "Who's your uncle?"

"Race Morgan."

"Really?" Rhett's lips puckered in speculation. "You need to get him to work on your car. He's fast."

I snickered, glancing at Teri Sue. Her peaches and cream complexion had flamed to pink. Rhett looked our way with a question in his eyes, but Cody laughed off the unintended burn, digging into the Tupperware container to grab one last cookie.

"Well, I gotta hit the road."

"Don't let us stand in your way." If he expected me to make a big deal about his leaving, he was in for a disappointment. I checked the fender to see if it was ready for a second coat of paint.

Rhett and Teri Sue became the picture of Southern hospitality, following Cody to his car and gabbing with him through the open window once he got in. When I heard the big engine roar, I glanced up to watch the Galaxie rumble down the driveway. No doubt about it. That was one fine car.

It wasn't until it had pulled onto Fox Hollow that I felt Teri Sue's eyes on me. I flashed her a scowl. "Don't you start."

\* \* \*

Even with Cody butting into our business, the time I spent at Teri Sue's was the most fun I'd had in years. Now that I had a week and a half under my belt, I no longer felt like a stranger at her house. The thought of doing this through September sent a shiver of contentment whispering along my skin as I drove to work Wednesday afternoon.

The rain had stopped that morning, so the roads were dry, in spite of the overcast. Rhododendrons blazed red and pink from people's yards, and the air held that mushroomy scent of damp forest. I reveled in the winding drive out Fox Hollow, windows down and stereo blaring *Cherry Cherry Coupe* by the Beach Boys. The bright energy in the hot-rodding songs from the sixties always gave me a rush. It was hard to believe music about cars had once been the rage. Too bad I'd missed out and had to be content with the occasional hit like Sammy Hagar's *I Can't Drive Fifty-Five*.

There wasn't much left to fix on the Camaro, but that was okay. After saying hello to Mark, who was weeding the flowerbed along the front porch, I joined Teri Sue in the barn.

"Hey, girl." She looked up from the carbon paper she was using to trace her sponsor's logo onto the newly repaired fender. A black smudge darkened one of her cheeks.

"Hey," I said, taking a seat on a toolbox.

As Teri Sue worked, we rambled about school, her upcoming graduation, and how fast the Camaro was going to be Saturday night.

"I'll definitely skunk Cody," she said, shooting a smirky little glance in my direction.

I grunted. "Bet you anything that jerk shows up again tonight."

"Told you he likes you."

I gave her a dirty look. "Wouldn't that just make my day."

"Why else would he hang around here so much?" Teri Sue lifted one edge of the paper to see how well her marks were transferring to the fender.

"Maybe he gets turned on by Southern accents."

"Could be," Teri Sue admitted, "but I wouldn't be interested. He's just a kid."

"He's only two years younger than you."

"Jailbait," she said, and we both laughed.

It felt so strange, having a conversation like this, and I couldn't believe it wasn't making me want to bite my fingernails to the quick. Teri Sue definitely had a talent for weasling under my radar.

She was pulling the carbon paper off the fender when Rhett wandered through the door wearing his Teenage Mutant Ninja Turtles T-shirt. This time, he hadn't bothered to bring an offering of cookies and drinks. He climbed into the hayloft and sat with his feet dangling over the edge, his brace banging against the ladder.

Teri Sue clenched her jaw against the noise and finally barked, "Don't you know any kids your own age?" She shooed me off the toolbox and rooted around in the top drawer until she found a paintbrush.

"I know loads of kids."

"So why don'tcha go play with 'em?"

"Okay," said Rhett, "but you'll have to let me borrow your truck. They live miles from here."

I laughed. "Aw, leave him alone, Teri Sue. He's not hurting anything."

"If that's what you think, you can take him home with you tonight." She stuck the paintbrush in my hand and gave me a gentle push toward the car.

"What—you want me to paint it? I can't paint."

"Why not? I already did the hard part." She slapped a can of Chrome Yellow 1-Shot into my other palm. "Now get to work."

I sighed and set the brush on the fender, grabbing a screwdriver to pry open the paint.

Not five minutes later, Cody's Galaxie roared up the driveway.

"There's your boyfriend," Rhett called from the loft, his mouth slanting up at one corner.

Oh man. Not him too. "Teri Sue, give him the keys to your truck."

"I'm just pickin'!" he said.

"If you keep talking like that, you'll be 'pickin'' yourself up off the floor."

Rhett giggled, clearly not impressed by my threat. "Hey there," he said as Cody ambled into the barn.

"Hey, Rhett. Cool T-shirt." Cody nodded toward the hayloft. His own shirt read, *Will race for food.*

"You like the Ninja Turtles?" Rhett asked as his new buddy dropped down on a stack of racing tires.

"The Ninja Turtles rock. Raphael's the best."

It figured he'd think so. Raphael was the crazy one. I rarely watched cartoons and never read comic books, but all those years of babysitting had left me familiar with the Turtles and their personalities.

"Michaelangelo's cooler," Rhett argued.

"Raphael and Michaelangelo have nothing on Donatello," I said, some momentary indiscretion prompting me to offer my opinion. Donatello was introspective and clever. He created all the Ninja Turtle inventions. "If you have to admire a cartoon character, you might as well go for one that has style."

Cody cocked an eyebrow at me as he tossed his dark hair out of his face, but he didn't comment.

For some reason, Cody didn't seem quite so obnoxious that afternoon. He and Rhett horsed around while I attempted to fill in the faint outline of the logo. After sending Rhett shrieking from a third wet willie, Cody paused to watch me struggle with the brush.

"Too bad Race can't do that for you. I've seen him knock out a fender like that in ten minutes." His hand flashed out and caught Rhett's just as it reached for the back of Cody's jeans.

"You want a wedgie?" he demanded, whipping around to paralyze Rhett with a ghoulish leer. "I'll give you a wedgie. I'm the Wedgie King." Cody yanked Rhett's underwear halfway up his back, the sound of tearing cotton audible over the poor kid's howl.

Teri Sue ignored their scuffling. "So give him a call," she said, eyeing my work with a grimace. It was almost enough to offend me. Hadn't I warned her I couldn't paint?

Cody watched as Rhett hobbled off behind the car to salvage what was left of his dignity and his underwear. After a long silence, he finally spoke. "He doesn't do that kinda thing anymore."

"Why not? I'd pay him."

"He can't." Something in Cody's tone—the faintest tremor in his voice—drew my attention. His confidence had crumbled, and seeing him without it was like looking at a sepia photo. The image might be intact, but the color had become a mere suggestion.

Interesting. With that cocksure attitude, I never would've taken Cody for caring about anyone but himself.

"There was this big wreck last year," he said, thumb and forefinger worrying at one of the buckles on his jacket. "Race got hurt—a head injury. It messed up his dexterity."

That accident had been big news for two reasons. First, Race's fearless driving and wise-cracking personality had made him the Sportsman class favorite. Second, it was rare for anyone to be seriously hurt at the speedway. Even the most brutal wrecks usually resulted in greater harm to the car than the driver.

I'd never learned the details of Race's injury, only that it was serious and he'd missed eight weeks of the season. The people who knew him best said he was lucky. Lucky to be alive and to still have his edge.

"I thought he recovered from that," I said. You sure wouldn't guess there were lasting effects from the way he drove.

"He did, mostly." Cody studied the dirt floor, shoulders slumped and voice hushed. "At least he can weld now. But he still gets headaches, and he hasn't done any drawing since it happened."

"Maybe he's scared he's lost his touch," said Teri Sue, who couldn't be bothered with tact.

Cody's eyes darted to her, and for a second I caught a glimpse of pain so deep and sharp it felt like it belonged to me.

Smacking a hand down on the Camaro, I hefted myself to my feet. "Teri Sue, you need to make up your mind about this fender."

For a flicker of a moment, Cody's eyes met mine. The gratitude in them pierced straight through me. I looked away, shaken by having my scorn vaporized in the space of a few heartbeats.

"Well, we might-could get some vinyl letters," said Teri Sue, still oblivious. She stepped closer to examine the mess I'd made.

"It's expensive," said Cody, his voice sturdier now. "That's what we did this year. They charge a ton to program everything into the computer the first time. After that, it's not too bad, but it wouldn't be worth it for one fender." The rush of words was like a broom, tidily sweeping his vulnerability off into a corner.

"Just call the guy who lettered it the first time," I suggested, careful not to let Cody catch my eye again.

"Reckon I'll have to."

I wet a grease rag with paint thinner and wiped off my scraggly letters. She didn't need to sound so disappointed.

\* \* \*

After a while, we sent Rhett to the house to round up a snack. He came back with a bag of Nacho Cheese Doritos and a pitcher of Kool-Aid.

"Hey, Jess, how 'bout you spend the night Friday?" Teri Sue suggested as Rhett and Cody fought over the bag of chips, scattering a few across the barn floor. Cody snatched one up and popped it into his mouth, citing the five-second rule while Rhett feigned retching.

"I dunno," I said. I hadn't spent the night at a friend's house since third grade.

"C'mon. It'll be fun. We can build a fire at the edge of the woods and camp out in sleeping bags."

"It'll probably rain," I said, though I knew it wouldn't. A high-pressure system was building off the coast, ensuring good weather was on the way.

"So we'll sleep in the hay loft."

"Can I camp out, too?" Rhett asked through a mouthful of Doritos, spewing orange crumbs. His upper lip bore a bright red Kool-Aid mustache.

"You kiddin'?" said Teri Sue, "I'm gonna handcuff you to the kitchen table so you can't come out and pester us."

"Oh yeah?" Rhett faked a karate kick at his sister, who didn't bother to duck.

"No, dude, it's like this." Cody demonstrated a kick that might have taken off Teri Sue's head, had it connected.

"*Cooool*," drawled Rhett. He attempted to copy Cody, but couldn't carry through with his left leg because of the brace. When he tried with his right, he lost his balance.

Cody's hand shot out to steady him. "Keep practicing," he said. "You'll have to compensate a little, but it'll come." He turned and fired a grin at me. "I could show you a few moves, too, Jess, for the next time you wanna beat someone up in the pits."

My cheeks flamed as Rhett looked from Cody to me, wide-eyed. "You beat someone up in the pits?"

"No." I glared at Cody.

Teri Sue tapped her fingers against the workbench, wrapped up in her own thoughts. "We could make it a party," she suggested. "Have a cookout. You can come too, Cody."

I could see I was about to be sucked in, and I didn't want any part of it. "Yeah," I muttered, "and we'll sit around the campfire singing happy little songs."

My sarcasm had all the impact of a snowflake falling into the Pacific.

"I'll bring some hot dogs and drinks," said Cody.

"And I know some real cool ghost stories!" Rhett added.

Wonderful. Now all of them were sold on the idea. I didn't have a prayer of getting out of it.

## CHAPTER 9

It surprised me to see Lydia's car in the parking lot when I got home. Most evenings, if she wasn't working, she was hanging out at the Springfield Tavern or one of her other haunts. A tingle of uneasiness played across my scalp as I walked up the stairs to the apartment.

Lydia slouched on the sofa, staring at the TV and sipping a Screwdriver. A bottle of orange juice and a half-empty fifth of Smirnoff's stood upright amid the clutter on the coffee table. "Where the hell have you been?" she demanded before the door even clicked shut behind me.

"At work."

"Bullshit. I called your manager, and he told me you quit over a week ago." She fixed me with a look that used to scare me to death when I was little. The one that meant alcohol had shanghaied every bit of her goodness, and I couldn't rely on love to hold her hand in check.

Standing a safe distance away, I waited. It was best to let her finish yelling before I tried to defend myself. Interrupting only aggravated her.

"Don't you have any respect for me?" she ranted. "All these years I've provided food for you to eat . . ."

*And a roof over my head.*

". . . and a roof over your head, and how do you repay me? You lie to me." She smacked her empty glass down on the coffee table.

"I'm not lying," I said as she topped off her drink, slopping orange juice and vodka on a stack of bills. "A girl from the speedway asked for help with her car. I'm making more money and getting better hours, too."

"I'll bet." Scorn twisted Lydia's face into a dark shadow of itself.

"What's that supposed to mean?"

"Admit it. If you weren't ashamed of what you're doing, you would've told me about it."

Anger swelled in me, hot and sudden. "That's stupid! Why should I be ashamed of doing something I'm good at?"

"You tell me," Lydia said, swirling liquid meanness in her glass. "You're the one who's running around behind my back, working on cars like some kind of dyke."

The words slammed into me like an avalanche, leaving me gaping. After a long, frozen moment, the shock of them faded enough to let my outrage through. "Since when does working on cars have anything to do with sexual orientation? Just because you don't know how to check your own oil doesn't mean you have to take it out on girls who do!"

Lydia's chin shot up and her blue eyes snapped. "Don't you use that tone with me, missy."

"Well what do you expect? How could you even say something like that?" I hardly ever stood up to her. It was so much simpler to let things slide. But I was fed up with her Jekyll and Hyde parenting, sick of tiptoeing around her feelings and playing the grown-up role.

"I must've struck a nerve if you're that upset," Lydia reasoned, her lips curling smugly.

"I can't believe this."

"Well, you don't date. I've never even seen you with a boy." She flourished her drink, sloshing it on the couch. "That seems just a *lit*-tle bit strange."

"Maybe I'm ashamed of what a boy would see if I brought him home!"

My statement rattled the room like a thunderclap. Uh oh. Big mistake. No matter how bad things got, some subjects couldn't be mentioned.

Lydia drew herself up with a look of raw anger that made me step back on instinct. In high school, she'd pitched for her softball team, and when she was mad, any available object might become a missile. But her rage fizzled almost instantly to dejection. "You're doing this to hurt me, aren't you? You just can't resist twisting that knife."

"Not everything is about you," I said quietly. "Or about Dad." That was what this came down to. Lydia had never coped well with him being on the road, and whenever he'd made it home, she wanted every bit of his time to herself. Each moment he'd spent working on his Mustang with me was a moment she'd been robbed of. And now, every hint that I liked cars was a reminder.

Lydia's gaze edged away from mine. She sighed and took another sip of Screwdriver. "Couldn't you find a job in a nice restaurant? Or maybe one of those shops at the mall?"

The note of concession in her tone tempted me to fabricate something to appease her, but I was tired of hiding. Why couldn't she accept me for who I was?

"I like this job. It's what I want to do." For the briefest second, I let myself hope she might actually hear me.

Lydia slammed back the rest of her drink. "It's no kind of work for a girl."

"Well, you'll just have to get used to it," I said, giving her a wide berth as I headed for my room. At least now she knew the truth, and I could stop worrying about her finding out.

Lydia's voice carried after me down the hall. "I expect you to give me your new work number before you leave here tomorrow!"

The next morning, I woke in a mood as dark and heavy as the clouds shadowing the sky. This spitefulness of Lydia's, this lying in wait to confront me, was something I hadn't seen before. No doubt she was headed for a crash. The only question was how much time I had before impact.

I scribbled Teri Sue's number on a scrap of paper and left if on the kitchen table, weighted down by a coffee cup. At least with this job, I might be able to keep us afloat without dipping into the money I had hidden.

The gloom hung on me all day, even once the clouds began to break up. After school, I got in the Pinto and sat behind the wheel, wondering what to do. We'd finished the repairs to the Camaro. I had no reason to go to Teri Sue's. And yet I found myself driving there.

"Didn't expect to see you tonight," she said. "But I'm glad you're here. You can help me haul the camping equipment up from the basement."

I tried to keep my solemn mood to myself as we set up the tent and unrolled the sleeping bags, but Teri Sue saw right through me.

"What're you all tore up about?" she asked after an hour of my one-word responses.

"Nothing. I'm just ... tired, I guess." It had been a mistake to come. I should've listened to my better judgment. But even in my lousy mood, it felt good to be here. Or it would, if I could just hang out without talking.

I sighed as I looked around at the house, the barn, and Mark's cheerful flowerbeds. In a couple of short weeks, I'd really gotten to like this place and these people. What was going to happen to all of it when Lydia hit bottom? What if I couldn't keep her problems hidden this time? Teri Sue had my phone number, and even though she hadn't called me yet, there was no telling when she would. All it would take was one conversation to ruin everything.

Why did my mother have to lose it now, when things were finally starting to go right in my life?

In the morning, I nearly tripped over a bag of Hershey's Kisses outside my bedroom door. One of Lydia's wordless apologies. Now I'd have to forgive her, or I'd be the one looking like a jerk. But for once, she was the least of my worries. Tonight I'd be sleeping at someone else's house. That hadn't happened in eight years. My stomach quivered at the thought. Making small talk with Teri Sue for an afternoon was one thing, but how was I going to fill up a whole twenty-four hours?

My thoughts drifted back to Lydia as I stuffed a change of clothes into my backpack. Was it even wise to leave her alone, as depressed as she'd been lately? What if she did something crazy? I dug an extra sweatshirt out of my drawer, telling myself not to be ridiculous. She and Jimmy were back together. She probably wouldn't even make it home tonight.

My qualms stayed with me all through school, but faded when I stepped outside into a perfect spring afternoon. Sunlight, blazing down from a startlingly blue sky, warmed my bare arms as I dashed across the parking lot. A whiff of newly mown grass stirred hazy memories of past summers, and for the first time, I considered the possibility I might enjoy the camp out.

Teri Sue was arranging rocks to create a fire pit when I got to her house. The heat of the afternoon had teased a delicious scent from the lilacs blooming beside the barn, and above our heads, the Douglas firs swayed in a slight breeze. I set down the bag of snacks I'd picked up on my way over.

"How's it going?" Teri Sue asked as I opened the cooler to shove a tub of dip into the ice.

"Okay."

"You had me sorta worried yesterday." She placed the last rock and sat back on her heels to study me.

Worried? What was there to be worried about?

"I haven't seen ya that tore up before," she explained.

I shrugged, surprised it was enough to bother her. "I wasn't tore up. It was no big deal."

"Well, okay. If you're sure." She squinted through the sunlight. "But if you ever need somebody to talk to . . ."

"Right." I gave her a nod as I turned to toss my backpack into the tent, hoping it would be enough to make her drop the subject.

"Jess! Hey, Jess!" Rhett hollered, bursting out of the house to come to my rescue. "I made cookies."

"Yeah? What kind?"

"No-bake Chocolate Oatmeal."

"Mmmm. Chocolate's my favorite," I said as he rushed up beside me. "I can taste them already."

Rhett's face lit up like high noon in July. "Want me to get you one?"

"How 'bout you round us up some firewood, instead?" Teri Sue suggested, standing and brushing the dirt off her knees.

"Okay. Wanna help, Jess?"

"Sure." No sense taking a chance his sister wasn't done grilling me.

It was cooler beneath the firs and hemlocks, and I could smell green in the air. Rhett dashed ahead, hunting through the sword ferns for downed tree limbs then running back to stack them in my arms. By the time Cody showed up, we had a huge pile of wood.

"Looks like you guys have been busy," Cody said. His T-shirt read *Ham and eggs—A day's work for the chicken, a lifetime commitment for the pig*. He opened the cooler and wedged two six-packs inside: Pepsi and Mountain Dew.

"Yeah, and look at this cool fire pit my sister built," Rhett said. "Hey, Teri Sue, can we light the fire now?"

She blinked lazily up at him from her reclining lawn chair, where she'd been soaking up the sun like a contented cat. "It's not even suppertime," she said. "Let's wait a while."

Rhett scowled before jumping right to the next idea on his list. "Okay then, how 'bout we play Hide and Seek?"

Teri Sue groaned.

"Dude," said Cody, "I don't think I've played that game since I was ten."

Rhett held his ground, cajoling his sister until he coaxed her out of her chair. For the next couple of hours, we were transported back to grade school days, first hunting each other down in the woods, and then following Rhett to the creek to see the "town" he'd built along the bank for his Matchbox cars. It had been ages since I'd goofed off like a little kid, but I had to admit, it was fun.

When we got tired of hearing Cody complain about how hungry he was, we headed for the campsite. Teri Sue built a fire, while I passed out plates, drinks, and Ball Park Franks.

The boys drew Teri Sue into their banter as we cooked and ate our hot dogs, but I was content to sit back and listen. I couldn't remember the last time I'd felt so relaxed.

When Rhett broke out his cookies, I glanced across the fire at Cody, who'd plowed through three dogs, a bag of chips and an entire plate of Teri Sue's potato salad. A lightning bolt zinged through me when I realized I didn't hate him anymore. Somewhere between watching him horse around with Rhett, and hearing him talk about his uncle's wreck, I'd started seeing the humanity under all that cool.

Dusk whispered in to fill the void of the setting sun, darkening the trees across the highway to silhouette. We melted in our lawn chairs under the mesmerizing warmth of the fire. A bat bobbed and darted over our heads while we watched, lulled into silence by an overdose of food. This was the sort of thing normal kids got to enjoy all the time. But a tiny nagging feeling lurked at the back of my mind, telling me not to make the mistake of thinking I could stay in this world.

"Hey," Rhett said, his voice loud over the crackle of flames. "Y'all wanna see my hay fort?"

His sister groaned. "I'm too full."

"Aw, come on." Rhett grabbed her hand and tugged.

He led us into the barn and made us follow him up the ladder with only a flashlight for illumination. We waited while he pushed aside a bale to reveal the mouth of a tunnel where the roof met the hayloft floor.

"Y'all coming?" he asked, peering over his shoulder before dropping to his hands and knees.

The tunnel skirted the back wall of the hayloft then turned to the right. A few yards later, it ended.

"Up here," Rhett said. The hollow space opened above me, with the pathway resuming on top of the bales. We followed him around another bend, where the tunnel doubled back to run parallel to the one we'd crawled through. Finally, it dropped to floor level, opening into a space two bales high and six feet across. Rhett fiddled with something by the doorway, and light flooded the small room.

"Awesome," said Cody, studying the headlight Rhett had hooked up to an old car battery.

"Listen to this." Rhett twirled the dial on an AM radio pilfered from something that left Detroit prior to 1965. *La Bamba* blasted out at us. "The oldies station is the only decent one on AM," he explained.

"You call this decent?" asked Teri Sue.

"At least it's not country," Cody said.

It was the first he'd mentioned of her taste in music, and I bit back a chuckle, thinking of how much of it he'd endured over the past week.

For the next half hour, we sat around the perimeter of the room, backs against the prickly bales. The smell of hay hung sweet in the air as we listened to the radio and talked about things that didn't matter. I mostly stayed quiet, which prompted Cody to glance over at me, raising an eyebrow. My lips twitched a response that I immediately regretted. What if Teri Sue was right, and he actually liked me? The idea was so terrifying, it sent a shiver scurrying up my spine.

*Little Deuce Coupe* began to play, and Cody sang along. Even though it was one of my favorites, I didn't have the courage to join in.

Rhett's voice mingled with Cody's through the chorus, but he fumbled the rest of the words, and Teri Sue clapped her hands over her ears, moaning. Naturally, that made both boys sing louder.

When the song ended, Cody threw me a challenging look. "Betcha don't know what a flat-head mill is," he said, referring to the motor in the lyrics.

"Duh!" I gave him a dramatic eye roll. "It's an engine with the valves in the block."

Teri Sue shook her head. "I never understood what half that song meant. Not that I care," she added, making her voice go indifferent. "I try not to waste too much time listening to moldy oldies."

"I like car songs," I said, "no matter how old they are. I have a whole collection of them."

"Of course you do," said Cody, grinning. His gaze lingered on me a little too long, and I looked away, hugging my knees.

It was getting late by the time we crawled out of the hay fort. Rhett stood in the loft, holding the flashlight as I descended the ladder. I'd made it halfway down when the overhead lights flicked on, blinding me.

"So this is where y'all wandered off to."

I craned my neck to see Mark standing in the doorway.

"You have a phone call, Jess. It's your mama."

Panic spiked in my chest, ratcheting up my heart rate.

"Sounds fairly important," he added.

I dropped to the ground and looked up at Teri Sue. "Be back in a minute," I said. How could my voice come out sounding so normal?

"We'll get the stuff ready for S'mores," Rhett hollered, as if

Lydia's call was just a temporary interruption.

Outside, our fire had faded to embers. The moon, full a couple of days before, was rising behind the Douglas firs. It cast a ghostly glow over the front yard as I followed Mark, willing my heart back to an idle.

I stepped through the doorway into a house that felt stuffy after being outside.

"Phone's on the table, there by the sofa," Mark said, gesturing. He settled into a big leather chair and picked up the remote, un-paused the black and white movie he'd been watching. At least he didn't seem intent on eavesdropping. Teri Sue wouldn't have granted me the same courtesy.

I lifted the phone and stepped back toward the hallway, as far as the cord would allow. Drawing a deep breath, I place the handset against my ear. "Hello?"

"J-Jessica?" Lydia's voice, traumatized and tearful, grated in my ear. "I need you to g-gimme a ride."

Annoyance snuffed out my fear. This was nothing new. Every time Lydia had a few too many, the bartender took her keys and she called me to come get her. Up until this spring, it had meant walking to the bar and driving her home in the Buick.

"Where are you?" I made no effort to blunt the edge in my voice. She'd ruined my evening, and I wanted her to know it.

"D-downtown Eugene.... The police station.... They said I was driving d-drunk."

"What?" For a second, I forgot about Mark sitting a few yards away.

"Don' you take that tone with me ... missy!"

Mark glanced at me, and I wished I could die right there. Without saying anything more, I dropped the phone into its cradle and got out of the house, quick. He'd never seemed the meddlesome type, but this was big. I couldn't risk him butting into my business.

Back at the campsite, Rhett fumbled one-handed with a Hershey wrapper, trying to wiggle a piece of chocolate free without dropping the stick that held his nicely browned marshmallow. He smiled at me, serene and content. Firelight played across his face.

"That was quick," said Cody.

A swell of resentment rose to choke me. My night had been destroyed, and everyone else got to continue as if nothing had happened.

I snatched my backpack out of the tent. "I've gotta go."

A puzzled look rippled across Cody's face.

"What's wrong?" called Teri Sue as I bolted for my car.

Unable to answer, I jumped into the Pinto and roared away.

# CHAPTER 10

It was nearly midnight by the time I got to the police station. Another fight with Jimmy had triggered Lydia's binge. The cops had impounded her car and required her to sign papers saying she wouldn't skip town before her court date. She gave me an earful about these indignities on the way to the car, where she did a one-eighty and launched into her "I've-been-a-bad-mother-and-I'm-going-to-change" routine.

"I'm s-sorry, Jess. I-I ruined your evening, huh?" Lydia peered at me from the passenger seat, streetlights flashing across her face. Her bleached-blonde hair hung in her eyes, and dark mascara rivers ran down both cheeks.

There was nothing I could trust myself to say.

"I should do better," Lydia said, letting her head flop back against the seat. "It's jus' this Jimmy. He doesn't treat me right." She turned to face me. "D'you think he treats me right?"

"No." None of the guys she went out with did. But she wasn't very nice to them, either.

"They took my car. C'n you believe that? They had no right! How'my s'posed to get to work?"

I clamped my jaw tight. No way would I sympathize, and arguing would only get her more worked up. I didn't want to lie awake all night wondering if she was going to do something drastic.

"Why won'tcha talk to me?" Lydia demanded, her voice rising. "You hate me, huh? An' I deserve it. A good mother wouldn't get arrested."

I stared out the windshield.

"D'you hate me?"

"I don't hate you."

"You're dish-appointed. Dish-appointed 'cause I'm a bad

m-*mother*."

My fingers tightened against the wheel. "You're not a bad mother." How could she always manipulate me into telling her something I didn't believe?

"Y-yes I *am*." Her voice broke over a surge of tears.

I pulled my attention from the road to glance at her. "Just forget about it, okay? We'll work it out in the morning."

The night had grown cool and quiet by the time we got back to the apartment, but I could still smell spring in the air. It seemed like a million years had passed since I'd driven to Teri Sue's under the brilliant sun that afternoon. With exhaustion tugging at every muscle, I helped Lydia out of the car and up the stairs. She rested her weight against me, her crying now a soft whimper, as I fumbled with the keys.

Inside, I maneuvered her through the apartment to her room, where she flopped on the unmade bed the second I let go. I pulled off her shoes, tossed a blanket over her, and felt my way down the dark hall to my room.

Too tired to bother undressing, I sank into bed. I thought I'd fall right to sleep, but the pack of anxious thoughts running hot laps in my head wouldn't let me. What would Teri Sue, Rhett, and Cody think about my abrupt departure? How could I deflect their questions in a way that wouldn't lead to more?

After staring at the ceiling for an hour, I got up to slide my door lock into place, came back to the card table I used for homework, and turned on my desk lamp.

The shelf on the wall above held an assortment of college texts from the bargain bin at Smith Family Bookstore: Meteorology, Earth Science, Geology, and Physics. The lack of automotive books was my concession to Lydia. Those I kept under my bed, partly to appease her, and partly to insure they wouldn't wind up in the dumpster. The one thing that stood out among the heavy subjects was General Math. I'd bought it for a specific purpose, and it was what I pulled from the shelf now.

Sitting on the edge of my bed, I opened the book and flipped the first few pages to reveal the compartment I'd cut through the others. Inside was my insurance. Since my first babysitting job, any money left after paying bills and contributing to my car fund had been stashed for emergencies. I currently had almost four hundred dollars—more than enough to cover a month's rent.

As usual, counting the wrinkled bills made me feel better. They represented the power I hadn't had that first year after Dad left, when I'd constantly been on high alert, waiting for the landlord to pound on the door to demand the rent. They meant I no longer had to come home from school to find the phone disconnected or the electricity turned off.

I held them a while longer, reminding myself that things could be so much worse. Dealing with Lydia getting arrested, or lapsing into a paralyzing depression, was a challenge, but at least I wasn't powerless liked I'd been back then.

I put the money away, stuck the book on the shelf, and turned off the light. *Things will work out*, I told myself as I climbed into bed. *They always do.*

In the morning, I woke with snippets of a good dream flickering at the edge of my memory. But when I realized I was still wearing my clothes, last night's events rushed back like a flash flood.

Lydia I could handle. Teri Sue was another story. She'd expect an explanation, and this time a few words wouldn't be enough to convince her nothing was wrong. My best bet was to avoid her until it was time to go to the track.

After a quick shower, I made some toast and escaped the gloomy confines of the apartment. As I opened the door, bright morning sunlight dazzled me, instantly lifting my mood. The radio had said the rain threatening off the coast wasn't due to hit until late that night. It was a perfect day for exploring the logging roads I'd discovered south of town shortly after getting my license.

As I drove out Highway 58, alongside the Lookout Point reservoir, I rolled down the windows to let in the smell of the river and cottonwoods. Sunlight dappled the surface of the man-made lake, sparkling like a million stars. From my stereo, Robert Mitchum crooned *The Ballad of Thunder Road*. Of all the car songs I'd collected, the tragic story of a moonshine runner was one of my favorites, and today its melancholy tone seemed particularly appropriate.

After the lake narrowed to a slender white-water river, I spotted the dirt road I was looking for and turned onto it. The path began to ascend almost immediately as the forest closed in around my car. Forgetting my problems back in town, I inched the Pinto up the hillside, a steep bank on my left and a sheer cliff on my right.

For several hours, I explored the neglected trails, bumping over muddy ruts and stopping occasionally to get out and soak in the view. As the afternoon wore on, and the sky hazed over, the majesty of the lush second-growth forest soothed away my irritability.

When I headed back to town, I felt like myself again.

At four o'clock, I pulled up in front of the Clines' barn to see the #70 Camaro already loaded onto the trailer. Teri Sue and Rhett were piling toolboxes and tires into the back of the pickup. I'd figured if I could stave off Teri Sue's questions until we got to the track, she'd be too busy to grill me. Unfortunately, she wasn't the only one I had to worry about.

"Hey, Jess!" Rhett said. "Why'd you run off last night?"

"Hush," said Teri Sue, surprising me. "It's none of your business."

Rhett gawked first at her and then at me, mouth open. I knew how he felt. Since when did his sister care about other people's privacy?

Teri Sue squinted at the sky. "Think the rain'll hold off? On TV they said it's not supposed to start till after midnight."

Grateful for the reprieve, I studied the clouds. They'd thickened and dropped, but weak sunlight still glowed through. "Did they say anything about the barometer?"

"Like I'd remember if they did?"

"Well, unless it's dropping like a rock, we're okay."

Teri Sue nodded. "Good. Then if you wanna grab the ice chest, we'll be ready to go."

At the track that night, whenever Cody wasn't busy with his own car, he was over by ours. After giving me a questioning look and getting a scowl in return, he didn't touch the subject of the campout.

We got off to a rough start with a blown tire in practice, but Teri Sue turned things around by finishing second in both her dash and her heat.

"Hoo-eee!" she hollered as she pulled herself through the window of the Camaro. "This baby's runnin' like a scalded cat!"

I didn't know how she could look so good after climbing out of a race car, but somehow she managed to glow, rather than sweat. I gave her a high five, and we were still whooping it up when Cody strolled over, the top of his firesuit open to reveal a T-shirt that read, *Drive it like you stole it*. The hair at his temples was sweated into dark curls, and his rooster tail bangs had been smashed down by his helmet.

"Pretty decent, Teri Sue," he said, not revealing the slightest hint of embarrassment over his last-place finish.

"Thanks."

"But be forewarned—I plan on winning next week."

"Uh oh," I said. "I guess we'd better bolt some nerf bars to the doors."

Cody quirked an eyebrow at me as he boosted himself onto

the hood of the Camaro. "Maybe I oughta spin her out again in the main," he suggested. "It seems to make her faster."

"I'll pass." Teri Sue dug into the pocket of her firesuit and pulled out a wad of crumpled bills. "I'm getting a Pepsi. Y'all want one?"

"Sure," Cody said.

I shrugged. I could hardly refuse now.

"Better get Jess a Hershey bar, too," Cody said, studying me with a sidelong glance. "She looks like she could use a chocolate fix."

Teri Sue walked away, taking my confidence with her. For a second I thought about hollering "wait up," but I didn't want to give Cody the satisfaction of knowing he intimidated me. I snuck a look at him, and he grinned, patting the spot to his right.

"Come sit down. I've had all my shots. Race insisted on it before he'd let me out in public."

Against my will, a smile crept over my lips.

"C'mon," he repeated, slapping the hood again. "The view's awesome from up here—seriously."

I climbed up beside him, careful to keep plenty of distance between us.

Out on the track, the slow Sportsman heat was just beginning. We watched for several moments in silence.

"You doing okay?" Cody asked, keeping his attention on the race.

I stared out at the track. "Yeah."

"Liar.... But I guess I'd lie, too, if I wanted people to mind their own business."

I glanced at him, barely turning my head. "So why'd you ask?"

He shrugged.

A burst of shouting drew my attention as Rick DeHoyos took the checkered flag. The fast Sportsman heat was up next, but Jack Benettendi's Chevelle had spewed antifreeze down the backstretch on the final lap. The cleanup crew was spreading cat litter on the spill when Teri Sue returned from the concession stand. She handed out drinks, dropped a Hershey bar in my lap, and hopped up onto the hood, shoving me closer to Cody.

"Looks like it's fixin' to rain," she said.

I tilted my head back to see the sky. It was almost too dark to be considered dusk, but I could still make out the threatening clouds. A cool, damp wind blew from the southwest. No doubt, that low pressure system was moving in. I pulled my feet up, tucking my chin into my knees and wishing I hadn't left my sorry excuse for a jacket in the pickup. It didn't help that Teri Sue was crunching her ice. That sound would make anyone shiver.

Cody shifted, his leg and shoulder pressing against me. "Race is gonna kick butt," he said as the six cars of the fast Sportsman Heat pulled onto the track. "How much ya wanna bet?"

I snorted, itching to scoot away, but trapped by Teri Sue. "What kind of idiot do you think I am? Betting against Race would be throwing away my money."

"Addamsen timed in faster," said Teri Sue through a mouthful of pulverized ice as she fired a smirk in Cody's direction.

The pack circled the asphalt, dust from the grease sweep drifting over the wetlands that surrounded the track. Engines growled as the cars weaved back and forth to warm their tires. Finally, the flagman snapped the green and Race shot between Jim Davis and Holly Schrader to duck to the inside. I could've sworn he was going to swap paint with them—there didn't seem to be room for a Dart to slink between the two cars—but he made it. Just like always.

"Ha!" said Cody, casting a triumphant look at Teri Sue.

The cars rounded the corner and roared down the backstretch. Race nosed the Dart under Denny Brisco's Camaro, with Jerry Addamsen, his rival, glued to his bumper. Through turns three and four, Addamsen's Firebird tapped at the back of the Dart. But nobody intimidated Race. He glided smoothly out of the corner to pass Tom Carey and take the lead.

"Yes!" Cody sprang up to balance on the bumper, thrusting both fists in the air. The car bounced under us as he hooted and hollered.

Raising her foot, Teri Sue planted it neatly on his rear end and shoved. If she'd tried that with me, I'd have done a face plant. Cody caught himself mid-fall and jumped to the ground with barely a stumble. As he spun around, he skewered Teri Sue with that cocksure look he'd used on me the week before. Seeing him direct it at someone else sent an odd little zing through me.

When he was safely out of reach of Teri Sue's feet, Cody turned back to the track to watch the remaining laps. With Addamsen held up by Tom Carey, Race was able to pull ahead. He threw the Dart into the corner sideways, breaking the rear-end loose in a controlled drift.

"He's showing off," said Teri Sue.

"Yeah," Cody sighed, voice thick with envy. "But it looks *so* cool."

It did. I couldn't watch a four-wheel drift without getting a flutter in my gut.

Addamsen finally made it around Carey, but he didn't have time to reel Race in before the checkered flag fell. The Dart led the Firebird across the finish line by a good half car-length.

"What did I tell ya?" Cody asked, turning to face Teri Sue.

"Let's see you do it," she challenged.

"All right, Street Stocks, let's get moving!" Ted Greene hustled down the pit road, bellowing in his usual belligerent fashion. I tried to fade into the shadows as Teri Sue and Cody scrambled to get into their cars. Fortunately, Ted didn't seem to notice me.

Whatever luck Teri Sue had been blessed with earlier, faded during the main. It almost looked like she was taking lessons from Cody on how *not* to win a race.

"Eleventh?" she demanded, voice pinched with disgust as I took down the window net.

"You'll make up for it next week."

"Sweet Jesus, I hope so! Rhett coulda done better."

At least she'd finished ahead of Cody. As we jogged up to the pit wall to watch the Limited Sportsman main, I puzzled over his driving. It was strange how he qualified well then choked in traffic. If he'd been the nervous type, it would've made sense, but after seeing how expert he was at keeping his cool, I didn't know what to think.

The last thing I wanted was to go home to deal with Lydia, so I didn't say no when Teri Sue invited me to the Little R.

We picked a booth, and Rhett tried to sit by me, but Teri Sue shook her head and made him slide in on her side. A few minutes later, when Cody showed up and dropped down beside me, I understood the scheming behind that seemingly innocent maneuver.

While we waited for our food, I slumped in my seat, the Lydia-induced lack of sleep catching up with me. Like last night, I was happy to sit back and listen to the others. There was something comforting about being in the midst of a conversation without the pressure of having to participate.

The waitress finally appeared, loaded down with plates of burgers and fries, which she distributed around the table. I took my time with my food, listening to Teri Sue and Cody analyze the Limited Sportsman main, which Race had won. As Cody polished off two burgers and bragged over his uncle's driving, a twinge of envy tugged at me. What would it be like to have family you were proud of—family you didn't have to hide?

After a while, Rhett, who'd weaseled a fistful of quarters out of Cody and me, wandered off with a couple of kids to play video games in the other room. As soon as he was out of sight, Teri Sue waved a hand in my face.

"Hey, are you awake?"

I looked up from trolling a French fry through a lake of ketchup.

Teri Sue had that no-nonsense look on her face, the same one she'd worn the day she gave George the boot. "So what happened last night?"

The abruptness of the question hit me like a snowball full in the face.

"You didn't get in trouble, did ya?"

"No." I dropped my attention to the table, picking up my burger and tearing off a bite so she couldn't expect me to talk.

"You sure got us curious, the way you took off."

I could feel Teri Sue's stare boring into me, but I didn't look up. Chewing deliberately, I made my mouthful last.

"So ... you got any plans for your car this week?" Cody dropped the comment into the conversation as smoothly as his uncle took a corner. My eyes caught his across the table in a quick look of appreciation.

"Don't change the subject," said Teri Sue.

Why was she being so damned persistent? Couldn't she see I didn't want to talk?

"Maybe she doesn't wanna talk," Cody suggested.

"Why shouldn't she?" Teri Sue leveled a glare at him before zeroing in on me. "Jess, what's going on? You in some kinda trouble or something?"

"I told you I wasn't."

"What about your mom? Is she—"

I slapped down my burger, nearly upsetting my Mountain Dew. "Look, I don't want to talk about it, okay? Haven't you heard of the concept of privacy?"

Teri Sue drew back, blinking. "Okay! Don't get your panties in a wad. I was only trying to help."

"I didn't ask for help."

"Jess ..."

Without waiting for her to say another word I got up, tossed a five-dollar bill on the table, and walked out.

## CHAPTER 11

Outside, a light mist haloed the streetlights. I stood in the parking lot, considering my options. There weren't many. I could humble myself to Teri Sue or walk to her place for the Pinto.

I shivered as dampness coated my sweatshirt like dew. My jacket was still in the truck, but I'd be damned if I'd go back into that restaurant. Even though it was a good nine or ten miles to the Clines', I started walking.

A cold fury smoldered in my gut, growing stronger with every step. What right did Teri Sue have to pry into my life? Did she think our friendship entitled her to an account of my personal business? Well, she could stuff her damned job. I hated the idea of crawling back to Burger King, but I couldn't take another chance with her. Anybody that bent on nosing into my business was too much of a security risk.

Footsteps slapped the pavement behind me. Oh man. Didn't she know when to quit? "I don't want to talk to you, Teri Sue."

The breathless voice in my ear wasn't the one I expected. "I'm not Teri Sue."

I shouldn't have been surprised, but I was. Turning, I snapped off a warning look at Cody. "I don't want to talk to anyone."

"Okay. But how about letting me give you a ride back to your car?" He studied me, his dark eyes saying more than his words.

I hesitated. The mist had turned into a drizzle, and water was oozing through the hole in the bottom of my left sneaker. I'd be soaked by the time I got to Teri Sue's. Still, I hated to give in. "I don't think so."

"It's a long walk."

"I've walked farther."

Cody shrugged, moisture glistening off his leather jacket in the pinkish glow of streetlights. "Well, okay. But don't say I didn't offer." With no further argument, he turned and started toward the restaurant.

I watched for a few seconds, waiting to see if he'd come back or at least look over his shoulder. When he didn't, I resumed my pace.

Cars whooshed by on Highway 99. The drizzle intensified to rain. My sweatshirt grew cold and heavy, and water dripped from the bill of my Eugene Speedway hat. I shivered as icy droplets wicked from the bottom of my ponytail, trickling down the back of my shirt. *Keep walking.*

This was my own damn fault. I'd known all along it was foolish to let my guard down.

I'd gotten soft and now I'd have to suffer the consequences—no job and an empty spot where Rhett and Teri Sue had been. I never should've trusted her. How stupid could I be?

*Just forget it*, I told myself as my sneakers smacked the asphalt. I should consider myself lucky. I could've wound up like Billy Evans. Just because I was sixteen didn't mean the state wouldn't be all too happy to butt into my business.

I thought back to the scrawny kid in fourth grade who'd always come to class in grubby clothes. Half the time he didn't bring a lunch, and the night of the spring concert, his dad had showed up smelling like my mother did after she came home from the bar. When Billy got yanked out of school and sent to live with strangers, it was my first hint to keep Lydia's drinking a secret. Nobody had to give me a second one.

A car passed, slowing as it pulled to the shoulder. The distinctive taillights of a '65 Galaxie blazed scarlet through the falling rain. I had every intention of walking right around that big Ford, but as I stepped into the weeds to pass, I couldn't help looking inside. Cody leaned over to pull up the lock button. For a moment, I stood trembling and dripping. Then I opened the door. The distinctive smell of old car wafted out to tickle my nose.

"Heat'll be going pretty good in a couple minutes," Cody said. "Let's go."

I pushed aside a stack of books, crinkly in their plastic covers. Library books. Huh. Who'd have thought Mr. Cool would be the scholarly type?

My jeans caught on the cracked vinyl as I slid inside. Cody hit the gas almost before I had the door closed. His take-off pressed me against the seat. With his eyes on the road, he reached down onto the floorboards and groped for a T-shirt that looked like it had found new purpose as a grease rag.

"Here," he said, thrusting it at me with a lingering glance. Something gentle flickered in his eyes, a look of protectiveness. It rattled me to realize I was the object of that concern. What reason had I given Cody to show me kindness?

His fingers, warm and dry, brushed against mine as I took the shirt. No amount of willpower could still the shivers that shook me head to toe as I wiped the rain from my face and blotted my ponytail. Under the dash, the heater whirled away, struggling to take the nip out of the air.

"Thawing out?" Cody asked, his attention back on the road.

"Yeah."

"You suck at that, you know."

"What?"

"Lying." He leaned forward, wiggling his arm out of one sleeve of his jacket, then the other, while holding the wheel with the opposite hand. "Put this on," he said, tossing it in my lap.

Too cold to argue, I draped the jacket around my shoulders, pulling it closed from the inside with icy hands. Cody's warmth clung to the lining, along with the faint scents of leather and motor oil. I closed my eyes and leaned back, comfort warring with uneasiness inside me.

For several miles we rode in silence, tires hissing over the wet street.

"It doesn't go on forever," Cody said finally, both hands on the wheel as he stared straight ahead.

"What doesn't?"

"The bullshit. It seems like it'll never end, but it will."

I snorted, turning to pierce him with a look. "You don't have any idea what you're talking about."

"Oh?" Cody met my glare and held it. "You've got brick walls around you a mile high, and something going on that you'll walk ten miles through the rain to keep hidden. It's not hard to guess things aren't all kittens and cupcakes at home."

Kittens and cupcakes?

"Look, I'm not gonna pry. I understand how bad family stuff can get. But it doesn't have to go on being that way."

For one fleeting instant, I felt a pang of hope, but then it smacked headlong into reality. "Easy for you to say."

"What's that supposed to mean?"

"Not everyone has an uncle like Race to sweep them off to a better life." The bitterness in my voice was thick, and I hated myself for being weak enough to let it show.

Cody's fingers flexed against the steering wheel. "You think I don't have problems?"

"I think you have more options than other people."

"Everyone has options."

"*I* don't." I turned to stare out the passenger window, hoping he'd take the hint.

"But—"

"Just drop it!" Whipping around, I glared at him, temper shooting into the red zone. "I don't need sympathy, I don't need help, and if people think they can butt into my private life after hanging around with me for a few days, then I don't need friends, either."

Cody drew back, momentarily taking his hands from the wheel in a gesture of surrender. "Whoa—okay. I'm sorry, Jess."

When I didn't answer, he sighed and returned his attention to the street. We drove through town, finally turning onto Fox Hollow, with only the murmur of the engine and the occasional tick of turn signals interrupting the silence. Cody edged a few glances at me, but he didn't say another word.

As the Galaxie swept along the twisting country road, headlights illuminating evergreens and spreading oaks, my anger faded. I shouldn't have yelled at him. He'd stepped in to head off Teri Sue's attack, and even after he had me captive in his car, he hadn't demanded any explanations. My conscience needled me to apologize, but I couldn't force words into that sheltering silence.

It was nearly midnight when we pulled into the Clines' driveway. With the engine idling, Cody waited for me to get out. His eyes, dark and solemn, tugged at something deep inside me, and I couldn't look at them for long.

"Thanks for the ride," I said, sliding his jacket off my shoulders and setting it between us on the seat.

"No problem."

The chrome handle chilled my hand. I pushed against the door and stepped into the night. Cody didn't complain as I lingered beside the car, letting out the heat. I had to give him points for not pressuring me. And for offering help I could accept with dignity. I rested a hand on the rain-slicked roof, leaning in to face him, not ready to be left alone in the darkness.

"What is it?" he asked.

"My mom drinks."

I looked him in the eye, challenging him to abuse my trust. He didn't flinch, didn't attempt any sappy expression of sympathy.

"That sucks."

"Yeah."

For a moment I hesitated, overcome by both vulnerability and relief. Then I realized I was shivering. "I better go."

My fingers felt strangely reluctant to part with the Galaxie as I slammed the door and sprinted through the rain to my car.

## CHAPTER 12

Sunday was Mother's Day, but Lydia was asleep when I got up. She hadn't been home when I'd returned from the track the night before. With her Buick impounded, that most likely meant she'd made up with Jimmy. A cold flutter went through me as I remembered what I'd told Cody, but I sensed he wouldn't make me regret it. I left a Mother's Day card and some chocolates on the kitchen table, ate a quick breakfast, and took off.

After two weeks of spending my free time at Teri Sue's, I wasn't sure what to do with myself, so I drove through town without a destination. It soothed me to explore new neighborhoods and cut down alleys, forgetting myself for a while. Eventually I wound up at the deserted speedway. With the wetlands hushed, and traffic whispering by far off on West 11th, it seemed like a good place to think.

I parked on the track and climbed into the stands, dropping onto a board that felt damp from the previous night's rain. The chilly air seeped into my bones. I should've brought something warmer than the sweatshirt I'd pulled on that morning. What I needed was my jacket, but I'd sooner freeze than call Teri Sue.

Above me, clouds hung low and gray as my mind idled, kicking up one idea after another. I could try to get my old job back at Burger King. Or I could see if the parts store by the college was hiring. Too bad I didn't have the nerve to do what I really wanted to—ask Kasey McCormick for work. As a woman, she was the only person who might give me a chance. But she also had the reputation of being one of the most promising new restoration artists in the Valley. What would she see in me?

Tires crunched gravel, and I stood to peek over the back of the stands. A yellow '65 Galaxie. How did Cody know I'd be here?

The Ford pulled onto the track, parking beside the Pinto. Cody got out, cut around the end of the fence, and jogged up the steps, taking them two at a time. With his leather jacket zipped, I couldn't read the lettering on his T-shirt *du jour*.

Why wasn't I nervous? He'd tracked me down when even *I* hadn't known where I was going. Shouldn't that be freaking me out?

"Hey," Cody said, reaching into his coat pocket and pulling out a bag with a familiar gold foil seal. "I thought maybe you could use a pick-me-up."

"Euphoria chocolate?" I made no move to take it. "That stuff costs a fortune." Every once in a while, I stopped by the shop on 17th to breathe in the incredible scent that hits the moment you step through the door, but I couldn't afford anything more extravagant than their chocolate-covered graham crackers.

Cody shrugged and thrust the treat in my direction. "It's no biggie. I only had to sell a pint of blood. It's not like it cost me a limb."

His joking cut through my uncertainty, just as it had last night. But I didn't take the bag.

When he rattled it in my face, I sighed and pulled it from his hand. "Thank you." I pried the seal loose without tearing it to reveal a truffle—the big kind that had to be refrigerated because it was made with real cream.

"Amaretto," Cody said, sitting down. "It's Kasey's favorite. I kinda like the Cookies and Cream, myself."

I bit into the smooth shell, catching crumbs in my hand as they fell away from the filling. Rich sweetness melted over my tongue, the flavor so intense it sent a shiver through me. *Wow*. Hershey's would taste like a stubby old crayon after this.

As I savored the truffle, Cody hunched forward, arms resting on his thighs and hands dangling between his wide-spaced knees. The quiet that hovered between us felt safe.

"What made you think I'd be here?" I asked as I licked the last of the chocolate from my fingers.

His shoulders scrunched up. "I dunno. Just a guess."

Well, *that* didn't make me the least bit uncomfortable. I picked at a splinter on the wood plank beneath us.

Cody bounced his foot and looked out over the track. After a few moments, he slanted a glance at me, the damp wind blowing his hair into his eyes. "Come down to the pits for a second."

"What for?"

"There's something I wanna show you."

I laughed, folding the bag from my truffle and tucking it into my back pocket. "You think there's anything down there I don't know about?"

"Yeah. C'mon." He gave my sleeve a tug. Without waiting, he got up and tromped down the bleachers. I watched until he was halfway to the bottom before giving in and following.

In the infield, we stayed on the asphalt because when the clay soil got wet it glommed onto your shoes, making you look like Bigfoot. Cody stopped at the far side of the pits, near turn three, where he crouched to pluck something from the close-cropped weeds.

"Here. Smell this."

Cutting him a doubtful look, I took the sprig and sniffed. The scent of mint hit me like an electric shock, current ricocheting along every nerve as I was jerked back into a night of racing. This was what I'd smelled whenever someone spun out.

"Cool, huh?" Cody's grin seemed a little unsure of itself. "I guess it grows wild around here. Every time I catch a whiff of it, I think of last season when I moved in with Race."

"Huh. I never even knew this was here."

Cody scuffed a Converse high top against the pit road, his eyes ducking away from mine. "Well, I guess I'm kind of weird for noticing stuff like that."

"No—" I looked up quickly. "I mean, it's cool. It makes me feel sort of ... nostalgic."

Cody's smile re-emerged, like the sun burning through clouds. "Yeah," he said, nodding. He crouched to pluck another piece of mint before sitting on the cracked asphalt.

Hoping I wouldn't regret it, I lowered myself down across from him. "So how'd you end up with Race? That is, if you don't mind me asking."

Cody hooked his arms around his raised knees, holding the mint to his nose. "It's not exactly classified information. I got busted for graffiti, and my dad wanted to ship me off to military school, but in a rare moment of humanity, Mom conned Race into taking me instead."

A rare moment of humanity? I wanted to ask what he meant, but couldn't pry after he'd been so respectful of my privacy. "So those rumors I've heard are true."

Cody flipped his bangs out of his eyes. "What—about me being a total pain in the ass? Yeah, they're true. I was never a candidate for Citizen of the Month, but after Mom ditched us, I kinda lost it." He twirled the mint between his fingers, attention fixed on the spinning stem. "It's not like we were ever a real family—just three strangers living in the same house—so I don't know why I gave a damn. I guess I was pissed 'cause she could walk away, and I was stuck with the mess she'd made."

So his parents were divorced. Maybe he *did* understand what I had to put up with. A breeze stirred around us, and I leaned forward to hug my legs.

Cody sighed. "Some of the crap I pulled probably wasn't fair to my dad. I mean, even though he always looked the other way when Mom cut me down, it's not like he hit me or anything. Some people have it a lot worse." His eyes met mine.

Oh man. That better not be a hint. "Your mom cut you down? Does she drink or something?"

"Nah, it's just her natural, sweet personality. She thinks I'm a loser." Cody pinched the mint between his thumb and forefinger until there was nothing left but a pungent odor and a wad of green mush. "After Race's wreck, she tried to con me into moving to Phoenix with her, and when I refused, she pretty much disowned me. I haven't heard from her since."

Wow. He had me beat in the worthless parent department. At least Lydia was only mean when she was drunk. I rubbed my shins, trying to generate enough friction to counteract the cold. "I guess you're glad to be living with Race then, huh?"

"Best thing that ever happened to me. Mom was crazy to think I'd leave." Cody flicked his fingers to get the mint off of them. "I gotta give her a *little* credit, though. It couldn't have been easy, convincing Race to take me in the first place. He hadn't spoken to her in five years."

"Really? Five years?" As difficult as Lydia was, I couldn't imagine turning my back on her.

"He hadn't talked to *any* of the family in that long. And they deserved it for the way they treated him while he was growing up. You think my mom sounds bad, you don't even wanna *hear* about my grandpa." Cody wiped his fingers on his jeans, leaving behind a green streak. "The whole Morgan clan is about as screwed up as you can get. Financially loaded and emotionally bankrupt—though I guess that's not entirely true. Grandma let Race down when he was a kid, but she's been busting her ass to make things up to him since the wreck. And she convinced Dad to let me drive the Dart." He stopped talking abruptly and glanced at me, his face twisting into a grimace. "Sorry. I didn't mean to bore you with the sordid family history."

"That's okay. It's interesting. I never knew my grandparents."

"What happened to 'em?"

"The ones on my dad's side died in a car accident before I was born, and my mom never talks about her parents." I shifted my hips, the dampness of the asphalt seeping through the seat of my jeans.

"That's kinda harsh."

"It seems normal to me."

Cody picked up a pebble and skipped it across the asphalt. For a few moments, we sat without speaking. It should've been awkward, being alone with a boy this close to me, but somehow Cody's presence was like an extra blanket on a chilly night.

He tossed another pebble, landing it in a puddle. "So how'd you get into cars?"

"My dad. One day he was changing the oil in my mom's Buick, and I kept bugging him, so he let me help." I could still feel the hardness of the creeper under my back, see the alien landscape of the engine's underside as Dad pointed out the oil pan, drain plug, and filter. "Every time he opened the hood after that, I had to be there. He used to call me his little Grease Monkey." My voice stretched thin as I spoke the nickname. It had been so long.... But as mad as I was at my father for leaving, I couldn't hate him the way Lydia did.

Cody rested his chin on his knees, huddling against the growing wind. "You said 'was.' What happened to him?"

"He took off when I was eight."

"That why your mom started drinking?"

I nodded, staring down at my worn-out sneakers.

"Musta been tough. I mean, being eight years old."

"It's still tough." The words came out almost a whisper. "But back then it scared the hell out of me. It was like I had to become an adult all of a sudden, you know?" I raised my head, risking a look at Cody. His brown eyes were serious, his mouth relaxed from its nearly perpetual grin.

I've never told anyone about this," I said.

"I kinda thought that might be the case."

The way he was watching me, I knew he'd sooner die than repeat a single syllable. It was strange, how safe I felt with him.

Like I could tell him anything. I glanced back down at my shoes, pulling a stray bit of grass from one of the laces. "You know the other night?"

"Yeah?"

"My mom got arrested. DUI. I had to pick her up at the police station."

"Shit. No wonder you didn't wanna talk about it."

I nodded, shivering as I waited for Cody to say something more, to ask what I was going to do now. But he kept quiet.

"Why'd you come looking for me?" I asked. "I've been a total jerk."

Cody shrugged. "I dunno. I guess you kind of intrigued me. I've never had a girl try to hit me before."

*That* intrigued him? He must have a couple of his plug wires crossed.

"And you didn't give up. Not even after I knocked you on your butt."

"So stupid people intrigue you?"

He grinned. "Nah. Just gutsy ones. To tell the truth, you reminded me of Kasey."

"*Riiiiight.*" I drew the word out. "I can just see her going psycho on some guy for spinning Race."

"That's not what I meant. It's just ... Kasey's stubborn. Focused. And she's always gotta be in control." He shoved his dark hair out of his eyes, but the wind blew it right back in.

"Seems like you're the one who's always in control," I said. "When I went after you, you shrugged it off like it was nothing." Normally, admitting my respect would send me too far beyond those brick walls Cody had accused me of having. Yet with him, the words slipped right out.

He laughed and shook his head. "I can't believe you see me that way. I don't *feel* in control. I feel like everyone can tell I'm about to lose it. It's not so bad anymore, but I used to go into these huge rages."

"Really?" My skin prickled as I remembered my own humiliating fury. "But you're not like that now."

"That's because I did something stupid—something I could've regretted the rest of my life. It made me realize I needed to get a handle on my temper." He went silent, brooding over that long-ago mistake. "So, enough about me," he said abruptly. "What about you? You gonna give Teri Sue another chance?"

"Are you kidding?" A sudden gust of wind yanked at my Eugene Speedway hat, and I clutched the bill. It was going to rain soon. I could smell it.

"I know she pissed you off, but she didn't mean to. She just doesn't know when to quit. All she wants is to be your friend."

"I told you last night how I feel about friends."

If he didn't watch out, taking Teri Sue's side would cost him the points he'd made with me.

"All right. Fine. The thing is, you really like that job. And it's a helluva lot better than working at some burger joint."

Well, that might be a legitimate argument. Short of building the Pinto, nothing had ever given me as much satisfaction as working on the Camaro.

"You should talk to her," Cody said, his expression so earnest it made me wonder why he cared. "She won't nag you anymore."

I grunted. "What makes you such an authority?" A few drops of rain spattered the asphalt, and I tugged the sleeves of my sweatshirt down over my hands.

"You were pretty persuasive, walking out the way you did last night. I'll bet she never so much as asks you how it's going again."

"Right." How naïve did he think I was? Nothing short of a two-by-four would knock a dose of sensitivity into Teri Sue.

Cody sighed, pulling the collar of his leather jacket up around this neck. "I swear, you're as stubborn as Kasey. Look, my butt's getting numb, and you're obviously freezing. Let's go over to my place and watch the race. The Busch guys ran at Nazareth yesterday and Race taped it."

We didn't have cable, so the only time I got to watch NASCAR was when it was on network TV. But the thought of going home with Cody made my stomach quiver. "I think I'll pass."

He pushed himself up off the asphalt. "Come on. It'll be fun. Race and Kasey always get into arguments over who's gonna win. I think it's kind of a hold-over from the rivalry they've got going between OSU and the U of O." He tugged my ponytail, and I tossed my head to make him let go.

"Kasey will be there?"

"Of course she will. It's her place." His forehead wrinkled into frown lines, then a flash of understanding ironed them out. "Oh—you didn't know we live with her. I guess you think she's nothing more than Race's sponsor." He grinned fiendishly. "That'd be one helluva sponsorship package."

My face heated up.

"Let's go," Cody said. "I know you're anxious to see Race again, him being your hero and all."

My cheeks flared hotter. How had he figured *that* out? "Race is the last person I want to see. He'd probably slam the door in my face."

"Because you went ninja on me?" Cody laughed, reaching out to help me up. When I ignored his hand, he retracted it smoothly. "Don't worry. He thought that was funny."

"I didn't. It was embarrassing."

"Well, you don't have to worry about him giving you a hard time. He's too nice a guy." Cody rocked forward on his toes, sticking his hands in his pockets. "So how 'bout it? Kasey wants to see your Pinto."

Lips pursed, I squinted up at him. "How would she know anything about it? *You* haven't even had a close look."

"I don't need one to know there's no four-banger in that thing. You made it clear when you tore out of Teri Sue's the other night." One corner of his mouth hitched up in a grin. "Whatcha got in there? A 302?"

I fought back a smile. "351 Windsor."

"You gonna let me see it?"

"I guess."

The wind whipped around us, driving a few scattered raindrops into my face as I followed Cody to turn one. When I popped the hood, he studied the engine compartment, hands spread out over the fender.

"Wow. Kasey would go nuts over this," he said, shaking his head. "If she saw it, she'd probably offer you a job."

"Yeah, that'd be the day." I shut the hood with a thump.

"Let's get to my place" Cody said. "I'm starving. Besides, it's gonna start pouring any minute."

I looked up at the angry, gray nimbostratus clouds above us. "I should go home," I said, weighing the appeal of meeting Kasey against the swirl of uncertainty in my stomach.

"Aw, c'mon," Cody wheedled. "It'll give you a chance to see Kasey's Charger. It's got a Hemi in it."

Automotive lust overpowered my hesitation. I'd never seen one of the famous Chrysler hemispherical head engines. How could I pass up a chance like that?

## CHAPTER 15

Anxiousness ate away at me as I followed Cody through town and up 27th to the part of Spring Boulevard on the butte above the college. The Galaxie pulled up a steep, narrow driveway to a house covered in cedar shingles. The back of the lower level disappeared into the hillside, while the front stood above ground, leaving the main floor high over the sloping driveway. A staircase led up to a deck that extended the length of the house.

With rain falling soft but steady, Cody didn't give me a chance to look at the Charger. He led me up the stairs, taking them two at a time, and I had to be content with glancing back at it over my shoulder.

"Hey, guys," he said as he flung open the front door. "I brought Jess home to watch Nazareth with us."

Nothing like a grand entrance.

Race was lounging on the couch in sweat pants and a University of Oregon Athletic Department T-shirt, watching TV. It was strange, seeing him without his firesuit.

"Good," he said, "I was wondering when you were gonna get back."

Kasey appeared in the kitchen doorway, bits of auburn hair escaping her ponytail to fall in curls around her face. Like me, she was wearing a T-shirt and jeans, but on her they looked cute instead of sloppy. The fact that she could be a mechanic and still come across so girly drove home my complete hopelessness in the style department.

"Kasey, this is Jess," Cody said. He glanced toward the couch. "I guess I don't have to introduce her to you, Race."

"No, we've met." He fired off a full-throttle grin and exchanged a look with Cody that made me suspect I'd been a topic of conversation. My face turned thirteen shades of red.

"Sit," Cody said, giving me a light shove toward the couch.

I sat.

Being a mere two feet from The Legend turned my insides to Jell-O, but just as predicted, he had the good grace not to dwell on the incident at the track.

"Teri Sue sure was running strong last night," he said.

"Y-yeah." My brain stalled, and I swallowed, trying to remember basic English. "She had her best finishes yet in the dash and heat."

"Want something to drink?" Cody asked, his smirk telling me he knew how nervous I was.

"Uh ... Sure."

"There's some chocolate zucchini cake in the kitchen," Kasey said.

Cody perked up like a dog hearing its name. Raising an index finger, he gave me a solemn look. "I'll be right back."

Great. Now I was alone with both of my heroes. Who'd have thought I'd ever consider Cody a source of refuge?

Kasey sat in an easy chair across the room, tucking one foot beneath her. "I've noticed Teri Sue's qualifying times have improved. It's nice to see she's found good help."

"Uh ... yeah." My face flared so hot it was a wonder they couldn't feel the heat shimmering off of it.

"Getting rid of some of the oversteer seems to have helped," Kasey said. "That Camaro was awfully loose at the beginning of the season."

Now *that* was something I could comment on. "Adding a bigger sway bar and reducing the stagger took care of a lot of it. And we've been experimenting with lead ballast. What I'd really like to do is get a heavier spring for the right front, though."

Kasey nodded. "Be careful. People have been seriously hurt swapping those out. If you decide to give it a try, be sure to use a good spring compressor. I can lend you one."

"Thanks." Much as I appreciated the offer, I didn't think I'd have the courage to ask when the time came. Renting one would be so much less intimidating.

A big cat strolled into the room, brown tabby markings on his upper body and pure white fur on his stomach and legs. As I reached down to pet him, he tilted his head to let me scratch his chin. Apparently satisfied with the sample, he jumped up beside me and flopped over, weight dropping against my leg like a rock.

"You must be a cat person," Kasey said over the animal's impressive purr. He sounded like an unmuffled engine turning a good 7,000 rpms.

"Not really. My mom's allergic, so we never had pets."

Cody came through the kitchen door with two slices of cake. As he passed the couch, Race swiped a finger through the frosting on one of them.

"Hey!" Cody said, giving him the evil eye. "Get your own." He handed me the piece of cake that hadn't been accosted before going back to the kitchen for two glasses of milk. As soon as I took one, the cat was up on his haunches, nose twitching as he rubbed against my arm.

"No, Winston! You're fat enough," Cody said.

Who'd have thought cats were capable of dirty looks? Winston jumped off the couch, flicked his tail, and strode from the room.

"I swear that cat must be pregnant." Cody wedged himself between Race and me and took a huge bite of cake.

"Impossible," said Race. "He's been fixed."

I glanced sideways at him. His expression was serious as a thrown rod.

Kasey shook her head and smiled. "You'll get used to them."

"What's to get used to?" Cody asked, licking frosting from the back of his fork.

"Really." Race got up and fed a tape into the VCR.

For the next three hours, we cheered our favorite drivers. Cody and I pulled for Chuck Bown, an Oregon native, while Kasey put her money on Jimmy Hensley, and Race rooted for Tommy Houston. Cody wasn't kidding about Race and Kasey's rivalry. They went at each other like Rhett and Teri Sue.

"Did you see that?" Race demanded, berating one of Hensley's passes. "It's a wonder he hasn't taken out the whole field."

Kasey grunted. "At least he knows the difference between the throttle and the brake."

"Yeah, he knows the brake because he can't stay off it."

Hensley piloted his Oldsmobile across the finish line first, giving Kasey the last laugh, but Race wouldn't let it go.

"How can anybody badmouth Tommy Houston? He's made every single race since he start—"

"So, Jess," Kasey said, looking across the room at me. "I understand you have a Pinto I should see."

"You only interrupt because you know I'm right," said Race.

"I interrupt because no one can get a word in edgewise." Kasey grasped the arms of the chair and boosted herself up. "How about it, Jess?"

Proud as I was of the Pinto, I wasn't sure I trusted my work to her expert eyes. "Can I see your Charger first?"

"Certainly." Kasey headed for the door, narrowly ducking the OSU Beavers pillow Race chucked at her. "Keep that up," she called over her shoulder, "and you'll be cooking your own dinner tonight."

Race waited until she'd turned away to bean her with a second pillow.

Outside, the air was heavy with moisture, but the rain had stopped. The Charger sat proudly in the driveway, a '68 RT with Plum Crazy purple paint, tasteful black Mopar police wheels, and fifty-series tires that seemed almost as wide as they were tall.

"Do you really have a Hemi in this?" I sounded like an excited little kid, but I didn't care. The Hemi was a legend among engines. It caused a political uproar in NASCAR back in the sixties because it was so fast.

"Of course. I dropped it in about six months ago."

"Sweet. I've been wanting to see one for years."

Kasey chuckled. "Cody certainly has you pegged."

I wondered just what it was Cody had been saying, then Kasey pulled the hood release and I forgot everything else. The Hemi straddled the engine compartment, an orange, cast iron monster boasting five hundred horsepower. The wrinkle-black valve covers were so wide you could practically bathe a baby in them.

"It's beautiful," I murmured.

Kasey laughed. "Now can I have a look at your car?"

Reluctantly, I pulled myself away. "Okay."

I chewed a thumbnail as I led Kasey down to where I'd parked in the street. What if she noticed the dust in the paint on the valve covers, or the mickey mouse throttle spring attachment I hadn't gotten around to fixing? I raised the hood and stood back, holding my breath.

Kasey moved closer. She glanced at the engine, then at me. "The obvious choice would be a 302, but something tells me this is a 351."

The comment surprised me, since the engines were virtually identical on the outside. "You're right."

Time dragged as she leaned over the grill to scrutinize the engine compartment. I waited, willing my fingers not to tap the fender. My shop teacher said I'd done a great job, but he was comparing my work to what other kids had done. I wanted to be a good mechanic, period, not a good mechanic for a teenaged girl.

Kasey dropped to the ground, heedless of the wet asphalt. She peered under the Pinto at the transmission and rear end. After another millennium, she pulled herself up, the knees of her jeans soaked through.

"You did all of this yourself?"

"Yeah."

She shook her head, smiling with her whole face, the way my dad used to. "You've invested a lot of time in this project."

"Uh huh." I glanced down and ran my hand over the fender. "I've been working on it for two years."

"It's very clean. It's evident you pay attention to detail."

My cheeks burned. No one had pointed that out before, but it was true. When it came to anything mechanical, I'd didn't allow myself to do a slap-dash job.

"Where did you learn how to do this kind of work?"

I shrugged. "Books and magazines, mostly. I've been reading about cars for years. In fifth grade I got sent to the principal's office because I wouldn't put away the service manual for my mom's Buick during social studies."

Kasey's lips twitched before pulling into a thoughtful frown. She studied me, and then she said the magic words.

"If you could fit another job into your schedule, I'd love to take you on."

## CHAPTER 14

"I can't believe it," I said as Cody drove me to the shop. Excitement sparked and crackled inside me like the air around a lightning bolt.

"You already said that," Cody pointed out. "Five or six times, in fact." He angled a look at me, his brown eyes shimmering with the grin he'd managed to keep off his lips.

"Do you know how long I've been trying to find this kind of work? Everyone's laughed at me before."

"I didn't hear Kasey laughing. In fact, she usually doesn't get that excited about anything that doesn't have four wheels. Except maybe Race. And he damn near had to get himself killed to get her attention."

I glanced across the seat of the Galaxie, surprised. "They weren't together before the wreck?"

"Nah, Race was totally hot for her, but she wouldn't give an inch. He had to settle for being her best friend." Cody shook his head. "I used to give him so much crap about it."

"It's amazing he kept you around."

"Well, he was practically begging for it. Race may act cool, but he's totally gullible. The perfect target for a bad ass juvenile delinquent like myself." Cody's smirk made it clear he was amused by his own reputation.

"So why didn't Kasey want to get involved with him?"

"Beats me."

"But the wreck changed that?"

Cody grunted, a shadow flickering across his face. "It changed a lot of things."

We rode the last half-mile in silence. Signaling a left, Cody cut across traffic into the Eugene Custom Classics lot. A row of cars sat out front: a rusty mid-'60s Comet, a '65 Dodge Coronet, and a '70 El Camino.

"Sweet," I said as I got out of the Galaxie.

"Just wait'll you see what's inside."

Cody unlocked the door and flipped the breaker, bringing a bright red '58 T-bird into view. A '69 Z28 Camaro sat beside it, with an early '50s flatbed GMC in the third bay.

I drew in an appreciative breath. "Be still, my heart."

"Yeah," Cody said, laughing. "I figured you'd have that reaction."

I glanced around before looking over my shoulder to where he stood beside the door, hands tucked into the pockets of his leather jacket. "This place is great. It must've cost a fortune to get started."

"Well, Kasey's not hurting for money. When she was getting her engineering degree, she designed some logging equipment and sold it to a lumber company. Made enough for this and her house."

"Wow."

"Yeah, she's pretty amazing."

Cody gave me a tour, starting with the paint booth at the far end of the building. The primered shell of a '55 Chevy Bel Air sat inside. "Kasey does a lot of the body work, but Jake handles most of the painting. He's, like, in his forties and kinda quiet, but he's cool. Eddie's the other mechanic. He graduated from the automotive program at Lane last year. He deals with welding the sheet metal, since all that stopping and starting takes a lot of dexterity. But Race handles the heavier stuff. In fact, he's boxing the frame of this beast over here." Cody led me back to the flatbed.

"So what do you do?" I asked. Despite the hours he'd spent at Teri Sue's the past week, I knew he had a job at the shop.

"Whatever Kasey tells me to. Usually the grunt work." He continued past the Camaro and T-bird to open the back door. "Out here is where we keep spare parts and scrap metal."

Along with the mini-junk yard, the small lot held Kasey's car trailer and the early '70s Dodge pickup she used to haul Cody's Dart to the track.

Cody pulled the door shut and continued the tour, pointing first one direction, and then the other. "Parts washer, where I spend most of my time. Bathroom, I guess that doesn't need any explanation. And this," he said, leading me into a smaller room, "is the office. Race's domain when he's not making sparks and noise or helping with the mechanical stuff."

"Race runs the office?"

"Yeah." Cody sat on the edge of the desk. "Since he couldn't go back to doing graphic design, Kasey gave him a job sorting out her records, and it kind of expanded from there. Race knows a lot about business—took some classes before he quit trying to please Grandpa." He shook his head, his face clouding over. "I don't know why he bothered. He could've become president of IBM, and that asshole still would've found a reason to tear him down."

Cody's bitterness tugged at something inside me. How could I have been so wrong about him?

"Well," he said, slamming the door on his emotions as he pushed away from the desk, "I guess I better get you back to your car." Forcing a grin, he reached out to pull my ponytail. "So what do you think of the place?"

I rolled my eyes. "You have to ask?"

When I opened the apartment door late that afternoon, a rich, meaty scent greeted me, stirring memories that flitted away the second I tried to place them.

"Lydia?" I called.

"In here, sweetie."

I followed her voice to the kitchen and did a double take. She stood at the counter, washrag in hand, sweatshirt sleeves rolled above her elbows and hair pulled back in a pink bandana.

The mess of boxes and canisters that normally crowded the countertops now covered one end of the table.

"What are you doing?"

"Just a little spring cleaning. I'm glad you made it home for dinner. I made beef stew."

The puzzle piece of memory snapped into place. No wonder I hadn't been able to identify the scent. The last time she'd cooked stew was before Dad left.

"Sit down," Lydia said. "I'm almost done here. We'll have dinner together."

Sit? I was so shocked I could've fallen. I pulled out a chair and eased into it. "What's going on?"

Lydia rinsed her dishrag and draped it over the faucet. When she turned to face me, her eyes reflected a steadiness I hadn't seen in a long time. "The other night was a wake-up call, Jess. It's time to make some changes." There was something different in the way she held herself. A kind of confidence. "I know it's not going to be easy," she continued, scooping stew into bowls and setting one in front of me. "But with the support the county's offering, I think I can do it this time. Last night I talked to a woman from AA, and she was really encouraging."

My hand stopped midway to my spoon. AA? She'd talked to someone from Alcoholics Anonymous? As often as she'd promised to get her life together, she'd never gone that far.

"You mean you weren't out with Jimmy?"

"No. And I won't be until he stops drinking. Things are going to be different from now on."

I stared down into my bowl, thoughts swirling in that limbo between doubt and hope. It wasn't the first time I'd heard those words, but she'd never backed them up with clean counters and beef stew before.

Teri Sue left a couple of messages with Lydia while I was gone Sunday, but I didn't call her back. I needed time to think. Now that I had another job, I could afford to lose hers. I just wasn't sure I wanted to.

After school Monday, I reported to work at Kasey's shop, where I was greeted by the scents of primer, carburetor cleaner, and hot engine oil. My idea of Heaven. Race herded me into the office to fill out employment paperwork. Immediately, I dropped the pen he handed me, then blushed and fumbled as I bent down to pick it up. Why did I have to be so nervous around him?

With the forms complete, I went out to ask Kasey what she wanted me to do.

"You can help me with this Z28," she said, straightening up from the engine compartment. "We're doing a complete body-off restoration. We'll need to bag and tag everything as we disassemble it. Can you write legibly?"

"Um, yeah. But..."

She tucked the bolts she was holding into a sandwich bag on the fender. "But what?"

"Well, I just figured you'd put me to work washing parts or something."

"You'll get your share of that too, believe me."

"Anyway, that's what she's got me for," Cody added, coming across the shop with five bottles of 30 weight oil.

I chewed my lip as I looked at the car. The '69 Z28 was one of the most desirable Camaros. I knew I wouldn't mess up, but I couldn't believe Kasey was willing to give me the chance to prove it. "Are you sure you want to trust me with something like this on my first day?"

Her eyes caught mine in a firm, no nonsense look. "Why wouldn't I? I've seen what you're capable of. That Pinto is an impressive resume."

"Yeah, but..."

"Jess, I didn't hire you to do grunt work, I hired you so I could teach you. I was fortunate enough to have good people to show me the ropes when I was young, and that's why I've been successful."

"Okay," I said, nodding. "Just tell me what to do."

We spent the next two hours stripping the engine compartment. As we worked, I noticed Kasey was as obsessed with details as I was, taking photos before she disassembled anything, and meticulously labeling the bolts, brackets, and other small pieces. She spoke throughout the process, not just about what we were doing, but also about restoration principles and the history of the car. It was the most fun I'd ever had working. Better even than helping Teri Sue.

What was I going to do about *her*? Guilt nagged me as I washed the grease from my hands, preparing to go home. I thought of all the times she'd pulled me effortlessly into conversations with her easy, chatty nature. Of how problems just seemed to roll off her back. And then there was Rhett, sneaking into the barn and giving us that cheeky grin whenever his sister tried to chase him off. Could I really walk away?

Maybe, if I had some reassurance Teri Sue wouldn't nose into my business again, I could forget what happened Saturday night.

I got into the Pinto and backed out of my spot. It would be wrong to leave her hanging. Irresponsible and mean. I sighed as I reached the end of the parking lot and hit the brakes. Instead of turning right to go home, I turned left and headed for Fox Hollow.

When I pulled up in front of the Clines', Mark was on the porch in one of the Adirondack chairs. His feet, tanned and dusty in their Birkenstocks, stretched out into a pool of sunlight. The gentle music that played from the boombox on the table at his side made me think of old growth forests and wind-blown beaches.

He looked up from the book he was reading—a skinny little

paperback with Asian lettering on the cover. "Hello, Jess. Teri Sue's in the kitchen fixing supper."

"Thanks." I waited for further comment, wondering if he knew about the trouble between us, but nothing came.

Uneasiness slowed my steps as I went inside. I pushed through it, not stopping until I reached the kitchen doorway. Teri Sue stood at the stove, stirring something that smelled as wonderful as Lydia's beef stew.

"Hey," she said. "Didn't think I'd see you again."

I let my weight rest against the doorjamb. "It seemed wrong to walk away without saying goodbye."

"Is that what you're fixing to do? Walk away?"

"I guess that depends on you."

Teri Sue laid the spoon down and stuck a lid on the pot. "If you mean am I gonna poke my nose into your affairs again, you can stop worrying. I might not be the sharpest knife in the drawer, but I can see when I've botched things." She leaned back against the dishwasher, her hands braced on the counter to either side. "I'm sorry, Jess."

The apology was more than I'd expected. A jumble of feelings crowded my brain, and I looked down at the worn linoleum, struggling to voice them. "I-I'd like to keep working for you. I just need to know you won't push me like that again."

Teri Sue grunted. "Well, you've seen how I am about running my mouth. 'Bout all I can promise is that I'll back off if you set me straight. Think you can live with that?"

Her brutal honesty coaxed a smile out of me. "I guess I can give it a shot."

When I got to Eugene Custom Classics the next day, Kasey was nowhere in sight, and Cody was arguing with Race.

"Dude, just go home. You look like hell."

He wasn't exaggerating. Crouched inside the frame rails of the flatbed in his welding leathers, Race was pale, his posture rigid. "I will," he said, "as soon as I'm done here. Kasey needs this bay."

Cody's face twisted into a scowl. "And she can't wait until tomorrow? It's not worth torturing yourself over."

"Don't you think that's my business? I've only got a couple hours of work left. Even less if Jess helps out." Race used the truck's frame to lever himself up and turn my way. "You'll give me a hand, won't you, Jess?"

"Uh ... yeah. Sure." I glanced from him to Cody, who was giving me a look of death. Now what? It wasn't like I could say no.

"If you wanna speed things up, you can take the van and go get some acetylene," Race told him. "I'm almost out and the spare tank's empty."

"Fine." Cody held out his hand. "Keys?"

Race dug them out of his pocket and slapped them into his palm.

As Cody stalked away, Race caught my eye. "You don't need to look at me like I'm gonna croak. It's just a headache. Lord knows if I went home every time I had one, I'd never get anything done."

"Um ... okay." I'd feel a lot better about this if Kasey was here. Where was she, anyway? And why couldn't Jake pull himself away from sanding that Bel Air to intervene?

"Cody worries too much," Race continued, glancing after him. "Which is why I'm glad to see him finally making some friends. That kid spends way too much time obsessing over things that can't be changed."

I rubbed the back of my neck, focusing on the truck. "So ... uh ... what do you want me to do?"

"Cut some steel plates that'll fit the frame while I weld the ones I've got. You know how to use a cutting torch?"

"Yeah, I learned in shop class."

"Good."

I got busy, nervous both from working in close proximity to the driver I'd spent four years practically worshipping, and because I didn't know whether I should be siding with Cody or with Race. The stress turned me into a klutz, and I dropped the welder's chalk at least three times. When the piece of steel slipped out of my hands, landing on the floor with a clang that made Race wince, I told myself to get it together. Race was an ordinary human being. The sooner I got that through my head, the better.

Over the next couple of days, I struggled to find my footing at the shop, and to renew it with Teri Sue. From three-thirty till six, I worked for Kasey, and then I went to the Clines', staying until dark.

Teri Sue bent over backwards to stay out of my business, often catching herself in the middle of a sentence with an, "Oops, sorry. Forget I said that," even when the comment was so innocent I hadn't noticed it. Her efforts impressed me so much that on Friday, when I forgot my peanut butter sandwich, I accepted her invitation to stay for dinner.

The next day the races got rained out, so I caught up on the homework I hadn't managed to squeeze in between my two jobs. Being home had been more pleasant lately, with Lydia sticking by her promise to change. She'd joined AA and continued to meet with Judy, the woman she'd spoken to the night after she got arrested. I saw no signs of Jimmy or alcohol. But, as encouraging as this was, I couldn't let myself believe it would last.

By the middle of my second week at the shop, my new routine became second nature. I even stopped dropping things around Race. Cody and I had worked into a friendship that in many ways was closer than the one I had with Teri Sue. He was the only person I trusted with anything private, and I had a good idea that some of the things he said to me, he'd never admitted to anyone else.

I could see exactly what Race meant about Cody worrying too much. He agonized over anything that threatened his uncle in the least—even the things Race brought on himself. Uncomfortable as that was to watch, I could understand it, because I knew where it came from: Cody's fierce loyalty to this person who'd been so compassionate toward him. I'd never had that kind of connection with anyone, and I envied it. But sometimes Cody's efforts to smooth the wrinkles out of Race's life made his own a lot more difficult.

I got a dose of that on Thursday, when we were alone in the shop, closing up. Cody had been out of sorts since witnessing an argument between Kasey and Race an hour before. It hadn't seemed like much of an issue to me. Race told the grease rag vendor he'd have to run it by the owner before he could authorize changes in their service. But Kasey got annoyed with him for not making the decision himself.

"I wish Race would let go of his damn pride, once in a while," Cody said, crouching down to sweep under a '52 Packard. "Sometimes I think he needs a good swift kick in the ass."

"Because he won't upgrade the grease rag service?" I couldn't understand why he was so worked up about it.

"Because he won't make *any* business decision without Kasey's approval." Cody straightened up, waving one arm at the open bay door while leaning on the broom with the other. "You see those cars in the parking lot? The reason they're there is because of Race. Sure, Kasey's great with a wrench, and she's got a lot of artistic vision, but she hates any part of the business that takes her away from the cars. This place was really suffering until Race took over the office."

I plucked a half-inch wrench off the inner fender of the Packard and added it to the collection in my hands. "But if it's her money and talent that got the place started, I can see why he'd feel uncomfortable making decisions for her."

"She'd be *glad* if he made the decisions. It's not like she sees herself as his boss. Last fall she even offered to make him a partner."

"I take it he didn't accept," I said, heading for the toolbox with my collection of wrenches.

"He totally went ballistic. To him it was just more charity."

That was something Cody didn't have to explain. He'd already told me how Kasey had taken them in after the wreck, when his grandma was worried about them going back to the rundown trailer they'd been living in. Between the job and place to live Kasey had given Race, and the loan his mother had forced on him, I didn't blame him a bit for feeling like a charity case.

"I don't think Race's pride is worse than anyone else's," I said, placing each tool in its slot. "I'd feel the same way."

Cody sighed. "I know. I would, too. I just hate to see him making things so much more complicated than they need to be."

## CHAPTER 15

On Friday, another low-pressure system slipped over the Coast Range from the Pacific. We were all disappointed by our second rainout in a row, but Rhett took it particularly hard.

"This weather sucks!" he said as we moped in the barn late Saturday afternoon. He'd pulled off his brace and was sitting on one of the toolboxes, massaging his leg.

I shook the last few M&Ms out of the king-sized bag Cody had brought me and popped them into my mouth. With a push, I uprooted myself from the workbench and went to peek out the door. Again. The chilling drizzle hadn't eased up, and low clouds now cloaked the tops of the Douglas firs.

"Might as well get used to it," I told Rhett. "This is typical for springtime in Oregon."

"Yeah?" His face looked as overcast as the afternoon. "Well y'all can keep it. Give me a good thunderstorm that's over in fifteen minutes any day."

"Sorry to disappoint you, but we hardly ever have thunderstorms. Western Oregon isn't the place to go if you're looking for extreme weather."

"So what do y'all have? You don't have lightning bugs! You don't have sweet tea!" Rhett's lips bunched up in a pout and his green eyes narrowed.

"We have Jess," Cody said. He raised his head and grinned roguishly at me from where he was sprawled across the hood of Teri Sue's race car. "Doesn't that make it all worth it?"

Rhett scowled. "No. Why does it have to rain so much here, anyway?"

"It's the mountains," I said. "As a storm comes in from the ocean, the air mass has to rise to go over the Cascades. When air rises, it cools, but when it cools, it can't hold as much water.

The water vapor condenses and falls as rain."

"Oooh, check out Miss Wizard!" Cody teased.

Teri Sue flipped an old spark plug at him, and it caught him on the shin.

"Ow!" he yelped, jerking his leg up to his chest.

"At least she has a brain," said Teri Sue.

Cody moaned, rolling back and forth across the hood of the Camaro like he was trying to out-do William Shatner in an old *Star Trek* episode. The sheet metal buckled and popped under his weight, prompting Teri Sue to curse him and throw another plug. This one bounced off the hood of the car, chipping the paint.

"Ha!" Cody hooted.

"Get off my car."

He smirked at her. "Make me."

Teri Sue lurched halfway up off her stack of tires with a menacing look then sank back as if following through wasn't worth the effort.

"How come you know so much about the weather, anyway?" Rhett asked.

I shrugged and leaned back against the open door frame. "It's just interesting. Don't you like to learn about stuff that's interesting?"

"I reckon."

"You don't think it would be cool to be able to predict the weather?"

Rhett worked his leg back into his brace. "Even the weatherman can't do that. It was supposed to be sunny today."

"*I* knew it was going to rain."

"How?" Rhett's face twisted as he tightened the straps on his brace.

"Well, there were high clouds yesterday morning. That's the first sign a storm is on its way. It isn't a sure bet, because it's not unusual to see high clouds on a nice day, but the barometer was falling, too. That told me a low pressure system was coming in."

Teri Sue faked a snore.

"So how come the guys on TV didn't figure that out?" Rhett asked.

I shrugged. "Who knows? They said it was going to rain Sunday, so they weren't exactly wrong, just off with their timing. Forecasting isn't an exact science, you know. And meteorologists aren't gods. They just have better equipment to work with than people like you and me."

"I don't have *any* equipment," Rhett said.

Cody snickered, and I threw him a dirty look. "Neither do I. I just check out the news to find out what theirs says and watch the sky. I've always wanted my own weather station though."

"I've always wanted my own pizza," Cody said wistfully. "A big one with nothing on it but pepperoni. All for me." His eyes went dreamy. Either the spark plug hadn't hurt him much, or the mere thought of pizza had healing qualities.

"When I was in sixth grade," I said, "my teacher gave me a book about meteorology. It explained how to build a weather station from stuff you have around the house. But I never tried because there was no place to put it, living in an apartment." The thought of my teacher's generosity still boggled my mind. I knew she'd been trying to encourage my fascination with science, but who'd spend that much money on a kid like me?

"You could build one here," Rhett suggested, sitting forward on the toolbox. "We've got plenty of room."

I held back a smile. "Keeping good records is a lot of work. You have to take readings first thing in the morning and again during the hottest part of the day. It's not something I could do by myself."

"I'll help!" Rhett's skinny chest and shoulders perked up like an exclamation point.

Teri Sue laughed, shaking her head. "How much would I

have to pay you to teach me how to manipulate him like that?"

"I didn't *manipulate* him," I said, placing a hand on my chest in mock offense. "I encouraged his natural tendencies. Besides, it wouldn't work for you. You're his sister."

Either Rhett didn't think he'd been exploited, or he didn't care. "When can we get started?" he asked.

"How about in the morning? I'll get some stuff together and bring it over."

Sunday morning, Rhett and I built our weather station. It consisted of a rain gauge, a barometer, and an anemometer—a device to measure wind speed. Over the next few days, I showed him how to take readings from each piece of equipment, record the information in a notebook, look for patterns, and make predictions. He was so intrigued by the process, I lent him my meteorology book.

"I'll take good care of it, Jess," he said, cradling it against his chest. "I promise."

At home, things were going better than I ever could've hoped. Jimmy had stopped by a couple of times, but Lydia was only seeing him at the apartment, and as far as I could tell, she hadn't touched a drink since the night she'd been arrested. She had her rough moments, but at those times she'd turn to Judy instead of heading for the Springfield Tavern. Even though Judy wasn't her sponsor, Lydia had found a close friend in her, something that hadn't happened with another non-drinker for as long as I could remember. I wanted to cross every available appendage for luck. My mother had never gone this far in her efforts to get sober. Was it possible she'd actually make it this time?

On Tuesday, Teri Sue had to study for a big test, so I got home early. Not feeling up to doing my homework, I turned on the television and found an old movie on KPTV, the independent station out of Portland. The comfort of the couch pulled me in, and the next thing I knew, Lydia was shaking my arm.

"Wake up, sweetie! Look what I've got."

I blinked in the dim blue glow of the TV. When Lydia reached over and flicked on the end table light, I noticed the huge bag with a Sears logo in her hand.

"What's that?"

"It's for you." Lydia thrust the package at me, pride and excitement lighting up her face. "Go ahead, look."

I took it and pulled out a flannel-lined denim jacket, one of those baggy ones covered with pockets and brass buttons. All the seams were double-stitched with rich, rust-colored thread. It was exactly the kind of thing I would've chosen for myself.

"Wow!"

Lydia grinned like a kindergartener receiving her first gold star. "Do you like it?"

"I love it," I said, pulling my gaze away from the jacket to look up at her. "But how can you afford something like this?"

She clapped her hands together. "That's the best part! I started a new job today."

"Really? Where?"

"Sears. In Women's Wear. They're giving me better hours than I was getting at the restaurant."

I studied her face. The glow stretched from her smile to her eyes, erasing all the normal distress. How could I snuff that out by mentioning the foolishness of spending money she hadn't yet earned?

"That's so cool, Lydia. I'm really proud of you."

They were the best words I could have chosen. My mother's eyes glistened, and she quickly looked away. "Well, the weather's been so terrible this spring. I wanted you to be warm."

I glanced down at the jacket in my hands. "It's perfect, Lydia. I mean it."

\* \* \*

May gave way to June, and the end of the school year rushed into sight. Teri Sue was the most excited of any of us. She graduated on June first, a proud member of South Eugene's class of 1990. If she was disappointed about not finishing school with the people she grew up with, she didn't let it show.

"I'm just glad to be done," she said after the ceremony. Then she went off with some kids in her class to celebrate. It didn't surprise me that Teri Sue had made so many friends in the few short months she'd been in Oregon. If she were shipwrecked on a desert island, she'd probably manage to befriend the natives within a day, despite not being able to speak their language.

The morning after Teri Sue's graduation, Rhett called early to give me his weather forecast. "We won't get rained out tonight," he said as I stood at the phone in the kitchen, still in my nightshirt and bare feet. "The barometer's reading 'high' and it's not a bit cloudy. Besides, there was dew on the grass this morning, so that means it can't rain till at least noon." He'd become so obsessed with meteorology I'd had to take him to the library to get more books.

"Great!" I said. "I'll see you guys after lunch." I figured I'd better give Teri Sue some time to recover. Her graduation party had been an all-nighter.

That evening, in spite of a lack of sleep, Teri Sue finished a respectable second in her dash, third in her heat, and seventh in the main. Cody, who'd showed up at the track excited after earning his green belt in karate that afternoon, qualified well but did poorly in all three races. As we were packing everything up to go home, Teri Sue speculated about that.

"Maybe he's chicken. Look what happened to Race last year. Cody might reckon he's next."

I thumped the lid of the toolbox shut and swung around to face her. "Teri Sue, couldn't you at least *pretend* to have some tact?" Even though I knew she wasn't entirely serious, her choice of words made me want to shake her.

"I was joking!"

"It's nothing to joke about. Race almost died. Anyway, a wreck like that's a fluke, and Cody knows it. He's not chicken." Even thinking of him in those terms made me feel traitorous.

"Knowing a thing's a lot different than believing it," she said, raising her chin. Occasionally, Teri Sue could come off sounding almost wise. I guess it came from having a father who went around quoting the *Tao te Ching*.

"Cody's not chicken," I repeated.

Teri Sue grinned slyly. "Why Jessica DeLand," she said, batting her eyelashes and making her drawl go all syrupy. "I do believe you're smitten."

School ended the following Friday, and I came home that evening to find Lydia and Jimmy in the kitchen. My stomach froze into a hard little lump when I saw the Budweiser can in my mother's hand.

"Aw, c'mon," Jimmy said. "Sun, surf, and sand. What more could you want?"

"You know I can't," Lydia said, darting a glance in my direction.

This scene shouldn't have surprised me, shouldn't have fazed me in the least. I'd watched my mother fall off the wagon more times than I could count. So why did I feel like I'd lost the lottery by a single digit?

Jimmy turned in his chair, eyes meeting mine momentarily before sliding away. He pushed back from the table and stood up. "I gotta get going. See you tomorrow, Lydia."

It wasn't until he'd pulled the door shut behind him that I spoke. "I thought you'd quit drinking."

"Don't you start. One beer never hurt anyone." Lydia's commanding tone would've carried more weight if she'd had the courage to look at me.

"One beer leads to another. You know that as well as I do."

She got up and snatched the cans from the table. "You don't know everything, missy."

As I drove to Teri Sue's Saturday morning, warm sun pouring through the windows of the Pinto, I tried to reassure myself. Lydia was in AA now. She could call her sponsor for support. If she didn't, I'd get in touch with Judy and tell her what was going on—explain what a bad influence Jimmy was. Maybe the peer pressure would be enough to pull her back into line.

I didn't believe a word I was telling myself, but I was sick of Lydia's problems. I didn't want to think about any of that on a gorgeous day like today. For once in my life, I just wanted to be a normal girl, on her way to hang out with her friends.

When I got to the Clines', Rhett was in the front yard, jotting down a reading from his min-max thermometer. I'd bought it for him a few days before. Rather than just showing the current temperature, it held a separate fluid that registered the highest and lowest readings of the day.

"Looks like it'll be nice again," Rhett called as I crossed the lawn, the dewy grass wetting my worn-out sneakers.

"How hot is it going to get?"

Rhett's face puckered as he studied the clipboard in his hands. "I'm gonna say 85."

I draped my arm around his shoulders. "Sounds like great racing weather. Let's go drag your sister out of bed."

It turned out to be *perfect* racing weather. That night, Teri Sue won her heat, finishing just ahead of Kit McKenzie. Since they didn't give trophies for the heats, she drove straight back to the pits after taking the checkered flag.

"Yeee-HAAAA!" she hollered as she braked sharply, sending up a cloud of dust.

Grinning, I unhooked the window net. "I take it that was a traditional rebel yell?"

"You got it."

As she crawled out of the car, I slapped her on the back. "That was awesome," I said, borrowing one of Cody's words.

"Even though I beat your boyfriend?"

"Cody's not my boyfriend." I said, feeling a blush spread over my face. I didn't know exactly what he was to me, but boyfriend was not the word I'd use.

"*Riiiiight . . .*" said Teri Sue, giving me a wink.

"If I wasn't so ecstatic over you winning, I'd smack you."

Teri Sue grinned like a Jack-o-lantern as she danced off to get us some hot dogs.

Later that night, the rush of Teri Sue's win was still with us as we watched the Limited Sportsman main from our perch on the hood of Cody's car. Teri Sue was ribbing him like she always did, but at the halfway point, Race's Dart remained in the lead.

As Colby Carter clipped the wall and spun coming out of turn four, a shout went up from the crowd. The two cars directly behind Carter rammed him, blocking the front stretch. A third plowed through the infield dirt in an effort to avoid the pile-up, filling the air with dust and obscuring the view for the rest of the pack. The front-runners, who were about to lap Carter, screamed out of the corner into almost blinding conditions.

Race got his car stopped without hitting anyone, but Randy Whalen, directly behind him, did not. His red Firebird crashed into the back of the Dart, slamming it against the outside wall with an impact that rattled the lights on the pole above—along with every nerve in my body.

"Holy—!" Cody sprang from beside me, and Kasey barely managed to catch hold of his wrist before he could leap the infield wall.

"Damn it, let go!"

His eyes shot fire at her as he gave his arm a violent shake.

But Kasey held on.

"You're not going out there. Not until they get the cars stopped." The emotions playing across her face were so raw, I had to look away. For the first time, I truly understood what the two of them had been through.

"Get your hands off me!"

"Just calm down," Kasey said. "He's all right."

"You don't know that!" Yanking free, Cody vaulted the wall. Fortunately, the cars had stopped by then. He zig-zagged between them, reaching the Dart just as Race pulled himself through the window.

I drew a breath to quell the shock of witnessing Cody's panic and crowded the wall, along with a dozen others.

The wreckers swooped in. Officials jogged across the track. Within moments, the announcer gave word nobody was hurt. When a tow truck yanked Randy Whalen's car away from Race's, I cringed at the shriek of tearing sheet metal and exchanged a look with Teri Sue.

"Damn," she said, "that's gonna take all week to fix. And Race was only leading by three points."

But the cold, tight knot twisting my stomach was there for a different reason. Without Kasey to stop him, Cody would've run right out into the chaos on the track. I'd never seen him lose his cool like that, and glimpsing the angry, wounded kid he'd once been had felt like an invasion.

A wrecker pulled up hauling Race's car. Teri Sue swore in appreciation. "Sweet Jesus!"

The right front fender was wadded like tin foil, with the suspension folded against the frame. The left rear quarter panel, shoved in and upward, looked nearly as bad.

Race followed the wrecker, amped up on adrenaline and jabbering at Cody, who trailed him like a thunderstorm ready to cut loose. I cringed, waiting for the explosion. No doubt the only thing stopping it was the crowd of drivers and crew who'd gathered to marvel at the damage and consolingly slap Race on the back.

When the mob began to break up, Race flashed Cody a jittery grin. I stepped back, holding my breath. My hands found the cold, chipped concrete of the wall behind me and clutched it tight.

"Guess I'm gonna need your help this week, kid." Race caught Cody's glare and his smile faded. "Hey, what's—"

"Fix it yourself."

"Cody ..." said Kasey, while I froze, wishing I were anywhere but here.

"I'm sure as hell not gonna help him get himself killed!"

Race's eyes went wide, but he kept his tone light. "It was just a little tangle up. Nothing to get upset about."

Mouth twitching, Cody gave Race a look that could've leveled an entire city block. Without another word, he turned and stalked away.

## CHAPTER 16

The shouts of racers, tow truck drivers, and officials filled the night, but without the usual engine noise and bellowing from the crowd, the speedway seemed eerily hushed. Race watched, eyes wide and jaw slack, as Cody strode across the infield toward turn one.

"He'll be all right," Kasey said, resting her hand on the back of Race's neck.

Doubt flickered across his face, and my stomach twisted. It seemed so wrong to see him and Cody like this.

"I'll go talk to him," I said.

Race's eyes caught mine, his faint, sad smile appearing and vanishing so quickly I almost missed it. "Thanks, kiddo. I appreciate it."

The clean-up crew was still busy on the front stretch, so nobody paid attention as Cody crossed the track and I followed. At the dusty entrance road, he cut into the tow-vehicle parking area, ducking between trucks and trailers until he came to Race's van. After leaning against the chalky green paint for a moment, he slid down to sit with his back against one of the Econoline's rear tires.

"Cody?"

He scowled through the fading twilight, breath coming hard. With a toss of his head, he flipped the hair from his face. "What do you want?"

The harshness caught me like a slap, and a cold rush of uncertainty rattled my resolve. "Nothing. Just to sit with you. Okay?" After years of avoiding people, I had no idea how to comfort them. I wasn't even sure why I was trying.

Cody sniffled and pulled the back of his hand across his eyes. "It's a free country."

Oh man, what had I gotten myself into? My heart thumped an anxious staccato as I stepped around a trailer and sank down beside him. Now what?

The side of the van felt cool through my T-shirt, but the sun had dropped below the horizon only half an hour before, so the air still held its warmth. In the west, the last hints of sunset cloaked the sky, staining it faintly orange and purple.

Cody sat beside me, his breathing still ragged, elbows propped on his knees and head clasped in his hands. For a long time, neither of us said a word. The stars grew slowly brighter against the darkness. Tiny Pacific tree frogs croaked in deceiving big frog voices. Then the roar of the resuming Sportsman race drowned out the sounds of nature.

"I remember the stupidest stuff about that night," Cody said, his voice so soft I could barely make sense of the words. He pulled his hands away from his face and stared off across the field. "We had this blue Nerf football, and we were tossing it around. I was hassling Race, trying to scam a few bucks out of him for a cheeseburger. Just doing normal stuff and having a good time. Then two hours later, I'm thinking he's gonna d-die." His voice cracked on that last word, and he fell forward, wrapping his arms around his knees.

Oh wow. What was I supposed to say? Paralyzed, I sat beside him. Waiting. Not knowing what to do.

Cody shut his eyes and inhaled deeply, his shoulders shaking. "The whole time I'd been living with Race, I thought it was my choice. Like I controlled it and could leave if I wanted. . . . I even ran away and he came after me, so I knew he wasn't gonna be the one to give up. But it never once crossed my mind that he could get . . . killed." The words choked off, and his head fell back against the van, tear-streaked face tilted up toward the sky. "I mean, who ever thinks about something like that?"

His raw pain cut me deep, making my throat cinch up. Until this moment, in spite of everything I'd been through with

Lydia, I'd never realized it could be harder to watch someone else hurt than to be hurting myself.

"It was so out of control. One minute everything's great and the next it's just ... gone. The doctor in the emergency room wouldn't even let me see him. I was so freaked, I started yelling. I figured he was lying to me—that Race was already dead. Then he told us he needed surgery, but even that might not help."

He hunched forward, forehead on his knees, arms curled around his head. I ached to touch him, felt the need so powerfully it caught in my chest as a sharp, bright pain. But still, I couldn't make myself reach out.

"Why won't it go away?" he demanded. "I keep having these nightmares. Keep seeing the Dart roll ..." His breath caught in a sob.

My fingers reached out on their own, going to his arm before my fear could stop them. With a strangled sort of cry, Cody fell against me, and somehow my arms knew what to do. Closing around him, they pulled him close. Where did that instinct come from?

"Damn, Jess, it was awful. You'd think by now I'd be over it. You'd think—" he broke off and gulped at the air. "But it's still that night. Those tow truck lights flashing, all that noise..." He shuddered fiercely, and then his voice dropped to a whisper. "*I was so afraid he was gonna die.*"

There were no words, no words at all to fix this, so I drew him closer. I'd never held anyone like this. Not in my whole life. But it felt so right.

Cody shook in my arms. "I've never been that scared. Even Kasey was crying, and I knew it had to be bad if she was upset. Finally the doctor said Race had made it through surgery, but he still might not live ... and even if he did, he could have permanent brain damage. Then they told us to go home. Can you believe that crap?" The anger in his voice was so fresh, it might've happened yesterday. "When someone you care about is messed up that bad, you can't just leave 'em!"

My arms tightened around Cody, my cheek resting against the softness of his hair. An hour ago, I couldn't have imagined holding someone like this. Now I didn't think I'd ever want to let go.

"We weren't gonna leave—no way in hell—so we stayed all night. Kasey kept crying, real quiet. Watching her was like seeing the earth stop turning." The trembling had slowed, and Cody's voice sounded stronger now. "We spent all of Sunday waiting to hear something. You don't know how many damned seconds are in a day until you have to wait through every one of 'em like that. Kasey kept going to check on Race in ICU, and finally she came back and told me he was doing better. Then the fear just evaporated and I got pissed. I was so mad at him for scaring us like that."

Cody sagged in my arms, finally going quiet. I held him for a long time as his breathing became regular and easy.

At last, he sat up and pulled himself away, wiping his eyes with the sleeve of his firesuit. He shoved the dark hair back from his forehead and turned to face me.

"Jess..." he said. No one had ever looked at me the way he did now, eyes gentle—wistful. He put his hand over mine and squeezed. "Why'd you follow me?"

"I had to."

His eyes stayed locked on mine, so dark, so full of feeling. "I've never told anyone before. I mean, the facts, sure, but not—" he hesitated, his Adam's apple dipping as he swallowed. "It's different with you. Everything's different."

A surge of heat went through me. My voice came out in a hush. "It's like that for me, too."

On the other side of the grandstands, the crowd cheered, and the thunder of engines died away as the Sportsman main came to an end.

"We'd better go back," Cody said. Holding my hand firmly, he stood and pulled me to my feet.

He didn't let go the whole way back to the Camaro.

Teri Sue greeted me with nothing more than a raised eyebrow, and neither of us said a word about Cody's outburst as we watched the Super Stock main. I fidgeted through the whole thing, pacing along the pit wall and chewing a thumbnail. Every cell in my body was vibrating, both from the shock of witnessing all that emotion, and the sheer thrill of being so close to Cody. I wished I could go someplace quiet to sort it out. I suspected I couldn't chalk it up to friendship, but what did it mean?

After the race, Teri Sue went to get the pickup and we began loading the gear. Kasey walked up as I was piling racing tires into the bed of the truck.

"Jess? Do you have a minute?"

I glanced at Teri Sue, certain the restraint she'd been showing had consumed every bit of her willpower. She surprised me by nodding and heading off toward the Porta Potty.

I turned back to Kasey. "Is Cody all right?"

"He's fine. I just wanted to let you know how much Race and I appreciate you being there for him tonight."

"Oh. Okay. Well ..." I shifted from one foot to the other, hoping we could leave it at that.

Kasey's smile told me she understood. "I know this is all new territory for you, Jess. You're a private person, and you don't give yourself away easily. But there are some things I should let you in on, because I'm not sure Cody can."

I pivoted the toe of my sneaker in the powdery infield dirt, raising a dusty scent. "He told me about the wreck."

"That's good. I don't think he's opened up to anyone about that. He doesn't have an easy time letting people get close." Kasey sighed, the shake of her head barely noticeable in the pale glow of the overhead lights. "Cody's got a big heart, and the only thing he's ever wanted is a family to belong to. But his mom was too selfish to give him that, and his dad never knew how. Race was the first person he connected with."

And now he was connecting with me. Was this swirl of emotion fear, or something else?

"It's always hard when someone you love gets hurt," Kasey said, "but for Cody—well, it was the only time he'd let himself care about anyone. It was particularly difficult for him to get over the wreck."

My hands spread out on the cool steel of the tailgate as I eased my weight back against it. Cody's grief was so fresh in my mind, I could feel my arms around him, even now. "I wouldn't exactly say he's over it."

"No," Kasey agreed. "He's not. I don't think any of us are, but it's worse for him because of how deeply he feels everything." She shook her head, a far-away look on her face. "I've seen him struggling, but honestly, I've been so consumed with giving Race what he's needed, I haven't had much left for anyone else."

I ran my fingers over the pickup's smooth paint, recognizing the note of regret in her tone. Sometimes, no matter how hard you tried, you couldn't keep all the balls in the air. And when you dropped one, the only thing you could see was your failure.

"You shouldn't feel bad about that," I said. "It's hard, taking care of people."

Kasey's eyes met mine with a question in them, and I realized I'd said too much.

"You don't need to worry about him," I added, even though I was a little worried myself. "He's got me and Teri Sue, and even Rhett. We'll look out for him."

"I'm not worried," Kasey said, reaching out to touch my arm. "After what I saw tonight, I know he's in good hands."

\* \* \*

Our celebration at the Little R that night was particularly rowdy, due both to Teri Sue's victory, and to the Limited Sportsman pile up. Drivers were as apt to brag about their wrecks as their victories, I'd discovered. Still revved up from the crash, Race rattled on about what it was like to come out of turn four into a blinding cloud of dust.

Cody was quieter than normal, but he put away his usual amount of food and didn't flinch at Race's story. Whether that was because he was okay with it, or because he was so accomplished at projecting an air of composure, I couldn't tell.

It was after midnight when the festivities wound down. As Teri Sue drove us home from the Little R, Rhett fell asleep slumped against me with his head on my shoulder and his neck at an awkward angle. A streak of mustard from a speedway hot dog blazed across the front of his Ninja Turtles shirt. His hands, grubby as usual, curled limply in his lap.

"Seems like Cody bounced back all right," said Teri Sue. She peeked across the cab, waiting to see if the subject was still off limits.

I was too tired to protest, even if I'd wanted to. "He's very good at acting cool."

The sounds of Rhett's gentle snoring and the hum of the pickup's engine were hypnotic as Teri Sue navigated the nearly deserted streets.

"I'da never thought he was still so tore up about what happened to Race. Makes me feel foolish for what I said last week." Teri Sue sounded genuinely sorry. "I didn't mean to be hateful."

I smiled at her over Rhett's disheveled hair. It was easy enough to forgive her now. "I know—you were just pickin'."

Teri Sue chuckled and shook her head. She glanced at me thoughtfully. "You're sweet on him, huh?" For once, there was no teasing in her tone. It was a simple question, presented with

141

a gentleness Teri Sue generally lacked.

"I don't know. I don't want things to get weird." I didn't tell her what it had been like to have my arms around him, or how seeing him so miserable had made me feel protective. All that was still too fresh and new.

"Ah, the age old dilemma. Keep him as a friend and never know romantic fulfillment, or go for broke and risk losing your buddy. Might as well take the romance, Jess. It's impossible for a guy to just be friends with a girl."

"It is not!"

Rhett stirred beside me, mumbling something about thunderstorms.

"Sure it is. Ask any guy."

"I don't believe that."

Teri Sue shrugged. "Suit yourself. But you'll only be disappointed."

"All the people I hung out with at school were guys."

"And they were all secretly hoping they were gonna score."

I rolled my eyes. "That's the most ridiculous thing I've ever heard. In case you haven't noticed, I'm not exactly most guy's idea of a perfect ten."

"You're Cody's, and he's the only one who counts. Besides, it's not like anyone beat you over the head with an ugly stick. You're actually kinda cute."

I laughed. There was no way she'd convince me of that, but it was pointless to debate the issue. Cody would win a main event before anyone won an argument with Teri Sue.

The apartment was dark when I got home, and the door of Lydia's room hung open, revealing an empty bed. It was the first time she'd been out past ten in weeks. I knew what that meant. What I couldn't understand was why it bothered me so much.

I crawled into bed and stared up at the ceiling, where the

lights of an occasional car flashed over the textured surface. Feelings chased through me, a tumultuous rush of angst and excitement that wouldn't let me sleep. One thing was certain. There was no longer any denying that I cared about Cody—more than I'd cared about anyone in years. But where did that leave me? I didn't know the slightest thing about romantic relationships. Lydia certainly hadn't provided any decent examples. And if being more than friends meant I was going to have to become a blushing, giggling idiot like so many of the girls at school, then I didn't want any part of it.

    I sighed and rolled over, wadding my pillow up under my head. The whole idea of having a boyfriend made me feel like I was slowly disappearing. But what if Teri Sue was right?

## CHAPTER 17

The next morning, while I was making breakfast and trying to sort out my feelings about Cody, Lydia shuffled into the kitchen in a nightshirt and slippers. Her spacey look told me she'd had too much to drink and hadn't completely sobered up.

I went back to buttering my toast.

"I'll need your car today," she said.

What? No one borrowed my car. Lydia knew better. She'd never so much as asked.

"You can't drive," I said, concentrating on getting the margarine all the way out to the edges of the bread. "Your license is suspended."

"I didn't ask for your opinion."

The bite of her words tore my attention away from the toast. Lydia stood glaring, arms folded across her chest, head cocked at a challenging angle.

Okay, time to fall back and regroup. "If you're tired of taking the bus, I can give you a ride to work."

"What work?" Lydia flung her arms out. "Damn bitch fired me yesterday. So I was late a couple of times. So what? I told them I wasn't a morning person." She let her weight thump back against the counter as she ran a hand through her sleep-muddled hair.

A couple of times? That meant the drinking must've started before Friday. My hopes crumbled. A beer or two with Jimmy was something she could spring back from, but this … "I thought you liked that job."

"What difference does it make? What's done is done. Now gimme your keys." She thrust a hand at me.

"You're not driving my car without a license."

"Whether or not I have a license is none of your business."

"It's my business if it's my car." I dropped my gaze, snapping the lid onto the margarine. The knife clattered as I tossed it in the sink.

Grunting, Lydia pushed away from the counter. "Maybe instead of wasting money on that jacket for you, I should've gotten my car out of hock."

My skin flashed cold. "Maybe you should have."

The Buick had been impounded for almost a month. The first week, she didn't have the money to get it out, and by the time she'd received her paycheck, the storage fees were so high she couldn't afford to.

"Look," I said. "I'm sorry about your job, but I don't know how to fix this. You need to talk to Judy."

Lydia barked out something between a laugh and a snarl. "As if she could find the time. She's too busy packing—gonna move to Florida to take care of her damn mother. Like the nursing home can't do that for her."

Oh no. A cold wave of apprehension swept over me. With Judy gone, there wasn't a chance of Lydia getting things under control.

"Family obligations," she muttered. "Always getting in the way. Just look at me. If I didn't have a kid to take care of, I could do something with my life. Go someplace where it doesn't rain nine months out of the year."

Anger crackled inside me, springing out before I could get a handle on it. "Since when did you make motherhood a priority?"

"Since my whole damn life."

The audacity knocked me breathless, a series of memories snap-shotting through my head. My eight-year-old hands shaking her rag doll body as I begged her to get up and go to work. My feet climbing onto a chair so I'd be tall enough to stir the Ramen noodles on the stove. My arms straining to drag back the door of the Springfield Tavern so I could peek through the dimness inside to find her.

"Right. Like you're the one who does the babysitting around here." Playing the grown up was bad enough. Having her lie about it, deny it entirely, was just too much. Something inside me snapped. "You know what? I'm sick of this. You're supposed to be my mother! Mothers don't get arrested for drunk driving. Mothers don't get fired for coming in late!"

"Don't you backtalk me, missy." Lydia's lips tightened into pale, straight lines. She took a step forward, and I inched away, feeling the countertop bite into my back.

Lydia's breath, stale with sleep and old booze, puffed warm against my cheek. "Give me your keys."

"No." I ducked aside an instant too late to avoid the hand that grabbed my upper arm. Lydia's fingernails sliced through my skin. That might've been an accident, but instead of easing up at my surprised yelp, she tightened her grip.

"Let go!" I jerked loose and dashed for the door.

Out in the bright spring sunshine, I rushed down the steps and took refuge in the Pinto. My hand shook as I worked the key into the ignition.

I was halfway to Teri Sue's before I realized how much my arm stung. I looked down at the five half-moon punctures, now puffy and oozing blood. With one hand, I rooted in the glove box for some fast food napkins. The blood wiped away, but the marks stood out like neon.

Sighing, I clamped the wheel with trembling hands. There was nothing I could do but hope Teri Sue would go on minding her own business.

I was still rattled when I got out of my car at the Clines'. Taking a deep breath to draw in the calming scents of cut grass and Mark's roses, I started for the porch.

"Hey, Jess!" Rhett yelled from above. I squinted through the morning sunlight into the branches of the alder beside the house. He was perched halfway up, constructing a platform from two-by-fours. One thing I could say for the kid, he never let that brace slow him down.

"Y'all gonna work on the car today?" he called.

"I don't know. Why?"

"I sorta wanted to go swimming at Fern Ridge. It's going to be hot this afternoon. Eighty-five."

I smiled. Already, his sunny energy was burning through the clouds Lydia had cast over my morning. "And you 'sorta' need a ride."

"Yeah."

"I'll talk to your sister."

It wasn't a bad idea. The more I could distance myself from what was happening at home, the better.

Half an hour later, Teri Sue had packed us a lunch. At her insistence, I'd called Cody, tracking him down at the rental shop on Bertelsen where he and Race kept their cars. He turned down my invitation. There was too much to do on the Dart if Race wanted to compete next Saturday, and that was okay by me. I still wasn't sure how I felt about last night.

"Let's take the Pinto," I suggested as Teri Sue brought a pile of towels out onto the front porch. She and her brother had never ridden in it.

"Yeah, cool," said Rhett. He helped me load up the trunk before scrambling into the back seat.

As I got in and turned the key, the chorus of *Dead Man's Curve* thundered out of the back speakers. Rhett cringed, slapping his hands over his ears.

"Oops, sorry," I said, hurrying to crank the dial to the left.

The song played on at a more reasonable volume, describing a drag race on the streets of Los Angeles that ended in a horrible crash.

"Who sings this?" Rhett asked.

"Jan and Dean. It's from the sixties. You like it?"

"Yeah."

Teri Sue flipped down the little mirror on the sun visor to check her hair. "Don't you have any country?"

"Luckily, no." In addition to putting up with her twangy hick music while working on the Camaro, I now had to listen to it at Kasey's shop. But there would be none of that in my car.

"I like Jan and Dean," said Rhett, sticking his tongue out at his sister.

Teri Sue returned the gesture through the mirror. "You would."

By the time we arrived at Fern Ridge reservoir, Rhett was thoroughly impressed with the Pinto, as well as my taste in music.

"That kid's totally in love with you," said Teri Sue as her brother ran off across the parking lot to claim his favorite spot along the bank. "You better play it cool, or you'll break his little heart."

The funky scent of the clay that lined the reservoir filled my nose, reminding me of long-ago days, when Dad would take Lydia and me swimming at the park under the Springfield bridge.

I opened the trunk, and Teri Sue pulled out the basket with the lunch in it. She handed it to me before loading up her arms with towels and a faded red blanket.

As we were crossing the parking lot, the horn of a big car blared behind us. Jumping, I turned to see the Galaxie with Cody grinning behind the wheel. Emotions cycled through me, shuffling like a deck of cards, but none of them stuck.

Cody threaded the Ford between a couple of rice burners and stepped out.

"I thought you were helping Race," I said, wondering when the awkwardness was going to hit.

"Yeah, that lasted until he realized who I'd been talking to and told me to get out here and have fun."

I mentally held my breath. Any second now, the reality of last night was sure to clobber me. As I tried to figure out how I felt, cottonwood fluff rained down from the trees around us. Summer snow.

"How's he doing today?" Teri Sue asked, adjusting her grip on the armload of towels. "I bet he's really feeling that crash."

"Yeah, he's creaking around like an 80-year-old man, but that didn't stop him from going straight to the shop to work on the car this morning."

Nervousness kept a lock on my tongue as the three of us walked down to the water's edge.

Fern Ridge wasn't much more than a giant mud hole. In winter, when they opened the floodgates, it dropped to a narrow channel. The rest of the lake was submerged wetlands.

Rhett didn't seem to care that the water was the color of heavily-creamed coffee. He shucked off his brace, shoes, and shirt and hobbled forward in his cut-offs. Sucking in his breath, he eased into the reservoir up to his waist. Teri Sue dumped the blankets and towels before wiggling out of her matching shorts and top to reveal an emerald bikini. Even a fashion idiot like myself could see the color was ideal for her. Bellowing, she dashed in after her brother, jumping him and forcing his head under water.

"I guess this is all part of that sibling rivalry thing," Cody said, glancing at me out of the corner of his eye.

I clutched the lunch basket to my chest. "I guess so."

Totally cool, Cody shook out the blanket Teri Sue had dropped and spread it over the grass. It was an old one, with the fuzz knotted up in little balls.

As I set down the basket, I did an internal freak-out check. Sure, I felt a little self-conscious, but it wasn't nearly as bad as I'd been expecting. Or as strong as the magnetism that drew me toward Cody. When he flopped on the blanket, leaning back on his hands, I sat down beside him.

A smile that was a shy cousin to his normal grin pulled at his lips. Then a frown swept it away. "What happened here?" he asked, fingers brushing my arm just below the crescent-shaped scratches. "Your mom?" His dark eyes rose to meet mine.

"Yeah."

A shadow flitted across Cody's face.

"She wanted to borrow my car," I said, shrugging—hoping this wouldn't be the thing that overtaxed his limits.

His voice came out in a grunt. "And she's still living?"

"Yeah. I took off."

"Lucky for her.... She doesn't hit you, does she?"

Uneasiness welled up inside me. I couldn't lie to him, but how would he take the truth? "Not anymore. I think she's afraid I'd hit her back."

A harsh glint rushed to fill Cody's eyes. "Maybe somebody should." Almost immediately, guilt erased the anger. He slipped his hand over mine, giving it a squeeze that sent shivers racing up my arm. "I'm sorry, Jess. I didn't mean to pull a Teri Sue on you."

"It's all right."

He looked away, out at the water, where Rhett's feet were poking up from the brown murk. "I'm sorry for last night, too." His voice was husky. Ashamed.

"You don't have to apologize for that."

"Yes I do." Cody pulled his hand away and dropped back on his elbows. "I freaked. I made a total fool of myself."

"You got upset. It's no big deal."

He shook his head, still staring out at the reservoir. "It happens too much. And I can't let it."

There was something big here, something deeper than what had taken place at the track. "Cody, nobody can lock up all their feelings."

His jaw hardened. "You don't understand.... I have to." He

sucked in a long breath and cut a look at me. "Remember how I said my temper made me do something I could've regretted all my life? I can't risk that again."

My hand found its way back to his. "Was it really that bad?"

"Yeah." He closed his eyes, his throat constricting as he swallowed.

I sat quietly at his side, waiting for him to find the words to tell me. Finally, he spoke.

"I didn't want to see Race right after he got hurt. At first I was too scared, and then I was too mad. But a few days later, Kasey made me go." He drew another tremorous breath. "I tried to keep my mouth shut, but Race wouldn't stop nagging me to talk, so finally, I let him have it. It was so wrong, Jess. I totally unloaded on him. He kept trying to get me to go over and sit with him, but I wouldn't. I just stood by the window because I knew he couldn't get up to come after me. And then he tried to . . ." Cody's voice pinched off, the ache in it tugging at me.

"He . . . he almost fell. And if he had—if he'd hit his head again—that would've been the end of it." For one slim second, Cody's eyes opened to allow his guilt to pierce me. "Damn it, Jess, I could've killed him. One stupid, selfish moment of anger, and I could've killed him."

My hand squeezed his, trying to convey the feelings I couldn't put into words. I wanted to tell him it wasn't his fault, yet I knew he needed me to see the truth.

His jaw went rigid and his shoulders shook as he fought to shove all that emotion back into its cage.

"I understand," I said. "But after what you've been through, last night would have rattled anyone."

"Right. And that's why Kasey was jumping over that wall, too." Cody slung a bitter look at me. "Damn it, I'm a guy. I'm not supposed to feel everything like this. I thought maybe I was getting over it, but when I saw Randy's car slam into the Dart . . ."

His words trailed off and he blinked to clear the dampness rimming his eyes. "It all rushed back. Not just the wreck, but what came later, too. For a long time, Race was a different person. I was so scared he was gonna turn into a stranger."

I thought about the Race I'd come to know—that gentle look he got whenever Cody started worrying, the way he found humor in every situation and rarely took anything, including himself, too seriously. I wasn't sure which would be worse, losing a person entirely, or watching the thing that made him special slip away.

"Do you ever talk to him about what happened?"

"No. Not since right after."

"Why not?"

Cody stared at the sky, where wisps of high cloud were beginning to obscure the blue. "I can't, Jess. He already feels guilty about what he put us through. It was partly his fault. He had this crappy helmet, and if it wasn't for that, things wouldn't have been nearly as bad."

Oh wow. It was awful enough, thinking about it as an accident. Knowing it could've been prevented added a whole new layer of pain.

"That must've been really hard to deal with."

"Yeah," Cody agreed, giving me a glance. "But at least Kasey and I didn't lose everything the way Race did. That wreck cost him so much. How could I bother him with my stupid worries when he was trying so hard to put his life back together?"

An ache swelled inside me. Poor Cody, keeping all this pain to himself. It was lonely, locking your troubles up tight, never letting anyone share the burden of your fears. And Cody's heart was so much bigger than mine.

He sighed and hoisted himself back up, releasing my hand. "I'm sorry. I'm doing it again. You must think I'm a complete wuss."

"No. I'm glad you're telling me. And I'm glad about last

night. I mean, not that it shook you up, but because . . . well, it made me feel . . . close to you."

"Really?" He slanted a look at me. "I was afraid it turned you off. My first girlfriend dumped me for being too needy."

"What a *bitch*." The words popped out without my permission, and my hand flew to my mouth to prevent any more from escaping. I never said things like that.

Cody laughed, the humor coming back into his eyes. "That's pretty much what I thought. She did it in the hallway at school. Total public humiliation."

Who *was* this girl? If I ever met her, I'd unleash a little of the wrath I'd shown Cody the night we met. And I wouldn't feel the least bit guilty about it.

"You're not needy," I said, my voice sharp. "You care about people. What's the crime in that? Anyway, seeing how you felt about Race was what told me I could trust you. Before that, I thought you were some jerk who was out to humiliate me."

A grin chased the last hints of self-consciousness from Cody's face. "Well, that explains the attitude."

## CHAPTER 18

Cody and I never made it into the water. I hadn't been about to go home to get my bathing suit after the fight with Lydia, and he'd driven straight out from Race's shop. Besides, we were content to sit on the grassy bank, talking.

Teri Sue, who snuck an occasional look in our direction, kept her brother occupied, dunking him under the surface every time he tried to get out. Naturally, each of her efforts resulted in another skirmish.

The scent of cottonwood, sweet and pungent, seeped from the surrounding trees as I lay back, studying the clouds that drifted in from the west to form a haze. Rhett was going to be disappointed. His weather forecast was doomed.

"So ..." Cody said, chewing a long stem of grass he'd plucked from the clumps growing around a nearby cottonwood. "Have you ever thought about going to an Em's game?"

"What?" He might as well have asked if I frequented yodeling competitions, for all the sense the question made.

"An Em's game. Have you ever thought about going?"

That was the nickname for the Eugene Emeralds, our minor league baseball team. They'd been dubbed such because our town was known as the Emerald City—a romantic way of saying it rained so much everything stayed green.

"Why would I?" Baseball was a snore compared to racing. The only thing that saw any speed was the ball.

Cody propped himself on one elbow. "I dunno. I just thought it might be fun. I can score tickets for Friday night. Kasey's getting 'em through some kind of business deal."

Uh oh.... Was he asking me for a date? Even after all I'd said to him, the idea made my insides twist like a bag full of pretzels.

"Race and Kasey are going, too," he added, plucking fuzz balls from the blanket. "But we can ditch 'em afterwards and get a pizza or something."

He *was* asking me out. My stomach shriveled, and the only thing that kept me from freezing up completely was seeing the muddle of self-consciousness and hope in his smile.

"Cody," I said, fighting the instinct to look away. "There's something I have to tell you."

"Yeah?" His hope faded a little.

"Well . . . the thing is, I've never had an easy time . . . letting people into my life. You're probably the closest friend I've ever had."

The smile vanished completely. Cody's brown eyes grew serious. "I know that, Jess."

For several endless seconds, I couldn't speak. "I guess I'm afraid something will mess that up."

Cody covered my hand with his, sending a minor quake through me. His expression melted into that tender look he'd given me last night. "I don't want to mess things up any more than you do. Let's go to the game and have a good time. If you don't like it, we'll just be friends. Okay?"

"Teri Sue says it's impossible for a guy to be friends with a girl."

Cody grunted. "Since when do you listen to Teri Sue?"

I felt a smile sneak over my lips. He had a point. Anyway, I could sympathize with how hard it must've been for him to ask, especially after revealing his deepest secrets. I didn't want him to think I was like that awful girl who'd humiliated him.

Drawing on all of my courage, I looked him in the face. "Okay," I said. "I'll go."

By three o'clock, the clouds had thickened enough to blot out the sun. Cody was anxious to get back to help Race and Kasey with the Dart, so we all decided to call it a day.

"What's the deal with this weather?" Rhett grumbled as we walked back to the parking lot. A corner of his towel trailed behind him through the dirt. "It was supposed to be eighty-five. The barometer was steady and it only got down to sixty last night."

"You can't get 'em all right," I said.

"Well, what happened?"

I shrugged. "Who knows. Maybe a butterfly flapped its wings in China."

"What?" Rhett looked at me as if I'd told him my parents had been abducted by aliens.

"It's Chaos Theory. The atmosphere is so complex, a tiny change in one part of the world can make a huge difference for the weather someplace else."

"Really?"

"Sure."

Cody yanked my ponytail. "Is there anything you don't know?"

"I don't know how to get you to stop pulling my hair."

"Like this, you mean?" Cody gave my ponytail another tug.

"Cut it out you two," Teri Sue warned, "There's a child present."

"I didn't realize hair-pulling was so scandalous." Cody snapped her bikini through her T-shirt.

With a giggle, Rhett tried to copy him.

Teri Sue caught her brother's wrist and twisted his arm behind his back, making him beg for mercy. "Y'all see what happens when you horse around?" she said, "My poor baby brother has to suffer the consequences."

"You're right," Cody said, stepping away and raising his hands. "That kid's suffered enough having you for a sister."

"Oh, you think you're smart, do you?" Teri Sue dropped Rhett's arm, snatched up her fallen towel, and twisted it into a weapon. Cracking it at the seat of Cody's pants, she chased him all the way back to his car.

It was almost four o'clock when we got to Teri Sue's. She opened her door and had just set one foot on the ground when Rhett shoved the seat forward, pinning her against the dashboard.

"You little creep!"

He darted out the door, laughing. Teri Sue pushed the seat back into place and shook her head. "I swear, sometimes I think that boy's about three fries short of a Happy Meal."

Rhett bolted across the lawn toward Mark, who was pruning rhododendrons and wearing his favorite hemp shirt. I remembered what Teri Sue had said the day he'd bought it: "Oh, Lord, your hippie town's corrupted my Daddy. He's wearing hemp!"

"Just be glad he isn't growing it," Cody had replied.

"Hey, Daddy," Rhett said now. "Did you know that if a butterfly flaps its wings in China, it can make it rain here? It's Chaos Theory—Jess told me."

"Is that so?" Mark snapped a spent bloom from the bush he was grooming and dropped it into the five-gallon bucket at his feet. Pausing, he studied his son. "You know, I have a Chaos Theory of my own. Want to hear it?"

Rhett regarded him with a wary sideways glance. "Not really."

"Well, it goes something like this: The more chaotic your room gets, the less likely you are to receive an allowance."

Rhett rolled his eyes and sighed. "I'll go clean it up." He dragged himself up the stairs and through the front door.

Mark pulled his pruners from the scabbard on his belt to trim a couple of branches that had been rubbing against the stones of the porch. "Chaos Theory, huh?" he said, glancing at me. "Where'd you hear about that?"

"Knowing Jess, she probably read it in some book," said

Teri Sue, fussing the tangles out of her damp hair.

"Uh . . . yeah, actually. The weather's a chaotic system, so any small change in that system—even a butterfly flapping its wings—can theoretically have a drastic effect on the end result—say the weather here in Oregon. That's why it's impossible to make an accurate long-range forecast. You can never take into account all the conditions."

"Oh, I'm familiar with the concept," Mark said. "I'm just impressed you would be."

"Well, that's my cue to go put supper on," said Teri Sue. "You staying, Jess?"

"Only if you've got enough."

"We've always got enough . . . and you aren't going to be a problem," she added, anticipating my next comment.

Mark laughed. Every time they invited me, I said the same thing. Even though I'd begun to occasionally accept, I didn't want them thinking I took their free meals for granted.

Teri Sue scooted up the steps to create another Southern culinary masterpiece, leaving me alone with her father.

"Chaos Theory," Mark repeated, shaking his head. "You never cease to amaze me, Jess." He took one last snip at the rhododendron he was pruning and moved to the next one. "I appreciate what you've been doing for Rhett, you know."

It didn't seem like I'd done that much. Just helped him put together the weather station and occasionally stood up for him against his sister.

"He's a good kid," I said. "I like having him around."

"He's a blessing," Mark agreed. "But he hasn't had an easy time of it."

"Teri Sue told me about the accident."

Mark eyed me solemnly. "And what did she say?"

"Just that her mom hurt Rhett, and afterward shut him out of her mind. It didn't make much sense."

Mark nodded. "It's hard enough to understand when you

have all the facts, and Teri Sue didn't give them to you. She wants someone to blame. In this case there is no one."

He sat down on the steps, patting the smooth concrete so I'd join him. "Janice—Rhett and Teri Sue's mama—is a gentle, beautiful soul, but she was never strong. The accident nearly destroyed her. You have to understand, Rhett was in ICU for over a week, and the doctors didn't hold out much hope he'd pull through. Janice's mind simply shut down."

Mark studied his pruners, absently flipping the lever to lock and unlock the blades. "She had to be hospitalized for several months. We thought she was making progress. Then she came home, and the first thing she did was ask Rhett whose little boy he was. Her way of dealing with the guilt was to erase him from her mind."

I stared at Mark, horrified, but his gaze remained fixed on the tool in his hand.

"It was an impossible situation. Rhett didn't understand, and Janice got upset every time she laid eyes on him. Poor Teri Sue was caught in the middle. She'd always been so close to her mama, but she adored her baby brother. When she couldn't make Janice see that Rhett really was her little boy, she washed her hands of the whole thing. To her it was a matter of weakness—her mama wasn't trying hard enough."

Oh wow. Teri Sue's actions seemed so harsh, and yet I could understand. Her easy-going, fix-it-up nature would've been completely staggered by something like that.

Mark let out a sigh. "The stress was tearing all of us apart, and Rhett had been through enough, so I spoke to Janice's parents. We decided it would be kindest for everyone if she went to live with them."

A swell of memory brought back the closeness I'd felt to Cody last night. My chest twinged at the thought of having something like that and then losing it. "You must really miss her."

"Every day. But I couldn't help her, and my children needed

me." At last, Mark looked up. His eyes held a sad honesty I wasn't used to seeing in adults. "Sometimes there aren't any good options in the choices we're given, Jess."

Wasn't that the truth. "Poor Rhett," I said, marveling at how he'd kept his cheerful energy in spite of everything he'd lost.

"Fortunately, he understands his mama's sick. But I worry over what it must be doing to him. No child should have to live with the idea that his mother doesn't know who he is."

In my mind, I saw Rhett crouched over the computer keyboard, heard his piping voice insisting his mother would write back. "He still hopes she'll remember."

Mark sighed. "Yes. And I can't take that from him, no matter how unlikely it might be."

When I got home at dusk, the apartment was dark and Lydia's door was shut. I didn't know whether to be worried or relieved. With Judy gone, my mother was sure to plunge back into depression. And there was nothing I could do about it. *Stop worrying,* I told myself. *You've got two great jobs. You can handle this.*

I picked up the chassis set-up book Kasey had leant me, hoping for distraction, but my mind kept drifting back to this morning and the connection I'd felt with Cody. As much as the rush of being close to him intrigued me, I couldn't help agonizing over our upcoming date. What if it ruined everything?

I finally gave up trying to make sense of the concept of roll center, put the book down, and went to bed.

Over the next few days, I worked mornings at Kasey's and afternoons at Teri Sue's, staying well into the evenings to hang out with her and Cody. Lydia was never home when I got in.

At first I didn't think much of that. It wasn't unusual for her to be out all night when she was on a binge, and there'd been times I hadn't seen her for days. But when I came home to darkness again Wednesday night, an uneasy feeling crept over me. Not only had I seen nothing of Lydia since Sunday morning, I hadn't detected any sign she'd been there while I was out. What if something had happened to her? What if she'd been arrested again and couldn't reach me?

An image of her lying in her room, dead of alcohol poisoning, flashed into my mind. Spooked, I hurried down the hall to check. I knew I was being foolish—that she'd probably been staying at Jimmy's—but I had to reassure myself.

When I opened the door, my stomach plunged. Lydia's empty drawers hung from the dresser. The pillows and comforter were missing from the bed. I robot-walked across the room and pulled back the closet door. Nothing, except some old clothes she hadn't worn in years.

It took me a second to notice the slip of paper taped to her mirror. I snatched it loose. Though Lydia's handwriting was perfect as always, the indent of the pen's strokes paid testament to her anger.

> *So you think you can do it all on your own, do you? Then why should I stick around? Maybe you're right. Maybe you'd be better off without me. You always acted like you didn't need me, and now you'll get your chance to prove it.*

Stunned, I sank onto the bed. Volatile and self-absorbed as Lydia might be, she'd never done anything like this.

## CHAPTER 19

I could only stare at the worn blue carpet in my mother's room for so long. Even before my stupor wore off, the gears in my head were meshing, driving my brain to come up with a plan.

The first thing was to try to find Lydia. I didn't have much hope for that. She wouldn't be stupid enough to admit she was ditching me then hang around town where she might get caught. No doubt she was long gone, enjoying that sun, surf, and sand Jimmy had mentioned last week.

I knew where Jimmy lived because I'd had to pick up Lydia there once, so I drove by, hoping to prove my hunch wrong. His truck wasn't in the lot, and when I peeked through the window of his apartment, it was completely empty. Even though I'd expected it, the sight sent a jolt through me.

*It's not that bad*, I told myself as I drove home. I was already paying at least a third of the bills. I could find a roommate, ask Kasey for more hours. It would be tough, but I could pull it off. Anyway, it was my fault. If I hadn't told Lydia how terrible she was as a mom, she might never have left.

The most important thing was to keep it a secret. I wasn't going to wind up like Billy Evans, pulled away from my friends and forced to live with strangers. Or Anna, the girl in my Freshman English class who'd been through five foster homes in four years and was treated like a slave in the most recent one.

Back home, I sat at the kitchen table and listed my expenses: rent, electricity, telephone, groceries, gas, car insurance. Next, I looked for costs I could trim. I didn't need the phone, and with Lydia gone, I'd save on the power bill. Food was another place I could scrimp. If I packed lunches instead of buying them, and took Teri Sue up on her dinner invitations a few nights a week, I could cut my grocery bill in half. I hated taking advantage of the Clines' hospitality, but if I wanted to pull this off, my pride would have to take a back seat.

I scribbled my adjustments and tallied the figures. The total wasn't impossible. If I wrangled a few more shifts at the shop and dipped into the money in my math book, I could manage until I found a roommate. By the middle of August, college students would begin flooding into town to hunt for housing. I'd have no trouble finding someone before school started.

Thoughts of Cody nagged me as I put away the notebook and got ready for bed. I wanted to be honest with him, but it wouldn't be fair to force him to choose between keeping my confidence and making sure I was okay. This wasn't as simple as a drunk driving conviction or a few scratches on my arm.

I turned out the light and crawled under the covers. Despite my carefully laid plans, whispers of worry crept into my head as soon as I closed my eyes. I tried to brush them aside. Everything would work out. It had to.

The next day, I asked Kasey if I could add a couple of afternoons to my weekly schedule.

"Are you sure that's a good idea, Jess? Between here and Teri Sue's, you're already working close to full time. You won't be a kid forever. You should take the opportunity to have fun."

"What could be more fun than working on cars?"

Kasey sighed and penciled me in for Tuesdays and Thursdays.

After I finished at Teri Sue's that night, I drove to the University, then Lane Community College, to check the bulletin boards in the student centers. There were only a couple of notices for people looking for rooms, and one guy needed a place that would take a dog. Our apartment required a deposit for pets. I tried not to let my lack of success bother me. It wasn't like I'd expected it to be easy.

The apartment was no different that evening than it had been the last four nights, but it seemed emptier now that I knew Lydia was gone. Even though I was furious at her for leaving me with nothing but a pile of bills and a nasty note, I couldn't help worrying. She'd gotten a double whammy, losing her job and her friend Judy in the same week. Last fall when she'd gotten into one of her funks, she'd huddled in bed for days, refusing to get up or eat and barely saying a word. Would Jimmy take care of her if that happened? What if he ditched her in some far off town?

*Stop thinking about it. There's nothing you can do.* I turned on the TV for some noise, but it didn't help.

Last night, with my plans and calculations, it had been easy to be brave. Now, I wondered if I could pull this off. The racing season would be over in September, and that would be the end of one source of income. Kasey would cut back my hours because she wouldn't want to interfere with my schoolwork. What if I couldn't find a roommate? There was no way I could handle the expenses on my own without working full time. And what if someone discovered I was living alone?

*Stop it! No one's ever paid attention to what goes on in this apartment. They're not going to start now.*

But the worries stuck with me all night, not the least bit intimidated by my logic.

The next evening, Cody picked me up at the Clines' for the Ems game. As the Galaxie pulled up in front of the barn, Teri Sue grinned and hooked her arm around my neck.

"Your first date. I'm so proud of you."

"Cut it out," I said, ducking away. Actually, I didn't have much complaint with the way she'd reacted to the changes in my relationship with Cody. For the most part, she'd been encouraging and respectful. Not that she didn't occasionally resort to teasing.

Cody got out of his car and sauntered around to open the door for me. He'd dressed up for the occasion in a crisp pair of black Levi's and a T-shirt that read, *Fasten your seatbelt—I wanna try something.* The best I could come up with was a pair of jeans that didn't have any tears or grease stains, and a logo-free T-shirt that fit.

"Y'all have her back by eleven, ya hear?" said Teri Sue. "Just because you're my friend doesn't mean I won't take you out behind the woodshed if you tarnish her reputation."

My face flared with instant sunburn as I ducked into the Galaxie.

"The only thing I'm going to tarnish is your butt with my foot if you don't stop embarrassing her." Cody leveled a glare at Teri Sue before glancing my way with an apology in his eyes.

"Aw, you know I was just pickin'."

"Uh huh." He circled to the driver's side and slid in next to me on the roomy front seat. "Just ignore her," he told me.

"Ignore who?"

Cody smiled as he poked a tape into the cassette deck, forcing the machine to swallow it. "Check this out. It's by the Beach Boys. I swear they were having a premonition about you."

He knew I collected car songs, so he was always on the lookout for ones I hadn't heard. Usually, I was familiar with whatever he played for me, but occasionally he'd come up with something new, like Queen's *I'm in Love with My Car.* This was one of those times. As we headed down the driveway, the speakers thundered a round of doo run runs then cut into the first verse describing a "car crazy cutie" with grease under her fingernails.

I looked across the seat at Cody, a rush of heat prickling my skin clear up to my scalp. He grinned around a mouthful of lyrics, pointing at me as he harmonized with the Beach Boys.

The song went on to tell the story of a girl who kicked butt at the drag strip, working on cars. It wrapped up with a line about how she was more interested in turning a wrench than getting a kiss.

"Admit it," Cody said, jabbing a finger at me as the song faded into another chorus. "That last part is definitely you."

"*Moi*?" I asked, placing a hand on my chest and laughing. "Well, maybe so, but that middle verse needs some help. Big blue eyes? Candy apple lips?" I shook my head. "So sexist."

"What's sexist about it? It's just a description."

"A description that materializes women. Guys are always so concerned with eye candy. What about substance? What about the fact that she knew how to gap the plugs?"

Cody turned to face me, mouth open to object, but his protest melted into a wanton smirk when he realized I was pulling his leg. "Well, with you, I get the whole package."

My cheeks caught fire. "Oh, shut up."

"What's the matter, can't take a compliment?"

"That was a compliment?"

Cody grinned like one of the roguish pirate heroes in the old movies Mark watched. "Yeah. It was."

"Well, I'm more than just a car crazy cutie."

"I know." Holding up a hand, he extended one finger at a time. "You're a mechanic, an amateur meteorologist, a Chaos Theory junkie, a substitute big sister, and a damned good friend.... Did I leave anything out?" He paused to slink a look over at me before adding one last item. "And you're also cute."

The baseball game wasn't any more exciting than I'd expected. After watching the Ems slaughter a team from Idaho, we parted ways with Race and Kasey to drive to Pietro's, a pizza place on West 11th popular with the racing crowd. Cody insisted Track Town was superior, but I was in the mood for a Great Northwest—a combination of pepperoni, ground beef, mushrooms, green peppers, and best of all, cheddar cheese.

I'd been waiting all night for things to get awkward, but being on a date with Cody wasn't much different than hanging around with him at the track or Teri Sue's. Any shyness I began to feel was instantly snuffed out by one of his smart-assed comments.

My mouth watered when the guy from the counter placed our steaming pie between us. Cody spun it around to put my side within easy reach. We'd gone half-and-half because, as a pizza purist, he preferred boring old pepperoni.

"So," he said, settling back in his chair, "why'd you get so embarrassed when I said that you're cute?" He picked a stray mushroom off his half of the pizza, faked a shiver of horror, and tossed it onto my side before lifting a slice from the pie.

I shrugged.

"Good answer."

"Well, *I* don't know. Maybe because I don't believe it." I worked a piece free and took a bite. The savory tang of tomato sauce, pepperoni, and cheddar cheese melted over my tongue.

Cody gave me a wide-eyed look. "What's not to believe?"

Was he seriously that bewildered, or was he just trying to be nice? "Oh, come on. I'm plain and I'm a slob. I haven't got a clue about how to use make-up."

"You don't need make-up. And who said you're a slob?"

"No one had to. I can tell from the way the girls at school look at me."

Cody took a monstrous bite and spoke through it. "Are you kidding? Listen, Jess, there's nothing wrong with you. If girls are looking at you funny, it's because they're jealous." He waved the pizza slice to emphasize his point, slopping sauce on the table.

"Jealous of what? The grease under my fingernails? Or maybe my stylish wardrobe, complete with oil stains?"

Cody's forehead creased in annoyance. "Get real."

"Well what, then?"

He blew out an exaggerated breath. "Okay, maybe you don't know the first thing about clothes or makeup, but you've got class. No matter what you're doing, you look good. I bet other girls have to work their butts off at that."

"Yeah, sure." I licked sauce from my fingers. Those bimbos probably fell out of bed in the morning looking perfect.

"I'm serious. A lot of girls are totally obsessed with their appearance, but you don't care. And you can get guys to gawk at you *without* caring."

I savored a bite of pizza. It was the cheddar cheese that made it. Cody didn't know what he was missing. "I haven't noticed anybody gawking," I said.

Cody smiled. "*I* have. Damn, Jess, you've gotta be crazy, thinking you're not cute." He gave me a once-over that left me completely self-conscious.

Dropping my gaze, I studied the pizza in my hand. Since sixth grade, girls had eyed me like something scraped off the bottom of a cafeteria table. And while the boys in auto shop were cool enough, they treated me like one of the guys. There was no way I could buy into this totally skewed image Cody was presenting.

"What's it gonna take to convince you?" he asked, reaching for another slice of pizza. "A notarized document from your peers?"

I twisted my lips to one side, thinking it over. "That would be a start."

Cody grinned. "I'll see what I can do."

## CHAPTER 20

Saturday night, Teri Sue won her first trophy dash, sending us whooping.

Race had his car back in top shape, winning the main and making up a couple of the points he'd lost to Jerry Addamsen the week before. In spite of it, Cody was anxious, totaling up the margin between them, the weeks left in the season, and how many times Race would have to finish ahead of Addamsen to claim the championship. After seeing victory snatched from his uncle last season, he couldn't stop obsessing. But I knew Cody's nervousness wasn't just about what was happening in the Sportsman class. His dad had driven down from Portland to watch the races, cranking up his pressure to perform.

Though Cody's fears played out with three mediocre finishes, he held his head up while his dad chatted with us in the pits at the end of the night. I had to admire him for that. It couldn't be easy, being Race's nephew and having everyone compare the two of them.

On Monday, the electric bill arrived. I took it and the phone bill to the bank so I could cash the paycheck I'd been carrying in my pocket and purchase a couple of money orders. It shocked me to see the two payments eat up most of my check. In spite of my planning, I hadn't expected it to cost so much just to survive.

Over the next couple of days, I tried to convince myself I was okay with Lydia's absence. And to some degree I was. I'd spent plenty of time alone in the apartment, and I'd been making sure the bills got paid for years. But I'd never before had to deal with all of it, every tiny detail, knowing I didn't have backup.

Wednesday night, someone banged on the door. I jumped up from the kitchen table so violently I nearly knocked my chair over. With my pulse racing through my veins, I laid Kasey's chassis book on its face and went to answer.

A glance through the peephole revealed the landlord. *Oh crap.* Had he figured it out already?

I forced myself to swing the door wide open. Nothing to hide here.

The landlord stood looking at me expectantly, hands in pockets, jingling change. "Your mom home?"

"No, she's at work."

"Huh." He glanced past me, into the apartment. "I've been trying to track her down for three days now. Seems like she's never around."

Could he hear my heartbeat? It sounded like a jackhammer to me. "She just got a new job. She works different hours now."

"Oh. Well tell her she needs to get me the rest of last month's rent. She still owes me twenty bucks."

Relief sluiced through me. Was that all? I reached into my back pocket with a trembling hand to pull out some cash. "Sorry. She asked me to take care of that." I peeled a twenty away from the remaining ten and ones. "I'll make sure it doesn't happen again."

When I shut the door, all my strength whooshed away. I walked back to the table on Gumby legs, lecturing myself about being more careful, more vigilant.

One tiny slip-up, and it would all be over.

On Thursday, the summer solstice, Cody talked me into a second date. He wanted to take me to Cougar Hot Springs, a place in the mountains about an hour east of town. It was a popular hangout for college kids and Eugene's hippie element. A popular *naked* hangout. Unsure of Cody's intentions, I resisted until he assured me we could wear bathing suits.

"You'll love it, Jess. It's not as scandalous as everyone says. The reason I like it is because it's way out in the woods. When you lie in one of those pools with the steam rising around you, and look up at the stars through the trees, it makes you feel . . . like . . . timeless."

I gave in, but named my conditions—this time I wanted to drive.

At eight-thirty, I pulled into the parking lot of Eugene Custom Classics. Cody leaned expectantly against the front fender of the Galaxie, looking cool as usual. The sun was still up, but it would be twilight by the time we made the hour-long drive to the east. The hot springs, Cody had informed me, were best after dark.

"So I finally get to ride in the infamous Pinto." He opened the door and had to remove a pile of school stuff from the seat before he could sit down. At least he made the effort. Teri Sue had simply sat on the papers when we went to Fern Ridge last week.

"Jeez," Cody said, shaking his head in mock disgust. "You're even messier than Race."

"I'm not messy."

"Yeah? The inside of this car looks worse than his trailer ever did. You shoulda seen that place."

"You've told me about it." I wasn't pleased with the comparison. The Pinto got cluttered when my life was busy, but it wasn't *that* bad. Only a couple pieces of clothing, and one or two car parts, littered the back seat. I kept most of the trash in a plastic bag on the front floorboards.

"School's been out for almost two weeks," Cody reminded me, waving the papers in my face. "I'm surprised you haven't burned this crap."

I pulled out onto East Amazon. "The last thing I want to think about right now is school, so if you're done criticizing my housekeeping skills, throw that stuff in back."

As Cody made an exaggerated flourish to toss the papers over his head, something made him stop. "Is this what I think it is?"

The note of trouble in his tone drew my attention from a right turn onto 30th.

Grinning triumphantly, he held my report card in both hands.

A tornado of emotion ripped through my chest, not just anger but something that felt an awful lot like panic. Another blunder on my part. Sure, my grades weren't exactly a national secret, but if I got careless about this, I could get careless about anything.

"Put that down!" I snatched at the paper, which he pulled out of reach. "Damn it, Cody!"

I could've gotten more response pleading with a rock. The car behind me honked, and I jumped, realizing I'd let up on the gas.

"Eyes on the road," Cody said, solemn as a driving instructor. He scanned the card, holding it off to one side where I couldn't reach it.

Swearing, I squeezed the accelerator, but not before the guy behind me roared past, flipping me the bird.

"Let's see," Cody said. "'A' in auto shop... well, that's a no-brainer... 'A' in trig, 'A' in physics..." He cocked an eyebrow at me. "You took trig and physics? I thought those were for juniors."

"So I'm a genius."

"Oooh, maybe not. You got 'C's in English and history."

"Give me that!" I grabbed for the paper again, but Cody pulled it away.

"You shouldn't be so self-conscious."

"I'm not self-conscious. That's just private."

"Not anymore. Let's see, an 'A' in health and... what's this...

a 'D' in art? How can anybody get a 'D' in art?" He clicked his tongue and shook his head. "Race would be soooo disappointed."

Outrage swamped the circuits of my brain, shorting out the last of my restraint. I whipped the Pinto to the shoulder of 30th Avenue, tires screeching as I locked up the brakes. The momentum threw us forward against our seatbelts.

"Damn it, Cody, I'm serious!"

He blinked at me, shocked, then with uncharacteristic meekness folded the paper and handed it over. "I was just teasing, Jess. You don't have to get so upset."

"You'd be upset, too, if I was butting into your private business!"

Cody shrank back. "Okay, you're right! I'm sorry."

For several long seconds, I glared at him as the stink of burning rubber wafted in through the open windows. How could he keep pushing, knowing how I felt about my privacy? Couldn't he see that enough was enough?

"Look, Jess, I'm sorry." Cody placed his hand over my knuckles, which stood out like knots of ivory against the black steering wheel. His eyes held the appropriate remorse, but if he expected me to let him off the hook, he'd have to promise he wouldn't try anything like this again.

As if sensing his touch wouldn't melt me, Cody pulled his hand away. "Okay, how about this—I'll tell you something private about me."

"Like what?" At the moment, I wasn't sure I wanted to know anything private about him.

Cody's eyes darted off to examine the dashboard, then the view through the windshield. "Well," he said finally. "I like to read. ... Not just comic books, but stuff like *The Old Man and the Sea*. And not just for school, either." He snuck me a sideways look.

"You think that's a secret?"

"Well, there's something else." His voice went soft, and he hesitated, looking down at the jumble of papers in his lap. "I . . . I write stuff."

I glanced at him. "What kind of stuff?"

"Short stories, song parodies . . . things like that. And I was on the school paper last year."

"So why didn't you tell me before?"

He shrugged. "I dunno. I guess I didn't want you to think I was a geek."

Seriously? "Cody, you have library books in your car."

"Yeah, well . . ."

"Why does it even matter what I think?"

"I dunno. I guess it's the same reason you were afraid to ask Kasey for a job. It sucks worse to lose some things than others."

My anger fizzled. He was worried about losing me? I pulled in a breath and looked at him. "So are you ever going to let me read something you wrote?"

"That could be arranged." Once more, Cody's hand closed around mine. "Do you forgive me?"

I sighed and put the Pinto into first gear, looking for a break in traffic. "Yeah, I forgive you. Just don't do anything like that again, or I'll shove you out on the side of the road."

Cody nodded somberly. "That's something I don't doubt for a second."

By the time we got through Springfield and out onto the McKenzie highway, the bright summer evening had soothed us back into our normal rhythms. Cody sang along with my favorite tape of car songs. I simply drove. The cottonwoods and Douglas firs along the riverbank cast long, cool shadows over the twists of highway. Occasional glints of sunlight from low in the west danced across the river.

We were so caught up in enjoying the drive we almost missed the Cougar Reservoir turn-off, a narrow secondary road that led south from the main highway. It wound around the side of a mountain with the river a skinny bent twig far below.

After what seemed like an hour, we reached a gravel turnaround.

"Park here," Cody said.

I pulled into the lot and we stepped out of the car, where the mild night air hugged my bare arms. The sun had set, and violet shadows of dusk cloaked the wilderness, but I could make out the huge reservoir beyond the parking area. It stretched still and silent to the north and south.

Cody pulled a Mini-Mag flashlight from his back pocket. "Okay, this way," he said, cutting across the deserted road. We backtracked several hundred feet, climbed over the guardrail, and started up a dirt path I wouldn't have noticed on my own.

As we hiked, the citrusy scent of Douglas fir fragrant in the air, the wilderness began to work its magic on me. We were deep in the forest, miles from the McKenzie Highway. Other than our footsteps, no human sound broke the nighttime rhythm of nature. The golden beam of the flashlight bounced off sword ferns and the roots of mammoth firs, illuminating the woods. The night closed in like a cave, with hugeness all around and only a small visible circle at our feet.

Cody turned to face me after scrambling over a big log that had fallen across the path. "You feel it?"

I nodded.

"This is real. This has been here forever. Not like apartment buildings, and freeways, and cable TV." He reached up to take my hand as I climbed through a notch someone had hacked in the center of the log. I didn't need the assistance, and would've been insulted if anyone else had offered it, but I slipped my hand into Cody's and left it there.

"Here we are," he whispered a few minutes later when a tiny, cedar-shingled hut came into view. A rail fence, constructed from smooth logs, framed the last part of the path.

Beyond that, the trail dropped away to a series of six steaming pools carved out of a rocky hillside and ringed with stones. Water flowed from a crack in the cliff.

"The top pool's the hottest." Cody spoke in a hush, so as not to disturb the people soaking below. He pointed to a small cascade flowing from a log that protruded over the bank. "That stream mixes with the water as you go further down. It's cold. Just a regular creek. People stand under it to cool off when they get too hot."

He stepped beneath the shelter and stripped down to his cut-offs, hanging his clothes on one of the fence rails. "We're really not supposed to be here at night. Race said they changed the rules a couple years ago because of partying, but no one pays attention."

I pulled off my T-shirt, jeans, and shoes, shivering in my bathing suit. Bits of gravel stuck to the bottoms of my feet as I tiptoed after Cody down the slabs of log placed in the embankment to form steps to the spring.

Only two other groups sat in the water. Three college kids occupied one of the lowest pools, while a middle-aged hippie couple lounged in the highest one, passing a can of Foster's Lager between them. The light from the stars was faint, but the hippies had set two stubby candles on the rocks. Steam rose around the candlelight, drifting into the trees.

"This place sure has atmosphere," I whispered.

Cody nodded and led me to the second pool. It swallowed us up to our necks when we sat. I leaned back against the roughness of rocks and turned my face to the sky, the tantalizing warmth permeating my muscles. Towering Douglas firs surrounded us, but directly above, a patch of clear night showed through. The stars were a brilliance of icy specks against the darkness. I felt the calm of the wilderness seep slowly into my body.

"You like it?" Cody asked.

I took a deep, settling breath. The air smelled of sulfur, moist earth, and fir needles. "Oh yeah."

Cody smiled in the dim light. His hand felt for mine then grasped it under the water. "Me too. It's one of my favorite places."

We soaked for over an hour. There was no need to speak, no need to do anything but enjoy the evening and each other's company.

It was late when we finally toweled off, shivering in air that felt nippy after the heat of the pools. Cody's hand reached for mine as we started down the trail.

"That was nice," he said softly, as if speaking in a normal voice would spoil the magic.

"Yeah."

We walked in silence, the flashlight beam pouring from Cody's hand to spread in a luminous pool before us.

"I'm sorry about earlier," he said when we were halfway to the car. "I know what it's like, letting people see your personal stuff." He hesitated, and the forest noises closed in around us. "I never let anybody read my writing till last year. I figured my friends would give me a hard time, and I knew my parents wouldn't understand."

"What about Race?"

"That's who I finally trusted. But it wasn't easy. My mom used to give me crap for reading so much. She said I was a wuss. I thought anyone else who found out would, too."

If I hadn't maintained a strict policy of not slamming other people's parents, I would've had a few things to say about Cody's mom.

"What made you change your mind?"

"Mostly, it was what happened to Race. At first I didn't know his dexterity was messed up. He didn't want people feeling sorry for him, so he tried to hide it. But when I asked him to sign a release form for karate, and he couldn't, I figured it out." Cody slowed as we approached the downed tree in the path. "He seemed so vulnerable, you know? So exposed. I felt like I had this advantage over him, and I wanted to make things equal."

"So you showed him one of your stories?"

"Yeah."

I squeezed Cody's hand. It was hard to imagine I'd ever considered him too aloof and self-centered to care about anyone but himself.

He struggled to keep his grip on me as he climbed the fallen log. When he jumped down to the other side, the flashlight beam bounced crazily over the vegetation. I dropped beside him, and as he turned to continue along the trail, I held back, tugging his hand.

"What?" He pivoted to face me, dark eyes fixed on mine.

I drew him close—reached for his other hand. The flashlight fell to the ground.

"Cody," I said, my fingers tightening over his. "I think I'm starting to like you."

Around us, the night closed in, quiet and deafening at the same time. Full of things that were real.

Then Cody leaned forward, and his lips brushed tenderly against mine.

## CHAPTER 21

Up until the night at the hot springs, I could delude myself into believing I had an out—that if things got too uncomfortable, I could jam my relationship with Cody into reverse. But after he kissed me, there was no going back. I had a boyfriend, whether I wanted one or not.

Fortunately, the idea had begun to grow on me.

I'd thought being more than friends with Cody would mean losing what I already had with him. What I hadn't anticipated was that instead of giving something up, I was gaining so much more. It was like spending a lifetime eating dry cake, and then discovering this amazing thing called frosting.

In one way, nothing really changed after the night at the hot springs. But in another, everything was different.

That Saturday, Teri Sue made it into the fast heat, so she didn't get to participate in the 'B' dash, which was limited to the top four qualifiers in the slow one.

"No big deal," she said. "All I care about is getting faster."

And she was. Fast enough to finish fifth in the main.

"Teri Sue sure has been kicking butt these past few weeks," Cody said as we watched Race whittle another two points off Addamsen's lead by winning the Sportsman main. His hand had found its way around mine. "You're doing a great job on her car, Jess."

I dodged the compliment, not knowing how to respond. If I told the truth—that Teri Sue's success was as much due to her driving as my improvements to the Camaro, it would only put Cody's lukewarm performance under the spotlight.

The sad thing was, I knew he had it in him to be a good driver. I'd seen it the night we met, just before he took out Teri

Sue in the main. But since then, his only glimmers of talent had come during practice, or time trials, or when he was angry.

It seemed odd that a guy who made such a point of maintaining control was actually faster when he lost it.

The following Monday dawned with that somber, dry sort of overcast that sometimes creeps over western Oregon in June. I drove to the shop in a mellow mood, glad it was payday. In only a week, the rent and car insurance would be due.

At lunchtime, Cody came up behind me and pulled my ponytail.

"You going to Teri Sue's today?"

"Yeah, later. I have to cash my check."

"I guess I'll swing by after dinner to see you." He tugged at my hair again and sauntered off to the Galaxie.

I forced down a PB & J—less than enthusiastically, considering how many I'd consumed in the past couple of weeks—then ran errands and let myself into the apartment. After sticking the milk in the fridge, I headed for my room to stash my money. Time to break the habit of carrying a pocketful of cash. The encounter with the landlord had taught me one simple mistake could derail my carefully constructed plans.

I pulled General Math from the shelf and flipped the cover. My brain took an extra second to process what my eyes were seeing. Or not seeing. The compartment I'd cut through the pages was empty.

Panic swelled as I flipped the book over and shook it, as if six hundred dollars could somehow get stuck inside. How had Lydia discovered my hiding spot? I'd always been so careful.

"Damn it, Lydia!" I threw the book against the wall. It hit with a bang and slid to the floor, like a bird after flying into a window.

Struggling to rein in shock and fear, I braced myself against the wall as my heart did a drum solo in my chest. Lightheadedness swept me. My hands and feet went tingly. Panting, I fought for air, lungs tight.

*Get a grip, Jess. You're hyperventilating.* Funny how the lessons of health class could come back at a time like this. I lowered myself onto the bed, forced myself to inhale deeply, holding each breath before I released it. After several moments, the lightheadedness faded.

Okay, this was a setback. A big one. But I could get through it. I could figure it out.

The determined words fell flat. What good were they, with the rent due in five days? Even after Teri Sue paid me, I'd only have half of what I needed. My heart started to thunder.

*Cool it. Just breathe.* I closed my eyes and began counting to give my brain something to focus on.

After everything I'd been through, this was so incredibly unfair. All my fighting, all my practicality, all my scrimping and saving—they meant nothing now. And as familiar as I was with my mother's flaws, it hurt to see how easily she'd done this to me.

A sudden thought cut its way through the mind-numbing stupor. I was supposed to meet Cody at Teri Sue's. Oh hell. I pulled myself to my feet. This was too big to fake my way through. I'd have to call and say I couldn't make it.

I drove to the local mom and pop market because I'd had the phone disconnected the week before. Teri Sue was easy, but Cody wanted an explanation. A stream of nonsense about Lydia needing something flowed readily off my tongue. Did he buy it? It was hard to tell. I hated lying to him, and he always seemed to catch me at it.

Brushing aside guilt, I went home and let myself into the apartment. Now what? I sank onto the couch. The remote lay in front of me on the coffee table, so I picked it up and turned on the TV. I'd never been a big television junkie. There were always so many other things to occupy my time. But today, all I wanted was an escape.

I watched all afternoon: soap operas, sit-coms, the local and national news. It only left me feeling more hopeless. At six-thirty, I dragged myself to the kitchen for something to eat. Dazed by the afternoon's events and my TV binge, I pulled open the refrigerator door. All I saw were a couple of eggs, the milk I'd bought earlier, a tub of margarine, and five cans of Budweiser.

Somehow, I hadn't noticed the beer before. Its eternal presence had rendered it invisible in the past. Now it seemed to glow, promising a sweet oblivion the television had failed to deliver.

I pulled a can from its clear plastic webbing, opened the tab, and took a sip. The taste nearly gagged me. But what did it matter? I tipped back my head and chugged the whole thing.

With a rib-shaking belch, I tossed the can into the sink. "What do you think of *that*, Lydia?"

My stomach rumbled disapproval, reminding me I was hungry. I scrounged a sleeve of Saltines from the cupboard and took them to the living room. Halfway there, something slipped inside my head. Giddiness washed over me, and my lips stretched into a smile all on their own. I sank onto the couch, falling back against the cushions. No wonder Lydia drank. This felt great!

With the addition of alcohol, TV seemed a lot more entertaining. I settled back to watch. Half an hour later, a stroke of genius hit me. If one beer was this good, two would have to be awesome. I went to the kitchen to grab another can. Big mistake. Two thirds of the way to the bottom, anxiety swept in to snuff out my euphoria.

*The rent. What am I gonna do about the rent?* Part of me couldn't care less, but a bigger part panicked, propelling me up off the couch to pace around. *What am I gonna do? What am I gonna do?*

If I could only think. Maybe seeing it on paper would help. I stumbled to my room for my notebook. *Gotta study those numbers. Gotta come up with a plan.*

But the beer wouldn't let go of my brain.

*Concentrate Jess. You can shake this. Coffee. Coffee's s'posed to help, right?* I brewed a pot and drank half of it, but all that did was throw my stomach into a tantrum and make me have to pee. Why couldn't I strong-arm myself sober? It was like some alien force had claimed control of my body.

*C'mon, c'mon, there's gotta be something that'll work.* I stepped into the shower and turned it on cold. Nothing. My brain still scrambled behind a hazy web that kept it from getting at the facts.

Not that the facts were my friends. Even drunk off my ass, I could see that. I was screwed, plain and simple. There was nothing I could do but move out.

## CHAPTER 22

The next morning I woke on the couch, the place I'd slumped in surrender when I couldn't wish my way out of being drunk. Groaning, I sat up and turned off the TV. Never again. The helplessness of being that out of control was something I had no intention of repeating.

As I got ready for work, I agonized without coming up with a solution. No money was no money. There wasn't any way of getting around that. Then, when I was in the Pinto, headed for the shop, I figured it out. If I didn't have an apartment, I'd eliminate my biggest expenses. I could sleep in my car and save money. In a month or so, I'd have enough to rent a room with some college students. They wouldn't have to know I was still in high school.

The plan was only a beginning, but it made me feel better.

That night, it was a struggle to act normal as I ate dinner with the Clines and tinkered with the Camaro. My body might be at Teri Sue's, but my mind was back in the apartment. The first thing I'd do was pack my stuff and stash it in the Pinto. After that I'd box up everything else, call Goodwill to haul it away, and scrub the apartment. If I worked hard, I could be done by Saturday, the last day of June.

There was no room for doubt in my head. If I gave in to that, I was a goner. So each time a ghost of anxiety whispered in to haunt me, I exorcised it with another item on my to-do list. Staying busy was my only hope.

I got off at noon on Wednesday, raided the recycle bin behind Safeway for empty boxes, and headed home. Sorting through the apartment and deciding what to keep was a monumental task. How could I walk away from ninety percent of my life? I kept coming across things that reminded me of good times with Dad or Lydia, but the one that sent the sharpest pang through me was my old, beat-up copy of *Green Eggs and Ham*. Instantly, I was transported back to a time when Lydia was the kind of mother who taught me how to sound out words, bake cookies, and draw handprint Thanksgiving turkeys. I could almost feel her arms around me as I sat on her lap a lifetime ago. Lately, we might not have had the perfect relationship, but we'd had *something*. Why did she have to abandon me?

I finally narrowed my belongings down to what would fit into the trunk and backseat of the Pinto. By that point, it was time to go to the speedway to meet Cody and Teri Sue for practice.

They were already on the track when I arrived. I waited at the edge of the asphalt for the cars to roar past before crossing. It was still early, and only a few other drivers had shown up, none of whom were in the Street Stock class. I parked beside Teri Sue's pickup, where Rhett sat perched on the hood.

"Hey, Rhett," I said, boosting myself up beside him.

He stared out over the track without a glance in my direction. "Hey."

"What's up?"

He shrugged, eyes locked on the cars.

"You bummed about something?"

Again, his shoulders lifted. I reached over to tickle him out of his bad mood.

"Quit, Jess." He jerked away, giving me a quarrelsome look.

"Did I do something wrong?"

"No. Just leave me alone."

"If that's what you want." I slid off the truck and went to lean against the pit wall to watch the action on the track. Cody charged after Teri Sue with an aggressiveness he rarely displayed in competition. Why was it so hard for him to transfer that to an actual race?

Five minutes later, the two cars pulled into the pits

"Hey," I said, circling the Camaro as Teri Sue extricated herself from it. "What's up with Rhett?"

She slid him a look as she blotted sweat from her forehead with the sleeve of her firesuit. "Aw, he's ticked at me."

"Why?"

"We got into it on the way out here." Teri Sue pried open her cooler and fished out a Gatorade.

"You two are always getting into it. It's never upset him before."

She focused on her drink, spinning the top off the bottle and taking a long swig. When I continued to stare at her, she sighed. "Okay, fine. He kept pestering me to stop at the store, but he wouldn't say why. Turns out he wanted to buy a birthday card for Mama. I don't know how many times I've told that boy she won't write back." Fierce as her scowl was, it couldn't counter the way she ducked her eyes. "I didn't mean to say what I did, but he gets me so riled."

I glanced at Rhett's slouched figure. "What did you say?"

She fiddled with the lid of her bottle, twisting it on and off.

"Teri Sue, what did you tell him?"

"That Mama doesn't read his letters.... Grandpa's afraid they'll spook her, so he puts 'em away in a box."

*What?* I wasn't sure which shocked me more, this act of deceit, or the fact that Teri Sue had so ruthlessly revealed it to him.

"Look, I'm sorry," she flustered. "And I told him that. But it's just as well. Maybe now he'll stop wasting time on her."

A thousand sharp replies jumped to my throat, forming a traffic jam. I swallowed them and turned away. For the next few minutes, I busied myself checking tire pressures and temperatures. Teri Sue stood back and watched.

"You think I'm being hateful," she said. "But you don't know the whole story."

"I know enough. Your dad told me."

"I'm only looking out for Rhett."

I nodded toward the track. "Maybe you should concentrate on looking out for yourself. The fast cars are almost done. If you want to hot lap, you better get lined up."

Teri Sue pinned me with one last beseeching look before sliding into the Camaro. Without a word, I clicked the window net into place. She pulled away, and I went back to the pickup to climb up beside Rhett.

As the Sportsman and Super Stocks filed into the pits, we sat in silence. Rhett pulled his good leg against his chest, swinging the other one back and forth, the heel of his dusty sneaker bouncing against the bumper. His chin sank down to rest on his knee.

"Your sister told me what happened," I said, as the chief steward waved Cody and Teri Sue onto the track.

Rhett snorted. "So now you're gonna give me a hard time, too?"

"Since when have I ever given you a hard time? I know Teri Sue doesn't understand how you feel about your mama."

"And you do?"

"Maybe. I've got a mom too, you know. And believe me, she has her problems." Memories flickered through my head, of Lydia making accusations, getting arrested, stealing my money, and running away. In spite of it, I missed her. I didn't know why Rhett, Cody, and I had gotten stuck with second-rate mothers, but I understood why Rhett couldn't stop wanting his.

He turned toward me, the hardness fading from his green eyes. "What's wrong with your mama?"

"She drinks." I knew he'd understand my jumbled feelings, so the words slipped out easily. "She's hopeless at taking care of anybody, including herself, and I never know what to expect from her. One minute she's hollering that I'm no good, and the next she's buying me a present."

Rhett nodded as if that made perfect sense. "But she's your mama."

"Yeah."

He sighed and fiddled with a shoelace, chin dropping back down to his knee. "At least she didn't forget you like mine did."

"No, but my dad took off when I was a couple of years younger than you, so I understand."

"It's not the same if you still get to see him."

"I don't. I haven't even heard from him. He called a couple of times right after he left, but he didn't want to talk to me."

Rhett tilted his head, the last of the surliness melting from his expression. "Wow. At least with Mama I know it's not her fault."

The words sprung something loose in my chest. I turned away and stared out at the track, where Teri Sue held the lead. As she exited turn four, Cody nosed underneath to challenge her down the straightaway.

"It's okay," I said. "Eventually, you learn to accept people for who they are, and then it doesn't hurt so bad."

Rhett's pursed lips said he knew a load of crap when he heard one. His sneaker went on thumping the bumper. "You reckon my mama will ever get better?"

"I don't know. I guess it's possible."

"Teri Sue doesn't think so."

"Teri Sue doesn't know everything."

Rhett sighed. "I'm probably being stupid."

"No, just human." I scooted over to drape an arm across his bony shoulders. "She's your mama, and you love her. There's nothing wrong with that."

Rhett ran his fingers along the top of his brace, casting me a sad, sidelong glance. "Teri Sue says it's dumb to be crazy about her when she hurt me."

The statement stirred a whirlwind of annoyance. Why did she have to be so thoughtless and stubborn? "She's wrong. You just said it wasn't your mama's fault. Don't let your sister tell you otherwise."

"But she's right about one thing. Mama doesn't love me anymore."

How could I argue with that? I didn't want it to be true, but I couldn't lie to Rhett. "That doesn't mean you have to stop loving her. You know what I heard? When abused kids get taken away from their parents, they want to go back to them. I guess when you care about someone, you keep forgiving them again and again, no matter how much they hurt you."

Rhett frowned. "That sounds crazy."

"Yeah."

"Life's crazy."

"Uh huh. Sometimes it is." I pulled him closer, resting my cheek against his silky red-gold hair. "You know what, though?"

"What?"

"You can talk to me about it whenever you want. I'll never give you a hard time."

Rhett sighed and snuggled against my chest. "Yeah," he said. "I know."

# CHAPTER 25

The next two days flashed by like a Super Stock setting fast time. After working at Kasey's, I went directly to Teri Sue's. The 4th of July was the following Wednesday, which meant three races in eight days. The car had to be ready.

Both nights I worked on the apartment until two a.m., cleaning, packing, and throwing things away. The late nights took their toll, causing me to drag into work exhausted. When Cody noticed, he questioned me, but amazingly, he accepted my lies.

Saturday, I allowed myself to sleep late before finishing the apartment. At noon I was ready to leave for good. I stuffed my key into an envelope and dropped it through the slot in the landlord's door. After tossing the last of my stuff into the Pinto, I left without a backward glance.

The unnerving reality hit me on the way to Teri Sue's. When the races were over tonight, I wouldn't have a home to go to. I still hadn't worked out the details of sleeping in my car. Where would I park? Places like the mall had security guards, and smaller store lots would be too conspicuous. A public area like Hendricks Park might draw the attention of the police. That left finding a spot along the road.

Well, I wouldn't have to worry about that until tonight. For now, it was enough to be out of the apartment. Satisfaction swelled inside me—I hadn't left a single clue behind to arouse suspicion.

After Teri Sue and I loaded the Camaro onto the trailer and the equipment into the pickup, she wrangled up a plate of homemade oatmeal cookies and a pitcher of sweet tea. The Southern drink had come to rival Mountain Dew for the honor of being my favorite.

As we sat on the porch, performing a disappearing act on the cookies, Teri Sue attempted to weasel juicy details out of me about Cody. Now that I'd admitted to liking him, she was always speculating about what he'd do next to impress me and commenting on how sexy he looked in a firesuit. The whole sisterhood thing was alien to me, but I enjoyed it.

With my waking hours caught up in work and packing, there wasn't much new to say. Teri Sue had to satisfy herself with reminiscing about her own love life. She hadn't found a real boyfriend since moving to Oregon, so she told me about the one she'd left behind, and about her first love, a slow-speaking teddy bear named Bobby who'd been crushingly shy but devoted. He'd slipped wildflowers and love notes into her desk all through sixth grade.

"Do you miss your old boyfriend?" I asked, setting my empty glass on the little wooden table between our chairs.

"Sometimes. But it wasn't true love. Not like with you and Cody."

True love. Was that what you called this thing that was happening to us? It sounded way too serious.

"It seems funny now," I mused, "the way I hated him at first. I still don't understand it."

"You didn't hate him. You hated the thought of liking him. You control freaks can't hack it when your hearts traipse off on their own without paying no never-mind to your brains."

The idea set off a tremor that rattled my reality. Teri Sue's relationship savvy could be downright unnerving. How could she be so smart about romance, and so clueless when it came to her own family?

"Why don't you spend the night?" She stretched her legs till her bare feet rested on the sun-warmed stone wall that encircled the porch. "We can have a sleepover—while away the hours painting our toenails and talking about boys. It'll be like junior high." Her face scrunched up in a grin. "How 'bout it?"

"Sounds good," I said. Anything to delay the inevitable for one more day.

That night, the announcer hyped the 4th of July race, intensifying the charge of the speedway atmosphere. Teri Sue qualified for the fast heat once again, besting her previous time by four hundredths of a second. A shiver rushed down my neck as the numbers crackled from the loudspeaker. With improvements like that, she stood a good chance of making it into the 'A' dash by the end of the season.

Cody's performance was far less spectacular—last in the 'B' dash and fourth in his heat. That was nothing out of the ordinary, so I didn't think much of it until the main, where he came in a dismal twelfth. As Teri Sue climbed out of her car, ecstatic about another fifth place finish, Cody's window net banged against the door of the Dart. I jumped, startled both by the noise and the rare display of temper. When he yanked off his helmet and tossed it on the floorboards, I exchanged an *uh-oh* look with Teri Sue.

"I should've stuck to karate," he grunted as he pulled himself out of the Dart.

Teri Sue raised an eyebrow and handed back the unopened bottle of Gatorade I'd just given her. "I think I'll run and get us a couple'a hot dogs."

She hurried off to the concession stand, while I studied Cody across the roof of the Camaro. He slouched against his car, thumbs hooked over the door and fingers drumming the outside. In a sad coincidence, he'd chosen today to wear his *I suffer from occasional delusions of adequacy* T-shirt. Part of the slogan peeked through his unzipped firesuit.

What was I supposed to say? Everything was bound to come out sounding patronizing, but I couldn't just stand there doing nothing. "I know a finish like that is hard to take," I finally managed. "But you'll do better next week."

"Unless I don't." Cody's eyes flashed and his knuckles went white against the door. "Maybe it's time to face the fact that I suck."

"You don't suck. You always qualify well, and you were doing great the night you got into it with Teri Sue."

He choked out a laugh. "Only because I was pissed at her for being better than me." His heel kicked against the Dart's rocker panel, leaving a dusty footprint. "I don't know what the deal is. Everything's fine during time trials, then it all goes to hell during the race. I'm so worried about screwing up, I can't drive worth a damn."

I spread my hands out over the roof of Teri Sue's car, the steel cool beneath my fingers. "What does Race say about it?"

"That it's no big deal. He figures things will sort themselves out when I get more seat time."

"Maybe they will."

Cody snorted, glancing up just long enough to blast me with scorn. "Get real, Jess."

The defeat in his eyes pulled me to him. I circled the Camaro, edging in at his side and slipping my hand over his. "You'll always be the most important person in my life, even if you never win a race. But I still believe one of these days you will."

Cody shook his head, jaw rigid as he glared out at the front stretch, where his uncle was deftly wresting the lead from Jerry Addamsen. "I sure hope you're right."

It was a pleasure to wake up Sunday morning surrounded by bright cheerfulness. I'd always loved Teri Sue's bedroom, where light poured through the south-facing windows from sunrise to sunset. But as I stretched luxuriously in my sleeping bag, memories of the day before slipped into my head, fading the warm brilliance. Tonight I'd be sleeping in my car.

I spent the whole day at the Clines', fiddling with the

Camaro and helping Rhett with his latest project. Inspired by a friend and his father who'd dug their own pond back in North Carolina, Rhett had decided to widen and deepen a natural pool in the creek that ran through their woods. It was an ambitious project that would take weeks to complete, but I didn't mind lending a hand. Anything to take my mind off my problems.

"You wanna stay for dinner?" Teri Sue asked when Rhett and I dragged ourselves back to the house late in the afternoon, exhausted.

"Sure." I thought of sitting down at her kitchen table, dirty and sweaty, and then spending the whole night that way. It would be hard to find a place to wash up in the morning—something I hadn't considered when I made my plans. "Do you think it would be okay if I took a shower first? I'm filthy."

"Go for it."

When we were done with dinner, I dawdled for a couple of hours until I could no longer put off the inevitable. My fingers drummed the steering wheel as I drove back into town and cruised around, looking for a good spot to pull over. Nothing felt safe. Wherever I parked, I'd be right in the public eye. Anybody could walk by and see me sleeping in my car.

After half an hour of searching the neighborhoods around the University, I gave up trying to find the perfect location and picked a spot on Harris Street near some apartments. I curled up in the front passenger seat, tucking my head under the blanket to hide myself from passers-by. Since the seats didn't recline, I had to sit sideways across the two buckets. The hand brake dug into my thighs and the armrest poked me in the back, even through my pillow. As if that weren't enough to keep me awake, college students who'd stuck around for the summer were partying in the apartments, their music and noisy conversations too loud to ignore. I huddled on the seat, trying to wish myself to sleep. It didn't work.

Now that it was finally over, and I was out on my own, all the doubts I'd kept at bay slammed into me at once. And not just those, but others. Deeper ones. Two parents had left me. What if there was a reason for that? I wasn't exactly the lovable sort, the type to reassure Lydia when she'd been scared or depressed. Sure, I'd taken care of her physical needs, but I'd been an ice queen when it came to comforting her. Who'd want a daughter like that?

And while I'd never really thought I had anything to do with my dad leaving, I now started to reconsider. Maybe it wasn't just Lydia's constant complaints about him being on the road that had driven him off. If he could walk away without looking back, if he could tell my mother he didn't want to talk to me, maybe he had good reason.

## CHAPTER 24

At dawn, I gave up my uneasy dozing and headed for Kasey's shop. I stopped at a gas station to brush my teeth and splash water over my face in a tiny, grubby bathroom. After a week of late nights cleaning the apartment, the waking-up-tired routine was beginning to get old. For the first time in my life, I could sympathize with people who hated mornings.

It was seven o'clock when I got to the shop. I parked and listened to the radio while I ate a few handfuls of cereal straight from the box. Milk was too expensive and difficult to store. I'd have to watch my money if I wanted to rent a room later that summer and still be able to cut my hours when school started.

At 7:30, Kasey's Charger rumbled in beside me.

"Up early today," she said.

"Yeah." I wanted to ask her for more hours, but I knew she wouldn't give them to me.

"Well, come on in. We'll get started on the heads for that Javelin. I've been meaning to show you how to do a valve job."

Despite my fatigue, it didn't take more urging than that. But by noon, the lack of sleep caught up with me. I sank onto the couch in the office to rest for a few minutes before heading to Teri Sue's. The next thing I knew, Cody was kicking my foot.

"Sleeping on the job! What's up with you? You're always tired lately. You staying up all night partying?" He arched an eyebrow. "Or is there another boyfriend you're seeing on the sly?"

"Like you aren't enough to deal with?"

Cody held out a hand to help me up. "Let's go get something to eat. Or are you having peanut butter again?"

"No. I forgot to make a sandwich."

More accurately, I didn't have a place to make one. I

couldn't exactly stand on Harris Street with everything spread out over the hood of the Pinto as I put my lunch together. Just one more detail I'd have to work out. When I'd come up with the idea of living in my car, I hadn't realized how many everyday things would require so much planning.

All afternoon, I dreaded another night in my car. There had to be a better option than camping on the side of the road. Too bad I was too tired to think of it.

That evening, in spite of my exhaustion, I couldn't sleep. Doubts edged into my head, and when I finally achieved a state of semi-consciousness, squealing tires startled me awake. My heart pounded as I peered through the windshield. The taillights of a Firebird glared at me from the end of the street. Just some kids fooling around. Nothing to get upset about. I huddled back down in my blankets.

A little while later, a vehicle cruised by at half the normal speed. I waited for it to pass before I peeked out from under my blanket. A police car. Fear zinged along my spine. What if someone had reported me?

*Stop being so paranoid. It's just a routine patrol.*

The reassurance lasted until the car returned ten minutes later. Time to move on. Once it disappeared, I left. It was after two before I finally drifted off.

By the third night, I'd gotten used to the physical discomfort of sleeping in a car, but I couldn't overcome my nervousness. Sooner or later, someone was bound to discover me.

As I began to doze, suspended in that space between sleep and waking, disturbing thoughts swirled into my dreams. I was standing on the front porch of our house by the University, watching my father walk away. My little-kid hands reached out as I begged him not to leave. "Please, Daddy, please!" Tears filled my voice, sliding down to form an ache in my throat. But no matter how hard I pleaded, he wouldn't turn around. Lydia stood behind me, gripping my arm with knife-edged fingernails. "See," she whispered, scornful breath hot in my ear. "I told you he didn't want to talk to you."

I woke with a yelp, sweating and twisted in my blankets. The streets lay dark and quiet around me. Untangling myself, I adjusted my pillow so the armrest didn't dig into my back. Something had to change. I couldn't keep this up much longer. Cody pestered me daily about being so tired, and before long, Kasey and Race would notice, too.

If I could just find a safer place to park—somewhere private. Then it came to me. The gravel lot behind Eugene Custom Classics. It was such an obvious solution, I couldn't believe I hadn't thought of it sooner. I scooted behind the wheel and drove to the shop, creeping around back to tuck the Pinto in beside Kasey's old Dodge pickup.

Sleep came as soon as I stretched out across the seat. I didn't wake up until my alarm went off the next morning.

With the shop closed for the 4th of July, I was able to sleep until nine o'clock. I woke refreshed and optimistic for the first time in days. After brushing my grubby hair into a ponytail, I slapped my Eugene Speedway cap on to hide it and headed for Teri Sue's. Sometime today, I'd have to figure out how to get cleaned up. I hadn't had a shower since Sunday, and I could feel the sheen of sweat and grime building up on my body. I just hoped I didn't smell as disgusting as I felt.

The spicy scent of baking greeted me the second I walked through the Clines' front door. I followed it to the kitchen, where Teri Sue was preparing a picnic to take to the track. A sweet potato pie sat cooling on the counter, with a jar of pickled eggs beside it.

"You must've gotten up early," I said.

"Seven o'clock." Teri Sue gave me a face-splitting grin. "Pick your chin up off the ground, girl, it's not like I turned water into wine."

We spent the next few hours making biscuits, baked beans, potato salad, and Southern fried chicken. Most of my previous cooking involved things that came out of a box or can, so helping her prepare everything from scratch proved educational.

"You think this is going to be enough?" I asked.

"Unless you plan on feeding everyone in the pits."

"No, just Cody."

Teri Sue laughed. "Could be I'm gonna need a couple more chickens."

The 4th of July race was a huge event at the speedway. In addition to a Demolition Derby and fireworks, all the divisions were awarded double points. Cody and I had convinced Mark to sign a stack of release forms so Rhett could get into the pits. Teri Sue hadn't been thrilled about the idea, but we gave her no choice.

At four o'clock, we loaded up and headed to the track. Rhett bounced on the seat, so excited he couldn't sit still. Teri Sue had to keep shoving his legs out of the way to shift gears.

"Just don't think you're gonna make a habit of this," she warned. "It's a special occasion."

Rhett grunted. The faraway look in his eyes told me he was already plotting how to get himself into the pits for the rest of the season.

When we arrived at the speedway, the stands were filling up, even though it was only four-thirty.

"Damn," said Teri Sue. "Looks like we're gonna have a full house."

"It's always like this on the 4th. I hope your dad gets here soon, or he'll be standing by the fence all night."

We pulled up beside the two Darts. As soon as the pickup came to a stop, Cody draped his arms over the door and leaned in the driver's window. He wore a T-shirt that Kasey had banned from her shop: *I couldn't repair your brakes, so I made your horn louder.*

"Did you bring the food?" he asked with the faintest note of worry in his voice.

Teri Sue grinned. "Is a frog's butt water-tight?"

All the hoopla must've distracted Teri Sue, because she wasn't as fast as usual. She qualified right at the cut-off point between the two heats and wound up in the slow one.

When it was time for the 'B' dash to line up, Rhett proudly assumed my job of fastening the window net. Moments later, he crowded beside me against the front wall as Cody, Teri Sue, and the other two drivers growled out onto the track.

"My sister's gonna win it."

"I'd be a fool to bet against you."

As wild as Cody got pulling for Race, he had nothing on Rhett. From the moment the green flag dropped, the kid howled so loudly they could've heard him up in the announcer's booth.

Teri Sue shot forward, squeezing her #70 Camaro between Cody and Danny Lamar before they even reached the first corner.

"Yee-haw!" shouted Rhett, jumping on my foot.

Lamar had to back off, but Cody held his own through turns one and two. Teri Sue got the pedal down a little faster than he did and stole the lead as they pulled onto the backstretch. After that, no one could touch her. She crossed the finish line half a lap ahead of Lamar.

"And taking the checkered flag," bellowed the announcer, "is our very own Southern Belle, TERI SUE CLINE!"

"Did you see that?" Rhett shouted. "Did you *see* that?" He hopped up and down like a Mexican jumping bean.

As always when a woman won a race, there was confusion about who should award the trophy. The flagman or a driver from a higher class usually got the honor, since the trophy girl hardly seemed appropriate. This time, Ted Greene approached Race.

"Morgan," he barked, "they want you to do the honors."

"No problem." Race hopped over the pit wall and jogged onto the track.

"And presenting Miss Cline with her award," bawled the announcer, "is our Limited Sportsman points leader, RACE MORGAN!"

One of the officials slipped the golden figurine to Race, while Teri Sue pulled off her helmet and crawled out of the car. The photographer ushered them into the proper positions and snapped a shot as Race placed the trophy in Teri Sue's hands. When Race leaned in to give her the customary peck on the cheek, she slung her arms around his neck, award and all, and pulled him close. The kiss she planted on him almost sent him sprawling.

Whistles, shouts, and applause erupted from the stands as Teri Sue continued kissing, and Race stood there taking it.

I slunk a look at Kasey, who was shaking her head and smiling.

"Damn," said Cody. "She sure knows how to put on a show. I hope you're not gonna kill her for this, Kasey. Jess would be really bummed about losing that job."

A few minutes later, Teri Sue pulled into the pits, her face glowing like a set of overheated headers. She fanned herself with one hand as she wriggled through the window of the Camaro. "Whew," she said, "He can give me my trophy any ol' time."

Later, while the Street Stocks were being herded off to line up for the main event, Rhett and I joined Race and Kasey along the front wall. On the track, the clean-up crew was spreading cat litter over the oil one of the Super Stocks had belched down the front stretch.

"That was some kiss Teri Sue gave you," I said to Race.

"Yes it was," agreed Kasey with a quirk of a smile. "I notice she didn't kiss Jerry Addamsen that way when he presented her trophy a few weeks ago."

"I'd like to think that means she has good taste," Race said. He grinned and shook his head. "But I've gotta say, she's no rookie. Some poor Southern boy must've cried all night when Teri Sue Cline left North Carolina."

"Gross!" Rhett hollered. He hunched over the wall, scanning the front stretch, his skinny shoulder blades poking through his T-shirt. "Aren't they done yet? I wanna see the Derby and fireworks."

"Have you ever been to a Derby?" asked Race.

"No."

"You'll like it. Lots of noise and destruction."

"Have you ever driven in one?" Rhett turned to look up at him.

"No, but I've seen a lot of 'em. I've been coming to the speedway since I was your age. I had to hitch rides until I started crewing for Denny Brisco. He ran a Street Stock back then." Brisco, one of Race's close friends, now competed against him in the Sportsman class. I didn't realize he'd been driving that long. It must've been fifteen years since Race was Rhett's age.

"Why'd you have to hitch?" Rhett propped an elbow against the pit wall. "Didn't your parents wanna go?"

Race laughed. "My parents are rich high-society types. They wouldn't have been caught dead at a stock car race."

"But your mom sometimes comes now." I'd met her a few weeks ago. When Cody had introduced her, gushing as if she were one of the Beatles, her military posture had made me feel like I was about to get sent to the principal's office.

"She's changed a lot since I was a kid." Race glanced at the front stretch then over his shoulder toward the line of Street Stocks. It was taking an awfully long time to get the track in shape. I wondered how Cody was feeling, strapped into his car. He'd once told me that was the worst part of competition. The longer he had to sit anticipating the action, the more nervous he got. I was about to walk over to give him some moral support, but Rhett's next question stopped me.

"If your parents hated racing so much, how come they named you Race?"

"They didn't. My uncle gave me that nickname when I was a kid."

Rhett squinted at him. "So what's your real name?"

"I try not to let that get out."

When Kasey chuckled, Rhett's eyes slid between her and Race.

"Why not? How bad can it be?"

"Pretty bad."

Rhett chewed his lower lip. "Will you tell me if I guess?"

"Prob'ly not."

"Can I guess anyway?"

Race grinned. "It's not like I can stop you."

"Is it Sigmund?"

"No."

"Herbert?"

"No."

"Leonard . . . ? Alvin . . . ? Wilbur . . . ?" Rhett went on and on, listing the most horrible names he could come up with. Race denied each one, while Kasey and I nearly choked ourselves laughing.

"Rhett," I said, struggling to catch my breath. "None of those names sounds even remotely like 'Race.'"

He frowned and pursed his lips, reconsidering. "I know . . . Rachel!"

Race groaned.

"Oh, come on," said Rhett. "Just say it. I won't tell anyone!"

"You swear?" Race's voice dropped to a whisper. He regarded Rhett with the utmost seriousness, as if he were about to impart a national secret. "I can't have the announcer finding out and broadcasting it over the loudspeaker. It'd be the end of my reputation."

"I swear." Rhett drew a finger across his chest in an X.

"It's . . ." Race paused for dramatic effect. "Horatio."

Oh man. It wasn't as bad as Sigmund, but I still wouldn't want to be stuck with a name like that.

"Horatio William Morgan the sixth."

"No way!" shouted Rhett, collapsing against the wall, his whole body shaking. It took everything I had to keep a straight face.

"Yup. There's been a grand tradition of saddling every first born son in the Morgan family with that name for generations."

My lips quivered as I fought off a smile. "Wow," I said, "I'm really sorry, Race."

He grinned at me. "Just don't spread it around."

A short while later, the clean-up crew finished with the oil spill, and the Street Stocks were waved out onto the track. Their main event got off to a roaring start, with Teri Sue blowing by three slower drivers on the first lap.

"She's tearing it up, tonight," observed Race.

"I wish Cody was." Unfortunately, he was one of the drivers Teri Sue had passed.

Race shrugged off my concern. "One of these nights, something's gonna click for him, and then it'll be a whole new ball game."

This wasn't going to be the night. By the fifth lap, Cody was in tenth place. Teri Sue, on the other hand, had battled her way into second. She didn't stay there long once the quickest cars worked through the pack to challenge her, but she managed to hold off points leader Ward Cooper for a full lap—no small accomplishment.

By the halfway mark, it looked as if Teri Sue might finish fourth. Then, on lap eleven, Danny Lamar's Camaro overheated, spilling water down the backstretch. Todd Griffin hit the slick spot and spun, blocking half the track. The cars behind him took wild evasive action.

As Kit McKenzie locked up her brakes, Cody was left with nowhere to go. He plowed into the rear of her Camaro, steam billowing from his radiator in a searing white cloud. Jack Baumgartner flew out of the corner straight into the mess. His Nova rammed Cody with such force it levered the back of the #13 Dart right up off the ground.

"Oh shit," Race said as my breath seized in my chest.

## CHAPTER 25

"Whoa!" shouted Rhett, scrambling up onto a stack of tires for a better look.

Race craned to see the backstretch. He didn't bolt for the track as Cody had a few weeks ago, but with his jaw tensed, and his face a twist of worry, he looked like he wanted to.

"He's okay," Kasey said, her fingers settling lightly on his shoulder.

Race caught me with an anxious glance.

Even though it was scary to see someone I cared about take a hit like that, I was sure Kasey was right. Wrecks always looked worse than they were. Race should know that as well as I did. But maybe being involved in one of the worst crashes in track history had skewed his perspective. "You go," I said. "I have to be here if Teri Sue comes in."

He took off, while I stood on tiptoes to see over the cars in the pits. Even from the opposite side of the infield, it was clear the Dart had suffered serious damage. Maybe more than could be fixed by Saturday night.

"Race is really shook up," I said, watching him jog out to where the tow truck was hooking up to the 13 car.

Kasey steadied Rhett with one hand as he wobbled on his precarious perch. "He feels responsible for Cody. When you assume the role of parent, it changes everything."

Like I'd know about that.

"I don't think I fully understood it until Race and Cody moved in with me," Kasey added. "But it can be frightening to know you're responsible for another person's well-being."

It was frightening to know I was responsible for my own well-being.

Rhett swayed on the stack of tires.

"Get down," I said, offering him my hand. "If your sister sees you up there, she'll kill me." Refusing my assistance, Rhett grumbled as he scrambled to the ground. Stubborn kid.

The tow truck headed toward us, its revolving light intermittently illuminating the pits in a sickly yellow glow. Race trailed behind, leaning close to talk to Cody, his hand resting on his shoulder.

When the wrecker pulled up to deposit the Dart, Kasey shook her head at the damage.

Rhett peered up at her with worried eyes. "Can you fix it before Saturday?"

"We'll have to see how bad it is."

"I'll help," I said, "as long as Teri Sue doesn't pile her car up tonight."

"Me too," said Rhett.

Cody and Race reached us just as the tow truck finished unhooking the Dart. Though he was rambling a mile a minute, Cody seemed otherwise unscathed.

"You sure you're okay, kid?" Race asked. "You got hit pretty hard."

"Dude, for the hundredth time, I'm fine! It's the car that's totaled. We'll probably never get it back together. I'll be out the rest of the season. Just look at this!" He waved his hand at the crumpled Dart. "Doesn't anyone know what brakes are for?"

"Take it easy," Kasey said. She draped her arm around Cody's shoulders. That calmed him, at least for a moment. A stern look in Race's direction got him to shut up, too.

"We'll fix the car, all right?"

"Can we?" The second Cody opened his mouth, he started babbling again. "It looks pretty bad. Damn, I tried to stop. I woulda been okay if—"

"Cody!" Kasey's voice was so arresting even Rhett, who'd been circling the wounded Dart, jumped. "We'll fix it. Believe me. Now go sit down and try to unwind, okay? Jess, get him something to drink."

I was already fishing in our ice chest for the spare bottle of Gatorade.

"And Race," Kasey added, "if you don't get lined up for your main, Ted will make you sit it out." That got his attention in a hurry. Fortunately, with fast time, he was at the back of the pack of cars already parked near the rear pit exit. He buckled himself into his Dart and sped away.

As the clean-up crew continued to deal with the mess on the backstretch, I took the Gatorade to Cody, who'd seated himself on Race's toolbox. "I guess we've established the fact that you're okay, then?"

His hands shook as he unscrewed the lid. "Well, I did bang my elbow on the door bars, but it's nothing a kiss won't cure." He flashed me a hopeful grin.

"I don't think I could manage one that could compete with Teri Sue and Race's."

"That's okay," said Cody, "I'll make do." He tugged at my T-shirt, and I bent down to give him a quick peck, blushing at the thought of everyone watching.

"Yuck!" said Rhett. "What's with all the kissing tonight?"

Cody sighed, giving me a rapturous look. "If only you knew."

Teri Sue scored a fourth place finish once the main restarted, sliding neatly into seventh in the championship. With the derby and fireworks, it was after midnight by the time we left the speedway, so we bypassed the Little R. I picked up my car at Teri Sue's and drove back to Kasey's shop. Whether because the long day had worn me out, or I finally felt less vulnerable, sleep came easily. The disturbing thoughts that had plagued me the past three nights barely troubled me at all.

The next morning, my wind-up alarm woke me at 7:00. I went down the street to the nearest gas station, put five dollars worth of fuel in the Pinto, and got the key to the bathroom. The icy water raised goose bumps on my bare skin, and the miniscule size of the sink made it hard to wash my hair. Better than spending the day feeling filthy, though. I'd never worked up the nerve to ask Teri Sue if I could use her shower yesterday.

After pulling my damp hair through the back of my Eugene Speedway cap, I returned the key and headed for work. Cody was at the shop when I got back. He tugged my ponytail as I came through the door.

"Hey, why's your hair wet?"

"Our blow dryer's broken." Just one more lie. Even the little ones felt like a betrayal, but at least I was getting them by Cody.

"Bummer. Good thing it's not winter, huh? Hey, check out this bruise." He held up his elbow, which sported a mark the size and color of a ripe plum.

"Ouch."

"Now don't you feel guilty for only giving me a little peck last night?" His bottom lip protruded in a pout, and his dark eyes melted me like a Popsicle.

"People were watching."

"No one's watching now."

True. Kasey and Race were in the office, and the other mechanics hadn't shown up yet.

"Well?" said Cody.

Fine. If he wanted a real kiss, I'd give him one. I grabbed his shoulders and yanked him toward me. My brazenness brought a startled look to his eyes, but his lips recovered the second they met mine.

"That," said Race, his tone dead serious, "is completely inappropriate workplace behavior."

*What?* Mortified, I jumped back to see him standing behind Cody. Where the heck had he come from?

Race smirked as if he'd just learned Jerry Addamsen had been busted for running an illegal set of heads.

"She's only making my boo-boo better," said Cody, raising his arm as evidence.

Race stepped past us to open the bay doors. "It didn't look to me like it was your elbow she was kissing."

Impatient to begin the repairs to his car, Cody was almost useless at work. At three o'clock, Kasey took pity on him and let us leave. I gave Teri Sue a call before following Cody to the shop near the speedway where he and Race kept their cars. Her pickup pulled up a few minutes after we got there.

"Where's Rhett?" I asked as she got out.

"I left him home. He'd just get in the way."

"Oooh. I'll bet he took that well."

"He's not talking to me," Teri Sue admitted with a shrug.

Cody pulled the chain to open the bay door. His Dart was still up on the trailer, where it would have to stay until Kasey and Race got there with the van.

"Wow," said Teri Sue, inspecting the damage. Last night it had been too dark to see the full extent of it.

"Let's get busy," I said. "While we wait, we can make a list of what needs to be done."

As I fought the twisted hood, prying it loose with an ear-splitting shriek, Cody hunted down a notepad.

"Looks like we'll need a new bumper, radiator, and core support," I dictated as he took notes. "We can pull out the hood and left fender, but the right one's toast. And Race is going to have his hands full, repairing these frame rails." As a unibody car, the Dart didn't have a true frame. More like a couple of layers of sheet metal folded over to form a box, though Race had reinforced what was there with steel plate.

"I don't know about the suspension," I continued. "Looks like the right side took most of the impact, but we'll have to get it up on jack stands to be sure." I went around to the back end and got down on my hands and knees.

"This wheel and tire need replacing. The rear-end looks okay, though, except for the front spring mount on the left. That's pretty mangled. Another job for Race."

I crawled out from under the car to find Teri Sue watching me, arms folded over her chest and a smirk plastered across her face. Cody stood beside her, grinning.

"What?" I said, glancing from one of them to the other as I slapped dust off my knees.

Teri Sue laughed, her head wagging back and forth.

"Why are you guys looking at me like that?"

"Oh, no reason," said Cody. "It's not like you walked in here and took charge or anything."

Heat flooded my face. Oh man. He was right.

"Hey, I'm not criticizing," Cody said, affection mellowing his grin. "It just cracks me up. You're all business."

I pinned my gaze on the car, cheeks still humiliatingly warm. "Well, somebody should be if you want to run this thing Saturday night."

"I won't argue with that."

We got to work pulling the hood and fenders. Race and Kasey arrived a little while later. As Race backed up to the trailer to help Cody and Teri Sue unload the car, I went over our list with Kasey.

"Looks like we've got our work cut out for us," she said, her expression settling somewhere between serious and determined.

She ordered a couple of pizzas so we wouldn't have to leave the shop, and we spent the evening removing damaged parts. As we worked, Kasey jotted down everything we'd need, while Cody stressed at each additional setback.

"Are you kidding me?" he said when I discovered the left upper control arm was tweaked. "There's no way we can get this thing back together by Saturday night."

"It'll be fine, kid," Race said. "I've dealt with worse." But his expression lacked its usual confidence.

When he and Kasey headed out at ten o'clock, the rest of us stayed to close up the shop.

"You think those two'll ever get hitched?" asked Teri Sue. Filling her usual supervisory role, she leaned against a workbench while Cody and I wiped down tools and put them away.

"Maybe," Cody said. "If Race ever gets his head together."

"What's that supposed to mean?"

Cody scooped the grinder up off the floor. "He still thinks he's gotta prove himself."

"Prove himself how? He seems like a hot ticket to me." Teri Sue cocked a salacious eyebrow, no doubt re-living that kiss. "Smart, good-looking, a total badass on the track—what more could a girl ask for?"

Cody's eyes glinted as he wrapped the cord around the grinder. "That's not how he sees it. Ever since the wreck, he's considered himself damaged goods. He looks at how much Kasey's accomplished and figures he doesn't have anything to offer."

"Oh—so he's good enough to date her, he just can't marry her?"

*Way to go, Teri Sue. Turn it into something shameful.*

Cody shot a scowl in her direction. "It's not like that. He *wants* to marry her, he just feels like he's gotta earn it."

"And how's he gonna do that? Win the championship?"

"I dunno. Maybe." Cody shrugged and stuck the grinder on its shelf. "Or get the business to where it's making a bunch of money."

"That's really sad," said Teri Sue, shaking her head.

Cody sighed. "Tell me about it."

# CHAPTER 26

Friday afternoon, Cody and I drove out past the speedway to Roscoe's wrecking yard on Danebo. We'd swapped vehicles with Race so we'd have room for the bumper, fender, and hood. Kasey had called ahead, so the body parts, control arms, radiator, and core support were waiting for us when we arrived at 12:30. Impressive. When I went to a wrecking yard, I had to pull my own parts.

"I think the radiator's good," Roscoe said around the toothpick he was gnawing, "but you should get it tested. Wouldn't hurt to have it rodded out, either. Prob'ly fulla rust." He scratched his scruffy beard as he shuffled one-handed through the papers on the counter for our receipt.

When Cody pulled out a handful of cash, Roscoe waved him off.

"Kasey had me put it on her tab. Said she'll take it out of your paycheck." He leered, revealing gaps where he was missing a couple of teeth.

Back outside, Cody shook his head at the huge pile of parts. "Lotta work here. You think we can get it done by tomorrow night?"

Even with Race taking half the day off, and Teri Sue coming over to join us, it seemed like a stretch. But how could I admit that? "Sure. It'll be close, but we can pull it off."

When we got to Race's shop, we found him torching away the damaged parts of the frame and roll bars. He stopped and pushed the tinted goggles up off his face as we began unloading the van.

"Go ahead and trim that fender for tire clearance," he said. "Then see if you can straighten the rear quarter panel out some. Teri Sue called to say she's on her way. We'll have her take the radiator over to be serviced. She can get the control arms cleaned up when she gets back."

We spent the afternoon and evening scrambling to repair the car. The sense of urgency and resulting camaraderie fused into something I'd never felt before—the rush of being a vital member of a team. When Kasey said it was time to pack it up at ten o'clock, I didn't want to leave.

Cody echoed my sentiments. "Aw, c'mon. Just one more hour." He rubbed his forehead with the back of an arm, his face slack with exhaustion. "We're never gonna get this done."

"We've got all day tomorrow," Kasey said. "And I'm more on top of my game in the morning than at this hour."

"Fine. You go then. I'll stay by myself."

"No you won't, kid." Race clapped a hand down on Cody's shoulder. "I know you're stressed, but you're not gonna stay here half the night then drive home in a stupor. We'll get it wrapped up tomorrow."

I glanced at the Dart, which now resembled the picked-over carcass of a Thanksgiving turkey. For Cody's sake, Race better be right.

First thing in the morning, Teri Sue and I loaded up the Camaro. We hauled it with us to Race's shop so we could work until we'd have to leave for the speedway. Rhett whooped when he heard the news, thrilled at the chance to help with the Dart.

It was a long, stressful day, all of us worrying about whether we'd have time to finish. And with everyone except Race working on the front end, we kept tripping over each other. But by four-thirty, we'd bolted the hood in place and were ready to load up.

The officials allowed us just a brief practice session, so Kasey only had time to make a few minor adjustments. There was no telling how the car would perform.

"Are you nervous?" I asked Cody as he slid through the

window to line up for time trials.

"If I am, I'm too tired to feel it."

I wasn't sure whether to consider that a good thing or a bad thing.

When the Street Stocks began qualifying, I jotted down the numbers. Teri Sue had her best run all season, claiming fifth fastest time and missing the 'A' dash by two-hundredths of a second. Cody didn't even make it into the 'B' dash. He groused about that when he came in from the track, but Kasey silenced him with a wave of her hand.

"Don't even start. After what you and that car have been through, it's no wonder things are a bit off. You've only had a half dozen laps to sort it out."

"It's too loose," Cody said, rubbing the back of his neck and eyeing the car as if it had growled at him.

Kasey nodded. "I could see that. I'll adjust the torsion bars and we'll try a little less stagger. That should help."

It did, but not enough. The rear end still wanted to come out from under Cody in the corners. He barely squeaked by with a fifth-place finish in his heat. And he only did that well because Jack Baumgartner hit the wall and Billy Harris's engine was running like an out-of-balance washing machine.

Again, Kasey reassured Cody. "When a car's been wrecked this badly, you can't slap it together in three days and expect it to run at the front of the pack. I'll try the heavier sway bar, and if that doesn't help, we'll work it out in practice next week. These things take time."

"Or maybe I just suck," said Cody.

"I'm not even going to honor that with a response." While Kasey's tone remained level, her eyes revealed that her patience was slipping. "Now go do something to unwind, and I'll see to the car."

"Eat a cheeseburger," suggested Teri Sue, who knew as well as I did what a motivational force food was in Cody's life. "I'll even buy you one." She strolled off to the concession stand and returned a few minutes later with a burger, popcorn, Pepsi, and three candy bars. "This oughta take your mind off things," she said. "Though I still say they can't make a decent burger in this state." Almost weekly, she offered the same complaint. Apparently the ones in North Carolina came stock with coleslaw. Even Cody found that idea disgusting.

The Super Stock heats went by without a hitch as Cody plowed through the food Teri Sue had bought him. Then it was time for the two of them to line up for their main event.

"I think I'm gonna puke," Cody groaned.

Race slid the window net into place. "Now you know why I don't stuff myself before getting into the car. Why don't you try those breathing exercises you use in karate?"

"I already did. They didn't help."

"Well," said Race, "if at first you don't succeed ..." He slapped the roof of the Dart. "Now get out there and kick some butt."

Cody started the race on the outside of the second row. The green flag seemed to catch him off guard, and before he could recover, half the pack thundered by on the inside. When he finally made it down to the low groove, only a few of the slower cars were still behind him. In the course of a single lap, he'd dropped from fourth place to eleventh.

"C'mon, kid," Race muttered, pacing along the pit wall.

But Cody now seemed so determined not to let anyone else slip underneath that he failed to swing high enough on the straightaways. Two more cars plowed around him on the outside.

"He's not going to be easy to live with when this is over," I said.

Race kept his eyes trained on the black Dart. "There's sixteen laps to go. Anything could happen."

The next time around, something shifted. Cody still wasn't

squeezing everything he could out of the car, but he settled in, driving a smarter line.

"That's the way to do it," said Race.

But now the lead cars were threatening to lap the slowest ones. Neither the points leader, Ward Cooper, nor his closest challenger, Dallas Sauter, seemed concerned about the two stragglers limping through turns one and two. They howled by them, three wide through the corner, which was never a good idea on that narrow track. The maneuver sent Sauter wide on the backstretch. His Monte Carlo bounced off Cooper's #52 Camaro. The two cars were still fighting to recover as they overtook Cody going into three.

Even on his best day, Cody qualified five or six tenths of a second slower than the leaders. It made for a big difference in cornering speed. As the faster drivers screamed by the #13 car, Cooper took the proper high line. But Sauter tried to sneak underneath, his inside tires way off in the dirt. Both cars swapped paint with the Dart, and in the scuffle, Cody lost control.

As the Dart spun to the infield, the two slowest cars rumbled past.

Oh man. As if things could get any worse.

The flagman threw the caution, dropping everyone to a crawl. Cody roared back out onto the speedway. When he caught up with the rest of the pack, he was waved ahead of Sauter by one of the officials.

"Good thing they sent that jerk to the back," I said. "No way was that a legal pass."

"Shoulda docked him a lap," grumbled Race.

The flagman held his arm high, raising an index finger to indicate one lap before the restart. The strung-out line of cars bunched together. This time, when the green whipped out over the front stretch, Cody got the jump on two of the guys ahead of him. Sauter was just as quick. He charged past the Dart, crowding three abreast under the flag tower. Remarkably, the pass didn't fluster Cody. He tore around the track, his black Dodge looking more and more like his uncle's as he picked off three of the slower cars and moved into tenth place. The Dart was still loose, but Cody had adapted. He hung the back end out through the corners, taking the rear tires up to the limit of adhesion.

"Now *that's* driving," said Race.

Pride swelled in my chest. But we hadn't seen anything yet. Cody was just catching up to his real competition. He hounded Danny Lamar down the front stretch, his bumper a few scant inches from the Mustang's. As they tore into turn one, Cody slipped expertly underneath to claim the groove. Holding his own through the corner, he charged onto the backstretch in search of his next victim.

Mike Williams and Steve Sabrinski, two of the faster drivers, hovered just ahead, engaged in heated battle. Sabrinski tapped at Williams' rear bumper, while Williams weaved back and forth, blocking the groove. Wisely, Cody held off. After a lap and a half of putting up with Williams' checkerboarding, Sabrinski shoved his car up under William's Nova. When Williams lost control, the two of them spun, coming to rest at the entrance to turn three. From where I stood, it didn't look like there was room to squeeze between the two disabled cars, but Cody must've seen a gap. He zipped ahead, barely letting up on the gas. Amazingly, he made it through. Lamar, who was right on Cody's tail, wasn't so fortunate. His Mustang caught the bumper of Williams' Nova, sending it sliding up into the Dart.

I held my breath as Cody's car zigzagged toward the exact spot where he'd spun earlier. Plowing through the weeds, he narrowly missed the drainage culvert. Somehow he managed to keep control. Dirt and grass flew from the rear wheels as the Dart straightened out and snarled back onto the track.

"Woo-hoo!" I hollered. Cody hadn't lost a single position to the cars behind him.

The caution flag flew again. Now Cody was in seventh, right behind Kit McKenzie, and two cars back from Teri Sue. I was grinning so hard my face hurt.

Beside me, Race let out a whoop that would've put Rhett to shame. "I knew the kid had it in him!" He pulled Kasey into a crushing bear hug then turned to squeeze the breath out of me.

"Morgan!" Ted Greene appeared scowling behind us. "Just because you're points leader doesn't mean you can play the prima donna. Get your butt over there and line up."

In the excitement, we'd completely forgotten to make sure the #8 Dart was in position for the next event. Race hopped into his car and drove to the back of the pack of Sportsmen, where he pulled himself up onto the door to watch the rest of the race.

Cody looked positively cocky now, weaving back and forth to keep his tires warm while the track was cleared. He crawled up on the bumper of Kit McKenzie's bright purple Camaro, and when the race restarted, attempted the same maneuver he'd pulled on the slower cars. McKenzie was too quick for that. She held him off through turns one and two, swinging wide as she exited the corner. But even when Cody was forced into the gravel at the top of the track, he refused to back off. Racing Kit neck and neck down the backstretch, he finally overtook her.

Next on his list was Teri Sue.

Cody didn't have to go far to catch up. The four lead cars were duking it out just ahead of her baby blue Camaro, blocking the track. With three laps left, Cody swooped up behind them. He tormented Teri Sue for the rest of the race, but couldn't find a way around her. As the checkered flag fell, Cody pulled across the finish line in sixth place.

Race's joyous howl traveled all the way across the infield, and he no doubt heard Kasey's and mine as well.

Astounded by Cody's turn around, I didn't even think of getting Teri Sue her Gatorade. Instead, I waited with Kasey. When the Dart rumbled to a stop beside us, I unbuckled the window net and let it fall inside the door.

"That was absolutely phenomenal! I knew you had Morgan blood in you."

Cody pulled off his helmet, unbuckled his harness, and climbed out of the car, dropping lightly to the ground. "You liked that, huh?" His brown eyes gleamed with cockiness.

"What happened out there?"

"I'm not sure. It's like wrecking changed everything. Maybe that's what's been holding me back—worrying about busting it up. I guess I was so afraid of losing control I couldn't drive as hard as I needed to." He shook his head, as if he still didn't quite understand it.

But I did. Once you'd seen the worst that could happen, you didn't have to be afraid any more.

I hugged Cody hard. "I'm glad you got it figured out. I've never been so proud of anyone in my life."

## CHAPTER 27

In the days following Cody's breakthrough, my life began to feel like a fistful of dry sand, slipping through the cracks between my fingers. The lot behind Kasey's shop took care of my need for a place to stay, but sleeping there had its issues. I had to be awake before anyone showed up in the morning, and I worried somebody in one of the neighboring businesses or the houses behind the fence might notice me. While I slept better, I didn't have my normal energy, probably because I could never relax. Every moment was spent on high alert against doing or saying anything that might give me away.

Rhett was too young to pick up on my edginess, and Teri Sue continued to mind her own business, but I wasn't fooling Cody. Almost daily, he asked if things were okay at home. Each time, I'd insist everything was fine. If that didn't persuade him, I'd mumble some vague untruth that left me feeling guilty.

My tiredness wasn't the only thing Cody noticed. "What's all that crap in the back of your car?" he asked one afternoon.

My pulse revved, trying to supercharge my brain into coming up with an answer. "Oh, just some stuff Lydia wanted me to take to Goodwill."

"So you're giving it a scenic tour of the city first?"

"Maybe," I said, wondering where I could store it to avoid further questions. "You got a problem with that?"

Lying to Cody bothered me more than almost anything I'd had to deal with since April. He'd always been so honest with me. But I couldn't suck him into the mess Lydia had left behind. It wouldn't be right to ask him to keep such a secret from Race and Kasey.

Over the next two weeks, the stress of secrecy drained all the fun out of my life, but I continued to pull off the charade.

Just one more month and I'd have the money I needed to rent a room. Then everything could go back to normal.

A little relief came the third Friday in July. After three weeks, Rhett had finished digging his pond and closed off the bypass channel. He'd badgered Teri Sue into holding a camp-out to celebrate. The morning dawned hot and dry, with a forecast of several days of temperatures in the upper 90s. Late in the afternoon, Cody and I headed out to the Clines'.

Rhett poked his head through the passenger window of the Pinto before I'd completely rolled to a stop. "The pond's filling up," he said. "Come see."

The three of us followed him through the woods to a clearing dominated by a gaping brown hole. The creek ran down one side to form a small pool at the bottom. Amazement swelled in me, as it had each time I'd given Rhett a hand with the fifteen-foot-wide, four-foot-deep pit.

"You dug this?" Cody asked, turning to him with new respect.

"Well, Jess helped."

I laughed. "Don't let him fool you. He did eighty percent of it while I was at work."

"Impressive," said Cody. "Now I know where you got those linebacker shoulders."

Rhett absently ran a hand along his muscles, his face a shy twist of smile as he looked out over his masterpiece.

"Good job, squirt," said Teri Sue.

Remarkable as Rhett's accomplishment was, watching the pond fill up got old in a hurry. We filed back to the campsite through woods scented by sun-baked Douglas fir needles. Teri Sue crumpled newspapers and built a fire. As we waited for a bed of coals to form, Rhett entertained us with his latest interest—tales of extreme weather and the resulting disasters it produced.

Teri Sue put a quick stop to that. "Okay, who's ready for

dinner?" she asked, reaching into the cooler for the hot dogs.

"I am!" shouted Rhett. "I want the kind with cheese in the middle."

"Too bad. Those are mine." Teri Sue jammed a stick through one and held it over the fire.

Poking his tongue out at his sister, Rhett got his own and waved it in her face to show it had a cheesy center. As he sat down to cook it, he described the events of the Columbus Day storm, which had hit the Pacific Northwest in 1962.

Though the trees now blocked the sun, cutting the worst of its swelter, the fire made up the difference. I hung back as far as I could and still warm my dinner. When my slightly scorched hot dog was ready, I plopped a spoonful of Teri Sue's homemade potato salad beside it on my plate. Neither looked appetizing. Maybe it was the heat. Not that it seemed to be affecting anyone else. Teri Sue was already on her second dog, while Rhett and Cody raced to see who could finish their third the fastest.

"I won!" Rhett hollered, showering us with bits of soggy bun.

"Cheater!" said Cody.

"Am not! I beat you."

"Oh, come on," I said, shaking the debris from my clothes. "How could he cheat?"

"He stuffed part of his bun down his shirt. I watched him."

Rhett's outrage brought him to his feet. "You lie!"

"Really, I saw it," Cody insisted.

When Rhett pulled up his grubby T-shirt to prove him wrong, Cody leapt forward and tackled him, tickling his bare belly.

"Sorta makes you wonder which one of 'em's the ten-year-old, doesn't it?" Teri Sue asked as they rolled through the dust and fir needles.

"You mean one of them's older than that?"

Cody sat up and gave me a frosty look. In a flash, he'd abandoned Rhett to attack me. My plate flew into the air as I slid off my seat, flailing to avoid his tickling fingers.

"Quit!" I yelled, grabbing at his wrists. As if I had a chance of stopping him. Nobody was going to pin Cody. Rhett jumped on his back, making a valiant but ineffective effort to rescue me. Finally Cody relented.

"Look what you did," Teri Sue accused. She scooped my paper plate off the ground and picked twigs out of the potato salad. "Jess was trying to eat this, y'know."

"I think it'd taste better without the dirt," said Cody.

Teri Sue didn't waste any words on a response. "You want another hot dog, Jess?"

"No, I'm okay," I said, still fighting to catch my breath.

"You didn't eat much."

"Jess never eats much," Cody said. That wasn't exactly true. I skimped when it came to breakfast and lunch, but not because I wanted to. The more money I saved, the closer I got to renting a place, and I was damned tired of living in my car.

"You're getting too skinny," said Teri Sue. "I reckon you think no one can tell, what with those baggy T-shirts you wear. But it's pretty obvious when you have to hike up your britches every five minutes."

A shimmy went through my stomach. As if I didn't have enough to hide without her noticing things like that.

"It's from helping Rhett with the pond," I said. "I've gotten more exercise in the past few weeks than I've ever have in my life."

The glance Teri Sue and Cody exchanged across the flames chilled the heat right out of the evening.

That night was the kind you remember later as a classic summer evening, full of warm, gentle breeze, chirping crickets, and shimmering campfire. It was after midnight when we finally went to sleep.

I woke with a start some time later, surprised to find I wasn't cramped in the front seat of the Pinto. My heart thumped as wisps of nightmare flitted away before I could make sense of them. Above, the stars glowed with a silvery brilliance, faintly illuminating the yard. They'd shifted in the sky since I'd fallen asleep.

I drew the balmy night air deep into my lungs. The dream was completely gone now, leaving only fear and an overwhelming sense of loss.

*It's not real*, I told myself. *Things always seem worse at night.* Trembling, I curled into a tight ball under my blankets and tried to wish the sadness away.

"Jess?"

Cody's murmur was almost indistinguishable from the whisper of breeze tossing the fir branches above.

"Jess? You okay?"

"Yeah.... Just a dream."

Cody scooted across the grass and snaked one arm out of his sleeping bag to draw me close. The moment he touched me, I knew the feeling of loss was connected to him.

"Must've been some dream," he said, his voice husky. "You're shaking."

"I'm sorry I woke you up."

"*Shhh.* Don't worry about it."

My eyes felt suddenly warm and wet. I swallowed hard to hold back tears. It had been forever since I'd cried, but Cody's gentleness crept right under my defenses. Kindness had always been the hardest thing to guard against.

"Jess, tell me what's wrong. Please."

If only he knew how much I wanted to.

"I'm worried about you. Really worried." His warm breath whispered against my ear. "You haven't been yourself in weeks. I know you're hiding something."

I was so tired of the secrecy and deception—of the constant struggle over things everyone else took for granted. In that moment I almost told him. But before I could find the words, good sense reminded me of why I had to stay quiet.

Cody's forehead pressed against the back of my neck, the scent of his hair gel stirring another whisper of loss. "Something happened between you and your mom, didn't it? Something bad."

The accuracy of his suspicion sent my heart thundering. But it was only a guess.

"You know you can trust me, don't you?"

"Of course."

"So tell me."

I hated hearing his anxiousness and knowing I was the cause. But giving in would cost me so much.

For the longest time I stayed silent, and when I spoke, it was another lie. "There's nothing to tell."

Cody sighed. "Please, Jess. Let me help."

"Just hold me."

His grip tightened around my shoulders, and his lips brushed against my hair. The gentle rhythm of his breathing joined with mine to soothe me.

For the first time in weeks, I almost felt safe.

## CHAPTER 28

The next morning, I woke with Cody still snuggled beside me. My head ached and my brain felt so prickly hot it didn't seem like I'd slept at all. Not wanting to invite the ribbing that would result if Rhett and Teri Sue saw us like that, I wiggled out from under Cody's arm and got up.

As the local meteorologists had predicted, the day broiled into another scorcher. By early afternoon, the temperature had inched into the mid-nineties. That evening, Teri Sue was the only one in the pits not complaining.

"This is nothing," she scoffed. "It isn't even humid. Try spending a summer in North Carolina. Then you'll know what hot is."

By that point, I didn't care if I ever made it to the South. I was worn out, my head hurt, and it was damned hot enough for me.

Teri Sue qualified for the fast heat and came in fourth. Cody, driving expertly in both his dash and heat, eked out a second and third place finish. The main proved less impressive, but Teri Sue took sixth, and Cody seventh—far from an embarrassment.

"Now that's a little more like it," Cody said as he climbed out of his car. While he'd been carrying himself with a cocky little swagger all evening, there was no mistaking the hunger in his eyes. Only one thing would completely satiate him—his first win.

Throughout the Limited Sportsman main, Cody and Teri Sue kept up a good-natured squabble about Addamsen's recent success, which brought him to within two points of the lead. Like Cody, I wanted to see Race win this championship, but right now, the only thing I could think about was getting back to the Pinto and going to sleep. I propped my butt against the front of the Camaro, my eyes on the track.

"Something wrong, Jess?" Teri Sue asked, her words cutting through the steaming fog in my head. "You've been grumpy all day."

"It's just too hot."

Teri Sue laughed. "You Yankees." But Cody's eyes lingered on me, dark with concern.

Much as I wanted to go straight back to my car after the races, I forced myself to be sociable when Cody introduced me to his Goth friend Heather, who'd come out to watch. Teri Sue gave her the evil eye on my behalf. But even if Cody hadn't assured me in advance that Heather held the same schoolfriend status as his buddy Quinn, I wouldn't have been able to conjure the energy to feel threatened.

We finally got everything loaded up and took off. After the brief bliss of Teri Sue's air-conditioned pickup, the doors of the Little R opened into a furnace.

"Sorry folks. The AC's on the fritz," the waitress said as she rushed by, arms overloaded and face a shimmer of sweat.

I sagged into a booth and bided my time until I could escape. The milkshake Cody forced on me helped only a little. Welcome as the iciness felt, slipping down my throat, my stomach wasn't quite sure what to think about it. Cody snuck me worried looks the whole fifty-three minutes we sat there.

When I finally got back to the Pinto, I left the windows down. It was too hot to worry about predators. But sleep eluded me. I couldn't stand to have the blankets over me, and without them I felt naked. The best I could manage was an edgy sort of semi-sleep.

Lately, it seemed like even Mother Nature had to get her licks in.

Sunday morning, while the relative coolness of daybreak still tempered the air, I headed for the Clines'. Mark answered the door in cut-offs and a tie-dyed Grateful Dead shirt.

"Teri Sue's asleep—no surprise there—and Rhett's down at his swimming hole," he said. He'd apparently just discovered what his son had been up to, because the next thing he did was launch into a lecture about the illegality of constructing a pond without a permit.

Who knew you needed permission for something like that? I mumbled an apology and escaped to the woods, hoping we hadn't messed things up too much for the aquatic life forms Mark seemed so concerned about.

When I pushed through the bushes surrounding the clearing, Rhett was crouched on the dirt mounded at the lower edge of the pond, cobbling something together from scrap lumber.

"Hey," I said, flopping beside him.

"Hey." He glanced at me but didn't set down the hammer. "You like my deck?"

"It's cool." The dull throbbing in my head had returned, so I scooted into the shade of the cottonwoods to stretch out. At a few minutes past nine, sweat already coated my skin.

"My sister still asleep?"

"Do you have to ask?"

Rhett reached up under his T-shirt with the hammer handle to scratch his back. "We could wake her up."

"Don't you think that might shorten your life expectancy? Anyway, I'd rather lie here and relax. I didn't get enough sleep."

"Me neither. It was too hot. Daddy said he's gonna buy an air conditioner. Up till now, he didn't reckon we were gonna need one."

"Guess again."

Rhett went back to his deck building, and I pulled an arm over my eyes, drifting into a light slumber, in spite of the pounding. An hour later, the shuffle of Teri Sue emerging from the woods pulled me back to consciousness.

"Hey, lazybones," Rhett said around a mouthful of nails. "Wanna go swimming?"

"Maybe in a little while." Teri Sue plopped down beside me. "Lord, it was miserable last night."

I shifted my arm so I could peek at her with one eye. "I thought you said it didn't get hot here. I thought it only *really* got hot in North Carolina."

"Yeah, well, we had air conditioning back there," Teri Sue admitted, stretching out like a cat.

We lounged in the shade, an easy conversation drifting between us as Rhett hammered away. When lunchtime came, he was the only one with enough energy to trudge back to the house. He returned with Cody, whose eyes sparked with a mixture of worry and annoyance.

"What the hell's going on, Jess? I called your house and got a recording that said your number wasn't in service."

"What?" His words pulled me into a sitting position. When I'd had the phone disconnected, I hadn't thought he or Teri Sue might attempt to call. They hardly ever had in the past.

"I tried three times and got the same recording."

Oh man. How was I going to get out of this? My thoughts were too muddled by heat and headache to line up in a neat, orderly pattern. "I guess they finally cut off our service." The lie, once begun, took care of itself. "They've been threatening to do it all month. Lydia was late paying the bill again."

Cody's gaze pinned me, piercing deep, like he could see every thought in my head.

I didn't allow myself to look away. "Well, I'm not going to bother having them hook it back up. I hardly use it anyway. If Lydia can't live without a phone, she can deal with it herself."

Cody folded his arms across his chest, shifting his weight to one foot. "What if someone needs to get a hold of you?"

"I guess they'll call me here or at the shop. That's where I usually am, anyway."

Rhett glanced uneasily from me to Cody. "Let's go swimming," he said, peeling off his T-shirt.

"Great idea." The throbbing in my head put me at a serious disadvantage for a full-on argument.

"You've gotta wait an hour," said Teri Sue, not bothering to open her eyes. "You just ate," She, at least, seemed unconscious of the tension crackling through the air.

"You gonna stop me?"

Teri Sue grunted.

"He'll be okay," I said. "I'll keep an eye on him."

I'd put on my bathing suit under my clothes that morning, and Rhett and Cody were both wearing shorts, so no one but Teri Sue needed to change. And after sticking one foot in the icy water, she decided she wasn't that hot after all.

Rhett cannonballed off the deck, with Cody following. I slipped in more cautiously, letting the pond claim me inch-by-inch. After the clinging heat of the past three days, the chill was a delicious relief.

When Teri Sue noticed we were having more fun than she was, she went back to the house for her bathing suit. By the time she returned, I'd had enough. I pulled myself out of the water and slumped on the sun-warmed boards, thoroughly drained.

Heat shimmered over me, baking my muscles and drying my skin. I soaked it up as the others squabbled in the water and birds chittered from the trees. I'd almost dozed off when a splash cut into my consciousness. A shadow swept across my face, and icy drops shocked the skin on my arms and legs. Eyes flickering open, I saw Cody standing over me, skin taut against muscles defined by his karate classes. He tossed the wet hair off his forehead and sat down.

"You okay?" he asked, his voice low and his gaze trained on Rhett and Teri Sue.

"Yeah, sure. The water's too cold, that's all."

Cody's face clouded over with that doubtful expression I'd seen so much of lately. "I wish I could get you to trust me, Jess."

"I do trust you."

"Then tell me what's going on."

I glanced toward the pond where Rhett was spitting water in his sister's face.

"Cody..."

He sighed and lay down on the deck beside me. "Okay, I know. Not now. But someday, Jess, you're gonna have to let me in."

## CHAPTER 29

I spent the rest of the day at the Clines', where the pond and woods helped ward off the smothering heat. Something shifted between Cody and me that afternoon, opening a void that swallowed all the eager energy he'd been focusing on me for so long. Only one thing would bridge that gap, and it was the one thing I couldn't do.

Leaving him to goof around with the others, I crept off to the shade to lie down. The forest floor, cool and padded with duff, was a welcome contrast to the hard warmth of the deck. But by that point I could've slept on a pile of rocks.

I woke refreshed an hour later. The temperature had dropped by a good five degrees, and cumulonimbus clouds billowed in a threatening mound to the southwest. The air hung dead still around me.

"Hey, Rhett," I called. "Can you feel that?"

"Yeah."

There was something different about the atmosphere, a sort of electricity. As if noticing at that exact moment, the birds burst forth with a clamor of fervent squawking. A gust of wind kicked up, tossing tree branches and buffeting the undergrowth.

"Look at the clouds. I think we're going to have a thunderstorm."

Rhett scrambled out of the pond. "Let's go check the weather station."

"You two are warped," said Teri Sue from the deck, where she lay with her lower legs dangling in the water. But, with dinnertime closing in, she and Cody followed us back to the house.

Rhett scurried through the yard, checking his instruments

as thunder rumbled in the distance. Recharged by my nap and the excitement of the impending storm, I shadowed him.

"Woo-hoo! Look at this." Rhett's homemade barometer registered its lowest reading yet.

The sky grew darker and the wind picked up. Lightning flashed. Rhett's anemometer spun like a merry-go-round.

"Whoa!" he said. "That was a thirty mile an hour gust!"

"Hot diggity," grunted Teri Sue, rolling her eyes as she disappeared into the house.

It was the last reading Rhett got from his wind gauge. Seconds later, it flew apart, raining Dixie cups and plastic straws across the yard.

"Guess we'll have to build a new one," he said with a shrug.

Lightning sizzled across the sky. Wind whipped the Douglas firs, bending their tops. Cody watched from his seat on the steps as Rhett and I dashed through the yard, dancing in the wind, counting seconds between lightning bursts and claps of thunder.

"It's five miles away," crowed Rhett.

The rain began, stirring a scent of dampening dust. We ran around, getting soaked and not even caring.

"It's two miles away!"

Small hail beat down around us to shroud the lawn in white. Alders shivered angrily, displaying the pale undersides of their leaves.

"Woo-hoo!" cried Rhett, holding his arms out as he spun. A blaze of silver lit the sky. The next instant, thunder boomed. Rhett threw back his head and howled. The storm was right overhead.

I felt alive, invincible, like no mundane human problem could touch me. Cool rain pounded over us, running down our faces, getting in our eyes. We laughed and danced, giddy from the current in the air.

In the shelter of the porch, Cody watched with the faintest

hint of a grin. "You're crazy, Jess," he called out over the noise of the storm.

"Yeah? So?" I shouted back.

Cody's next words came at me softly, more a thought mumbled aloud than a declaration. I couldn't quite hear them, but somehow I could read his lips. "And I'm crazy about you."

I stopped short in the middle of my happy dance. If only those whispered words were enough to melt the tension between us. If only he'd step down from the porch and pull me close. But it couldn't happen. Cody's grin had already faded. Now a sad sort of acceptance filled his eyes.

Thunder boomed one last time as the storm rumbled away, sucking with it the energy it had so fleetingly bestowed. And I was left standing on the lawn, breathless and soaking wet, feeling the distance grow between us as Cody turned and walked away.

Sunday night was no more comfortable than Saturday had been, and now I had Cody's disappointment to keep me awake. But as much as it hurt to see him pull away, keeping quiet was the only choice I had.

I woke the next morning before the alarm sounded. Already, it was uncomfortably warm in the Pinto, making it impossible to go back to sleep. As soon as I sat up, the pulsing in my head returned. Wasn't this heat ever going to end? I switched on the radio to hear the weather report.

"Is it hot enough yet for ya folks? If not, you'll be happy to know we've got another scorcher on tap. Temperatures will remain in the upper nineties all week. Almost makes you miss that rain back in May, doesn't it?"

I groaned and switched off the key.

At seven-thirty, Kasey pulled in. She was always the first one there, which gave me a few minutes to hang out with her before everyone else showed up.

She grimaced as she stepped inside, carrying her traditional Monday morning donuts for the crew. The heat had been building in the shop since noon Saturday.

"I've got to get air conditioning in this place," she said.

I laughed. "The other day, Teri Sue told me it doesn't get hot in Oregon."

"The other day?" Kasey flipped on the lights and pushed the buttons to open the bay doors. "What's she saying now?"

"That she misses the air conditioning she had down South."

"I miss the air conditioning at my place, and I only left it twenty minutes ago."

I followed Kasey into the office and dropped onto the couch, while she started her coffee. Every morning, she went through a ritual of brewing it from freshly ground beans. A gourmet and an addict, she wouldn't have anything to do with the stuff that came out of a can. Though how she could stand to drink something hot when it was well over eighty in that office, I couldn't fathom.

"Want a donut?" she asked, sliding the box across the desk.

My stomach, dazed by the heat, clenched at the suggestion. I shook my head. All I wanted was to spend the rest of the day right where I was, flopped on the couch. Of course, I wasn't going to admit it. I'd never seen Kasey slack off because she was too tired or hot. If she could handle the heat, I could too.

"You look worn out, Jess," she said, glancing up after filling her Kliban cat mug. "You should take some time off. Go have fun with Cody."

No point telling her he was mad at me. It would only invite questions I had no intention of answering. "I'd rather work."

"I know you would, but you're pushing too hard. And I'm not the only one who's noticed. Teri Sue called last night. She's worried about you."

"What?" Raw anger surged through me. How dare Teri Sue get into my business? Hadn't the first time taught her anything?

"That's crazy."

"I don't think so," Kasey shook her head, eyes disturbingly intent on me. "She's right—you've lost weight and you look exhausted."

*Great. The first time Teri Sue notices something outside her little bubble, it has to be me.* "I'm fine. I just need to earn money while I've got the chance so I can paint the Pinto. And I'm only tired because I've been helping Rhett with his pond."

Kasey pulled out the desk chair and sat down. "I'm not going to let you run yourself into the ground, Jess. I can't control how many hours you put in at Teri Sue's, but I can regulate what you do here. I'm taking you back down to mornings. Twenty hours a week is plenty, with the time you're putting in on that race car."

She was cutting my hours? Panic crawled up my throat to choke me. How was I supposed to make my plan work without money? "Kasey—"

Her free hand rose to halt my protest. "Don't bother arguing. It won't do you any good. I was just as driven as you are when I was your age, so I know exactly what you're going to say."

"But—"

"I know. You enjoy working hard and think you can handle it. It's what you have to do to get ahead. I was in the same position. I wanted to learn about cars, and because I was a girl, nobody but my dad would take me seriously."

"So if you understand, why are you fighting me?" Somehow, I had to persuade her to let me keep those hours.

"Because I was wrong back then. I spent all my spare time working. From the age of thirteen, I helped in my father's shop. He taught me about paint and bodywork, and when I insisted on learning how to turn a wrench, he persuaded a friend to give me some hours in his garage." She sipped her steaming coffee and looked at me over the cup.

"What's so bad about that? It was what you wanted to do, right?"

"Of course." She nodded. "But I took it too far. And not just with cars. When it came to school, I was even worse. With six kids in my family, I knew the only way I'd get to college was on a scholarship, so I took studying very seriously."

I rubbed a hand across my face, wiping away dampness. "You did what you had to. I can't see a problem with that. Aren't adults always telling kids they need to buckle down if they want to get ahead?"

"They're also telling them they need balance in their lives." Kasey took a long drink and eased back in her chair. "With all that working and studying, I never had much chance to date or spend time with my friends. It took its toll."

I shook my head. "That's not a problem for me. I have more friends now than I ever did. And I love this job."

"You can love it just as much at twenty hours a week." Kasey finished her coffee and glanced at the clock. "We'd better get started. I have to run up to Portland on Wednesday to look at a car. It's going to kill most of the day, so I can't afford to waste time."

Right. She cuts my hours then obsesses about a few unproductive minutes.

I un-stuck my bare arms from the imitation leather and pushed up from the couch. Fine. If she wouldn't give me the work I needed, I'd get it from Teri Sue. Just as soon as I wrung her neck for ratting me out.

I spent the morning trying to convince myself I could make up the hours I needed at Teri Sue's, but that was a bigger con job than the ones I'd been pulling on everyone else. There wasn't that much to do on the car. I'd have to find some other way to earn money. If I worked on the Camaro in the afternoons, and took off as soon as I was finished, I could get a fast food job in the evenings. Not ideal, but it would have to do.

Just before lunch, Teri Sue called me at the shop. "Jess, you're gonna be here this afternoon, right?"

So now she was feeling guilty? "Where else would I be?"

"I dunno. I just wanted to be sure. Rhett's a mess, and I need you to talk to him."

"What's wrong?" She'd better not be hassling him again, too.

Teri Sue hesitated. "Well, his birthday's tomorrow."

"Yeah, I know." He'd been talking about it all week. Did she think the rest of the world was as oblivious as she was?

"It's just that I got a letter from Mama today, and naturally, she didn't send him anything."

Oh man. Poor kid. "I'll be there right after lunch."

Cody, rather than trying to pester me into getting something to eat, went off on his own without saying goodbye. My insides shriveled as I watched him drive away. Was it that easy for him to turn his back on me?

I plodded across the sweltering asphalt to the Pinto. Even though the windows had been down all morning, heat shimmered up from the black interior when I opened the door. The throbbing in my head intensified, and my stomach went queasy as I got in. Usually hot weather didn't bother me. Why was this heat wave taking me to the mat?

I stewed about Teri Sue's interference the whole way to the Clines'. As if I didn't have enough to deal with, between Cody and this damn weather. By the time I arrived, my temper was boiling over. I strode across the grass to where Teri Sue sprawled in a shade-dappled lawn chair, listening to Reba McIntire.

"Uh oh," she said. "Why do I have the feeling that glare has nothing to do with Rhett?"

"Maybe because I made it clear two months ago you needed

to stay out of my business?" I planted my hands on my hips. "What's the big idea calling Kasey? She cut my hours."

"Really?" Teri Sue raised her sunglasses and squinted up at me. "I'm sorry, Jess. I didn't know talking to her would—"

"Who gave you the right to say anything to begin with? I needed that money. Do you know how much losing ten hours a week is going to set me back?"

Teri Sue's expression stiffened. "So what was I supposed to do? You're walking around in a daze and fighting with Cody and lately it looks like you're trying to starve yourself. If you're anorexic or something, I'm not gonna sit back and watch you do yourself in."

Was she for real? "How could I be anorexic? I stuff myself every time I stay for dinner."

"So maybe you're bulimic."

"Bulimic people make themselves throw up." Didn't she know anything? "You've never seen me do that, have you?"

"It's not like I watch you every minute."

*Ugh!* I tossed my hands in the air and raised my face to the sky. "I'm not bulimic. I'm just trying to save money, and your stupid meddling cost me a bundle."

"All right. I'm sorry. I can give you the hours, if it's that big a deal. Why are you so hard up for cash, anyway?"

I sighed and folded my arms across my chest. How could she shake this off so easily? Couldn't she see life wasn't that simple? "My mom and I are just having a hard time," I said. "And it's nobody's business but ours, so don't even ask."

Teri Sue shook her head, tilting her sunglasses up off her eyes. "Okay, I won't. Don't get your panties in such a twist. I was just looking out for you."

"I can look out for myself. And don't think you're off the hook. Unless you really tear up the car, you don't have ten hours to give me, so I'm still in a mess. Now where's Rhett?"

"Down at the pond."

I turned to walk away.

"I'm sorry Jess, really," Teri Sue called after me.

Ignoring her, I stopped to glance at Rhett's min-max thermometer before leaving the yard. Ninety-eight degrees. After the heat of our argument, it felt more like a hundred and ten.

The woods were only slightly cooler than the Clines' front yard. I trudged down the well-worn path to find Rhett floating on an inner tube in the pond, his eyes closed against the blistering sun.

"You're going to look like a lobster if you don't watch it," I said.

He didn't turn to face me, didn't even open his eyes. "I'm wearing sunscreen."

At least he was willing to talk. Good. The showdown with Teri Sue hadn't left me with enough energy to fight him. I peeled off my shoes and socks, plopped down on the shaded corner of the deck, and sank my feet into the soothing pond. What I wouldn't give for a cool place to spend about ten hours sleeping.

Rhett drifted toward me, eyes closed and hands trailing in the water. "My sister sent you out here, didn't she?"

"Yeah."

"It's her fault. If she wasn't so mean to Mama, maybe we'd still have her around."

I circled my legs under the surface, letting the pond draw the heat out of them. "You know better than that."

"Teri Sue hangs up on her. She never answers her letters."

"It's nobody's fault. Your mama's sick."

Rhett's eyes snapped open and he scorched me with a glare. "I know that! But it's not fair. She's supposed to love me. She loves Teri Sue, and Teri Sue doesn't even care about her."

An echo of my own loss ricocheted through my chest. Flawed as Lydia might be, she was still my mother. How much worse would it be if I was barely eleven?

"You're right. It isn't fair. I'm sorry, Rhett."

"Everyone's sorry, but no one can fix it." His eyes brimmed, and he stared hard at me through the tears. "Why won't she get better? I thought if I loved her enough, she'd get well."

"Love can't fix everything."

"It should!"

The fierceness in his eyes seared straight through my heart. "Come here," I said.

Rhett dawdled, only reluctantly propelling himself across the pond to rest his feet on the deck. His bony knees poked up out of the inner tube, the scars on his leg stark against his tanned skin. Why did life have to be so screwed up? He was just a little kid. Kids shouldn't have to deal with things like this.

I squeezed his foot. "I know it's hard. I really do. But it'll get easier if you stop trying to make your mama into someone she isn't."

Rhett scowled and turned away. "You sound like Teri Sue."

Just what I wanted to hear. "You can't force people to change, Rhett. I ought to know. I kept—I keep hoping my mom will stop drinking, but she never does. Expecting people to be something they're not only makes things harder."

It was good advice. Too bad I couldn't apply it to my own life.

"So that's it, huh?" said Rhett. "Just suck it up?"

"Unless you want to keep hurting."

Rhett sank back against the inner tube, closing his eyes. "I don't think that's ever gonna stop."

## CHAPTER 30

The next day the temperature edged up past the century mark. Everyone in the shop was cranky. My body dragged like someone had strapped the lead weights from Teri Sue's race car to it, and the headache that had been bothering me off and on since Saturday swooped in with a vengeance. Even a simple brake job and tune up on a '68 Nova proved almost more than I could handle.

Cody hadn't shown up at Teri Sue's the day before, and I didn't ask him where he'd been. He was speaking to me only when necessary. The easiness we'd always shared had given way to a forced politeness. At noon he took off alone again, and a weird flutter went through me as the Galaxie sped away. I was losing him, just like I'd lost everyone else.

Wednesday morning, I woke up feeling like someone had beaten me with a stick. I considered leaving a message on Kasey's answering machine, saying I wouldn't be in, but immediately dismissed the idea. I couldn't stay behind the shop, and as hot as it was, I wouldn't get much rest no matter where I parked. There was nothing to do but go to work.

Lacking the energy to drive to the gas station and wash up, I tugged a clean T-shirt and jeans out of my duffle bag and crouched behind Kasey's pickup to slip them on. My head pounded as I bent forward to put on my shoes. I had to grab the fender to keep my balance. Damn Lydia! Why had she taken off? Why, for once in her life, couldn't she put me first? Tears welled in my eyes, and it took all my resolve to hold them back. I would *not* let myself cry. I hadn't in years, and I wasn't about to start now.

After driving the Pinto around to the front of the shop, I

dozed behind the wheel while I waited for Race to show up. At least I wouldn't have to bluff my way through the morning in front of Kasey. Knowing her, she'd left at dawn to check out that car in Portland.

Race's beat-up van rattled into the parking lot at a quarter to eight—early for him.

"You look like hell, kiddo," he said as he sorted through his keys for the one that would open the shop. "Why don't you take the day off?"

"I'm okay."

"Uh huh. Right." He glanced up from fumbling the key into the lock. "Let me tell you something—you're a lousy liar."

Funny how I could convince everyone but him and Cody.

As he stepped inside to turn on the lights, a wave of dizziness swept over me, and I gripped the doorway, trying to look casual about it. "I can't afford to take a day off. I need the money."

"You're sixteen, Jess. There'll be plenty of time to worry about money when you're out on your own."

He certainly had that right.

Race disappeared into the office, and I leaned against the nearest workbench to catch my breath. Who was I kidding? No way could I fake my way through until noon. Cody would see right through me, even if I managed to convince Race I was okay.

He poked his head through the office doorway, and I jumped. "Jess," he said, his voice gentle but firm. "Go home."

The order hit me like a car coming full-throttle out of turn four. Tears burned my eyes. Such a simple command, and yet impossible to obey. I stared at Race. Now what? It was one thing to follow the regular routine, but thinking was out of the question.

"Go," he said.

The words jarred me, compelling some primitive physical

intelligence to take over and force my body into action. Next thing I knew, I was in the Pinto, driving down East Amazon. Too bad I didn't have the slightest clue as to where to go.

I spent the day in Hendricks Park, dozing fitfully, sure someone would notice and give me a hard time. Finally, the sun disappeared behind the butte. I drove back to the shop and pulled into my spot beside Kasey's pickup, thankful the building shielded me from the slanting evening rays.

Shade or no, the heat wouldn't let me drift off. I shifted on the seat, unable to find a comfortable position, the open windows failing to provide even the slightest relief. After midnight, it cooled down, but my rest was still broken by crazy, frightening dreams.

And then someone was jostling my shoulder.

"Jess, wake up!"

Hard as it had been to doze off, it was even more difficult to fight sleep's grip. I opened my eyes to sunlight glaring off the hood and immediately shut them. The air hung hot and stuffy around me. Even with the windows down, the inside of the Pinto was a blast furnace.

"Jess!" Cody shook me again.

Groaning, I pulled away. Every part of me ached, and the shaking didn't help. Through the haze that cut me off from all that must've happened just yesterday, a single thought stood out. *I forgot to set my alarm.* One moment of stupidity and it was over.

"What time is it?"

"Almost nine-thirty. I've been half crazy wondering where you were." Cody's voice shrilled with panic. Why was he so upset?

"Lean forward and let me get the door open."

I shifted my weight, grappling for my bearings as Cody wedged himself between the seat and the dash.

"You scared me," he said, his eyes huge. "I swear I hollered, like, twenty times before you woke up."

I stared at him in a daze. *Excuse. You've gotta come up with an excuse.* My brain ignored the command.

Cody rested his hand across my forehead and swore. "Damn, Jess, you're really sick." Chewing his lip, he studied me. "C'mon, let's go inside. It'll be cooler there."

He slid out of the car and gripped my upper arms. I let him help me from the Pinto, let him steady me when my legs went weak. Maybe later, I'd be sorry he'd found me like this, but right now it was a relief to be rescued.

"Race!" Cody hollered as he shoved open the back door with his foot.

Strong hands grabbed my other arm.

"What's going on, Jess?"

I blinked up at Race. How could I even begin to answer?

"She was out back, sleeping in her car." Cody's tone still held that anxious edge.

Race frowned. "Why were you sleeping in your car?"

"It's your mom, isn't it?" Cody asked. "Did she kick you out?"

I shook my head.

"Let's get her in the office." Race scooped me up like I was still five years old. Ducking in front of him, Cody cleared a pile of magazines and maintenance manuals off the couch.

Where was Kasey? Up in Portland? No wait, that was yesterday.

"Cody, grab the fan, will ya? And get Jess some water." Race eased me down on the couch, its imitation leather cool against my skin. He brushed the hair back from my forehead. "Damn, kiddo, you're burning up."

My eyes stung, tears welling at his kindness.

Cody came back with the fan and plugged it in behind the desk. Air washed over me, warm, but at least not still, as he dashed back out of the office and returned with a mug of water. It took every ounce of my energy to sit up long enough to drink it.

"I knew something was wrong," Cody said as he pulled the empty cup from my hands.

I slipped down against the cushions. "Nothing's wrong."

The distress in his eyes hardened to anger. "Get real, Jess. I found you sleeping in your car. Are you gonna deny that, too?"

"Easy, kid," Race said. "Don't get excited."

"*Don't get excited?* She's been bullshitting me for weeks!" Cody slammed the mug on the desk, rattling a cup of pens and pencils, along with my frazzled nerves. I steeled myself for the onslaught of his temper, but it didn't come. Instead, a look of comprehension spread across his face.

"You're *living* in your car, aren't you?" He sank down beside me on the couch. "That's why you've been so worried about money."

The sudden understanding nudged me closer to tears. After days of dealing with coolness and disappointment, I couldn't handle his sympathy.

"Jess?" His hand slipped over mine.

Damn it, why couldn't he leave me alone? I closed my eyes tight.

"Why would she be living in her car?" asked Race.

"Her mom drinks."

How could he go blabbing that? I pulled away, burrowing against the back of the couch, wishing I could crawl behind the cushions and hide.

"Well, that explains the deer-in-the-headlights look she got when I sent her home yesterday," Race said. "But I still have the feeling I'm missing something. What haven't you told me?"

Cody filled him in on everything I'd said about Lydia, even the parts that weren't accurate due to my lies. The long silence that followed was broken only by the peaceful undulation of the fan.

"Jess," Race said, his tone gentle. "You need to tell us

what's going on."

But still, I couldn't.

"She's not gonna tell you anything," Cody said.

"Then maybe I should call her mother."

Cody grunted. "Good luck. The phone's been disconnected."

Tears leaked from my eyes. Much as I hated myself for being such a baby, I was too tired to hold them back.

"I could drive by her place," Race suggested. "See if anyone's home."

Cody snorted. "Even *I* don't know where that is."

"It's easy enough to figure out. The address will be on her W-4."

A desk drawer shrieked, and the noise set me bawling. Race was right. My address was on that W-4. If he went to the apartment, he'd find out someone else lived there now.

"Good going, Race." Cody squeezed my shoulder. "It's okay, Jess. Everything's gonna be fine."

But now that I'd started crying, I couldn't stop. I curled up tighter against the back of the couch. Why couldn't they just go away?

"What's going on in here?" The sound of Kasey's voice fueled a fresh round of sobs. Against her, I didn't stand a chance. I'd be in some foster home by the end of the week, and I'd never see any of them again.

"Cody found Jess sleeping out back in her car," Race said, "He thinks she's been living in it."

Amazing, how effortlessly he could put into words the thing I'd been hiding for weeks.

"She's sick," Cody added. "And she won't tell us anything."

"What do you mean, she's been living in her car?" Kasey's no-nonsense tone stood out sharply against Race's compassion and Cody's alarm.

"From what Cody's been able to piece together, things are pretty bad for her at home. Apparently her mom's an alcoholic, maybe even abusive."

No wonder I couldn't stop crying, with people saying stuff like that. Didn't Race know how naked and ashamed he made me feel, talking about me as if I were some helpless victim?"

"Well, it's obvious you two are only making things worse," Kasey said. "Go get started on that Merc and let me talk to her."

"I'm staying." Cody's grip tightened on my shoulder, and a sob broke from my chest. What had I ever done to deserve that kind of loyalty?

"No you're not, kid. Kasey's right—we're botching this."

Reluctantly, Cody's hand pulled away. The couch shifted as he got up and Kasey settled in his place.

"Try to relax, Jess. Whatever it is, I'll help you work it out." Her hand made soothing circles on my back, but how could I believe her? No one could fix this mess.

I went on crying as Cody and Race left the office. Kasey continued to murmur comforting things. Her hand felt so steady, so calming, and yet I couldn't get a hold of myself. At last, exhaustion put the brakes on my tears.

Kasey squeezed my shoulder. "I'll be right back."

She was gone only moments. "Can you sit up a minute?"

When I rolled over and levered my weight away from the couch, she handed me a fresh mug of water and a couple of Tylenol.

"Jess, I know it's difficult for you to ask for help," she said as she sat down. "You're used to doing things for yourself, and you're amazingly adept at it. But eventually everyone comes across a problem they don't have the resources to fix."

Wasn't *that* the truth. No one would've convinced me of that in the past, but this kind of defeat had a way of shaking up your reality. I swallowed the pills, drained the cup, and sagged back against the couch.

Kasey took the mug from me. "Do you realize, in all the time I've known you, I've never once heard you ask for help?

Believe me, I understand. I value self-sufficiency as much as you do. But sometimes even the strongest people have to rely on others. There's no shame in that."

To Cody, it seemed to be all about trust. Like if he could prove himself, it would be enough to make me talk. But Kasey got it. Asking for help was damn near impossible.

"Tell me what's going on, Jess," she said.

"I can't." The words came out in a whisper, and I squeezed my eyes shut. As right as she was about me, there was so much she didn't know. And how could I explain?

"What is it you're so afraid of?" Kasey's hand reached straight through the crumbling walls of my boundaries to grip mine.

*Damn.* How did she do that? Somehow, I had to try to tell her. After all she'd done for me, she deserved that much.

"It's not just asking for help," I said, stopping to steady myself with a breath. "It's you. You and Race and Cody …" I wanted to go on, but couldn't squeeze the words out.

"What about us?"

"It's … you're like family. I can't … I don't want to … If I tell you …"

"You're afraid you'll lose us."

I nodded, cowering behind closed eyelids, feeling naked even though she'd been the one to say it. Why was it so damned hard to tell people how I felt?

"Jess, it's okay to admit it."

I knew that. I honestly did. But knowing didn't make it any easier.

"We care about you, too," said Kasey, her hand tightening around mine. "A whole lot. I don't know why you think you're in danger of losing us, but the one thing you have to realize is we would never, ever, let anyone take you away from us against your will." The intensity in her voice made it clear she meant it. "Do you understand that?"

I nodded.

"Do you trust me?"

My throat cinched up. I wanted to, but how could I? Fierce as Kasey sounded, there were some things even she couldn't fight. Like the system the government had for dealing with kids like me.

"Trust is a delicate thing, Jess. It's difficult to build and easy to destroy. And it's not always about believing a person won't betray you. Sometimes it's about having faith in their ability to help, even when you don't think they can." Kasey paused a moment to let that sink in, her hand steady and reassuring around mine. "You're a good kid, Jess. A tough kid. But if you want to be a whole, mature person, you're going to have to risk letting others in."

Like it was that easy. For eight years I'd done everything I could to keep people out, and now I was supposed to change?

*Well Cody did.* The thought blindsided me, but it was true. By trusting Race, he'd changed from an angry, desperate kid into a strong, compassionate person. And then there was Race, who still didn't have enough faith in himself to fully allow Kasey into his life. It was so sad, seeing what that did to the people around him. Is that what I was doing?

I'd never realized trust could mean having faith in other people's abilities. But maybe that was the key to fixing the mess I was in. I had to believe my friends could help. I had to stop trying to do it all myself.

Taking a deep breath, I looked up at Kasey.

"My mom's gone," I said. "I haven't seen her since the middle of June."

## CHAPTER 31

Kasey gaped at me. "You've been living in your car for a month and a half?"

"Just the last three weeks. . . . I tried to keep the apartment, but Lydia took all my money." Was I even making sense? With my brain in such a fog, I couldn't seem to come up with the right details.

"And you don't have any other relatives?"

"Uh uh. My dad's been gone for years. There isn't anyone else."

Kasey's tough but tender gaze held me as she thought that over. "Why were you so afraid to ask for help?"

"I can't get stuck in a foster home, Kasey. I just can't." Tears threatened, and I shut my eyes to hold them back.

"I don't think you're seeing this clearly," she said, giving my hand another squeeze. "What exactly do you think would happen if you wound up in a foster home?"

One more thing I couldn't put into words. No one was going to let a strange kid come into their house and make her own rules. I'd have to give up my freedom, ask permission if I wanted to work or go to the speedway. And foster parents could even keep me from seeing my friends. Kasey would understand if I could just say it right, but my head hurt, I was exhausted, and I couldn't think.

"I wouldn't get to be *me* anymore," I said, hoping that would be enough. Why wouldn't she stop drilling me? I'd told her about Lydia.

"Did you ever consider the possibility the state might place you with someone who'd understand your situation? Someone like me?"

I shook my head. It was foolish to be optimistic about

things I had no control over. Who needed that kind of disappointment?

Kasey studied me with a little half-frown. "There are a lot of options, Jess. Things you apparently haven't thought of. You've gotten yourself so worked up, you can't see this realistically."

*She* was the one who couldn't see it realistically. What did she think the state did with kids like me, put us up in the Hilton?

Sighing, Kasey patted my arm. "I can see this is more than you can deal with right now. You need some rest. You can come stay with us, and we'll talk more later."

"Aren't you going to call the police?"

"Of course not. The last thing you need is more stress. Besides, after all this time, a few more days won't make any difference."

Was she serious? "I thought that would be your first move."

"Like I said, you're not seeing this clearly." Kasey stood up. "I'll explain everything to the others so you don't have to go through it again, then Cody can take you to the house."

I drew in a deep breath. "He's going to be mad I told you and not him."

The sad look in Kasey's eyes said I still wasn't getting it. "I don't think so, Jess."

A thunderstorm rumbled inside my head, spawning lightning bolts of pain as Cody helped me into the Galaxie and closed the door. I shut my eyes against the blaring sun and slumped in the seat. I'd never felt so weak in my life. What if this didn't go away?

Cody didn't look at me as he slipped in behind the wheel.

"I'm sorry," I said. "Please don't be mad."

He gave me a quick look as he started the engine. "I'm not. At least not at you. I'd like to drop kick your mother into next week, though."

Right. "You've been mad at me for days."

"Hurt, Jess, not mad." Cody pulled out onto the street. His dark, somber eyes flickered from the road, to me, and back to the traffic ahead. "Anyway that was before I knew what was going on." He patted the seat. "Here, scoot over and lie down. You'll be more comfortable."

Sitting up took too much energy, so I stretched out beside him. He stroked my hair, teasing a few wayward strands away from my face and tucking them behind my ear. Like I deserved his kindness.

"I lied to you."

"Yeah, but I've done plenty of that myself, so I understand. Right now, the only thing I'm worried about is you being okay."

"I'm fine, Cody." Even *I* knew how stupid that sounded, but hiding my weak underbelly was a natural instinct.

Cody's hand tensed and he glanced down at me sharply. "No you're not. For once in your life stop fighting and let someone else help. You don't have to deal with everything yourself."

Exactly what Kasey had told me, and already I was blowing it. I closed my eyes, struggling not to cry. "I can't change just like that."

Cody's fingers fell back into their gentle motion. "No. I guess you can't." He stopped for a light, the Ford's big engine rumbling smoothly.

"I wish you'd been able to trust me, Jess, but I see why you couldn't. You were scared. I woulda been, too." The light went green, and he let off the brake. "I understand how it is, not knowing what's gonna happen to you because your parents are too messed up to put you first."

"I can't go to a foster home, Cody." Tears filled my eyes. All these years since I'd cried, and now I was practically turning into a river. Kasey was crazy to think it would all work out.

"*Shhh.* It's okay. I won't let that happen." Cody's hand

soothed my cheek, and he looked down at me with a fire that cut straight to my core. "There's no way I'm gonna let anyone take you away from me, Jess. No way in hell."

It felt so good to crawl into a real bed. Kasey's cat, Winston, curled up against my side the minute I was under the covers. All day, I drifted in and out of a feverish slumber, dazed and achy, yet so grateful to be in an air-conditioned house instead of the front seat of the Pinto. Cody was there each time I woke. Slouched in an easy chair he'd dragged in from the front room, he rested his bare feet on the bed as he read a well-worn copy of *The Red Pony*.

When night finally came, I dreamt I'd found Lydia huddled in an alley, her hair matted and her eyes hollow. I woke to the whimper of my own voice.

"Jess ..." Cody called from the easy chair, "are you okay? Did you have another dream?"

He was still there? "Yeah."

The chair creaked as he got up and came to sit on the bed. He stroked my cheek. Even in the faint light, I could read the concern in his eyes. Emotion rushed to the surface, my defenses stripped by the overwhelming events of the past few days.

"It's gonna be all right." Cody smoothed the tangled hair from my face, brushed away tears with a hand that felt cool against my hot cheek.

"I'm scared, Cody."

"I know." He stretched out beside me on top of the covers, one arm draped across me and the other curled protectively on the pillow above my head. His fingers stroked my hair in a tender rhythm.

Outside, floorboards squeaked. Kasey appeared in the doorway, illuminated by the dim glow of the hall nightlight. She glanced from Cody to the chair beside the bed, where his blanket and pillow lay in a tangled heap.

"What are you doing in here, Cody?"

"Jess had a nightmare."

Kasey smiled faintly and shook her head. "I appreciate the romantic nature of your vigil, but it's hardly necessary. You need to go back to sleep—in your own room."

"Aw, c'mon," he said, pushing himself up on one elbow. "Let me stay. Jess might have another bad dream."

Leaning against the doorway, Kasey folded her arms across her chest.

"I know what you're thinking," Cody said. "And you don't have to worry. It's not like I'm gonna put a move on her while she's sick." He looked down at me with the faintest grin. "She wouldn't be able to enjoy it."

"You're not funny," Kasey said.

But he was, and he knew it.

"Jess needs me. She feels safer when I'm here."

I hadn't said that, but it was true.

Cody cranked up the charm. "I'll bet it's been a long time since she felt safe."

True again.

Whether his words convinced her, or she decided it wasn't worth fighting over, Kasey sighed. "All right," she agreed. "But when I come back in the morning, I'd better find you sleeping in that chair."

## CHAPTER 52

I dozed through most of Friday, feeling as if I couldn't get enough sleep. But with the headache fading, it was easier to rest. Winston spent the entire time tucked into a furry ball against my leg, while Cody continued his watch from the chair beside the bed.

It wasn't until after dark that I fully woke, no longer feverish and disoriented. I still felt tired, but it wasn't the sagging kind of weariness that had hung on me all week.

Cody slouched in the easy chair, legs drawn up in front of him as he scribbled away at a notebook that rested against his knees. He wore a pair of lime and purple board shorts under a T-shirt Kasey found distasteful and Race thought was a riot. It read, *If it's called tourist season, why can't we shoot them?*

"Hey," I said.

Cody's pen hesitated mid-scrawl. His preoccupied frown softened into that tender, wistful look that made my insides melt. "Hey."

"You working on a story?"

"Just hashing over some ideas." He leaned across the arm of the chair to toss the notebook onto the nightstand. "How ya feeling?" he asked as he came over to sit beside me on the bed.

"Better."

"You hungry? Kasey saved you some dinner. I could heat it up."

"I'm starving."

Cody broke into a grin. "How 'bout a chocolate shake to go with it? I make a killer milkshake. Even Race says so."

"Sure. Sounds great."

Wonderful as it was to eat, I only got through about a third of the meal before my stomach protested. I set the plate on the nightstand and reached for the drink.

"You gotta eat more than that," Cody said, anxiousness wrinkling his forehead.

"I'm full."

"You've hardly eaten anything in days." He picked up the plate and held it out to me, but I pushed it away.

"Quit fussing and let me enjoy my milkshake," I said, raising the straw to my lips. Oh wow. Best one I'd ever tasted.

"Good, huh?" Cody grinned, totally pleased with himself. "I use chocolate ice cream *and* chocolate syrup."

"It's delicious."

He leaned back on one hand, his fingertips just touching my knee. "Teri Sue's really pissed y'know."

"She can get over it. I'm not exactly happy with her, either."

"Because she talked to Kasey? She was only watching out for you." He hesitated, his eyes meeting mine in a guilty look. "Maybe if I'd done the same, things wouldn't have gone this far."

So now it was his fault? "It wouldn't have made a difference. I wasn't going to say anything."

"You should've, Jess. I know you were scared, but Kasey's right. It's not as bad as you think. She'll work something out."

And I was supposed to be convinced?

Cody looked down at the rumpled blankets, shaking his head. "It kills me to think of you living in your car all this time."

"Everyone probably figures I'm an idiot, huh?" I took another sip, struggling to pull the rich sweetness through the straw.

"Not really. Kasey's been ranting about you not having any sense, but Race said what you lack in sense, you make up for in guts."

Embarrassed at the idea of my hero seeing me in those terms, I smiled and glanced away. "Race is crazy."

"Yup." Cody nodded. "Kasey thought that, too. He's got a

point, though. It's like this guy, Robert Louis Stevenson, said. 'Life is not being dealt a good hand, but playing a poor hand well.'" He caught me up in another look, this one full of admiration. "You've done a good job with the hand you were dealt, Jess."

I grunted. "Other than not having the sense to ask for help?"

"Yeah," Cody said, treating me to another grin. "Other than that."

Saturday morning, I woke feeling almost normal, except for having about as much spark as a dead battery. I glanced around the room and spotted the clothes I'd been wearing the other day, washed and neatly folded on the dresser. The keys to the Pinto sat beside them. Hazily, I recalled Kasey saying Race had brought my car back from the shop the other night. He was the only one who'd driven it but me.

When I stood up to get my clothes, my head whirled. I fought off the dizziness and took a few tentative steps.

"What do you think you're doing?" Kasey barked from the hallway.

"I was feeling better, so—"

"You won't be for long if you don't take it easy." She stepped into the room and placed a firm hand on my back, directing me toward the bed. "You haven't been eating properly, or getting enough sleep, and the pressure you've been under would be overwhelming to an adult, let alone a teenager. All things considered, I'm amazed you've shaken this off so quickly. Two days ago I wouldn't have predicted it."

I scowled. Did she think I was made of blown glass? "I appreciate everything you've done for me, but it's Saturday. Teri Sue will need my help."

"She'll survive." Kasey applied gentle pressure to my shoulder, forcing me to sit. "I can give her a hand if she needs anything."

"You're not saying you expect me to stay here tonight?" How could she even suggest it?

"That's exactly what I'm saying."

"But that's three cars for you to worry about!"

Kasey crossed her arms over her chest. "It'll be fine, Jess. Race managed on his own before he met me."

I stared up at her, stunned to realize she was serious.

"I know you don't like this," she said. "But I'm not giving you a choice. If you're tired of looking at these same four walls, you can come out and rest on the couch. At least that way Cody won't have to hide out in here to hover over you."

Annoyed as I was, the idea made me smile. "He *has* been pretty devoted."

"He'd put a dog to shame," Kasey agreed. "But I can see you tolerating it for about one more day before telling him to back off."

I laughed. Boy, did she have me pegged.

Kasey gave my shoulder a squeeze. "The towels are in the hall closet if you want a shower. Breakfast will be ready in about twenty minutes. That is, if I can get Race out of bed."

A shower had never felt so satisfying. After living in my car for three weeks, it seemed the height of luxury. But the thought of dealing with my problem dimmed the pleasure. The issue couldn't be put off much longer, and despite Kasey and Cody's optimism, I didn't see an easy solution.

Everyone was in the kitchen when I got there, though Race wore the dazed look I was used to seeing on Teri Sue's face when I showed up too early. I pulled out a chair and sat down, my body already protesting the small amount of exertion I'd demanded from it. Why did Kasey have to be right about everything?

"That little car of yours sure is a kick in the pants," Race said, yawning at me across the table.

My face warmed at the compliment. Even though I hated other people driving it, it didn't bother me that he had. "Better than that Pinto you stuffed into the wall a few years ago?" I asked, remembering an Enduro he'd competed in.

Race fired off a sleepy grin. "No comparison. That thing was lucky if it was firing on three cylinders."

Kasey set a plate of Belgian waffles, piled high with strawberries and whipped cream, in front of me.

"Wow," I said. "This looks delicious. Do you guys eat like this every morning?"

"Nah, Kasey's just showing off," Cody said, smirking at her. "Usually she only cooks breakfast for us on Sundays."

My stomach rumbled as I cut into a waffle with the side of my fork.

"All right, Jess," Kasey said, sitting down with her own plate. "It's time we discussed what to do about your situation. I'm still shocked you thought you could get away with living in your car, but we won't get into that. Let's just say it wasn't the smartest choice you could've made."

"She did the best she could," Cody said through a mouthful of strawberries and whipped cream.

Kasey waved her fork at him. "You're not in the clear on this, either. If you knew Jess was in trouble, you should've come to us."

"I was trying to get her to trust me," he said, eyes flickering in my direction before going back to Kasey. "How could I do that by narking her out? Anyway, she wouldn't have told you, either."

"Maybe not voluntarily, but I have leverage. I sign her paycheck."

My fork halted in mid-air. Whoa—ruthless.

"I didn't think about that," Cody said.

"It seems neither one of you did much thinking. Though, Jess, I suppose I can't blame you for being unable to see outside your own reality. Until recently, no one in your life gave you much reason to trust them."

A sneaker wave of self-consciousness crashed over me, and I looked down at my breakfast. But Kasey didn't give me time to dwell on my shame.

"I want you to tell us from the beginning how all this happened," she said, pouring herself some orange juice from the pitcher in the middle of the table.

It wasn't easy to put the experience into words, but I forced myself to do it. Every revealing detail. Cody listened wide-eyed, shaking his head from time to time, but letting Kasey and Race ask the questions.

"I've gotta hand it to you," Race said when I finished. "You're one tough kid."

"No kidding," Cody added. The way he was looking at me, you'd think I'd climbed Mt. Everest barefoot.

My face flushed hot, and I poked at my waffle.

"So you have no idea where your mother might be?" Kasey asked.

"Just someplace warm and sunny, like Jimmy said."

"Did you look for her anywhere other than his apartment?"

"Not really."

Kasey reached for her glass. "I think maybe we should."

"Why? She's long gone. Anyway, I'm not sure I could go back to that." I wanted to know Lydia was safe, but I'd never be able to trust her after this.

"I'm not suggesting you should live with her. I doubt the state would even let you. But what she did was against the law, and if she's as unstable as you say, it's in her best interest to get help."

I stared at my plate. Didn't Kasey realize how impossible that sounded?

"I know it's unlikely we'll find her, but we should try." She rested her hand on top of mine. "It might put your mind at ease. We could start by asking at the bars she frequented. Maybe she or Jimmy said something to one of their friends."

I swallowed hard and nodded. After that dream the other night, I'd feel better knowing I'd done everything I could to find her.

"What about your dad?" Race asked, helping himself to more juice. "Are you sure he's out of the picture? Cody told us he's a long-haul trucker. You'd think with a job like that, the police would be able to track him down."

I shook my head. "Lydia said they couldn't. They tried, because he never paid child support, but they didn't have any luck."

"Hmmm." Kasey took a bite of waffle and chewed thoughtfully.

"He wouldn't want to bother with me, anyway," I said. "Whenever he called, Lydia said he didn't want to talk to me. He never even sent me a letter or birthday card."

Kasey frowned at my dismissal, her brow furrowing. "Did your father ever tell you himself he didn't want to speak to you?"

"No. Just Lydia."

"The same Lydia who took your money and left you to fend for yourself?" asked Race.

I glanced between the two of them, wondering where they were going with this.

"She may not have told you the truth," Kasey said. "People often paint their ex-spouses as villains in order to get a child firmly on their side."

I'd never thought of that. A strange, fluttery feeling woke in my gut as I considered the implications.

"At any rate," she continued, "I spoke to an attorney friend of mine yesterday. He said foster care would be the normal course of action in a case like this, but it's certainly not the only one. You could also petition the court for emancipation, or—"

her pause made me look up from stabbing a piece of waffle, "—I could try to get custody of you, myself."

*What?* I gawked at Kasey. Letting me stay here for a few days was one thing, but volunteering to take full legal responsibility? Even my mother didn't want that job.

"Are you serious?" I asked when I figured out how to make my voice work.

"Of course." Kasey smiled and glanced across the table at Race, who was grinning at my reaction. "It's something I've given a lot of thought to. We discussed it last night. As long as you'd feel comfortable, we'd love to have you stay."

Oh man. How was I supposed to respond to that? I fidgeted with my fork, unable to look either of them in the eye.

"I think it makes the most sense," Kasey continued. "You'd probably have no trouble becoming emancipated, considering you're holding down two jobs and you've often taken up your mother's slack. But just because you're capable, doesn't mean it's the best thing for you."

"It wouldn't be all that different from how it was living with Lydia," I pointed out, laying my still-loaded fork across the plate. My stomach felt too stunned to allow another bite.

"Actually, it would be. When your mother was there, you had someone to share the responsibility. She might not have always done her part, but you weren't completely alone."

Considering I'd entertained that idea myself, right after Lydia left, I couldn't exactly argue.

"I know you're capable, Jess," Kasey said, her gaze intent. "And emancipation must sound like a wonderful option, but don't you think you'd be happier having other people around?"

A few months ago, I would've said no. A few months ago, I'd have insisted I didn't need anyone else. Now I wasn't so sure.

"Would the state let you take me? Couldn't they send me someplace else?"

Kasey shook her head, scooping up a strawberry and swooping it through the whipped cream. "It's not likely. The system is overburdened, and if Children's Services can find people willing to provide a home, they aren't going to turn them away. If I wanted compensation, I'd be required to take classes, but I'm not worried about the money. Without that detail, we could get the paperwork processed in a few days."

I hadn't even thought about the financial aspect. How stupid could I be? "You shouldn't have to support me, Kasey. You've done enough already."

"I'm not going to argue about that right now."

"But—"

"Jess, don't push me on this." The set of Kasey's jaw told me it would be a waste of time to keep fighting. "Now, if you're finished eating, go lie down on the couch. We can talk more about this later."

## CHAPTER 55

When Cody was done with breakfast—which meant polishing off all the leftover waffles—he came to join me in the living room. We spent the day watching TV and playing Nintendo. It didn't bother him at all, but it made me crazy. I wasn't used to sitting in one place that long, except at school. Even there, they let you get up and move every forty-five minutes. He finally took pity and broke out a couple of the stories he'd promised to let me read the night we went to the hot springs. I worried about what I'd say if I didn't like them, but his words hooked me from the first sentence. I made him dig out everything he'd written and spent the rest of the afternoon reading.

At four o'clock, everyone left for the track. I took a hint from Winston and stretched out on the couch to take a nap. With the house quiet, Kasey's words about my father flooded back into my head. Maybe she was right and Lydia had made up the whole thing. I'd been remembering it like an eight year old, but looking at it objectively, there was plenty of room for doubt. Lydia had held all the cards. Dad and I had been at her mercy.

I drifted off with Winston tucked against my leg, purring as smoothly as a Packard straight eight engine. When I woke several hours later, the television was on with the sound low, and a tousled, red-blond head poked above the arm of the couch beside me.

"Rhett?"

He turned around, beaming. "Hey, Jess! I didn't think you were ever gonna wake up."

"Why aren't you at the speedway?"

"Cody and I reckoned you could use some company," he said, boosting himself onto the edge of the couch.

"You reckoned right."

Rhett's smile faded as he studied me. "You're okay, aren't you?"

"Yeah, sure."

His jaw gave a faint quiver, and he blinked back tears.

"What's wrong?"

"Nobody would let me see you. It kinda freaked me out."

Oh man. My fingers went to his shoulder, clasping it tight. "There was nothing to get upset about. Anyway, it's not like I'd have been much company if they'd let you see me. Mostly I just slept."

"But Teri Sue wouldn't even tell me what was going on!" he hunched forward, angry tears slipping from his eyes and running down his cheeks. "I heard her talking to Cody on the phone, but she told me not to worry—that it was no big deal. Only I knew it was from the way she went and whispered to Daddy about it."

"Why didn't you call over here?"

"I did. Kasey explained everything, but she wouldn't let me talk to you. She said you needed to sleep." He sighed and wiped his face with the back of his arm. "I wish Teri Sue wouldn't treat me like a little kid. I reckon she didn't think I could deal with it, but I'm not five years old. She doesn't think I can handle anything!"

"I'm sorry, Rhett." I sat up and put my arms around him. "You're right, she shouldn't treat you like that. You've got a pretty darned good head on your shoulders. I'll talk to her about it, okay?"

"Okay.... She's mad at you, y'know."

"I'll straighten things out tomorrow."

Rhett let me hold him for a few more seconds before wiggling out of my embrace. Snuffling loudly, he turned and gave me an accusatory look. "How come you didn't tell me about your mama? I told you about mine."

"I almost did, that day at the speedway when you were so upset. But I was afraid if anyone found out, I'd end up in a foster home and never see you guys again."

Rhett's eyes went big. "Is that gonna happen?"

"No. Kasey said I could stay here."

"You could come live with us."

The idea was so typically Rhett, it made me smile. "Your dad might have something to say about that."

"He wouldn't care. He likes you."

"It's not that simple."

Rhett scowled, and I prepared for an argument, but he let it go.

"Was it scary, when your mama left?" he asked instead.

"Yeah, Rhett. It was."

"I bet you miss her, huh?"

I nodded.

"Yeah," he said with a sigh. "I know how that is."

The next morning, after providing a rundown of an uneventful night at the speedway, Kasey said she was giving me the week off. No amount of protest could sway her. When I told her I wanted to go to Teri Sue's, she insisted I get Cody to drive me.

"I know you feel fine," she said, raising both hands to stem my protest. "But I have this suspicion the minute you're out of my sight, you'll be trying a new setup on that Camaro, or helping Rhett with some crazy project. With Cody along, I won't have to worry about you overdoing it."

Sometimes, having her know me so well could be a serious handicap.

At the Clines', Cody stayed in the yard discussing that still elusive win with Mark, who was weeding his flowerbeds. I let myself into the house and tracked down Teri Sue in the kitchen. Even though it was almost eleven o'clock, she was just getting around to pouring herself a bowl of cereal.

"Hey," I ventured as I pulled out a chair.

"Hey." Teri Sue's tone put a chill on the late-morning warmth. She flipped through the Sunday paper and crunched her Corn Flakes, not bothering to glance up.

Startled by the un-Teri-Sue-like behavior, I fumbled at breaking the silence. Each attempt resulted in a one-word reply.

Well fine. If she wanted to be like that, I could pull out the heavy artillery. "You really should stop treating Rhett like a little kid, you know."

Teri Sue glanced up from the comics section. "He *is* a little kid."

"But he's not a baby."

"Huh." She returned her attention to *The Wizard of Id*.

"You should've told him what was happening, Teri Sue. You scared him."

Her green eyes snapped upward, full of anger. "No," she said in a tone that could've cut glass, "*you* scared him. And you scared me, too. What kinda idiot are you, trying to live in your car? You coulda been raped or killed! Cody said you were sleeping with the damn windows down, sending an invitation to any pervert who might come along." She practically breathed fire at me across the table. "You're really one to talk about telling people what's going on."

*Wow*. My brain was too stunned to come up with a response, but it didn't matter. She hadn't finished, anyway.

"I reckon you didn't give two second's thought to what it musta done to Cody, finding you so sick like that. 'Specially after what happened to Race last year." She slammed down her spoon. "Way to go, Jess. Hurt everyone who ever gave a damn about you."

Shame washed over me. The worst part was, I hadn't thought of it on my own. And Cody hadn't said a word. He'd just gone on being his loyal self.

I stared down at the tabletop. "I wasn't trying to hurt anyone."

"No, but the only person you were thinking of was your own damn self." Teri Sue shoved back, chair legs shrieking against the tile. She strode to the sink and dumped her bowl in. "You don't have the sense God gave a goat."

"I know. I'm sorry."

The apology seemed to siphon off a little of her anger. She looked across the kitchen, shaking her head. "Why didn't you come to me? You coulda stayed here. Didn't you ever stop to think?"

"I know it was stupid, but I'm not used to asking people for help."

"So it's better to half kill yourself and piss off your friends?"

"I'm sorry, Teri Sue."

She scowled, leaning backward to clamp her hands on the edge of the counter. "You better watch yourself, girl. Friends like me might be a dime a dozen, but you're never gonna find another guy as patient as Cody. I can't believe he's put up with your crap."

My throat pinched shut, and I hunched over the table, burying my face in my hands. Much as I'd expected her to be upset, I hadn't anticipated her laying into me like this.

"Oh Lord," said Teri Sue, "you aren't gonna cry on me, are ya? Don't go shattering my illusions about how tough you are on top of everything else."

If only she knew how much I'd already cried that week. I heard her footsteps on the tile, felt her hand on my shoulder.

"I'm sorry, Jess, I shouldn't have yelled at you like that."

"No," I said, my voice shaky, "you were right. And you're not a dime a dozen, either."

Teri Sue's arms went around me. She hugged me hard. "Next time you're in trouble," she said, "you damn well better say something."

\* \* \*

That evening, I wandered downstairs, exploring. With Kasey's house built on a slope, only the back of the basement sat completely underground. The opposite wall held a set of French doors that opened to a brick patio beneath the deck. The space in between was a huge entertainment area with a bar and fireplace. Apparently, Kasey used one corner as an office, because I found her down there sitting at a computer. It didn't look like a very private place to work, but the wainscoting, comfortable furniture, and warm maroon walls made it a cozy area, in spite of its size.

"Hey," I said. "Is it okay if I look around?"

Kasey's chair creaked as she swiveled to face me. "Of course. I've got some books down here you might find interesting." She motioned toward the north wall, which was taken up almost entirely by bookshelves.

I scanned the collection, noting it contained everything from fiction to philosophy to engineering. One section held nothing but college texts. I selected a calculus book and flipped through it. I'd been signed up to take the subject at my old school in the fall. Maybe they'd still let me when I transferred to South Eugene, the school I'd go to living with Kasey.

"Jess." Her voice pulled my attention away from the book. "I appreciate the restraint you've shown in dealing with my restrictions. It must go against the grain after fending for yourself for so long."

Not much I could say to that without sounding petulant. Kasey's restrictions were humiliating. But overprotective as she was being, it wasn't like she'd boss me around out of sheer enjoyment.

"I realize you can take care of yourself," she added, "but if I'm going to be your guardian, I have a responsibility to keep you safe."

"It's okay. I get it."

"And I have to consider the fact that you don't know when to quit."

Like she had room to criticize on that count. Besides, most people set the quitting point way too low.

Since Kasey seemed to be in a talkative mood, I closed the math book and took it with me to the computer.

A blueprint filled the screen—some kind of large bolt with internal threads. "What are you working on?"

"It's called a bump steer adjuster. I'm hoping to have these manufactured and sell them to drivers in the classes that won't allow Heim joints. You know what bump steer is, right?"

"Yeah, but we haven't gotten that far on the Camaro."

"One of these days, we'll get it over to Race's shop, and I'll show you how to make the adjustments. I'll borrow a set of scales, too, so we can fine-tune the weight placement."

"That would be great." It was a pain, trying to set up the car on that un-level dirt floor. Mark hadn't yet gotten around to having concrete poured in the barn.

As I glanced back at the monitor, something on the wall caught my eye. A collage of sketches. They were all Cody—practicing a karate stance, kicking back in a tattered chair with a book, slouching against Race's Dart wearing a James Dean sulk and dangling a cigarette from his lips. The sketches were simple but elegant, and even before I saw the signature, I knew who had drawn them. I stepped around the edge of the desk for a closer look.

"Beautiful, aren't they? Race really captured Cody's personality."

"I didn't know he was so talented."

Kasey sighed, her gaze locked on the drawing. "Was. That's the operative word." The sadness in her expression jolted me. How could someone as tough as her still be struggling with that wreck?

"It must've been really hard for him," I said. "I can't imagine having that kind of gift and losing it."

When Kasey's eyes caught mine, she made no effort to hide the pain lurking there. "The sad part is, Race doesn't know for sure it's gone."

"What? Cody made it sound like—"

"An absolute? Maybe it is." She shook her head, focusing once more on the collage. "Race's fine motor skills were certainly compromised. But whether that's permanent, or if it completely destroyed his artistic ability, I can't say. He hasn't tried to draw since the accident."

I stared at her, my chin dropping. "So he doesn't know?" How could Race let that uncertainty drag out for over a year? If it'd been me, I'd want the truth, one way or the other.

Kasey's chair squeaked as she leaned back, another sigh escaping her. "You have to understand, it's about more than just drawing. Race's confidence took a real beating last summer. If losing the championship wasn't disappointment enough, he had to accept financial assistance from a mother he hadn't spoken to in years. And in order to keep Cody, he had to let me give him a job and a place to live."

"Cody told me about that," I said, intrigued she'd allowed me to see this chink in her armor. Kasey was such a rock. The most in-control person I knew. Could she be as shook up inside as I was?

"Race really struggled with it," she said, running her fingertips along the edge of the desk. "And I didn't make it any easier, expecting him to be logical when he needed me to respect his pride. For a long time, he wasn't himself. That was the most difficult part for Cody and me. He eventually worked through it, but if he'd had to confirm the loss of his talent while dealing with everything else, well ..." She hesitated, searching for words, her eyes once more seeking mine. "It's about hope, Jess. People like you and me get by on sheer force of will, but it's optimism that keeps Race going."

A puzzle piece shifted and dropped into place. Rhett was like that, too. That's why he couldn't give up on the idea of his mother getting better.

Kasey eased forward in her chair, a forced smile evicting the melancholy from her face. "But none of this is anything you need to worry about," she said, the note of control returning to her voice. "Someday Race will pick up a pencil, and when he does, he'll be ready to deal with whatever he learns."

If I hadn't seen it, I wouldn't have guessed that just a moment before, Kasey had confronted one of her deepest regrets. Amazing, how she could be so tough, and yet so unashamed about revealing her vulnerability. Somehow, that made her seem stronger.

"So, you like math, eh?" she asked, startling me from my thoughts. I looked down at the textbook under my arm.

"What? Oh, yeah. Guess I'm weird, huh?"

Her lips pulled into an amused smile. "If you are, that makes two of us. How far have you gotten in school?"

"Through trig. I'm hoping to get into calculus this year."

Kasey opened a drawer, took out a spiral notebook, and handed it to me along with a pencil from the holder on her desk. "Why don't you try a few problems? See how it suits you."

The challenge of it, along with the appeal of impressing Kasey, prompted me to take the book to an easy chair near the French doors. Immediately, I got sucked in by the introduction, which explained the concepts of integration and differentiation. Math had always seemed like a puzzle. A new concept might baffle me at first, but working a few problems would line up the tumblers, releasing the lock. The best part was the challenge questions at the end of a chapter. They felt like a taunt from the person who wrote the book: *c'mon, I dare you to figure this one out.*

"So, what do you think of calculus?" Kasey's voice startled me, and I almost dropped my pencil.

"It's interesting. Not anything like algebra or trig."

"No, it definitely has a personality all its own." Kasey extended a hand for the notebook, and I gave it to her. As she took a seat in the chair near mine, she looked it over. "For someone who's never studied calculus, you're doing a great job. Have you ever considered going to college?"

I laughed. "Are you kidding? I have enough trouble with high school."

"Somehow I find that difficult to believe." Kasey handed back the notebook.

"Well, I do okay in math and science, but I get C's in just about everything else. And last year I almost flunked art."

She raised an eyebrow. "How can anybody flunk art?"

"That's what Cody wanted to know. But it was right after auto shop, so I was always late. And if I got really involved in working on my car, sometimes I didn't show up at all." I hid behind a sheepish grin, hoping she'd understand.

"Well, that explains it," Kasey said, chuckling. "So if you aren't going to college, what do you plan to do after high school?"

Good question. One that no longer had a simple answer. "I used to think I'd move down South and try to get a job on a Winston Cup crew. But now..." I shrugged. How could I walk off and leave Cody, let alone the rest of them? "I want to do something with cars—probably race cars. I really enjoy what I've done on Teri Sue's. Especially fabricating parts."

"That's engineering," Kasey said, nodding. "You might want to reconsider college. It's nothing like high school."

I made a face. Who needed four more years of sitting in classrooms? "You know what would be really cool? Having a shop like yours, only one that builds race cars."

Kasey leaned back, putting her feet up on the footstool. "That's a great idea, Jess. I've toyed with that concept, myself, but I have enough to keep me busy. It's possible I'd be willing to help someone else get started, though." She smiled. "Someone with a college degree."

Great. She just wasn't going to let that drop. "You're really big on this college stuff, aren't you?"

"If you want to run a business, your chances are much better with proper training. But mostly, I'd like to see you go on with your education because I think you'd enjoy it. With a science curriculum, you'd be like a kid in a candy store. You could even pick up a few meteorology courses as electives."

Meteorology courses? That *would* be interesting. Having an instructor to explain the difficult concepts in the books I'd read, or to bounce theories off of ... The daydream evaporated as I realized how pointless it was. "With my grades, there's no way I could get into college. And even if I did, I wouldn't be able to pay for it."

"You've got two more years of high school," Kasey said, giving me a no-nonsense look. "That's plenty of time to turn things around. And there are quite a few scholarships for girls who want to pursue degrees in science."

I ran my thumb along the metal coil of the notebook. "I can't qualify for a scholarship. You have to have, like, a perfect GPA for that." Wasn't she listening?

"Not necessarily. Many take into account other types of achievement, or they're based on ethnicity or involvement in some group. Besides, as strong-willed as you are, you shouldn't have any problem bringing up your grades." She pinned me with another look. "*If* you decide it's important enough, that is."

Nothing like a little manipulation. The funny thing was, it didn't bother me. Having someone worry about my future, urge me to make something of myself, felt kind of nice. And without the rent or electric bill to worry about, it wouldn't be that big a deal to put a little effort into studying.

"Think about it, Jess." Kasey swung her feet to the floor as she leaned forward to pat my knee. "Cody can help with English, and I'll tutor you in any other subjects you're struggling with. If it'll put your mind at ease, we can go to the college administrative office next week and talk to them about scholarships."

Was this for real? "I guess it wouldn't hurt to consider it."

For the second time in as many days, Kasey's concern overwhelmed me. And the most amazing part? She seemed to think I was worth it.

## CHAPTER 54

Kasey's attorney called the next morning, voicing misgivings that she and Race weren't married. Apparently, if my mother came back and took them to court, things could get ugly. Kasey said that's just how it was, and told him to proceed with the paperwork.

That evening, she visited Springfield Tavern and a few other bars, trying to track down information about Lydia. She returned with nothing, her expression somber.

"I'm sorry, Jess."

"It's not like it's a surprise," I said, shrugging. If we found her, it would only complicate things. Maybe it was wrong to write off my own mother, but for once, I had a shot at a normal life. I didn't want anything messing that up.

I'd thought not working that week would make me crazy, but Cody found plenty to keep us busy. After introducing Rhett and Teri Sue to the best recreation spots in the lower Willamette Valley, we took an overnight trip to the coast. Kasey wasn't happy about that until Race convinced her nothing out of line was likely to happen with a little kid along.

Late Friday afternoon, we dropped off the others and headed home. Cody pulled into the driveway to park behind the Charger, blocking everyone in. As the Galaxie's engine ticked under the hood, he turned to face me, eyes solemn.

"Jess..." he said. And then he was pulling me close.

His lips found mine, their caress sending a tingle along every nerve in my body. As we lingered over a kiss that tasted faintly of salt-water taffy, the lemon-vanilla scent of butterfly bush wafted through the windows on a warm breeze.

"I had a great time," Cody whispered, his fingers tracing my cheek in a way that left me lightheaded. "Someday we'll take a trip like that on our own."

His eyes held mine, dark and dreamy. Any fool could see he was about to kiss me again, and that if he did, he wouldn't stop there.

"Cody . . ." I said. The idea of something more was like the shriek of a race engine—intoxicating and dangerous. I eased toward him, almost powerless against the magnetism, but for once, Cody had more sense than I did. He drew back, conjuring a playful look to end the moment.

"See," he said, tugging the bill of my Eugene Speedway cap down over my eyes, "it's not so bad taking a vacation, is it?"

I pushed my hat back into place. "I guess I could get used to it."

Too lazy to unload the car, we made do with transferring the crabs we'd bought in Newport from the ice chest to a bucket. I followed Cody at a leisurely pace as he dashed up the front steps in his wide-open fashion.

"Hey, guys," he called, flinging open the door. "Look what followed us home. Can we keep 'em?" He tracked sand across the carpet to Race and Kasey, who sat on the couch watching the six o'clock news. "Awesome, huh?" He tipped the bucket on edge, nearly dumping crabs all over the coffee table.

Kasey glanced briefly from the TV screen, where the spotted owl controversy was heating up. "Put them in the refrigerator. I'll cook them for dinner Sunday."

"You kids wanna watch some movies tonight?" Race asked. "We rented the *Star Wars* trilogy."

"Every one of those things is at least two hours long," Cody said. "You're gonna be up half the night."

"Well, Kasey needs a Han Solo fix." Race cast her a mournful look and let out a sigh. "I'm certainly not going to stand in the way of her addiction."

Cody laughed. "You're just jealous 'cause his ship's cooler

than your race car."

"Maybe so," Race said, hooking a thumb at his chest. "But if *I'd* been flying the Millennium Falcon, it never would've got caught in that tractor beam."

"If *you'd* been flying the Millennium Falcon, it never would've made it out of Mos Eisley."

Before Race could sling a comeback, Kasey interrupted. "In the kitchen with those, Cody, before Winston claims them."

Caught up in swapping insults, Cody hadn't noticed the cat, who stood on the coffee table, nose twitching as he strained to paw the potential meal.

"No, Winston!" Cody jerked the bucket away. A crab sailed across the living room and landed under the TV.

"Honestly!" Kasey said. "Give me those. I have to go check the chili anyway." She got up and took the bucket from Cody, stopping on her way to the kitchen to scoop up the liberated crab. Cody flopped in her spot, and Race grabbed the remote.

"So, did you guys have a good time?" he asked as he commenced channel surfing.

"It was awesome." Cody launched into a detailed account of the places we'd stopped. Before he'd made it halfway through our adventures, Kasey poked her head through the doorway.

"Cody, I need to get my car out. I have to run to the store for some lettuce."

"Aw, just take the Galaxie," he said, tossing her the keys.

"What—you're gonna let someone else drive your car?" Race leered at him in mock astonishment.

"At least with her, I don't have to worry about it getting caught in some tractor beam."

After dinner, we made ourselves comfortable in the living room, where Cody turned Kasey's Han Solo infatuation into a weapon with which to torment his uncle. Race put up with the ongoing digs until the carbon-freezing scene, when Cody became so obnoxious he had to be smacked upside the head with an OSU Beavers pillow.

We were halfway through *Return of the Jedi* when Cody decided his non-stop snacking hadn't been enough to sustain him.

"I'm totally jonesin' for some ice cream. We got any?"

Kasey shook her head. "You used it up making milkshakes for Jess."

He'd fixed me one every night until we'd left for our camping trip. A few more days of that and my jeans would fit properly.

Sighing, Cody hoisted himself up off the couch. "Guess I'll have to make a Dari Mart run."

Race sat on the floor, rubbing Kasey's feet in an attempt to prove the advantages of a flesh-and-blood boyfriend. "Don't expect us to pause the movie for you. It's already twelve-thirty and we've got a race tomorrow."

"No biggie." Cody stood up and stretched, exposing a band of bronzed skin at his waist. "Those Ewoks were turning my stomach, anyway."

With him gone, we were able to watch the next twenty minutes of the movie in peace. Then the staircase shook with the pounding of his feet.

"Kasey!" he demanded as he burst through the door. "Did you change my radio station?"

"Of course. You didn't expect me to put up with that noise you listen to, did you?" She rarely took on Race or Cody directly, but her quiet way of settling the score always proved amusing.

"You coulda just switched it off."

"What, and go without music for a whole two miles?"

Cody parked his arms across his chest, the ice cream bag dangling from one hand. "All that country music soaked into the upholstery. I'll probably have to get my car fumigated."

"I can lend you the money," Kasey said with a straight face. "But it'll have to come out of your paycheck."

Race's snicker filled the room.

Snorting, Cody tossed the hair out of his eyes. "Well, I'm gonna forgive you this time, but only because that disgusting station you listen to gave me an idea. You know what IRN is?"

"Vaguely," said Kasey. "I've never really listened to it. Interstate Radio Network. Isn't that right?"

"Yeah. It's a program for truck drivers." He turned to look at me meaningfully. "*Truck drivers.*"

My stomach went cold and heavy at his emphasis. "So what's your point?"

A blast of noise from the television cut Cody off before he could explain. Race hit the pause button, stilling the battle for Endor.

"They have this service," Cody said. "If someone you know is a trucker, and you have to get a message to him, you call this 800 number. The DJ makes an announcement for so-and-so to call the station, and when he does, they give him the message." Cody thrust his hand at me. "Here's the number."

Eleven digits stood out across his palm in a scribble of black ink. Speechless, I stared at them. A picture flashed in my head. A snippet from that dream of my father walking away. Emotions swooped in—loss, abandonment, betrayal. All so powerful they sucked me right back to that moment. But the dream was a lie, wasn't it? A fabrication conjured by my mind, based on hateful things Lydia had said.

"Well?" Cody prompted, hand outstretched. Eyes full of expectation.

I blinked at him, woozy, like I'd been swept back from another world.

"Damn, kid," Race said, his warm-hearted voice a comfort. "Give her a chance to take it in." His gaze held mine, empathizing. At least he got it.

Ironically, Kasey didn't. "It's quite a long shot. No one's heard from Jess's father in years."

"But it's worth a try," Cody argued. "What does she have to lose?"

What *did* I have to lose? If I was lucky, the fear my father didn't love me. If not, the hope he still did.

Race opened the end table drawer to fish out a notepad and pencil. "Here," he said, tossing them to Cody. "Write down the number and give Jess some space. She obviously needs time to think about it."

I shot him a grateful glance.

Cody transferred the number to the notepad and ripped off the page. Disappointment hung on him, not the least bit disguised by his attempt at indifference as he handed it to me.

"Your ice cream's gonna melt," Race said, clicking the remote. The shriek of blaster bolts filled the room. Much as I welcomed the distraction, I almost wished he hadn't restarted the movie. In a moment, the scene shifted to the reconciliation between Luke Skywalker and his father. Why couldn't Kasey have picked something else? I watched Vader throw the Emperor into the shaft to save Luke, heard the gentle strains of the Imperial March as the redeemed Anakin Skywalker died. And the whole time, I was acutely aware of Cody sneaking looks at me.

When the credits finally rolled, and the triumphant theme music surged through the room, I was no closer to understanding my feelings than I had been twenty minutes before.

Race yawned, stretched, and stood up. "Well, if Addamsen's gonna get his weekly butt-kicking, I'd better call it a night." He looked pointedly at Cody. "You might wanna consider that, too," he said before leaning down to kiss the top of Kasey's head.

Cody glanced at me and pulled himself to his feet.

"You do what you have to, kiddo." Race paused to give my

shoulder an affectionate squeeze then headed off to bed.

*Do what I have to.* But what was that? Even if my father wanted to see me, what chance was there that calling IRN would work? Dad might not hear the message. He might not even be driving a truck anymore. And what if he'd remarried and started a new family?

I sat on the couch for another half hour, mulling over the possibilities and trying to decide what I wanted. Race had put himself through a year of uncertainty when he could've picked up a pencil and found out the truth. A week ago I'd thought that was crazy. Now I understood.

I pulled the paper Cody had given me out of my pocket and stared at the numbers. What would I get if I called? Best-case scenario, what could I expect? A dad who'd walked out on me and hadn't come back. No matter what Lydia might've done to keep us apart, Dad didn't have to let that happen. He was a grown man. He could've come back and seen me for himself.

Unless he didn't want to.

I wadded up the paper and tossed it in the trash. To hell with him. What I had here, between this house and the Clines', was all the family I needed.

## CHAPTER 35

In the morning, Cody sidled up to me in the kitchen as I was pouring myself some Kix. "So ... um ... I don't suppose you happened to make that call last night?"

"No. And I'm not going to," I said, determined to put an end to this right now.

"But Jess—"

"I'm serious, Cody. Just let it go."

He stared at me, his dark eyes staging a battle over whether to keep pushing or honor my request. As sure as I was about this, I felt for him. It must be a huge letdown to find the key to my past and watch me toss it into the nearest blackberry patch.

Kasey filled her coffee cup and sat down at the table with the *Register Guard*. "It might not be a bad idea to try, Jess. Just so you have some closure."

Not her, too. "I don't need closure. I've had eight years to make peace with this, and I want to get on with my life."

"Okay," Kasey said, giving me a nod. She raised her cup, attention going back to the paper.

Cody muttered something under his breath, but he didn't bother me about it again.

That afternoon at the speedway, Teri Sue and I lounged on the hood of the Camaro, watching the Super Stocks hot lap and getting drunk on the aroma of racing fuel.

"Cody said there was a chance of you finding your daddy," said Teri Sue, her words almost lost in the shriek of high-powered engines.

Great. So now he was setting up sneak attacks. "Did he also say I told him to mind his own business?"

Teri Sue dipped her head at me. "Yup."

A car spun on the backstretch, careening toward the infield, and the roar tapered off until the driver limped back onto the track. I inhaled deeply as the scent of wild mint wafted across the pits.

"I don't need my dad," I said, sure Teri Sue would take Cody's side in this. "No matter what Kasey thinks about people lying to their kids, there's no reason he couldn't have tried harder. He didn't want anything to do with me, so why should I waste my time looking for him?"

"Hey, no need to convince me," said Teri Sue, swishing a hand through the air. "As far as I'm concerned, it's good riddance."

Relief rushed in to still my suspicions.

"But nothing's wrong, is it?" She squinted at me through the bright sunlight, shielding her eyes with one hand. "I mean, with you stayin' at Kasey's and all? That's not why Cody was looking?"

"Of course not."

"Oh. 'Cause I was thinking maybe you'd want to come stay with us. I mean, if it doesn't work out for you over there."

"Why wouldn't it work out?"

"Well, you know, if it got awkward living with your boyfriend and all." She fired off a devilish grin. "I bet you're riling ol' Cody up, prancing around the house in your baby doll pajamas."

Mortified, I slugged her in the leg. "You're not funny, Teri Sue!"

"Ow!" she hollered, rolling away from me and laughing. "I know, I know—you wouldn't be caught dead wearing baby doll pajamas."

"I don't prance, either," I said, slanting her a dirty look. "Unlike you, I'm sure."

Chuckling, Teri Sue rolled onto her back and shut her eyes against the sun. "Well, it's not just you and Cody. I'm thinking 'bout Rhett, too. I'll be moving into the dorms this fall, so it might be nice to have someone around to keep him company."

"You'll only be a couple miles from home. It's not like you're going to college in another state."

"Ha!" Teri Sue's laughter was sharp, even above the engine noise. "You think I'm gonna waste time hangin' out at the house when I'm living in a dorm full of cute guys?"

Good point. Still, when we'd talked about her going to the U of O, I'd never thought it meant she'd cut herself off from the rest of us.

"You and I will get together," Teri Sue reassured me, as if she'd heard my thoughts. "Heck, maybe I'll even sneak you into some wild parties. But I won't be home much. Rhett could use another big sister to look out for him. And he listens to you."

"He'd listen to you, too, if you treated him with a little respect." I gave her a reproachful look, but with her arm over her eyes, she couldn't see it. "You're always either bullying him or treating him like a baby. If he wants to go on loving his mom, it's his own business."

"I can't help it. He's my baby brother."

"Damn it, Teri Sue, you could at least give it a shot."

She huffed out an exaggerated sigh. "Okay, but you better think about what I said. You could have my room, and I'll use the guest room when I to come visit. I know how much you like all those windows."

Cody easily took second in the trophy dash. He missed winning the heat by half a fender length and returned to the pits wearing a serious look. While it was only a matter of time before he claimed a victory, I wished it would hurry up and happen.

Teri Sue eked out another top five finish, but it was Race who stole the show. On the last lap of the main, he swiped the lead from Addamsen just as the two cars took the checkered flag. A few minutes later, when Ted Greene hustled him into position for the trophy presentation, Race swept the microphone from his hand.

"Could I get my crew chief, Kasey McCormick, to come out here?" he asked.

The only thing unusual about the request was that Race put it into words. Family and crew always joined the winning driver for a photo.

"What the heck's he up to?" Teri Sue asked as Kasey swung her legs over the wall and headed for the track.

"I dunno, but I think I'll just wait here and see," Cody said.

When Kasey circled to the far side of the Dart, Race turned to greet her with his most alluring full-throttle grin. Then, eyes glowing in a rapturous look, he dropped to one knee.

"Holy—" Cody leaned forward, both hands on the pit wall, eyes wide.

Race pulled a small box from the pocket of his firesuit. "Kasey," he said, opening it and holding it out to her. "I know I'm about as hard-headed as they come, and sometimes I'm a monumental pain in the ass, but could you see it in your heart to marry me?"

An uncanny hush fell over the speedway.

Kasey smiled. "Of course."

All hell broke loose in the stands, but it was nothing compared to the hollering coming out of Cody. "He did it! He finally did it!" Cody turned to sling an arm around my waist and pull me close. "Can you believe it?"

I shook my head, staring at the unfolding scene as the photographer madly flashed shots of Kasey accepting the ring.

Beside me, Teri Sue practically swooned. "That," she sighed, "is the most romantic thing I've ever seen."

Cody couldn't stand still the rest of the night. He bounced around the pits, recounting the proposal to anyone who'd listen, even though they'd all seen it themselves.

"'Bout time he got around to it," said Race's friend Denny, slapping Cody on the back with a mammoth hand. "You don't know how happy I am to see it." As he lumbered away to offer Race and Kasey his congratulations, Cody went back to jabbering with Teri Sue, who was already speculating about wedding plans.

Later, as we were loading up our gear, Race drifted over and wrapped an arm around my shoulders.

"Thanks for the inspiration, Jess," he said, giving me a sideways squeeze. "I owe you one."

"What?" I peered up at him, totally confused.

Race just grinned before letting go and sauntering off toward his car.

Oh man. What did he mean by that?

Kasey wasn't the type to go giddy at a marriage proposal, but for the next couple of days she carried herself with a satisfaction that revealed how much Race's gesture had moved her. Her contented glow seemed to have as much to do with his renewed self-respect as the idea of getting married.

Cody was the one who couldn't stop talking about it, and Teri Sue, always the matchmaker, had plenty to add. You'd think it was their own wedding they were discussing, for as much as they kept bringing it up.

Even though I was glad to see everyone happy, the more I thought about what Race had said, the more it bothered me. Remembering the phone call from Kasey's lawyer, I worried it had somehow forced his hand. What if Race felt pressured into proposing because he thought I wouldn't be able to stay with them unless he and Kasey were married? I didn't want anything to do with that, and Kasey deserved better.

At work on Monday, when I managed to find him alone for a minute, I mustered up the nerve to talk.

"Can I ask you something?"

"Sure, kiddo, go for it." He hunched over the front fender of a Nova, fighting a stubborn exhaust manifold bolt. When it snapped, slamming his knuckles into the rusty surface, I winced.

"The other night at the speedway," I began, not daring to look him in the face. "The stuff you said about inspiration ... it wasn't because of what the attorney said, was it?"

Race laughed as he tapped the ratchet against the engine to knock loose the head of the bolt. "Are you kidding? Can you imagine what Kasey would've done if she thought that was my motivation?" He faked a shudder. "She'd have turned me down right there in front of God and everyone. Now *that* would've been humiliating. And don't doubt for a minute she has it in her."

I didn't.

Race stuck the ratchet on the remaining bolt. As I watched him work, I saw the faintest awkwardness in the way his fingers moved, like the difference between someone who's comfortable with tools and someone who's never handled them. If I hadn't known about the wreck, I would've assumed he was simply a little clumsy.

"I've gotta admit, the attorney made me think, but that's not the reason I proposed. It was just time. I shoulda done it months ago. God knows we've both been wanting it long enough." The bolt broke free with a crack, and Race worked it out of the head, pausing to look at me before wiggling the manifold away from the studs. "The thing is, Jess, I might not have realized it was time if it wasn't for you. Here I am feeling sorry for myself, and all the while you haven't made so much as a whimper about the crap your mom dumped on you."

Was he for real? "Nobody thinks you're feeling sorry for yourself."

"*I* do. I've spent the last year putting my pride before everything else, including Kasey's happiness. That's not what I'd call honorable behavior."

I traced my fingers over the top of the Nova's grill. "People understand," I said, sneaking a glance at him. "Anyway, you're still my hero."

Race shook his head as he lifted the manifold from the engine compartment. "Kiddo, getting in a race car doesn't make you a hero. There's no courage involved, just a lack of fear. What takes real guts is being scared spitless and doing what you have to anyway. And on that count, you're leading the pack."

My face flared red-hot, and I ducked my head.

"What's the matter?" teased Race. "Didn't you ever think you might wind up someone's hero?"

As a matter of fact, I never did.

Living in Kasey's house was one of the best things that ever happened to me. While spending so much time with Cody could occasionally be awkward, there was always something to laugh about with him and Race around. Best of all, I no longer felt the need to walk on eggshells, the way I had with Lydia.

Seeing how Race and Kasey got along, especially since Race's proposal, provided a whole new viewpoint on romance. The simplest things made it clear how much they cared about each other: a gentle touch in passing, an amused look across the dinner table, an off-hand kiss—the gesture so familiar it had become automatic. After years of watching my mother sabotage her relationships, I'd come to believe true love was a myth.

Thursday evening, I ruminated over this as Cody and I relaxed on the deck, watching the sun slip below the horizon. In the dwindling twilight, a lone cumulus cloud blazed with a fiery salmon glow. Could Cody and I have a relationship like Race and Kasey's? Could I ever be that lucky?

The lights of Eugene were just flickering on when Kasey

stuck her head out the front door.

"Jess?" she said, her smile brightening the dusk. "You're probably not going to believe this, but your dad's on the phone."

## CHAPTER 36

"What?" I bolted upright, every bit of peacefulness obliterated by a rush of shock. "What do you mean, my dad's on the phone? I threw away that number."

"We can discuss it later," Kasey said. "Right now you need to talk to him."

My stomach set up like concrete as I realized what had happened. "You called, didn't you? I thought you were going to drop it. How could you go behind my—"

"Jess! Just go talk to him. It'll be okay, I promise."

Furious, I stalked off to answer the phone. But I didn't quite have the guts to slam the door behind me.

My thoughts sputtered and my insides churned as I crossed the living room. Kasey should've listened to me. She had no right to make that call. But she'd found him, and he wanted to talk to me. What if . . .

My hand trembled as I lifted the receiver to my ear. I drew a deep breath. "Dad?"

"Jessie!" His voice came at me sounding exactly as it had when I was little. My mind whirled, ratcheting back and forth between then and now, trying to make sense of this detail that had no place in my current reality.

"Honey, I'm so sorry. I never meant for you to think I'd abandoned you. I swear I sent that child support check every month."

The line went quiet except for the hum and pop of the long distance connection, and I did nothing to fill the silence. Kasey must've told him everything.

"Jessie? Are you there?"

My tongue broke loose of its paralysis. "Lydia said there wasn't any child support. She said you just left, and she didn't know where you were."

"That's not how it was. I know your mom got those checks, because she cashed them."

The words hit my ears, but they didn't register. "Why didn't you write? Why wouldn't you talk to me when you called?" My heart pounded as I spit out questions that had gone unanswered all these years.

"Honey, I begged your mom to put you on the phone every time. She said you didn't want to speak to me. And I sent letters—dozens of 'em—but when she told me you wouldn't open them, I stopped. I always mailed a card on your birthday, though. Every single year." He hesitated, and a smile slipped into his voice. "I sent you a check for a hundred dollars just last March because I figured you'd be saving up to buy a car."

Something twinged inside me, but he wasn't getting off that easily. "I never got any cards or letters. Not one."

"I sent 'em, swear to God." The earnestness in his voice made it clear he was telling the truth. "It doesn't surprise me that Lydia never told you. After she lost the house, she refused to give me your new address. Everything went to a post office box."

A post office box. I'd never known she'd had one. I pictured Dad's letters carelessly tossed in some trashcan, and a white-hot rage filled my head. Kasey had been right. And Lydia hadn't just lied to me, she'd lied to Dad too, playing us against each other. Everything I'd believed since I was eight was wrong.

"I thought you didn't love me anymore," I said, my voice barely breaking a whisper.

"Aw, Jessie. I never stopped loving you, not for one minute. And I never will."

I sank down on the arm of the couch, so overwhelmed by the chaotic jumble of feelings washing over me that my legs wouldn't hold me up.

"Maybe I should've tried harder, should've come home and fought for you," he said. "But I couldn't take care of you, being on the road all the time. And I believed your mom when she said you wouldn't forgive me. I figured I deserved to be hated."

Part of me wanted to say I didn't hate him, but I couldn't. He had one thing right. He should've tried harder. All that crap about being on the road and believing Lydia was a lame excuse.

"I need to see you," he said. "And I'm gonna, just as soon as I can. I've got to deliver a load to Denver, but then I should be able to get some time off. If not, I'll talk to my dispatcher and ask if I can get a run out that direction."

My tiny glimmer of sympathy faded. Eight years, and he couldn't find a way to work me into his schedule? How could he expect me to go back to where we'd been?

"Look, Jessie, I'm sorry, but there's a line here at the pay phone. I've gotta let you go. How 'bout letting me speak to that lady you're staying with? I need to get the number for her lawyer and all."

That last bit zapped me like an electric shock. I was supposed to stay with Kasey. Go to school with Cody, bring my grades up, think about college. How would this affect everything?

"I'll call back in the next few days, all right? Maybe Sunday. I love you, honey."

How could I answer? I laid the phone on the end table and went out to get Kasey. As she slipped into the house, I let my weight fall back against the rough cedar shingles, eyes closed, trying to make sense of what just happened.

The deck creaked. Cody's arms went around me. He held me tight and didn't say a word.

For the next few days, I lived in a stupor, alternating between anger and hope, not understanding my feelings. Everyone seemed to think I should be overjoyed, and on one level I was. But I couldn't stop thinking about how easily my dad had given up, and I couldn't forgive Kasey for throwing a monkey wrench into our plans. After everything she'd done for me, I was afraid to come right out and confront her, so I avoided her as much as possible, brushing her off when she tried to explain.

Teri Sue stood staunchly in my corner, the experience with her mom making her side against my dad, but only Race seemed to understand my confliction. Saturday night at the track, he caught me alone by the Camaro while Teri Sue was off chatting with Kit McKenzie.

"Cody sure looked good out there in his heat," he said. "I expect him to win one any day now."

"I hope so." I busted loose the upper control arm bolts so I could add another alignment shim to the right front suspension. The tire temps on the outer edge were running a little high.

"You've been kinda quiet since your dad called. How are you holding up?"

I shrugged.

"It's a big change. Bound to be a shock after all these years."

"It didn't have to be. Kasey could've left well enough alone." I pried the control arm away from its mount on the frame, squeezing a spacer into the gap. "She made a mess of everything. I don't even know my dad anymore, and now he's going to barge back into my life."

Race sighed, spreading his hands out over the fender. "Honestly, kiddo, she didn't expect it to go anywhere, but she had to try."

"Why?" I looked up from fitting the wrench onto one of the bolts, my eyes meeting his dead-on. "I was happy the way things were."

"You don't steal someone's kid away without making every effort to find him. Kasey never could've lived with herself if she hadn't followed that lead."

Right. How could it be stealing if the victim didn't care about what was being taken?

"I was just getting used to things," I said. "I'm tired of my life changing every few weeks."

Race nodded, running a hand through his hair. "I hear ya, Jess. But it'll work out. Just because your dad's back in the picture doesn't mean the rest of us are going anywhere."

Dad called back the next day and told me he'd be in town the following weekend. "I can only stay a couple of days, but it'll give us a chance to catch up," he said.

The statement immediately drained some of my tension. If his job wouldn't let him get away for more than two days after not seeing me in all this time, what were the chances he'd mess up my life? Maybe he'd let me stay with Kasey, paying her for my room and board. Nobody would have to make any major changes.

Once I came to that conclusion, it was easier to focus on the good parts of seeing him again. Even though the idea made me nervous, I wanted to catch up, impress him with all I'd done on the Camaro. He'd been the one who'd turned me on to Fords. Would he be proud of the modifications I'd made to the Pinto? Was there a chance things would go right for a change?

By Friday night, the combination of hopes and fears had me so anxious I barely slept. I crawled out of bed at dawn, even before Kasey, who rose early enough to give the roosters their cue.

"Jess, quit pacing," she said a couple of hours later as the clock dragged its hands around to eight-thirty. Dad wasn't due until ten, but I couldn't sit still. What if this all fell apart—if he'd changed so much he wasn't the person I remembered?

The phone rang and I jumped.

Cody snatched it up. "It's for you, Jess. Teri Sue." He dropped the cool plastic into my hand.

Why was she calling at that hour? "Yeah?" I said.

"Jess, I know this is the day your daddy's s'posed to come into town," she said, her voice strained with tension. "But I really need your help."

"What's wrong?"

"It's Rhett again. He's up in his tree house and won't come down."

Oh man. What had she done to him now? "What happened?"

"Grandpa called last night. Mama had to go back to the hospital. She's been wandering off and getting lost. A couple days ago, someone found her standing in the middle of Highway 70. It was a miracle no one hit her."

"Wow. Poor Rhett. I can't imagine having to tell him."

"We didn't. When he figured out Daddy was talking to Grandpa, he snuck in the kitchen and picked up the other line. After he heard, he slammed down the phone and ran outside. I hunted forever till I found him in his tree house. He stayed up there all night."

A shiver scurried down the back of my neck. His fort was nothing more than a six-by-six platform. "And your dad let him?"

"Daddy's no good at climbing trees. He called up to him, but when Rhett didn't answer, he said we should leave him be, that he'd come down when he was ready." Teri Sue broke off to take a shaky breath, and when she went on, her voice quavered. "I'm worried, Jess. Rhett's never done anything like this before."

"Okay, I'll be right over."

Cody's eyes drilled me as I hung up the phone. "What's going on?"

I gave them a brief explanation, surprised by the relief that whooshed through me at the idea of putting off my reunion.

"Jess, your father will be here soon," Kasey said. "Surely they can deal with Rhett themselves."

"No they can't. He doesn't listen to Teri Sue. Besides, it's not like Dad's going to drive three thousand miles then just turn around and leave."

"All right," Kasey said with a sigh. "But try to make it quick."

\* \* \*

I pulled into the Clines' driveway to see Teri Sue peering up into the alder at the corner of the porch.

"He's just sitting up there like a statue," she said, giving me an anxious glance. "He hasn't said a word since last night."

"Don't worry, I'll take care of it."

I worked my way through the evenly spaced branches until I reached the platform where Rhett slouched, legs dangling over the edge.

"Hey," I said.

Rhett stared silently at the yard. His brace banged the framing under the platform as he swung his legs. His sorrowful mood seemed so out of place in the beautiful, blue-skied morning, with birds singing as the scent of Mark's roses drifted up from the flowerbed below.

I scooched over beside Rhett. "I'm sorry about your mama."

His brace banged louder.

"You wanna talk about it?"

"No."

"Okay," I said, cupping my hands over the edge of the platform and staring out at the roof of the barn. "Your sister's really worried, you know. Your dad, too."

"I don't care."

"What about me? Do you care if I'm worried?"

Rhett's knobby shoulders arced upward in a shrug.

"I know it's hard, hearing about your mama. But maybe going back to the hospital will be a good thing for her. Maybe it'll help."

His chin dropped against his chest. "It didn't last time."

The cynicism warned off further hopeful words, and I wasn't sure what else to say. Truthfully, I didn't believe his mom would get better any more than Mark did.

A breeze rustled the alder leaves, and dappled sunlight played over Rhett's tear-slicked cheeks. Hating to see him so defeated, I tucked an arm around his shoulders.

"It's my fault Mama's sick," he whispered.

"Of course it's not."

He began to shake. "She always said be careful, and I wasn't." A sob broke loose. "I-I made her hurt me. If she hadn't done that, she wouldn't be sick."

"Oh, Rhett!" I pulled him close, feeling his tremors as he wept and hiccupped. "You were just a little kid. She was the grown up. It was her job to look out for you, and she didn't."

"I should've been careful!"

"And she should've, too. She was the one driving. She was supposed to pay attention."

"I want her back, Jess." He gulped at the cool morning air. "I miss my mama!"

"I know, Rhett. I know."

He turned toward me, burying his face in my shirt, the tears coming fast and hot. For a long time he cried and I gently rocked him, wishing I could erase his pain. Finally, the sobbing gave way to whimpering, and then to sniffles. He pulled back, leaving a wet spot on the front of my T-shirt.

"I-I'm okay now."

"You sure?"

"Yeah." He rubbed the back of his hand across both cheeks before cutting me a sidelong look. "Jess … can I ask you something?"

"Sure."

His eyes darted away, fixing on his grubby jeans as he worked a finger through a hole in the denim. "When Teri Sue goes off to college, are you and Cody gonna stop coming around?"

"Of course not. You're our friend, too."

"But I'm just a kid. Y'all are gonna be so busy going on dates and stuff you'll probably forget all about me."

I reached for his hand, which now toyed with the frayed,

white threads around the tear. "You aren't just some kid to me, you're the little brother I always wished for. I could never forget about you."

"Promise?" His fingers gripped mine, and he looked up into my eyes.

I hooked my free arm around his shoulders. "I promise."

I figured Rhett could use some company, so I took him back to Kasey's. Having him around might make the meeting with Dad go easier. I wondered briefly if it was fair to force him to watch us reunite after what had happened with his mom, but I pushed the worry aside. Shielding him was where Teri Sue had made her mistakes, and I couldn't exactly hide the fact that my father was back in my life.

As I turned onto Spring Boulevard and caught a glimpse of Dad's red and silver Freightliner, a lightning bolt zipped through me. He still had the same rig?

"Is that his truck?" Rhett asked, voice bright with excitement.

"Yeah."

"Cool." His face twisted up in a lopsided smile. "You think he'd let me sit in it?"

"Of course."

All the nervousness I'd felt over the past eleven days came back a hundred-fold as I climbed the steps to the front door. Rhett almost stumbled over me when I reached the top and hesitated on the deck.

"What are ya waiting for?" he demanded.

"Nothing." My heart revved up to redline as I reached for the knob. Taking a deep breath, I opened the door.

## CHAPTER 57

As I walked into the living room, Race, Kasey, and Cody glanced up, interrupted in the middle of an animated conversation. Across from me, in the easy chair Winston usually monopolized, sat my father. At first I could only stare. He looked almost the same as the day he'd left. The wrinkle lines at the corners of his hazel eyes had grown more pronounced, and he'd gained a little weight, but other than that it was as if he'd never been gone. He even wore the Ford cap, threadbare and grubby now, that I'd bought him for Christmas the year I was seven. The sight of it made my stomach clench.

"Dad," I said, ten thousand emotions fighting for dominance inside me.

"Jessie..." A grin spread like wildfire across his tanned and weathered face. "Looks like my little Grease Monkey is all grown up."

The nickname sent another twinge through my gut. Part of me wanted to run to him and throw myself into his arms. Another part threatened to scream, "Where the hell have you been all this time?" Instead of doing either, I stood there and said nothing.

Dad got up and swooped me into one of his famous bear hugs, gripping me hard, as if trying to pack eight years of love into that single embrace. My arms responded in kind, even though my feelings still swung like a pendulum, back and forth between love and hurt.

"Cody," said Kasey, "why don't you and Rhett go in the kitchen for some cookies so Jess and her father can spend a little time together?" She stood and placed her hand on my arm. "Race and I are going down to his shop to get the car ready. We'll see you at the track."

The living room emptied, and I was left alone with my father. I stared at him, not having the slightest clue as to what to say. I wanted to forgive him, to enjoy this moment, but I couldn't let go of the smoldering anger.

"I can't believe you're still wearing that hat," I said. How could he keep it for eight years and yet not try to find me?

He smiled. "Of course I am. It reminds me of my little Grease Monkey."

A pang ripped through my heart, and that only stoked the fire. "It's disgusting," I said. "You should've thrown it out."

Dad flinched, but recovered quickly. "How 'bout showing me this Pinto your friends mentioned?"

The Pinto. Right. That would give us something to talk about. I led him down the steps to the driveway.

"I see your boyfriend has good taste in cars," Dad said as we passed the Galaxie.

The comment doused the flames a little. "What—you think I'd date a Chevy guy?"

I lifted the Pinto's hood and filled the silence by giving Dad a blow-by-blow description of the work I'd done. Watching his reaction, every head nod and smile, was like learning who he was all over again. And I kind of liked that person, sort of wanted to trust him. But I wasn't sure I could.

When I fired up the Pinto, Dad grinned and let out a little yip. "Sounds like music," he said, throwing a friendly arm around my neck.

I stiffened, but didn't duck away.

"How 'bout you take me for a spin?"

I drove him around the ritzy neighborhoods south of 30th, with their windy roads. Behind the wheel, I felt more at ease, so I answered Dad's questions about school, the speedway, and what had happened with Lydia. By the time we got back to Kasey's, he didn't seem like quite so much of a stranger.

Rhett was eager for a ride in the Freightliner, and Dad

wanted to meet Teri Sue and see the Camaro, so we climbed into the truck and headed for the Clines'. Rhett beamed the whole way, shouting, "Woo-hoo!" when Dad let him work the air horn.

Seeing how patient Dad was as he answered Rhett's babbled questions and let him crawl into the sleeper berth to look around, I was reminded of how he'd been with me when I was young. A little more of my resentment evaporated. Maybe this could work out.

At the Clines', I introduced Dad to Mark and Teri Sue before taking him to the barn to show him the Camaro. Rhett hardly let me finish before dragging him into the woods to see the pond, then around the yard to admire the weather forecasting equipment. When they came back, Teri Sue whipped us up some pulled pork sandwiches, and we ate on the front porch, enjoying the warm, fragrant afternoon.

Dad and Mark hit it off right away, which released a little more of the pressure. I sat back and sipped my sweet tea, letting my friends do the talking. By the time we left for the track at four o'clock, Dad riding with me in the Pinto, I almost felt comfortable with him.

At several points during the day, I considered asking Dad about living arrangements, but the few times somebody else wasn't around, I couldn't drum up the nerve. Things were going okay so far, and I didn't want to jinx it. I worried he'd bring up the subject, or Kasey would say something when we got to the speedway, but neither did.

Dad fit right in with the racing crowd, getting into a good-natured argument with Kasey over the merits of Ford versus Mopar, and discussing the latest Winston Cup standings with Race. He couldn't stop grinning at me as I prepared the Camaro for competition, which only made me self-conscious.

But soon enough, I had my hands too full to worry about

him being there. First, Race crashed during practice, tweaking the Dart's right front suspension. Then Cody's engine began to backfire through the carb on his second qualifying lap. Kasey couldn't help him because even though she'd cobbled Race's car together enough for him to time in, she still had to fine-tune the set-up.

"Jess?" Cody said, eying me hopefully. He was good at swapping out parts, but diagnosing mechanical problems had never been his strong suit.

I glanced at Teri Sue, wondering if she'd consider it a conflict of interests. She'd timed in poorly and was in the 'B' dash herself.

She shrugged. "Doesn't bother me."

"Okay, crank her up," I said. We had maybe ten minutes before time trials were over and their dash would begin.

Cody flipped the ignition switch and pressed the starter button, while I worked the throttle linkage from under the hood. The engine caught and the carburetor promptly let out a belch.

"Think it's a fuel problem?" Cody asked.

"No, it's got to be ignition."

Dad leaned over the fender. "That's what I'd guess."

"The coil?" Cody suggested, coming over to hover at my side.

"More likely the plug wires. You've got a cylinder trying to fire out of sequence." I chewed my lip. If it was dark, it would be easy to see a bad wire arcing, but in full daylight the only way to remedy the problem would be to replace them all. No time for that. I glanced at the distributor cap, wondering if I could manage. And then I saw it. One of the hold-down clips was sprung. Whoever'd taken the cap off the last time hadn't seated it properly.

"Kill it," I said. Cody obliged.

I popped the cap and wiggled the rotor loose. The metal

contact had been knocked off-center, cracking the plastic around it.

"Here you go," I said, showing it to Cody. "Did you have the cap off earlier?"

"Yeah."

"You must not have got it back on straight. The rotor probably hit one of the contacts."

Dad grinned. "Good call."

"Does Kasey have another one?" I asked.

"Kasey *always* has another one." Cody rifled through the milk crate that held their spare parts until he located a new rotor still in its box.

"Hurry," he said as I fumbled to open it. "They're almost done timing in the Super Stocks."

I glanced at the back pit exit. Only one car left to qualify. After that, they'd play the national anthem and Cody's dash would be up.

The part fell into my hand. Oh crap. A *Ford* rotor. Some bozo at the parts store must've stuck it in the wrong box.

"What?" demanded Cody with a hint of panic, obviously reading my distress.

"It's the wrong one."

"Are you kidding?" His voice squeaked like an eighth-grader's. "What are we gonna do?"

The parts store was right down the street, but there wasn't time to make the run. I glanced at Kasey. Distracting her could jeopardize Race's standing in the championship. I'd have to figure this out on my own. I spread my hands over the fender, staring down at the engine.

"Why did I have to run a Dodge?" Cody groaned. If he'd been driving a Chevy, we could've borrowed the part from practically anyone. As it stood, there was only one other Chrysler rotor in the infield.

"I know," I said as the opening strains of the Star Spangled

Banner crackled over the loudspeaker. "We'll use Race's."

Cody shook his head. "Uh uh. What if something happens to it?"

"Nothing's going to happen to it."

"No," Cody said, his tone resolute. "You didn't see what it did to Race, losing that championship last year. If it happens again, it's not gonna be because of me."

Oh man. Now what? It wasn't like I could miraculously heal a busted rotor.... Or could I? All it had to do was hold together for a four-lap race. "All right, I'll fix yours."

"Can you?" Cody's dark eyes pinned me in an anxious look.

"Sure," I said, dodging his gaze. "It'll hold through the dash, and Dad can get a new one between races." I forced the contact back into place, hoping I sounded confident enough to convince him. The rivet would keep the two pieces together, but with the plastic cracked, there was no guarantee the metal tab would stay properly aligned.

"You sure that's gonna work?"

"Positive," I lied as Teri Sue's Camaro rumbled by to line up. "Now get in the car."

While I replaced the cap and rotor, Dad helped Cody with his window net.

"Get a move-on, Everett!" hollered Ted Greene. The 'B' dash cars were already pulling onto the track.

"*Hurry!*" Cody shouted.

I slammed the hood. "Go!"

The engine howled to life and the Dart lurched forward, kicking up a cloud of dust.

"You know it'll take a lot of luck to keep that thing together," Dad said as Cody gunned it through the pits, swerving into the weeds to avoid the 'A' dash lined up at the track entrance.

"What else was I going to do?"

Dad squeezed the back of my neck and grinned. "You always

were my gutsy girl."

As Cody pulled onto the backstretch, the 'B' dash growled across the start-finish line for their warm-up lap. If he didn't catch up with them before they took the green flag, he'd be disqualified.

Kasey joined Dad and me in our sprint to the pit wall. The three cars in Cody's competition accelerated out of turn two. The Dart surged down the front stretch, and Cody slung it into the corner. He caught up with the others just as they headed into turn three.

"He made it," Race panted, having bolted across the pits after parking in the line-up for his own dash. "What was wrong?"

"Busted rotor," I said. "I hope it holds together. The spare was mis-boxed."

Out on the track, the green flag flew. All four cars raced into turn one bunched together. Coming out of two, Cody veered to the inside and got a nose under Danny Lamar. Though he couldn't swing wide enough to take advantage of the Dart's full power, he managed to pull even with Lamar's door. Teri Sue tucked in behind the Dart, forcing Todd Griffin to drop into last place.

"So far so good," I said, my ears straining for the slightest miss.

"Cross your fingers," Dad muttered.

The Dart swooped through the corner, edging ahead of Lamar. As it roared onto the front stretch, it left the Mustang behind.

Race howled in delight and turned to give me a high five. But Cody hadn't won yet. Now Teri Sue was challenging him down low. By the end of the straightaway, the Camaro's nose pulled even with the Dart's rear quarter panel. An unwritten rule stated that unless a car's bumper reached your door, the groove was yours. But nervous drivers often played it safe and gave away the line. Cody seemed through with being a victim of his doubts. Tearing into turn one, he dropped down to hold the lead.

Teri Sue burst out onto the backstretch, pulling alongside Cody again. This time her bumper crept up even with the leading edge of the rear tire before she had to back off.

Beside me, Race sucked in his breath. The cars were too evenly matched. If Cody didn't do something, Teri Sue would get around him on the next lap.

Anticipating the problem, Cody took a lower line zipping onto the front stretch. His position made it difficult for Teri Sue to get on the throttle down low, but didn't leave her space to sneak around on the outside.

"Smart driving," Race said.

Cody followed up by taking the next corner slightly wide. Teri Sue didn't have room to squeeze underneath, and couldn't find the horses to pass up high. Switching tactics, she went for intimidation. Through turns one and two, she dogged Cody's back bumper, riding so close I couldn't be sure there wasn't contact. In turns three and four, she went at him again. Cody didn't flinch.

Oh man. Who was I supposed to pull for? I hated to see Teri Sue lose, but my heart was one hundred percent behind Cody.

The white flag whipped over the track. One lap to go. Teri Sue made a bid to pass on the outside and failed. She dove into turn one up high, cutting a late apex to get a jump coming out of two. The rear end broke loose, and she had to back off.

"He's got it now!" Race said as the Dart screamed out of the corner.

Then the carburetor let out a series of pops.

Cody kept his foot in it, but as the 13 car sailed down the backstretch, it clearly lost power. To compensate, he cut low. If

Teri Sue wanted around him, she'd have to do it on the outside. Cody plowed into three with the Camaro only a fender-length behind.

All through the corner, the Dart backfired. I held my breath as Teri Sue edged ahead. The two cars roared out of turn four and sprinted toward the flag tower almost side by side.

"Come on, come on!" I muttered.

The checkered flag snapped wildly as the Dart screamed across the finish line, a mere bumper ahead of Teri Sue's Camaro.

"Yes!" shouted Race, shaking both fists in the air and letting loose with a westernized version of the Clines' rebel yell. Pride radiated from him with such intensity you'd think he'd just won his own first race.

Cody circled the track to park on the start-finish line. He pulled himself out of the car, gave the fans a sweeping look, and turned to grin at us. At his bidding, Race and Kasey scrambled over the pit wall for the photo. "You, too," Race called to me when I hesitated.

As I joined Cody beside the Dart, he slipped his arm around me, hand shaking with excitement.

"I always wondered what it would be like, having everyone cheer for me the way they do for Race," he said.

"So how does it feel?"

He didn't have to answer. His grin, blazing brighter than the flash of the photographer's camera, said it all.

## CHAPTER 58

Sunday morning, after Cody and I gave Dad a tour of both shops, he said he wanted some one-on-one time with me, so we took Cody home and went out to lunch. I chose Pietro's, since I seldom could convince Cody to go there instead of Track Town.

"Get whatever you want," Dad said as we stood at the counter, surrounded by the red faux-velvet 1800s saloon décor. "I'm easy."

I ordered a Great Northwest.

The comfortable energy we'd worked into yesterday had continued all morning, and we kept up an easy conversation about Cody's win as we waited for the pizza.

When it finally arrived, I slid a piping hot piece onto my plate and nibbled at it, trying not to burn the top of my mouth.

"Excellent choice," Dad said after taking his first bite. "You know what makes this so good? The cheddar cheese."

"Exactly."

We made our way through a couple of slices, talking about the races as I tried to work up the courage to tackle the one subject we hadn't yet broached.

Dad beat me to it. "So . . . I guess we should talk about what happens next."

"Kasey said I could stay with her," I said in a rush. "That's probably the best plan. I mean, so you don't have to spend a lot of money on an apartment or something."

"Whoa now. Hold up a minute. I know you're all settled in, but what about you and me? I haven't seen you in eight years." He pushed his plate away. "My cousin Dave has agreed to let you stay with his family back in Tennessee. That way I'll be able to spend more time with you."

"What?" Dread coursed through me in a gut-churning

wave. The pizza in my stomach solidified to granite. "You want me to move?" He couldn't be serious.

"Dave's family are great people—you'll love 'em. And you'll be right in the heart of stock car racing country."

That was supposed to sell me? What about my friends? What about my life? "I don't want to be in stock car racing country. I want to be here." I smacked my hand on the table. "Anyway, what does it matter where I live? You're on the road all the time. And you own your truck, don't you? Can't you just take runs on this side of the country?"

This couldn't be real. How could he expect me to leave? But I realized, on one level, I'd been worried about something like this all along.

Dad sighed and leaned forward, arms on the table as he played with the saltshaker. "It's not that simple, honey. Ninety percent of my work comes from one company, and they ship mostly on the other side of the Rockies. I get out here from time to time, but I'd see you a lot more if you were with Dave."

This was bullshit. "You haven't seen me in years, and suddenly you want to start being my dad?"

"Jessie—"

"You can't uproot me! This is my home."

Dad looked down at the saltshaker. "You wouldn't have to leave right away. School doesn't start until after Labor Day. You'll have a couple of weeks to finish up what you're doing with Teri Sue's car and say goodbye to everyone."

"I don't want to say goodbye! I have a whole life here. A boyfriend, and two great jobs, and people who treat me like family."

Dad finally found the guts to look up at me. "*I'm* your family, Jessie."

Seriously? He thought he could play that card? "Right. You should've thought of that eight years ago. If you were going to put up a fight, *that's* when you should've done it." I pushed away from the table. "I'm not going anywhere. You can get right back in your truck and drive to wherever the hell you've been all this time, because I'm not leaving."

I stood up and headed for the exit.

"Jessie!"

I kept walking, pushing through the front door and into the bright August sunlight.

"Jessie, please!" Dad followed me out to the parking lot. "Honey, stop. Just listen to me."

I turned around and let him catch up. "No, I'm not going to listen. If you care about me, you won't try to force me into this. You'll walk away and leave well enough alone."

"You know I can't do that. I love you. I've got eight years of catching up to do."

My hands found their way to my hips. "And whose fault is that?"

"I explained what happened," Dad said, raking his fingers through his sandy hair. "I had no idea your mom was lying to us. I just wanted to do what was best for you. She absolutely doted on you, and I thought she'd do a better job of raising you than I ever could."

Was that how he justified the whole thing? "She's an alcoholic, Dad. She didn't take care of me—I took care of her. Do you know what it's like to be ten years old and have to drag your mother home from a bar because she's so drunk they took her keys?"

"Honey, I had no idea."

"That's right," I said, pointing a finger at him. "Because you gave up. You took off and never looked back."

"Jessie—"

"You should've tried harder. Didn't you ever have a run to Oregon in all those years? Couldn't you have stopped here just once and tried to find me?"

Dad looked down at the weeds growing out of a crack

between the curb and asphalt, his shoulders in a slump. "I didn't have anything to go on. Not an address, not even a phone number."

"You had a PO box. Why didn't you go to the police and ask for help? Or try the schools? There's only so many around here. I had to be registered at one of them, didn't I?"

Dad's forehead wrinkled up in a dumbfounded look. "I never thought of any of that."

"Why not? I thought of it. How hard could it be?" Jeez. He was supposed to be the adult. Why had he given up so easily?

"Jessie—"

"You screwed up, Dad. Big time. You can't just come waltzing back into my life and expect me to forget all that. You can't take me away from the only happiness I've found in years."

"I don't want to take you away from anything," Dad said, rubbing his neck and giving me a pleading look. "I just want you back in my life."

"So to get that, you'll make me give up everything I care about? My jobs, my life, my boyfriend?" I swept my hands through the air. "Forget it. I don't need you. I'll get emancipated. And when the court hears how you abandoned me to a raging alcoholic, they won't let you drag me off to Tennessee to be dumped with strangers."

Dad took a step toward me, his hand out. "Look, honey, I'm sorry. Obviously we've got a lot to talk about, but now isn't the time. I've gotta be in Seattle this evening to pick up a load. Let's get in the truck and go back to Kasey's, okay?"

I locked my arms across my chest. "Right. Just take off again. You're good at that, aren't you?"

"You know I have to leave. I told you I could only stay two days."

"You mean one and a half?"

"Jessie—"

"Don't let me hold you up. I can find my own way home.

The busses in this town are a hell of a lot more reliable than you are."

I turned and strode across the parking lot, expecting him to try to stop me, or at least holler my name.

Amazingly, he let me go.

The bus ride to Kasey's neighborhood gave me time to cool off. I walked the last few blocks, spotting Dad's Freightliner in the driveway as I approached the house. Well, if he thought I was talking to him again, he had another think coming. I got straight into the Pinto and took off.

I had no idea where I wanted to go—just that I needed to drive. Some long, twisty highway that would let me become one with my car and forget everything else. As I sped away, the perfect road came to mind. One Cody had taken me down during my week's vacation.

I followed West 11th past the speedway, where I'd spent so many Saturday nights. I zipped by Fern Ridge reservoir, where Cody had asked me on my first date. Just past the little town of Noti, I turned north on Poodle Creek Road, a wonderful, winding highway with breathtaking scenery. Once off the main drag, I lost myself in the drive, exulting in the sweep of each corner, the rush of acceleration as I sped past slow moving motor homes and minivans.

When I came to the junction with 36, I headed west toward Triangle Lake, where Cody, Rhett, Teri Sue and I had inner tubed down the natural water slides a couple of weeks before. One of my happiest memories of the summer. All the bad parts of Lydia's abandonment behind me, the assurance of a place in Kasey's home, and no worries yet about the return of my father. I'd almost been like a regular kid.

How could Dad think he could take that from me? This was my home. These people were my friends. *Friends*. My heart seized at the thought. A few months ago, I didn't have a single one. Now I had half a dozen. How had that happened? Who'd have even thought it possible? One thing I knew for sure—I wasn't leaving them. Not for anything.

Kasey had said she wouldn't let anyone take me away against my will. Would she stand by that? Even if that person was my father? She'd been the one to call him, after all.

Resentment rumbled inside me. Why did she have to start all this? She owed it to me to set things right. But if she wouldn't, I'd take matters into my own hands. It shouldn't be too hard to get emancipated. Kasey had told me that herself. Things between us might never be the same, but I could salvage the rest of my life.

Highway 36 dumped back into 126 at Mapleton. By the time I got there, the long, meandering drive had calmed me and given me the confidence to do what had to come next. I headed east, back toward town.

My heart jumped when I saw Dad's truck still parked on the street outside Kasey's house. He hadn't left yet? What about his stupid load in Seattle?

The Galaxie was gone, which meant Cody was probably off hunting for me. If Dad had told him about his plans, he'd no doubt be desperate to track me down, stewing over how I'd reacted and scheming up ways for us to fight. Well, he had nothing to worry about. I'd tell Dad exactly what was going to happen and leave no room for doubt. Stealing myself against whatever arguments he had in store, I marched up the steps and into the house.

When I opened the door, Dad stood up from the couch, where he'd been sitting with Kasey. His face, creased with worry lines, seemed to have aged in the few hours I'd been gone.

"Jessie—"

"Don't even start," I said, lifting my chin and squaring my shoulders "I was serious. I'm not going anywhere. If Kasey doesn't want me here, I'll find my own place."

He raised his hands to subdue me. "Honey, I don't want to fight. I've been thinking a lot about what you said, and I understand how you feel."

"Understanding isn't good enough."

"I know that. Let's talk, okay?"

Right. So he could try another angle to convince me. "I don't need to talk. I've already told you what I think."

"Jess, just give him a chance." Kasey stood up. "Why don't you two go out on the back patio? It's a nice, quiet place for a conversation."

"Please, honey," Dad said, his eyes begging me.

I shook my head and sighed. "Okay, fine." I strode past him through the living room and into the kitchen, where I swooshed open the sliding glass door and stepped out onto the shaded patio.

Dad followed, pulling the door shut behind him.

The neighbor's lawn mower hummed, and the sweet smell of cut grass filled the air. "Okay, spill it," I said, arms across my chest. "I'm listening."

Dad sat down on the stone retaining wall, hands spread out to either side of him. "I'm sorry I didn't take your feelings into account, Jessie. Of course you want to stay with your friends. Kasey filled me in about how hard it's been for you to trust everyone. I don't think I really understood what it was like, growing up the way you did."

Was he for real? "But I told you, Dad. Kasey told you."

He nodded. "I know. And it should've sunk into this thick skull of mine, but it didn't. No dad wants to think of his baby girl having to put up with all that." He caught me in a look, his eyes piercing and sad. "I knew you were tough, so it didn't surprise me you could take care of yourself. But what it did to you—that's what I didn't get, honey. All those years you spent trying to hide everything—keeping your mom a secret. I didn't realize it meant you couldn't have friends."

His understanding bumped up against the wall I'd erected, swaying it a little.

"Well, you must not have wasted much time thinking about it."

He dipped his head. "You're right. I've only been thinking about myself. Now, and back then, too. All this time I've been trying to justify it, telling myself there was nothing I coulda done, and in the space of five seconds you came up with two ideas that might've worked. I don't know what to say, Jessie. I messed up. I let you down and there's no excuse."

Okay. Well, that sure wasn't what I'd expected to hear. It seemed like I should respond, but what was there to say?

Dad looked down at the concrete under his feet. "And if that wasn't bad enough, I had to come back here and try to take you away from everything you love. I'm sorry, honey. When I got that phone call and found out you still wanted me in your life, I was so afraid of losing you again. If I could've stuck you in that truck with me, I woulda done it. But even I wasn't crazy enough to think that could work, so I settled for the next best thing." He raised his eyes, looking at me with true regret. "I never thought of how it might affect you."

"Yeah, that was pretty stupid," I said, not yet ready to let him off the hook.

"Yup," he nodded. "It was. Guess I was still thinking of you as my little girl. But you're not little anymore. You're damn near a grown woman. You've been making your own decisions for years, and taking care of your mom on top of it. I was a fool to think I could come back here and change you."

My arms unclenched from their gridlock across my chest. "Does that mean you're okay with me staying?"

"That's what it means."

A tightness I hadn't even been fully aware of eased in my gut. I could have my friends and keep him, too?

"Kasey said you're welcome to stay with her," Dad continued. "I'm not sure I'm keen on the idea of you living with your boyfriend, but Kasey's got a good head on her shoulders. I trust her to keep you out of trouble. I'll send her checks for your expenses, and give you a little spending money along with it."

I slipped my hands into my pockets, the last of the tension draining from my body. "I don't need spending money, Dad. I've got two jobs."

"Well, I suppose that extra cash could go toward college." A tentative grin crept over his face. "Kasey told me she's pretty much got you convinced to give that a try. Says you're thinking about studying engineering."

I smiled. "Yeah, if I can get my grades up. Kasey doesn't think it'll be a big deal, but she's never read any of my English papers."

Dad laughed. "Honey, I have no doubt you can do whatever you put your mind to."

He looked so lonely, sitting by himself on the wall. I stepped closer and eased down beside him.

"So now what?" I asked, rolling a pebble back and forth under the toe of my sneaker. "You said you wouldn't be able to see me much if I stayed here. What exactly does that mean?"

"Well, I probably get a run out this way about once a month. The company I'm contracting with might be able to double that if I make enough noise, and if they don't, I can hunt down a few of my own jobs on the side. It's easier to let them feed me the work, but they can't insist on it."

"So I'll get to see you a couple of times a month?" I tilted my head in his direction. "For how long? A weekend?"

"Yup. About that."

"That's not much." I looked back down at the concrete.

"Yeah, that's what I thought, too. But you've worked hard to build a life for yourself, against some pretty stiff odds. I don't have a right to take that from you. And I know it's not in your best interest." Dad's hand came up to rub my back in broad, comforting strokes.

I closed my eyes and leaned against him. Funny, how in the space of two days, he'd stopped being a stranger and become my dad again.

"Thank you," I whispered, my voice nearly drowned out by the buzz of the neighbor's lawn mower.

He kissed the top of my head. "You betcha."

"I love you, Dad."

Hooking his arm around my shoulders, he pulled me close. "I love you too, Jessie."

## CHAPTER 59

Dad's departure left me strangely empty, despite my pure relief at having the uncertainties in my life put to rest. I spent the next morning at Kasey's shop, and the afternoon working on the Camaro, reveling in the security of knowing I no longer had to worry about losing everything.

The Clines invited me for supper, and afterward, as I pushed through the screen door to head home, Mark followed.

"Jess, could I speak with you a minute?"

"Sure." I took a seat on the stone railing, circling my arm around one of the columns.

As Mark settled into an Adirondack chair, the angled rays of early evening sun illuminated one side of his face and highlighted his hair in a golden glow. A crazy thought struck me out of nowhere. *This is what Rhett would look like in thirty years.*

"It's so good to hear you got things worked out with your daddy," Mark said. "He seems to care a whole lot about you."

"I'm just glad he backed down about trying to get me to leave."

"Me too. And that's what I wanted to talk to you about." Mark smiled in that calm, easy way of his. "I know things would work out just fine at Kasey's, but she says your daddy's a little concerned about you living with Cody. With Teri Sue going off to college, Rhett and I will be blowing around in this big old house like a couple of tumbleweeds. I was wondering if you might consider moving in with us."

Oh man. Couldn't people give me a few days to get used to the recent shakeups before throwing ideas like this at me? Not that it was a huge surprise, after getting the same suggestion from Rhett and Teri Sue.

"Wow," I said, wedging the backs of my sneakers into the rock wall. "That's a generous offer. But . . . well . . . I'm happy at Kasey's."

Mark stretched out in his chair, the soles of his Birkenstocks sliding across the smooth, dusty concrete. "I understand. The thing is, you and Rhett have a special bond. You've gotten through to that boy in a way no one else has, and he's grown a lot because of it. He's still got a ways to go, but now I'm confident he'll make it through with his sunny disposition intact." Mark looked at me with fatherly affection. "I owe a lot of that to you."

Not sure how to handle the praise, I leaned sideways against the stone column, the rocks cool against my face.

A breeze stirred the air, and a sweet fragrance, coaxed from the rosebushes by the day's heat, drifted across the porch. Mark took a deep breath, the scent bringing the same blissful expression to his face that I suspected the smell of racing fuel brought to mine.

"Jess, if this was one-sided, and Rhett was the only one getting anything out of it, I wouldn't be selfish enough to suggest it. But I think he's given you something, too. The pair of you are like littermates, sure as if you'd been born into the same family."

That idea twitched my lips into a smile. But Rhett wasn't the only person I felt a connection to.

"You're right, Rhett does mean a lot to me," I said. "But I can't walk out on Kasey. I don't think anyone's ever understood me the way she does, and she's the one who set my dad straight about why I needed to stay here. I can't walk out on her after she's gone through so much trouble for me."

The breeze picked up, stirring the branches of the alder beside the porch.

"I appreciate that," Mark said. "And it's an open invitation.

If it turns out you want a change, you're welcome to come stay with us."

When I got back to the house, I found Cody leaning over the deck railing, watching another perfect sunset. Crickets chirped from the tall grass growing along the road.

"Hey," he said, sliding his arm around my waist as I brought my elbows up to rest on the cedar rail. "I've been waiting for you." He nuzzled my neck with his lips, making me go ticklish.

I cast a nervous glance at the picture window behind us, but the living room was dark. As if cueing in to my uneasiness, Cody gave me a slight squeeze and let go.

"Mark just asked if I'd move in with them," I said. "He thinks it would be good for Rhett with Teri Sue going off to college." The words surprised me. Until they were out, I hadn't realized I was going to say them.

For a moment Cody didn't speak. The rhythmic chirp of crickets overpowered the evening.

"Maybe you should do it."

"What?"

He glanced at me with a doleful smile, delicately fingering the wisps of hair that escaped my ponytail. A shiver scurried down my back.

"You're making me crazy, Jess. Haven't you figured that out?"

I was beginning to get the idea.

"From that first night, when Kasey came in and found us together, I knew it wasn't gonna be easy," Cody said. "I joked about it, but even then I knew."

His touch sent a rush of giddiness through my already flummoxed brain. "And how's that going to be different if I'm living someplace else?" The temptation would still be there every time we got together.

Cody sighed and pulled his hand away. "At least it would give me some space. Race told me he'd break my damned neck if I ever did anything to hurt you, but if everyone expects me to be some kind of gentleman, I can't be around you twenty-four hours a day."

Dad was right. Mark was right. For once, even Teri Sue was right. Why hadn't I seen this coming?

"That's not the only reason, Jess. I could learn to live with it if I had to. But Mark has a point. Rhett needs you, and I think you need him just as much."

Once more, the universe smacked me upside the head. "Mark said that, too. But I don't have to live at the Clines' to spend time with Rhett."

"What about after Teri Sue's gone? You've gotta be realistic. I like the kid, too, and we'll have the best intentions of visiting him—we might even take him out for pizza a few times—but then it'll get to be a pain because we'd rather go by ourselves."

I gripped the deck railing, thinking of how much that sounded like what Rhett had said. "I'm not going to let that happen, Cody. I promised him I wouldn't."

"And you'll try to keep that promise," he agreed, his hand coming up to rest lightly on mine. "But you won't be able to. You think you'll have enough time for everything, but you'll be working, and hanging out with me, and trying to bring your grades up." He squeezed my hand. "There's no way you can fit it all in, Jess. You'll make yourself crazy trying."

Damn. He was right. I hated to admit it, but I could see things playing out exactly as he said.

Over the next couple of days, I couldn't stop thinking about what Mark and Cody had said. While there was no denying their logic, I'd just gotten re-settled into the idea of staying with Kasey. And she'd given me so much. How could I possibly turn my back on her generosity?

But the option kept nagging at me. Now that it had been thrust in my face, I realized it was the solution to my subtle worries about how Rhett would deal with my father's return, and my vague discomfort about always having Cody around.

By Wednesday, the idea had become too pervasive to ignore. After dinner, I went down to the basement, where Kasey was sitting at the computer.

"Uh ... Kasey?"

"Um hmm?" She typed quickly, attention focused on an assortment of hand-scribbled notes.

"I need to talk to you."

After rattling off a quick burst on the keyboard, she swiveled around in her chair. "Okay, what would you like to talk about?"

Right. Now that I had her attention, my nerve failed me. I stared down at the maroon carpeting between my sneakers.

"Is anything wrong?"

"Not really."

Kasey waited.

*Get with it, Jess. Grow a backbone, why don't you?* "I guess I was wondering how you'd feel if I decided not to stay here." I snuck a look at her, but she'd hidden her feelings behind her best poker face. "I mean, I really like it, and I'm grateful to you, but ... I think Rhett needs me."

A faint smile eased across Kasey's lips. "So you want to go live at the Clines'?"

I nodded. "If it won't make you feel bad."

"Jess," Kasey said, her eyes solemn but kind, "don't you think your main concern should be how it makes *you* feel? This is your life we're discussing."

Her question caught me off guard. She wasn't upset? Or disappointed? "It's just that I don't want ..." My words faded.

"I know—you don't want to hurt my feelings. Honestly, I

was wondering how long it would take you to bring this up. Mark talked to me yesterday."

"He did?"

"Yes. He felt you'd have a hard time telling me, so he wanted to explain it himself."

"Oh." My gaze dropped back to the carpet.

"It sounds like a workable idea," Kasey said. "He has just as much room as we do, and you and Rhett seem to fill a need in each other's lives. But it's your decision. I don't want to say anything to influence you one way or the other."

So that was it? She was okay with the idea? "It's just that you've helped me so much," I said, looking back up at her. "You gave me a job, and made me feel welcome, and put me back in touch with my dad. And then there's all the stuff Race and Cody have done."

Kasey rested her hands on the arms of her chair. "It goes both ways, you know."

"What?"

"You've given us as much as we've given you."

Yeah, right. How was that even possible? "I doubt it."

"Oh?" she crossed one leg over the other, leaning back. "What about the way you were there for Cody the night he got so upset? Do you think my comfort would've meant anywhere near as much as yours? And you're the one who provided Race the perspective he needed to get past his self-doubt. Cody and I had been working on that for months, yet you accomplished it without even trying."

"But I didn't do anything." Not the way she had, tearing down my walls and pushing me to be my best, or Cody had, putting up with my insecurity and lies.

"Sometimes just being who you are is enough. You never know how your life is going to touch someone else's."

The words echoed in my head, sending out ripples that put my whole concept of reality into a spin. Could it be possible I'd affected their lives as much as they'd affected mine?

I rubbed the back of my neck. "So it wouldn't upset you, if I went to live with Mark and Rhett?"

"Of course not. Our friendship doesn't depend on where you decide to live."

"Okay," I said, relief spreading through me in a warm rush. "But what about Race? I don't want to disappoint him, either."

Kasey grinned. "Something tells me that wouldn't even be possible."

"You *are* comin' back, aren't ya?" Rhett perched on the bed beside my duffle bag, my Eugene Speedway hat stuck backward on his head.

"Of course I'm coming back. School starts in nine days."

Rhett bounced lightly on the mattress. "Just checking."

Dad would be here any minute to take me on an East Coast run. We'd have seven days to get to know each other again while he treated me to a slap-dash tour of the country. I'd miss the second-to-last race of the season, but Kasey had assured me she'd fill in. Barring complete tragedy, Race had the Limited Sportsman championship locked up. Teri Sue solidly held seventh place in the Street Stock division, and it even looked like Cody might sneak up into tenth.

Less than a week had passed since I'd told my father what I wanted, and though I'd only been living with the Clines a short time, already I felt at home. Teri Sue and I were temporarily sharing her bedroom. Each day, it became more mine than hers as I unpacked my stuff and she boxed up things to take to college. Every morning, I woke to the sun streaming through those south-facing windows and felt like I'd been transported into the happily-ever-after of a fairy tale.

As I stood at the dresser counting out seven pairs of socks, Cody appeared in the doorway.

"Hey," he said, slouching against the frame in his best

James Dean impression.

"Hey."

"I got you a little going away present." With an air of nonchalance, he tossed a bundle of brown cloth at me.

I caught it in my free hand and shook it out. A T-shirt that boasted the slogan, *Chocolate, the OTHER major food group*.

Laughter pulsed up out of me, leaving a smile behind. "You certainly have a way with T-shirts."

"What can I say? It's a talent." Cody pushed away from the doorframe, giving me a roguish grin. "Well, I should leave you to your packing, but I didn't want you getting away without a goodbye kiss." Like the hero in one of Mark's old movies, he strode across the room and swept me into his arms. His dark eyes locked onto mine, then he kissed me with so much passion you'd think I was going off to war.

"Now you won't forget me," he murmured in a tone as dreamy as the look on his face.

I swallowed hard. "As if anyone could."

"My eyes!" Rhett cried, falling to the bed and writhing about. "I'm blind!"

Cody raised an eyebrow and released me. "Well, I guess that's my cue to take off." He tugged once on my ponytail and slipped out the door, throwing a sultry smile over his shoulder as he disappeared down the hall.

Needing to pull myself together, I sank onto the bed. Rhett continued to roll around, hands over his face, peeking between his fingers to see if it was over yet. When I glanced at him sharply, he stopped writhing and grinned.

"So are you gonna bring me something from New York?"

If he'd been anyone else, I would've strangled him for ruining the moment. "Sure," I said dryly. "How about the Statue of Liberty?"

Feigning thoughtfulness, Rhett rubbed his chin. "That'd be nice. But where would we put it?"

"I was thinking the bathtub—" The rumble of a big diesel engine sounded in the driveway.

Rhett jumped up and ran to the windows. "He's here!" he shouted. "I get another ride in his truck, right?"

I nodded. "That's what he told me."

"Well," Rhett said, "let's get going." He grabbed the rest of my clothes and jammed them into my bag. Then, slinging it over his shoulder, he made a dash for the door.

I shook my head as I watched him scramble down the stairs. An eleven-year-old bell boy with a dirty face, a brace on his leg, and red-gold hair spilling from under my Eugene Speedway hat.

Looked like a little brother to me.

## ABOUT THE AUTHOR

In addition to being a YA author, Lisa Nowak is a retired amateur stock car racer, an accomplished cat whisperer, and a professional smartass. She writes coming-of-age books about kids in hard luck situations who learn to appreciate their own value after finding mentors who love them for who they are. She enjoys dark chocolate and stout beer and constantly works toward employing *wei wu wei* in her life, all the while realizing that the struggle itself is an oxymoron.

Lisa has no spare time, but if she did she'd use it to tend to her expansive perennial garden, watch medical dramas, take long walks after dark, and teach her cats to play poker. For those of you who might be wondering, she is not, and has never been, a diaper-wearing astronaut. She lives in Milwaukie, Oregon, with her husband, four feline companions, and two giant sequoias.

Connect with Lisa online:

Twitter: http://twitter.com/Lisa_Nowak
Facebook: http://www.facebook.com/LisaNowakAuthor
Blog: http://lisanowak.wordpress.com/
Newsletter: http://bit.ly/LisaNowakNewsletter

If you enjoyed this book, please tell your friends about it.

## FREE EXCERPT: REDLINE

(Available Fall 2012)

My first mistake was answering the phone. My second was not hanging up when I heard my mother's voice.

"Jess? Is that you?"

The words sent a surge of octane through my veins, revving my heart into dangerous territory. Then anger flooded the system. "What do you want?"

"Just to talk to my daughter."

As if that were a reasonable request. As if *I* wanted to talk to *her*.

My fingers constricted around the telephone. "You gave up that privilege last summer."

In the long silence that followed I almost broke the connection, but something made me wait.

"Jess, I know you're mad, and I understand, but ..."

"You ran out on me, Lydia."

"It's not like you think."

"It's not? You mean you didn't take off without so much as a goodbye?"

"I left you a letter."

*Letter?* A splinter of laughter caught in my throat. I could see the words clearly—the insinuation that I deserved to have her leave me. The conspicuous lack of signature after four bitter lines. "Would that be the one you hid in your room so I wouldn't find it until you were long gone?"

She snuffled, and her voice tightened like an overstretched rubber band. "I was angry. You acted like you didn't need me anymore. I thought you wanted me to leave."

"Did you think I wanted you to take all my money, too?"

"Sweetie, I'm sorry. I figured you had more stashed away. You always do."

"Not this time."

The line went silent.

"I didn't know, Jess."

"Oh, like that makes a difference?" Another emotion swelled beneath the heat of my anger. I swallowed hard to keep it in check. "Who gave you this number?" I demanded, wondering how she'd tracked me down after I'd been so careful. "How did you know I was living here?"

"I didn't. I got the number from you last spring when you started working on your friend's race car."

My stomach seized as I realized what I'd just revealed. I rested my forehead against the wall, silently cursing myself.

"I went by the apartment," Lydia continued, "and I saw you weren't there, so—"

"How was I supposed to keep the apartment without any money?"

Lydia stammered, then went quiet, the void of silence drawing out for several breaths. "Well, it worked out, didn't it?" she said at last. "You found a place to stay."

"Only after I lived in my car for a month!" As much as I wanted to rub in the consequences of what she'd done, I couldn't say more than that. Couldn't admit to how badly I'd failed at fending for myself, how I'd almost destroyed my friendships because I'd been too scared and ashamed to ask for help.

"I have nothing more to say to you, Lydia."

"Please, sweetie." The defensiveness vanished from her tone, replaced by the apologetic whine I knew so well. "I messed up. I'm sorry. All I want is another chance."

I hung up, like I should've done in the first place.

It wasn't until I was back at my desk, staring at my calculus homework, that I realized how rattled the call had left me. The scribbles on my paper made no sense, and after reading a problem three times, I still couldn't comprehend it.

I needed to get it together. Lydia had done enough to foul up my life before she left. I couldn't let her ruin the good things I had going now. For the first time, I was making an honest effort in school and had a real shot at college. Once I completed a degree in Engineering, I could open my own shop and concentrate on the thing I liked best—building race cars.

I leaned back in my chair and looked out the window. The late afternoon mist should've dulled the rampage of fall colors. Instead it gave them a surreal glow. Big leaf maples blazed like golden torches between the Douglas firs, and the sumacs at the end of the driveway were glowing embers. My gaze slipped over the familiar features of the Clines' front yard—the barn where we worked on my friend Teri Sue's race car, the alder in which her little brother Rhett had built his tree house, the fire pit where we'd had our cookouts. It struck me that I felt safe here. So why did my heart seem to be on the verge of shorting out? It wasn't like Lydia had any authority over me, now that I'd found Dad. Even though his job as a long-haul trucker kept him on the road, I had his blessing to stay with Teri Sue's father and little brother.

Then I realized that being forced to leave wasn't what I feared. For the first time in years, I had an ordinary life. While Lydia had been gone I could pretend I was just like my friends, that homework and hanging out were the norm, instead of scrabbling to keep food on the table, or my mom out of trouble. But now . . .

I guess I should've known the idea of being normal was too good to be true.

As I leaned into my locker Monday morning, a hand pressed gently at the small of my back.

"Hey," said Cody, my best-friend-turned-boyfriend. "You get your essay done?"

"Fortunately." I found my psychology textbook and turned to meet his world-class grin. No matter how many times I saw it, it always sent a rush of warmth straight through me. "How'd things go with the bodywork?"

Cody's smile twisted back on itself. "I'll be lucky to get it done by Christmas." He'd spent Saturday evening and most of Sunday at his uncle's shop, doing bodywork on his '65 Ford Galaxie to prepare it for painting. I would've helped if I hadn't been stuck home writing an English essay and trying to fit my other assignments around it. I'd always been friendlier with numbers than with words.

"Next time I'll give you a hand," I said.

"I know." His lips perked up, and I could see they were itching to kiss me, but public displays of affection were frowned upon at South Eugene. Instead, his fingers sought mine, and his eyes, brown as the Euphoria chocolate he was always sneaking into my locker, said the forty-one hours since he'd last seen me were forty too many. He tossed his head to sweep his dark rooster tail bangs out of his face. "Anything exciting happen while I was so mercilessly separated from you? Alien abduction, maybe? Or a call from Dale Earnhardt begging you to be his next crew chief?"

My hand twitched in his at the mention of a call, and guilt sent my eyes scurrying away.

"What's wrong?"

I'd decided last night I wasn't going to say anything about Lydia. Cody hadn't met her, and I wanted to keep it that way. She'd probably never call back, and what was the sense of bringing up something so embarrassing when it had no effect on either of our lives?

"Nothing," I said.

"Uh huh. Then why'd you jump? Is everything okay with your dad?" Cody had always been able to read me, which made keeping things from him difficult. While his sensitivity and intuition had been big factors in winning my trust, he was a born worrier, and I hated to provide him with any fuel.

"Dad's fine. He just had to cancel his visit next weekend."

"Oh." Cody's fingers pulsed against mine. "I'm sorry, Jess."

"It's okay. I can wait another week." Much as I hated the delay, I was grateful for the excuse it provided. Cody and I didn't lie to each other, not since last summer, when I'd almost driven him away by neglecting to tell him about Lydia abandoning me. Living in my car had scared me half to death, but I'd been even more afraid of getting tossed into a foster home, of being separated from the first friends I'd had in years.

Of course this wasn't anything like that. I wasn't in danger. I just wanted to spare myself some humiliation, to go on pretending my life wasn't a broken, dysfunctional mess.

Cody closed my locker and circled his arm around my waist, directing me down the hall. "I know I'm no substitute for your dad," he said. "But I'll give you all my free time next weekend, okay?"

"Sounds like a plan."

A year ago, completely lacking in feminine charm and having the grease under my nails to prove it, I'd never have believed any boy would take interest in me, let alone a cute, sweet, funny guy like Cody.

Now if I could only convince myself I wasn't going to scare him away.

CPSIA information can be obtained at www.ICGtesting.com
Printed in the USA
BVOW071656030612

291631BV00001B/5/P